"Well, well, well," the Reaper girl hissed. "If it isn't Nike's Champion, slinging a sword like she actually knows how to use it. I was hoping I might run into you here."

"Yeah, it's me. Gwen Frost," I snapped. "Nike's Champion in the flesh. I know what you did to my mom."

The girl threw back her head and laughed. She just—laughed. Low, long, and loud. Like it was funny that she'd killed my mom in cold blood. Like it was the most hysterical thing *ever* that she and her Reaper friends had just done the same thing to a museum full of innocent people.

"Well, I should certainly hope so," she said. "Killing your weak, sniveling mother was the most fun I've had in *ages*."

Rage once again filled my heart, blocking out everything else. All my questions, all my worries, all my fears. There was only me and her and my desire for revenge, this burning, burning need I had to make her pay, to make her *suffer* for taking my mom away from me.

With a roar, I leaped off the dais, raised my sword, and rushed forward—and the Reaper girl stepped up to meet me.

Other Mythos Academy books by Jennifer Estep

Kiss of Frost

Touch of Frost

First Frost

DARK FROST

A Mythos Academy Novel

Jennifer Estep

KENSINGTON PUBLISHING CORP.
www.kensingtonbooks.com

K TEEN BOOKS are published by

Kensington Publishing Corp.
119 West 40th Street
New York, NY 10018

ISBN-13: 978-0-7582-6696-5
ISBN-10: 0-7582-6696-0

First Kensington Trade Paperback Printing: June 2012
10 9 8 7 6 5 4 3

Printed in the United States of America

As always, to my mom, my grandma, and Andre,
for all their love, help, support, and patience
with my books and everything else in life

And to Lucky, one of the best dogs ever.
Nineteen years wasn't long enough.
We'll always love and miss you.

Acknowledgments

Any author will tell you that her book would not be possible without the hard work of many, many people. Here are some of the folks who helped bring Gwen Frost and the world of Mythos Academy to life:

Thanks to my agent, Annelise Robey, for all her helpful advice.

Thanks to my editor, Alicia Condon, for her sharp editorial eye and thoughtful suggestions. They always make the book so much better.

Thanks to everyone at Kensington who worked on the book, and thanks to Alexandra Nicolajsen and Vida Engstrand for all their promotional efforts.

And, finally, thanks to all the readers out there. Entertaining you is why I write books, and it's always an honor and a privilege. I hope you have as much fun reading about Gwen's adventures as I do writing them.

Happy reading!

Library of Antiquities

1 Balcony of Statues
2 Check Out Counter
3 Artifact Case
4 Raven's Coffee Cart
5 Entrance
6 Book Stacks
7 Study Area
8 Offices
9 Staircase

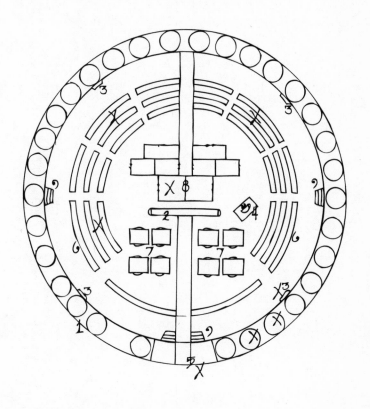

Chapter 1

"If you guys don't stop making out, I'm going to be sick."

Daphne Cruz giggled and laid another loud, smacking kiss on her boyfriend, Carson Callahan. Princess pink sparks of magic shot off my best friend's fingertips and flickered in the air around the couple, the tiny rainbows of color almost as bright as Carson's flaming cheeks.

I rolled my eyes. "Seriously, seriously sick."

Daphne quit kissing Carson long enough to turn and stare at me. "Oh, get over it, Gwen. We're not making out. Not in this stuffy old museum."

I raised an eyebrow. "Really? Then why is Carson wearing more of your lip gloss than you are?"

Carson's blush deepened, his dusky brown skin taking on a fiery, tomato tint. The band geek pushed his black glasses up his nose and swiped his hand over his mouth, trying to scrub away the remains of the lip gloss, but all he really did was get pink glitter all over his fingers. Daphne giggled, then pressed another kiss to the band geek's lips.

I sighed. "C'mon, c'mon. Break it up, lovebirds. The museum closes at five, and we haven't seen half the artifacts we're supposed to for myth-history class."

"Fine," Daphne pouted, stepping away from Carson. "Be a spoilsport."

I rolled my eyes again. "Yeah, well, this *spoilsport* happens to be concerned about her grades. So, let's go to the next room. There are supposed to be some really cool weapons in there, according to the exhibit brochure."

Daphne crossed her arms over her chest. She narrowed her black eyes and glared at me for interrupting her fun, but she and Carson followed me as I stepped through a doorway and left the main part of the museum behind.

It was a few days after New Year's, and the three of us were in the Crius Coliseum, a museum located on the outskirts of Asheville, North Carolina. Visiting a museum didn't exactly top my list of fun things to do, but all the second-year students at Mythos Academy were supposed to schlep over to the coliseum sometime during the winter holidays to view a special exhibit of artifacts. Since classes started back at the academy in the morning, today was our last chance to finish the assignment. It was bad enough that I and all the other warrior whiz kids at Mythos were being trained to fight the Reapers of Chaos. But homework over the holidays, too? That was *so* not fair.

Daphne, Carson, and I had gotten here about three

o'clock, and we'd been wandering around the museum for the last ninety minutes, going from one display to the next. From the outside, the Crius Coliseum looked like just another building, just another museum, tucked away in the Appalachian Mountains in and around the city.

Inside, though, it was a different story.

Walking through the front door of the museum was like stepping back in time to ancient Rome. The main room had been designed to resemble a grand coliseum, and white marble rolled out as far as the eye could see, broken up by towering pillars. Gold, silver, and bronze leaf glinted here and there on the walls before spreading up to cover the entire ceiling in dazzling disks of color. Sapphires and rubies burned like colorful coals in the necklaces and rings on display, while the fine silks and other garments shimmered inside their glass cases, looking as light and delicate as spun sugar. The museum staff even wore long, flowing white togas, adding to the effect.

But it wasn't just ancient Rome that was on display. Every room had a specific theme and displayed a different culture, from Norse to Greek to Russian to Japanese and all the lands and peoples in between. That's because the coliseum was devoted to members of the Pantheon. Gods, goddesses, ancient warriors, mythological creatures—the Pantheon was a group of good magic guys who'd originally joined forces to save the world.

Way back in the day, the evil Norse trickster god Loki had tried to enslave everyone and had plunged the world into the long, bloody Chaos War. But the members of the Pantheon had risen up to stop Loki and his followers, the Reapers of Chaos. Eventually, the other gods and goddesses had locked Loki away in a mythological prison, far removed from the mortal realm. Now, the coliseum showcased the artifacts—jewelry, clothing, armor, weapons, and more—that both sides had used during the Chaos War and other battles. Despite Loki's imprisonment, the fight between the Pantheon and the Reapers had continued over the years with new generations of warriors and creatures battling one another.

Of course, what most people didn't realize was that Loki was *thisfreakingclose* to breaking free of his prison and starting another Chaos War. It was something I thought about all the time, though—especially since I was somehow supposed to stop the evil god from escaping.

"This is cool," Daphne said.

She pointed to a curved bow inside a glass case. The bow was made out of a single piece of onyx, inlaid with bits of gold scrollwork, and strung with several thin golden threads. A matching onyx quiver sat next to the bow, although only a single golden arrow lay inside the slender tube.

Daphne leaned down and read the bronze plaque mounted on the pedestal below the weapon. "This says that the bow once belonged to Sigyn, the Norse goddess of devotion, and that every time you pull the arrow out of the quiver, another one appears to take its place. Okay, now that's *wicked* cool."

"I like this better," Carson said, pointing to a curled

ivory horn that resembled a small, handheld tuba. Bits of onyx glimmered on the smooth surface. "It says it's the Horn of Roland. Not sure what it does, though."

I blinked. I'd been so lost in my thoughts about Loki, Reapers, and the Pantheon that I'd just been wandering around, instead of actually looking at the artifacts like we were supposed to.

We stood in an enormous circular room filled with weapons. Swords, staffs, spears, daggers, bows, and throwing stars glinted from within glass cases and in spots on the walls, next to oil paintings of mythological battles. The entire back wall was made out of the same white marble as the rest of the museum, although a variety of mythological creatures had been carved into the surface. Gryphons, gargoyles, dragons, chimeras, Gorgons with snakelike hair and cruel smiles.

An ancient knight dressed in full battle armor perched on a stuffed horse on a raised dais in the center of the room. The knight had a lance in his hand and looked like he was about to charge forward and skewer the wax figure of a Roman centurion that also stood on the dais, his sword raised to fend off the charging knight. Other figures were scattered throughout the area, including a Viking wearing a horned helmet who was poised to bring his massive battle-axe down onto the shield of the Spartan standing next to him. A few feet away, two female figures representing a Valkyrie and an Amazon held swords and dispassionately watched the Viking and the Spartan in their eternal epic battle.

I stared at the Viking and the Spartan, and, for a moment, their features flickered and seemed to move. Their wax lips drew up into angry snarls; their fingers tightened around the hilts of their weapons; their whole bodies tensed up in anticipation of the battle that was to come. I shivered and looked away. My Gypsy gift, my psychometry magic, had been acting up ever since we'd entered the museum.

"Hmph. Well, I don't think that bow is so bloody special," a voice with a snooty English accent muttered. "I think it's rather boring. *Ordinary,* even."

I looked down at the source of the voice: Vic, the sword sheathed in the black leather scabbard hanging off my waist. Vic wasn't your typical sword. For starters, instead of having a plain hilt, the sword actually had half a face inlaid into the silver metal there. A single ear, a hooked nose, a slash of a mouth. All that joined together to form the sword's hilt, along with a round bulge of an eye. It always seemed to me like there was a man trapped inside the metal, trying to get out. I didn't know exactly who or what Vic was, other than rude, bossy, and bloodthirsty. The sword was always going on and on and *on* about how we should go find some Reapers to kill.

Actually, there was just one Reaper I wanted to kill— the girl who'd murdered my mom.

A crumpled car. A sword slicing through the rain. And blood—so much blood . . .

The memories of my mom's murder bubbled to the surface of my mind, threatening to overwhelm me, but I pushed them away and forced myself to focus on my friends, who were still staring at the onyx bow and ivory horn.

I'd brought Vic along today because I thought he might enjoy seeing the items on display. Besides, I'd needed someone to talk to while Daphne and Carson had been giggling and tongue-wrestling with each other. The two of them were so into each other that it was rather disgusting at times, especially given the sad state of my own love life.

"It's just a bow, after all," Vic continued. "Not anything important. Not a *real* weapon."

I rolled my eyes. Oh, yeah. Vic talked, too—mostly about how awesome he was.

"Well, some of us happen to like bows," Daphne sniffed, looking down at the sword.

"And that's what's wrong with you, Valkyrie," Vic said.

The sword stared at her. Vic only had one eye, and it was a curious color—not quite purple but not quite gray either. Really, Vic's eye reminded me of the color of twilight, that soft shade that streaked the sky just before the world went dark for the night.

"And you, Celt," Vic said, turning his attention to Carson. "Gwen told me that you prefer to use a staff. A staff! It doesn't even have a bloody *point* on the end of it. Disgraceful, the things they're teaching you warrior kids at Mythos these days."

Every kid who went to Mythos Academy was some sort of warrior, including the three of us. Daphne was a Valkyrie, Carson was a Celt, and I was a Gypsy, all of us the descendants of the Pantheon warriors who'd first taken on Loki and his Reapers. Now, we carried on that tradition in modern times by going to the academy and learning how to use whatever skills and magic we had to fight against the Reapers of Chaos. And we weren't the only ones. Vikings, Romans, Amazons, Ninjas, Samurais, Spartans. All those warriors and more could be found at the academy.

"Disgraceful, I say," Vic crowed again.

Carson looked at me. I just shrugged. I'd only had Vic a few months, but I'd quickly learned there was no controlling the mouthy sword. Vic said whatever he liked, whenever he liked, as loudly as he liked. And if you dared to disagree with him, he was more than happy to discuss the matter further—while I pressed his blade up against your throat.

Vic and Daphne glared at each other before the Valkyrie turned to Carson and started talking to the band geek about how cool the bow was. I wandered through the rest of the room, peering at the other artifacts. Vic kept up his running monologue about how swords were the only *real* weapons, with him, of course, being the best sword *ever*. I made agreeing noises when appropriate. It was easier than trying to argue with him.

Daphne and Carson continued to look at the bow, and Vic finished his rant and fell silent once more. I was reading about a ball of silver thread that had belonged to Ariadne, who gave it to Theseus to help him find his way through the labyrinth where the Minotaur was kept, when shoes tapped on the floor and someone walked up beside me.

"Gwendolyn Frost," a snide voice murmured. "Fancy seeing you here."

I turned and found myself face-to-face with a forty-something-year-old guy with black hair, cold blue eyes, and skin that was as white as the marble floor. He wore a dark blue suit and a pair of wingtips that had a higher polish than most of the glass cases in the room. I would have thought him handsome if I hadn't known exactly how uptight and prissy he was—and how very much he hated me.

I sighed. "Nickamedes. What are you doing here?"

"Overseeing the exhibit, of course. Most of the arti-facts on display are on loan from the Library of Antiq-uities."

Nickamedes was the head honcho at the Library of Antiquities, which was located on the Mythos Academy campus not too far away in Cypress Mountain, North Carolina. In addition to books, the massive library was famous for its priceless collection of artifacts. Hundreds and hundreds of glass cases filled the library's seven floors, containing items that had once belonged to everyone from gods and goddesses to their Champions to the Reapers they had battled.

I supposed it made sense that the Crius Coliseum had borrowed some artifacts from the library—that was probably the reason the Mythos students had been as-signed to come here in the first place. So they'd be forced to look at and study the items they walked past and ignored on a daily basis at the library.

Nickamedes stared at me, not looking a bit happier to see me than I was to have run into him. His mouth twisted. "I see that you and your friends waited until the last possible second to come and complete your myth-history assignment, along with a great many of your classmates."

Morgan McDougall, Samson Sorensen, Savannah Warren. I'd spotted several kids I knew roaming through the coliseum. All seventeen or so, like me, Daphne, and Carson, and all second-year students at Mythos, trying to cram in a visit to the museum before winter classes.

"I've been busy," I muttered.

Nickamedes let out a disbelieving huff. "Right."

Anger filled me. I had been busy. *Very* busy, as a matter of fact. Not too long ago, I'd learned that the Reapers were searching for the Helheim Dagger, which was rumored to be one of the Thirteen Artifacts that had been used during the final battle of the Chaos War. All of the Thirteen Artifacts had a lot of power, since they'd seen action during the climactic fight. But what made the weapon so important—what truly scared me—was the fact that the dagger could be used to free Loki from the prison realm he was trapped in.

I was determined to find the dagger before the Reapers did, so during the holidays I'd read everything I could get my hands on about the weapon. Who might have made it, how it might have been used during the Chaos War, even what powers it might have. But all the books and articles I'd read didn't tell me what I really wanted to know: where my mom, Grace, had hidden the dagger before she'd been murdered—or how I was supposed to find it before the Reapers did.

Of course, I couldn't tell Nickamedes all that. He

wouldn't believe I'd been doing something useful, something important, during the holiday break. No doubt Nickamedes thought I'd just been sitting around reading comic books and eating cookies like I did so many nights when I was working for him in the Library of Antiquities. Yeah, yeah, so maybe I wasn't all that dedicated when it came to my after-school job. Sue me for wanting to goof off and have a little fun before I had to face down another crazy Reaper who thought I was more powerful and important than I really was.

Still, despite the librarian's frosty attitude, I couldn't help glancing around the room, hoping I'd see a guy my age with him—a guy with the most beautiful eyes I'd ever seen and a sly, teasing grin to match.

"Is Logan here with you?" I couldn't keep the hope out of my voice.

Nickamedes had opened his mouth when a voice interrupted him.

"Right here, Gypsy girl." A low voice sent chills down my spine.

My heart pounding, I slowly turned around. Logan Quinn stood behind me.

Thick, wavy, ink black hair, intense ice blue eyes, a confident smile. My breath caught in my throat as I looked at Logan, and my heart sped up, beating with such force that I was sure he could hear it.

Logan wore jeans and a dark blue sweater topped by a black leather jacket. The clothes were designer, of course, since the Spartan was just as rich as all the other academy kids. But even if he'd been dressed in rags, I still would have noticed the lean strength of his body and his broad, muscled shoulders. Yeah, Logan totally rocked the bad-boy look, and he had the man-whore reputation to match. One of the rumors that kept going around the academy was that Logan signed the mattresses of every girl he slept with, just so he could keep track of them all.

I'd never quite figured out if the rumors were true or not, or how Logan would even manage to do that in the first place. Sure, I'd touched the Spartan and flashed on him with my psychometry, but I'd mostly seen his fighting skills, since that's what Logan had been thinking about and what I had needed to tap into at the time. I didn't know how many girls Logan had dated, but the rumors didn't matter that much to me because the Spartan was just a really, really great guy. Smart, strong, funny, charming, caring. Then, of course, there was the whole *saving-my-life-multiple-times* thing. Kind of hard not to like a guy when he kept you from getting killed by Reapers and eaten by Nemean prowlers.

Logan's eyes dropped to my throat and the necklace I wore there—the one he'd given me before school had let out for Christmas. Six silver strands wrapped around my throat, creating the necklace, while the diamond-tipped points joined together to form a simple, yet elegant snowflake in the center of the strands. The beautiful necklace looked like something a goddess would wear. I thought it was far too pretty and delicate for me, but I loved it just the same.

"You're wearing the necklace," the Spartan said in a low voice.

"Every day since you gave it to me," I said. "I hardly ever take it off."

Logan smiled at me, and it was like the sun had erupted from a sky full of storm clouds. For a moment everything was just—*perfect.*

Then Nickamedes cleared his throat, popping the bubble of happiness I'd been about to float away on. A sour expression twisted the librarian's face as he looked back and forth between his nephew and me.

"Well, if you'll excuse me, the museum's closing soon, and I need to make sure the staff is ready to start packing up the items for transport back to the academy in the morning."

Nickamedes pivoted on his wingtips and strode out of the weapons room without another word. I sighed. Yeah, I might not be the most dedicated worker, but I always felt like there was another reason that Nickamedes hated me. He'd pretty much disliked me on sight, and I had no idea why.

I put the librarian and his bad attitude out of mind and focused on Logan. He'd texted me a few times over the holiday break, but I'd still missed him like crazy— especially since I had no idea what was going on between us. Not too long ago, we'd shared what I thought was the kiss to end all kisses, but he hadn't exactly declared his love for me in the meantime—or even asked me out on a real date. Instead, we'd been in this weird holding pattern for weeks—one that I was determined to end.

I drew in a breath, ready to ask Logan how his winter break had been and what was going to happen between us now. "Logan, I—"

Shouts and screams ripped through the air, drowning out my words.

I froze, wondering if I'd only imagined the harsh, jarring sounds. Why would someone be shouting in the museum? A second later, more screams sounded, followed by several loud crashes and the heavy *thump-thump-thump* of footsteps.

Logan and I looked at each other, then bolted for the door. Daphne and Carson had also heard the screams, and they raced along right behind us.

"Stop! Stop! Stop!" Daphne hissed.

She managed to grab my arm and the back of Logan's leather jacket just before the Spartan sprinted out of the room. With her great Valkyrie strength, she was easily able to yank both of us back.

"You don't know what's going on—or who might be out there," Daphne warned.

Logan glared at her, but after a moment, he reluctantly nodded. I did the same, and Daphne loosened her grip on us. Together in a tight knot, the four of us crept up to the doorway and peeked through to the other side.

The Crius Coliseum was shaped like a giant wheel, with one main space in the middle and the hallways and rooms branching off like spokes. The doorway we stood in opened up into the center section of the museum. When Daphne, Carson, and I had walked through it a few minutes ago, folks had been milling around the exhibits, looking at the artifacts and browsing through the expensive replica jewelry, armor, and weapons in the gift shop. Besides the staff, most of the other people here had been second-year Mythos students, trying to get their homework assignment done, just like the three of us.

Not anymore.

Now, figures wearing long, black, hooded robes stormed through the coliseum—and they all carried sharp, curved swords. The figures swarmed over everyone in their path, their blades slashing into the students who'd been staring at the artifacts just a few seconds before. More screams and shouts tore through the air, echoing as loud as gunshots, as people realized what was happening.

But it was already too late.

"Reapers," Daphne whispered, voicing my own horrific thought.

The Reapers of Chaos ran their swords through everyone they could get their hands on, then shoved the dead and dying to the floor. The museum staff, adults, kids. It didn't matter to the Reapers who they killed. Wax figures, statues, and display cases crashed to the floor, splintering into thousands of pieces. Blood spattered everywhere, a cascade of scarlet teardrops sliding down the white marble walls.

A sick, sick feeling filled my stomach at the bloody chaos in front of me. I'd heard about Reapers, about how vicious they were, about how they lived to kill warriors—about how they lived to kill *us*. I'd faced down two Reapers myself, but I'd never seen anything like this. I was so shocked by the scene in front of me that I felt stuck in place, just like my friends. I knew we should be doing something, anything, to try to help the other students, but I didn't know what it could be.

Some of the Mythos students tried to fight back, using their fists or whatever they could get their hands on. But it didn't work, and one by one, the Reapers swarmed over the kids. Samson Sorensen fell to the floor, screaming and clutching his stomach, blood spurting out from between his fingers. A few Mythos students tried to run, but the Reapers just grabbed them from behind, rammed their swords into the kids' backs, and then tossed them aside like trash.

Out of the corner of my eye, I saw Morgan McDougall duck down and squeeze in between a tall, wide pedestal and the wall, putting her parallel to the doorway that my friends and I were next to. Green sparks of magic shot out of Morgan's fingertips like lightning, a clear sign of her surprise and panic, and she curled her hands into tight fists and tucked them under her armpits to try to smother the colorful flashes. Morgan knew as well as I did that if the Reapers saw the sparks, they'd find her and finish her off. The pretty Valkyrie spotted me watching her and stared back at me, her hazel eyes full of fear.

"Stay there! Hide! Don't try to run!" I shouted, although I didn't think Morgan could hear me above the screams and the alarms that had started blaring.

In less than a minute, it was over. The Reapers regrouped in the middle of the coliseum, talking to each other, but I couldn't hear what they were saying over the moans, groans, and whimpers of the dying kids on the bloody floor.

"Reapers," Daphne whispered again, as if she couldn't believe what she was seeing any more than I could.

It was almost like they'd heard the Valkyrie's low murmur because several of the black-robed figures turned and headed in our direction.

Chapter 2

For the second time, I froze. My mind just went blank, and all I could do was watch the Reapers head toward us, blood dripping off the ends of their curved swords. Maybe it was my imagination, but it seemed like I could hear every single scarlet drop as it hit the marble floor. *Plop-plop-plop.* I clamped my hand over my mouth to keep from screaming at the awful noise echoing in my head.

"Back, back, back!" Daphne hissed, once again using her Valkyrie strength to pull first Carson, then me, and finally Logan away from the doorway. "We have to get out of here!"

We turned around to run—and realized there was nowhere to go. There were no exits from this room to any other part of the museum.

"Trapped," Carson said in a bitter voice. "We're trapped."

Thump-thump-thump. Outside, the heavy footsteps continued, getting louder and louder as the Reapers marched toward us.

Desperate, I looked around, hoping there was a door, a window, or even a skylight that I'd missed before—or that maybe one would just magically appear and let us escape. That didn't happen, but my eyes landed on the wax figures of the Viking and the Spartan and the items they were holding—the Viking's axe and the Spartan's shield.

Weapons. My gaze flicked around the room. Swords, spears, daggers, staffs. We stood in a room full of weapons. The deadly points and sharp edges glittered underneath the lights, and one by one, the bits and pieces of metal winked at me, as if they knew exactly what I was thinking—and what we had to do if we wanted to make it through this.

"If we can't run, there's only one thing we can do— stand and fight," I said in a grim voice. "That's what we've been training for, right?"

Daphne and Carson stared at me, their mouths hanging open, but Logan had a different reaction. He actually *smiled,* and a fierce light began to burn in his eyes. Spartans were a little freaky in that they actually loved to fight, especially since they were the best warriors at Mythos—or anywhere else.

Not for the first time, I wished that I had Logan's confidence when it came to battling Reapers. With a shaking hand, I drew Vic from the scabbard strapped to my waist and held him up high. Vic's purplish eye met mine.

"Are you ready for this, Gwen?" the sword asked in a low voice.

"I guess I have to be, don't I?" I whispered back.

If he could have, I thought Vic would have nodded his half of a head in approval. "I'll be here with you, every step of the way. You're a Champion, Gwen. You'll be fine. You all will. Nike has faith in you, and so do I."

I nodded back, his words making me feel just a little bit better. I stood there a second, and I forced myself to breathe—in and out, in and out, in and out—just like my mom had taught me. Just like she'd always told me to do whenever I was scared, panicked, or upset. Yeah, I was all those things right now—and then some.

But there was no time to think about what I was doing, and no time to be cautious or quiet. I raced over to the case—the one with the goddess Sigyn's onyx bow and quiver in it—raised up Vic, turned my head away, then brought the sword down on top of the glass.

CRASH!

The case shattered with a roar, and shards of glass zipped through the air, stinging my hands and drawing blood. I thought that an alarm sounded, blaring together with all the others going off, but I was already moving over to the next case, one that contained a long wooden staff.

"Daphne! Carson! Logan!" I yelled. "Get the weapons!"

My friends scrambled forward, their shoes crunching on the shattered glass. I smashed another case, this one containing a sword with a dull bronze hilt. I used Vic to shatter the artifact cases, one by one, while Daphne, Carson, and Logan grabbed the items inside, as well as all the weapons they could reach on the walls and a few the wax figures were holding. We met in the middle of the room and quickly sorted through the weapons.

"We have to stick together and make a stand right from the start," Carson said, holding a staff in one hand and stuffing the ivory horn and a couple of daggers into the pockets on his khaki cargo pants. "We need to strike at them first. Otherwise, they'll overrun us."

Daphne strapped the quiver with its single arrow to her back, then tested the golden strings in the onyx bow. Satisfied, she bit her lip and looked around, the air around her cracking and hissing with pink sparks of magic. "Over there, behind the knight and the centurion. The Reapers won't immediately see us when they come in. Hopefully, I can pick a couple of them off before they realize what's going on."

"You three do that," Logan said, strapping the shield he'd swiped from the wax Spartan to his forearm. "I'll hide over there behind the Viking. When the Reapers move to attack you, I'll come up behind them. Divide and kill, right?"

I nodded. It was a good plan, even though my stomach twisted at the thought of Logan's being separated from the rest of us. But the Spartan was the best fighter at Mythos. This sort of situation was what he'd been training for his whole life—what we'd all been training for.

We scrambled up onto the dais and around to the far side. Daphne took up a position between the knight and the centurion, looking like another proud figure standing there, the golden arrow nocked and ready in the onyx bow. Carson moved to her left, while I stood on her right, the two of us flanking and protecting our archer, just like Coach Ajax had taught us to during all the mock fights we'd had in gym class. Across the room, Logan slid behind the wax Viking.

"We'll be okay, right?" Carson said, fear making his eyes seem more black than brown behind his glasses.

"Of course, we will," I said, trying to make my voice light. "Just think how jealous all the other kids will be when they hear that we took on a group of Reapers—and won."

Carson tried to smile at my lame pep talk, but his lips twisted into a grimace instead. I knew how he felt. After what I'd just seen, I didn't know if I'd ever be able to smile again. There would be no winning. Not today. Not with the other kids outside injured.

Not with so many dead.

Beside us, Daphne remained silent, although pink sparks snapped all around her now, cracking like fireworks, letting Carson and me know she was just as scared as we were. The Valkyrie stared at me a moment, then at the band geek, before turning her attention to the open doorway. Carson gripped his staff and pushed his glasses up his nose, while I tightened my hold on Vic.

I looked at Logan. Even from across the room, I could see the anticipation in his face. The emotion made his eyes glitter like ice. The Spartan was ready for the Reapers, ready to put his fighting skills to the test. Logan gave me a thumbs-up. His certainty in himself, in us, and in what we were about to do, made my stomach unclench the tiniest bit.

We hunkered down and waited for the Reapers to come.

Less than a minute later, the first Reaper stepped into the weapons room. The figure wore a black robe over his clothes and heavy black boots, but I thought it was a man, given how tall, thick, and strong his body looked.

But the most frightening thing about him was the mask.

A rubber mask covered the Reaper's face from his forehead all the way down to his neck, completely hiding his features. That was scary enough, but it took me a second to realize that the mask actually formed a specific, terrifying shape—the face of the evil god Loki.

Once upon a time, when the other gods had first imprisoned Loki for his many crimes, they'd chained him up beneath a giant snake that had continually dripped venom onto his face, causing him unimaginable pain. The venom had eaten away at the handsome god's features, melting them into something twisted, ugly, and utterly grotesque. That was the face the Reaper proudly sported over his own, and the sight chilled me to the bone—even more so than the bloody sword dangling from his hand.

One by one, the Reapers stepped into the room, until seven of them clustered near the doorway. Seven of them, four of us. Not the best odds, but not terrible either, considering it had looked like there had been close to twenty armed Reapers in the main part of the coliseum. Besides, we had Logan. With his fighting skills, the Spartan was worth a dozen Reapers.

I crouched behind the stuffed horse, my heart pounding, a tight grip on Vic, waiting for more of them to file into the room, but none did. I wondered what the other Reapers were doing, but I wasn't going to complain. I was just happy they hadn't all decided to come in here at once. We would have been killed for sure. Now, at least we had a fighting chance.

One of the Reapers stepped forward. "Spread out."

I blinked. That—that was a girl's voice. I shouldn't have been surprised, since Reapers could be anyone, from parents to teachers to students and everyone in between. The two Reapers that I'd battled before had been kids my own age. Still, something about the low, throaty voice bothered me. It almost sounded . . . familiar. Like I'd heard it somewhere before—

"Take anything that looks interesting or that has magic attached to it," she said.

I frowned. I'd thought the Reapers might have seen us standing in the doorway, that maybe that was the reason they'd headed in this direction, but it sounded like they'd just come in here looking for artifacts.

"And start searching for the Helheim Dagger," the girl continued. "They could have moved it here, according to our calculations."

My breath caught in my throat. The Helheim Dagger? How did she know about that? And why did she think it was here in the museum? My mind started churning. The girl barked out a few more orders, but I wasn't really listening to her words anymore. Instead, I concentrated on her voice, comparing it to another one—the voice I'd heard the night my mom had died.

The voice of my mom's murderer.

Where's the dagger? Where did you hide it? . . . Fool. There's no place you can hide it that we won't find it. It's only a matter of time. . . . The sneering voice rang in my head, the words playing over and over again.

Thanks to my psychometry magic, I never forgot anything I saw, heard, or felt when I touched an object. Not only that, but I could call up those memories whenever I wanted to and examine them the way someone might look at scenes on her favorite DVD. I suppose it was my own version of a photographic memory, only with perfect playback every single time.

A few weeks ago, my mentor, Professor Aurora Metis, had asked me to use my Gypsy gift on a Reaper boy named Preston Ashton. I got vivid enough vibes from objects, but I could get major whammies, major, major flashes of feeling from touching another person. I could see everything a person had ever done, from childhood to old age, all the feelings he kept locked away in the deepest, darkest part of his heart, and all the secrets he so desperately wanted to hide from everyone—even himself.

Professor Metis had wanted to know what Preston and his Reaper friends might be planning, what their next move might be against the Pantheon. So I'd taken Preston's hand in mine and used my Gypsy gift to delve into his mind.

I'd just never expected to see my own mom's murder.

For months I'd thought that my mom had been killed by a drunk driver coming home from work one night, but looking into Preston's mind had shown me what had really happened. How Preston had been there. How he'd caused the accident by ramming his SUV into my mom's car. How he'd done so on the orders of a mysterious Reaper girl—a girl who was Loki's Champion and was searching for the Helheim Dagger that my mom had hidden years ago. And then, finally, how the Reaper girl had plunged her sword into my mom's heart, killing her.

The same Reaper girl who was standing in front of me right now.

The awful pain of that moment, of reliving my mom's murder, knifed through my heart, splintering it into a thousand broken, bloody shards. I let out a noise that was somewhere between a whimper and a growl. But along with the pain came anger—more anger than I'd ever felt before. The rage quickly swallowed the pain, burning away everything else except my need for revenge.

"Gwen?" Daphne whispered, sensing the change in me. "What's wrong?"

For a moment, I couldn't speak; I couldn't move; I couldn't even think. There was nothing but the rage that filled every cell of my body. Finally, I forced the words out through clenched teeth.

"It's her," I muttered. "The Reaper girl. Loki's Champion. That's her right there."

The girl who killed my mom.

"Hey," one of the other Reapers said, staring down at

the glass that littered the floor. "Why are all the cases in here smashed already—"

"Now, Daphne!" I screamed. "Now!"

Everything seemed to happen in slow motion. Daphne rose up from her spot behind the stuffed horse, already drawing back her golden arrow and lining up her shot, aiming for the other girl. But the Reaper saw what she was doing, grabbed the man next to her, and shoved him in front of her, using him as a human shield. Daphne let go of her bowstrings.

Thwang!

My best friend's aim was true, but the arrow zoomed into the man's heart instead of the Reaper girl's.

A Valkyrie, I thought, making a mental note in the back of my mind. The Reaper girl had to be a Valkyrie, had to have a Valkyrie's superstrength, to shove a grown man around like he weighed nothing.

Beside me, a puff of golden smoke filled the air, and another arrow appeared in the onyx quiver strapped to Daphne's back. My friend had been right—that was wicked cool. Daphne saw me staring at her. She nodded, reached back, and grabbed the arrow.

"Kill them!" the Reaper girl bellowed over the noise of the still-blaring alarms. "Kill them all!"

The other Reapers didn't hesitate. Five of them charged forward while the Reaper girl stayed where she was. Two of the Reapers raced by the wax Viking.

With a loud battle cry, Logan leaped out from his hiding spot and rammed his sword into the Reaper closest to him, wounding his enemy. For a moment, there was mass confusion, before those two turned to fight Logan;

the other three hurried in our direction, one going right and the last two going left.

Carson and I stepped out from behind the stuffed horse to meet them, still keeping Daphne in between us. She put an arrow in one of the guys to the left, felling him just before he reached Carson. That was all that I saw before the Reaper on my side of the dais attacked.

Swipe-swipe-swipe.

The Reaper swung his sword at my head, but I parried his blows. I hadn't been going to Mythos Academy for very long, and I hadn't had the lifelong weapons training the other kids had had, but I'd gotten a crash course in learning how to stay alive these last few months. The Reaper raised his sword for another strike, but I ducked behind the figure of the Roman centurion, putting it between us. The Reaper wasn't quite quick enough to pull his blow, and his sword stuck in the wax that made up the Roman's chest. He frantically tugged on his weapon, trying to free it for another strike at me.

I didn't hesitate. It was kill or be killed, and if the situation had been reversed, the Reaper would have done the same to me. Still, that knowledge, that cold logic, didn't make me feel any better as I darted forward and shoved Vic into the Reaper's chest with all my strength. The Reaper screamed and clawed at the silver blade, trying to rip Vic out of my hands. I tightened my grip, yanked the sword out, then plunged it into his stomach. The Reaper screamed again and stumbled back. He sprawled to a stop on the floor below the dais, and he didn't get back up.

"Nicely done, Gwen!" Vic shouted, his mouth moving underneath my sweaty hand.

"Shut up, Vic!" I screamed back at him.

On the other side of the dais, Carson battled another Reaper, parrying the Reaper's sword with the staff he'd grabbed earlier. Daphne stood a few feet behind him, her bow up and ready, just waiting to put an arrow into the Reaper as soon as she got a clear shot. Across the room, Logan had killed the Reaper he'd stabbed before and was battling the second one.

My head whipped around to the seventh and final Reaper—the girl who'd murdered my mom. She stood in the same spot as before, a long, curved sword in her black-gloved hand. She stared at me, and through the slits in her mask, I saw the faintest glint of her eyes—and the spark of red that flashed in their depths. The angry, hate-filled flicker burned like a match underneath the twisted rubber covering her face.

"Well, well, well," the Reaper girl hissed. "If it isn't Nike's Champion, slinging a sword like she actually knows how to use it. I was hoping I might run into you here."

Her words made my stomach twist with fear, but I pushed the feeling aside. I knew the Reaper girl wanted to kill me. She'd threatened to do so in the memory I had of her stabbing my mom. I supposed I shouldn't have been surprised that she knew who I was and what I looked like. Professor Metis had once told me that Champions could recognize other Champions, that we were inevitably drawn to each other, attracting and repelling like magnets.

"Yeah, it's me. Gwen Frost," I snapped. "Nike's Champion in the flesh. I know what you did to my mom."

The girl threw back her head and laughed. She just— laughed. Low, long, and loud. Like it was funny that she'd killed my mom in cold blood. Like it was the most hysterical thing *ever* that she and her Reaper friends had just done the same thing to a museum full of innocent people.

"Well, I should certainly hope so," she said. "Killing your weak, sniveling mother was the most fun I've had in *ages*."

Rage once again filled my heart, blocking out everything else. All my questions, all my worries, all my fears. There was only me and her and my desire for revenge, this burning, burning need I had to make her pay, to make her *suffer* for taking my mom away from me.

With a roar, I leaped off the dais, raised my sword, and rushed forward—and the Reaper girl stepped up to meet me.

Chapter 3

I swung Vic in a vicious arc at the Reaper girl, trying to separate her head from her shoulders with one blow, trying to avenge my mom with one quick strike, trying to do something, anything to ease this intense ache in my heart.

It didn't work.

She easily blocked my attack and let out another mocking laugh. "Is that the best you can do, Gypsy? Pathetic. No wonder the Pantheon is doomed to fail, with you as Nike's Champion."

Then, the Reaper girl snapped up her gloved hand and hit me in the face. *Yep,* I thought, staggering back as pain exploded in my jaw. *Definitely a Valkyrie with a punch like that.*

I barely had time to blink the flashing stars out of my eyes before the Reaper girl came at me with her own sword. I lurched to one side, just managing to get out of the way of the whistling blade. The weapon stuck in the wooden base of one of the glass artifact cases I'd smashed. The sudden, jarring stop made the Reaper girl lose her grip on her weapon and stumble away.

Eyes wide, I stared down at the other girl's sword, which was a foot away from where my head had been a second before. Strange symbols gleamed on the surface of the blade, just below the hilt, each one of them outlined in the blackening blood that already coated the sword there.

Metis had told me that all the gods and goddesses gave their Champions a weapon, since Champions were those picked by the gods to carry out their wishes here in the mortal realm. The professor had also said that only a Champion could read the words on her specific weapon. *Victory always* was carved into Vic's blade. I wondered what the Reaper girl's sword said. Somehow I knew it had something to do with blood, pain, and death.

But that wasn't the only thing I noticed. Half of a face was set into the sword's hilt—a woman's face with a single crimson eye that was glaring at me. Hate made the orb burn as bright as a bloody sun.

I bit back a shriek and brought up Vic, so he could see the other sword.

"Lucretia," Vic snarled, apparently recognizing it.

"Vic," the other sword growled back in a low, feminine voice. "I'd so hoped that someone had finally melted you down and used you for scrap metal."

"Scrap metal!" Vic scoffed. "I'll show you scrap metal, you tarnished toothpick!"

Okay, so the Reaper girl had a talking sword, too, one that seemed to have just as much attitude as Vic did.

Super, super *creepy,* but right now, I was more concerned about not getting stabbed to death than about
the fact that her weapon was a mirror image of mine.

The Reaper girl surged to her feet, yanked her sword
free of the wooden base, and turned to face me once
more. Behind me, I could hear the *clang-clang-clang* of
a Reaper's sword hitting Logan's shield. Up on the dais,
Carson still struggled with the last Reaper, while Daphne
yelled at the band geek to get out of the way so she
could put an arrow through the Reaper's heart.

"Get ready to die, Gypsy," the Reaper girl snarled, as
she came at me again.

Clash-clash-clash.

Our swords rang together, and glass crunched like ce-
real under our feet as we battled back and forth across
the room. The other girl's Valkyrie strength gave her a
big advantage, and every single one of her blows threatened to tear Vic out of my sweaty, shaking grasp. Not to
mention that the Reaper girl knew *exactly* what she was
doing when it came to fighting. She moved from one attack position to the next, and she never stopped coming
at me—not even for a second.

Desperate, I tried to call up my memories of Logan
and the Spartan's fighting prowess, tried to tap into
those memories and Logan's skills with my psychometry
magic. But there was just too much going on, and I
couldn't focus the way I needed to.

Swipe-swipe-swipe.

The Reaper girl laughed again, her sword inching
closer to my throat with every single pass, and I got the
sense that she was just toying with me. That she could

have killed me anytime she liked but wanted to draw out the fight for as long as possible for her own twisted amusement—

"Carson!" Daphne screamed, her frantic voice penetrating my rage. "Carson!"

I looked at the dais just in time to see the Reaper there lunge forward and ram his sword into Carson's chest.

"No!"

I didn't know if I screamed or if Daphne did or if it was both of us together, but Carson crumpled to the dais, blood splashing everywhere. Logan increased his attacks on the second Reaper he'd been fighting so he could finish him off and rush over to help Carson, but I knew it was already too late.

"Awww, did one of your friends get hurt, Gypsy? What a shame," the Reaper girl mocked me.

Rage, fear, and adrenaline filled my heart, and I didn't think—I just acted. I threw myself at the Reaper girl, tackling her and driving her to the floor. The move surprised her, and she lost her grip on her sword, which clattered away. I could hear Lucretia shouting at the girl, but I didn't stop my attack. Even though I didn't have her Valkyrie strength, I raised Vic and smashed the hilt of the sword into the Reaper girl's face, hoping that I could break her nose underneath that hideous Loki mask.

"That's my girl!" Vic roared. "Keep it up, Gwen!"

But the Reaper girl wasn't done for. Somehow she got her arms in between us and shoved me off her. I stumbled back and landed on my butt, glass digging into my hands and even more slicing through my jeans.

The Reaper girl scrambled to her feet. In her haste to grab her sword, something soft and white fluttered out of the folds of her black robe and fell to the floor. The girl stretched out her hand, making a frantic grab for it, but I staggered to my feet, lurched forward, and swung Vic at her again, making her scuttle back.

The Reaper girl glared at me, her eyes flashing like rubies behind her rubber mask, and let out a vicious curse. Then, she did the strangest thing of all—she turned and ran out of the room.

"Where is she going? Why is she bloody retreating?" Vic snapped, echoing my own thoughts.

"I have no idea, but she's not getting away," I growled.

I took a step forward, ready to chase after her, when Daphne screamed again. This time, it wasn't a scream of fear—it was one of rage.

My head snapped around. While I'd been battling the Reaper girl, Daphne had stepped up to fight Carson's attacker, using her onyx bow as a shield to block his attacks and the latest arrow from the magical quiver as a makeshift sword. Over and over, the Valkyrie stabbed at the Reaper with the arrow, causing the man to back up. His foot caught on something I couldn't see, and Daphne stepped forward and shoved the arrow into the Reaper's chest. The man screamed and stumbled back, the arrow sticking out of his heart like a golden finger.

Daphne didn't care, though. She turned around and fell to her knees beside Carson. Tears streamed down her pretty face as she cradled the band geek's head in her hands. I hurried toward her. Across the room, I saw Logan kill the last Reaper and do the same.

"Stop, Gwen, stop!" Vic yelled at me.

I pulled up short of the dais, and Logan skidded to a halt beside me.

"What? What's wrong? Are there more Reapers?" Logan asked, his head turning back toward the door.

"No, it's the Valkyrie," Vic said. "Her magic is finally quickening. Just watch and give her a little room."

We did as he said. If Vic was right, then Daphne's hidden Valkyrie power—latent until now—was about to erupt in a big, big way.

I propped Vic up against the side of the stuffed horse so he could see what was going on. As we watched, more and more pink sparks began to flicker around Daphne, until a continuous stream of magic flowed out of her fingertips. Daphne cried the whole time, tears falling off her face and mixing with the magic in the air. Every time one of the Valkyrie's tears hit the stream, the magic sparked and cracked, taking on a rosy glow tinged with gold. That rosy glow just kept growing and growing, until it covered Daphne's entire body—and Carson's too.

"Carson," Daphne pleaded, staring down at the band geek. "Please, *please* don't die. You can't die. I won't let you. Do you hear me?"

I didn't know if the Valkyrie did it herself or if it was just her magic having a mind of its own, but something shifted at her words. The magic coalesced around her, no longer sparking and cracking, but instead filling the whole room with its warm power. Even though I was exhausted from my fight with the Reaper girl, something about that glow soothed me, made me feel stronger, more vibrant, more alive.

For the first time, I noticed that blood wasn't dripping out of the gaping wound on Carson's chest anymore. Instead, the warm, rosy gold glow of Daphne's magic had settled on top of his heart, right where the Reaper had stabbed him. The glow seemed like—like it was *helping* Carson. I watched while the rough edges of the wound drew together and then seamlessly healed. In a few seconds, it was like Carson had never been stabbed at all.

"Healing," I whispered. "Daphne's power is healing."

"Looks like she's doing a pretty good job of it, too," Vic said. "I think the Celt might make it after all."

Carson started coughing, almost like he'd heard Vic's words. For a moment, Carson's eyes fluttered open, and he looked at Daphne and smiled.

"Don't you ever do that again," Daphne whispered in a fierce voice.

Carson opened his mouth like he wanted to say something, but his eyes slid shut again before he could get the words out.

"You get Daphne," Logan said. "I'll make sure Carson's okay."

We stepped up onto the dais. Logan knelt down next to Carson and gently put his fingers on the band geek's throat, checking his pulse. Logan nodded at me, and I crouched down beside Daphne and reached for her hand.

My Gypsy gift kicked in the second my fingers closed over hers.

I'd touched Daphne many, many times before. I'd seen her memories and felt her emotions, but I'd never experienced anything like this. It almost seemed like I . . . *fell* into the Valkyrie, slipped into her body in a way that I never had with anyone else before, not even Logan. Her aura, her soul, her spirit, whatever you wanted to call it, my psychometry magic let me see Daphne's heart—the bright, pulsing pink spark that made the Valkyrie the strong warrior and vibrant person she was.

It was *beautiful*—so beautiful that I couldn't help myself. I reached out with my own magic, wanting to somehow touch that lovely spark, wanting to grab hold of Daphne's power and feel it for myself.

And I did.

The warm, pure healing power of Daphne's magic flowed into me, melting away all the aches and pains I'd gotten during my fight with the Reaper girl, healing the cuts on my hands and arms and the bruises on the rest of my body. The longer I held on to that spark, the better I felt—stronger and more alive than ever before. In a few seconds, I was completely well, and all of my injuries were gone, like I'd never fought the Reaper girl at all.

Daphne jerked, as if she'd just suddenly realized that

I was there holding her hand. Her fingers slid out of mine, breaking our connection, and the soothing feel of her magic vanished.

A second later, the rosy glow around her body winked out as well, and Daphne let out a long, tired sigh. Her amber skin looked almost as pale as mine, and her hand shook as she ran it through her blond hair.

"Daphne?" I asked in a low voice. "What did you do?"

"I have no idea," she mumbled.

Then, the Valkyrie passed out, her body pitching forward and sprawling on top of Carson's.

For a second, I didn't know what to do. Then, I lurched forward and grabbed my friend's shoulder.

"Daphne! Daphne!" I said, shaking the Valkyrie.

She didn't respond. Neither did Carson, although the wound in his chest was now completely healed.

Logan leaned forward and put his hands on my arms. "Relax, Gypsy girl, relax. They're both fine. Just unconscious. Carson because he was hurt so badly, and Daphne because her magic finally quickened. It's okay."

The Spartan's words penetrated my panic, and I looked at my friends. Their faces were pale, but their chests moved up and down with a steady rhythm. I watched them for a few seconds to make sure, but Logan was right. They were both okay. Yeah, what had just happened was totally freaky, but my friends were alive. That was what was important.

For the first time, I noticed the coliseum was utterly,

eerily quiet. The alarms had quit blaring, people had quit screaming, and I didn't hear the *thump-thump-thump* of the Reapers' footsteps anymore.

Had the Reapers left? Had they found the Helheim Dagger and disappeared with it? Was anyone still breathing in the museum besides us? Logan and I were fine, but Daphne and Carson needed help. With a jolt, I realized that so would the wounded kids outside—if any of them were even still alive. I'd forgotten about the other students and everything else while I'd been fighting the Reaper girl.

"Do you think the Reapers are gone?" I asked Logan in a low voice.

"I don't know, but we need to go see what's happening in the rest of the museum with the other kids." He drew in a breath. "And Nickamedes, too."

Nickamedes and Logan were so different it was easy for me to forget that the librarian was Logan's uncle and that the Spartan cared about him just as much as I did my Grandma Frost.

"That's all well and good," Vic piped up from his spot against the stuffed horse. "But first, don't you think you need to check the Reapers in here? Never turn your back on an enemy unless he or she is no longer a threat. You should know that, Spartan."

"He's right," Logan said, picking up his sword again. "We need to make sure this room is secure before we go see about the others."

The Spartan went one way, and I went the other, both of us moving through the room, swords in hand, checking on the Reapers lying on the floor.

They were all dead. I could tell by the weird angles of their arms and legs, the absolute stillness of their bodies, and the way their sightless eyes dully glinted through the slits in their rubber masks.

I looked around the room a final time to make sure I hadn't overlooked any of the bodies, and my gaze caught on something small and white lying in the middle of the glass and blood. I walked over and crouched down to get a better look at it.

A piece of paper folded into a thick square rested on the floor. So that was what had fallen out of the Reaper girl's robe while we'd been fighting. Weird. I would have expected her to have a dagger or two tucked into her pockets instead.

Since I wasn't sure what vibes were attached to the paper and what I might see if I touched it with my bare hand, I pulled my hoodie sleeve down and used the edge of the fabric to pick up the square. I couldn't open it, not without touching it with my fingers, so I settled for sliding the paper into my jeans pocket.

"What's that?" Vic asked.

"I'm not sure," I said. "But I'm guessing it's important since I almost took the Reaper girl's head off while she was reaching for it."

Vic sniffed. "And more's the pity you didn't."

Once the bodies were checked, I met Logan in the middle of the room. Daphne and Carson were still lying on the dais, but since there wasn't another door that led in here, they'd be safe enough while we figured out what was going on in the rest of the museum.

"You ready for this, Gypsy girl?" Logan asked in a soft voice. "Because it's not going to be pretty out there."

It wasn't pretty in here, but I didn't have to tell him that. He could see the blood and bodies as well as I could.

"I don't know that I'll ever be ready, but if there are people out there we can help, we have to try."

Logan stared at me, his eyes locking with mine. He put his arm around me and held me close. I closed my eyes and listened to the steady *thump-thump-thump* of his heart under my fingers. I could have stood there and listened to that sound forever.

"We're fine," he whispered. "We survived."

A sob rose in my throat at the thought of the horrible things that had happened, the horrible things that we'd all done, but I swallowed it down.

"I know," I whispered back. "I know."

Logan held me for another second. Then, he let me go, raised his sword, and eased over to the doorway. I tightened my grip on Vic and followed him. Together, we peered out into the main part of the coliseum.

Bodies sprawled across the floor, looking like larger pieces of debris next to the smashed artifacts. Glass, pottery, metal, and wood covered the marble like a ragged carpet. Everything that could have been broken was, and even the paintings had been torn off the walls and trampled. It looked like a tornado had ripped through the museum—it was just utter, bloody chaos.

But there were some survivors. A few students had

pushed themselves up into sitting positions, holding their hands over their wounds to try and slow the blood loss. Others slumped against the tall pillars, dazed, vacant looks in their eyes. Still more lay where they had fallen and quietly cried, their shoulders shaking and the tears slipping down their faces and mixing with the bloody debris on the floor.

"You check on the kids in here," Logan said in a low voice. "I'm going to the other rooms to see if there are any other survivors—and hopefully to find Nickamedes."

I nodded. The Spartan headed down one of the corridors while I stepped back into the main museum space. A few feet away, I spotted Morgan McDougall crouching over a body. Since she was the closest student to me, I headed in her direction, holding Vic and keeping an eye out for any Reapers who might still be lurking in the coliseum.

"Morgan?" I asked in a low voice. "Are you okay?"

The Valkyrie looked up at the sound of my voice, and I realized who she was crouching over—Samson Sorensen. The Viking was one of the cutest guys at the academy, but now he was dead, his handsome face pinched with pain, his empty eyes staring up at the ceiling and reflecting back the sheen of the metal discs there.

"It's okay," I whispered. "I'm here to help. Are the Reapers gone?"

"Yes," Morgan said in a shaky voice. "One of them ran out of the room you were in. A girl, I think. She shouted something at the others, and they all ran down one of the hallways. They left. They just left. Like they'd finally gotten whatever it was they'd come for."

I frowned. I hadn't seen Loki's Champion pick up any weapons or artifacts, and the other Reapers who'd come into the room were dead, so they wouldn't be taking anything out with them. Had the Helheim Dagger been in another part of the coliseum? Was that why the Reaper girl and her friends had gone in such a hurry? My head started to ache from all the questions that I just didn't know the answers to.

Morgan turned back to Samson, smoothing the Viking's sandy hair back from his bloody face. "I really did love him, you know? Even though he was Jasmine's boyfriend and we were sneaking around behind her back, I loved him the whole time."

Back in the fall, Morgan had been hooking up with Samson even though he'd been dating Morgan's best friend, Jasmine Ashton. What no one had known was that Jasmine was really a Reaper. Jasmine had been so upset when she found out Morgan was sneaking around with her boyfriend that Jasmine had tried to sacrifice Morgan to Loki. She would have, too—if I hadn't stopped her that night in the Library of Antiquities.

I started to answer Morgan, to tell her it was okay, that I understood how she felt about Samson, when I noticed a shadow on the floor beside us—one that was creeping closer and closer. Maybe the Reapers hadn't left after all. Fear flooded my body at the thought.

I waited a second, letting the shadow get in range, then I tightened my grip on Vic, whirled around, and raised the sword over my head, ready to bring the blade down on whoever was lurking behind me.

"Gwendolyn! Stop!" Nickamedes barked, taking a step back and holding up his hand. "It's just me."

It took me a second to focus on the librarian—and another one to notice all the blood on his clothes and the sword in his hand. Nickamedes's suit jacket was ripped and torn, his shirt was untucked, and his tie had been sliced in two, leaving only the knot hanging around his throat. Cuts and scrapes crisscrossed his hands like Xs and Os, and the right side of his face had puffed up with the beginning of a black eye.

I looked around the room again and noticed that several black-robed bodies littered the floor, along with those of the Mythos students. Nickamedes must have heard the commotion when the Reapers stormed into the coliseum and came out fighting. He would have too, since he was a Spartan just like Logan, with the same fighting skills and killer warrior instinct. Nickamedes had probably chased after the Reapers when they'd left.

The librarian looked just as wild and haggard as I felt, but concern filled his face as he stared at the blood on my clothes and on Vic. For the first time, I realized that maybe Nickamedes did care about the academy students after all—even me.

"Gwendolyn?" Nickamedes asked again. "Where's Logan?"

"He's fine. He went looking for you."

I slowly lowered my sword to my side, cold exhaustion filling my body like ice water being poured into a glass. I stared out at the dead students and all the other ones who were still bleeding and crying.

"Are you okay?" Nickamedes asked in a soft voice.

"I'm not hurt, if that's what you mean." I shook my head. "But I don't know that I'll ever be okay again."

Chapter 4

I don't remember much of what happened after that. Well, that's not exactly true. I remembered—I would *always* remember—even if all I wanted to do was forget.

Nickamedes called the Powers That Were at Mythos Academy, and thirty minutes later, other people started arriving. Most of them were professors at the academy, like Mr. Llew, my calculus teacher, Mrs. Banba, the economics prof, and Coach Lir, who oversaw the academy swim teams. Nobody called the cops. The regular mortal police wouldn't understand what had happened, and they just weren't equipped to fight Reapers—or to deal with the deadly destruction they'd caused.

Several other adults appeared as well, men and women dressed in heavy black coveralls. They opened the coliseum doors and pushed metal carts covered with black bags inside. I knew what they were here for—to load up the bodies and take them to the academy morgue. I shuddered and kept my gaze away from them.

Professor Metis and Coach Ajax showed up, too,

since they were part of the academy's security council. Metis and Ajax, along with Nickamedes, were responsible for keeping the students safe while they were at Mythos. But we weren't at the academy right now—and no one had been safe today.

What surprised me most was the fact that Raven came to the museum. Raven was the woman who manned the coffee cart in the Library of Antiquities, one of the many duties she seemed to have at the academy. She was an old woman with white hair, black eyes, and a face that was streaked with wrinkles. Raven sported a flowing white gown just like the ones the coliseum staff had worn, although a pair of black combat boots peeked out from underneath her long skirt.

Raven stood off to one side of the museum, gazing out at the destruction. Her arms were crossed over her chest, and I could see old, faded scars on her skin there, along with dark brown liver spots. She noticed me staring at her, and our eyes met. For a moment, her image wavered, like there was another, younger, prettier face beneath her wrinkles. But the really weird thing was that I felt something when I looked into her eyes—an aching wave of pain and sadness so intense that it made tears start to trickle down my own cheeks. Like somehow the attack today was all her fault. . . .

I blinked, and she was just Raven once more, the old woman who sold snacks in the library. The pain and sadness were gone and so were the tears I'd thought had been sliding down my face. I reached up, but my skin was completely dry. Weird. Really weird.

I looked at Raven, but she ignored me, walked over,

and started speaking to the woman who was loading Samson's body onto a metal cart. Raven moved through the crowd, talking to the adults who were here to clear away the blood and debris. Overseeing them must be another one of her academy odd jobs. I guess I shouldn't have been surprised, since she was on the security council with Metis and the others.

After another minute, I pushed Raven out of my mind. Her flickering face wasn't the most awful thing I'd seen today. My eyes lingered on a smear of blood on the white marble floor.

Not even close.

An hour after the attack, I stood in an office in the back of the coliseum, watching Metis examine Carson. The professor had made the band geek sit on a desk and take off his shirt. She'd spent several minutes peering at his chest, even though not a mark remained where the Reaper had stabbed him. After that, Metis had run her hands through Carson's dusky brown hair, looking for any head injuries. Now, she was shining a small flashlight into his brown eyes, watching them react to the glare.

"Is he going to be okay?" I asked.

I leaned against the wall next to Logan. Nickamedes was on the other side of the Spartan, while Coach Ajax stood in the doorway, filling the open space with his massive frame.

Metis clicked off the flashlight. "He's going to be fine. They both are."

The professor's green eyes drifted over to Daphne,

who was slumped in a chair. The Valkyrie had woken up by the time I'd taken Nickamedes to the weapons room, but she still looked exhausted. Every once in a while, a pink spark would weakly flicker on one of her fingertips, like she'd used up her energy for the day and that was all the magic she could summon up. I supposed that she had, healing Carson the way she did.

Metis nodded at Daphne. She'd finished examining the Valkyrie a few minutes ago. "You saved Carson's life today with your magic."

"I suppose this means I'll have to get you something extra special for Valentine's Day," Carson joked.

Daphne tried to smile, but pain filled her black eyes. She'd come so close to losing Carson—she couldn't just forget that, even if the band geek was alive and sitting right in front of her. I knew the feeling because I'd gone through it with Logan a few weeks back. Logan stared at me, and I could tell he was thinking the same thing—about how close Preston Ashton had come to killing us both, along with our Spartan friend, Oliver Hector.

Once Metis finished with Carson, the band geek put his shirt back on, even though it was as ripped and bloody as the rest of our clothes were.

"What do you suppose they were after? What did the Reapers want?" Coach Ajax asked, crossing his arms over his broad, muscled chest. The overhead lights made his onyx skin gleam like polished jet.

Nickamedes's mouth twisted. "You mean other than killing six students, five of the museum staff members, and injuring a dozen more? You don't think that was enough for them?"

Ajax shrugged his broad shoulders. For the first time, I noticed a weary look on his face. Normally, big, burly Coach Ajax reminded me of a granite statue more than anything else, something solid and unbreakable, but today he seemed small and deflated, despite his tall frame.

"The Helheim Dagger," I said in a quiet voice. "That's what they were after, that's what the Reaper girl told the others to search for. It was her, Loki's Champion. She came into the weapons room looking for the dagger. She's the one I fought."

Metis stared at me. "Are you sure it was her? And that she was after the dagger?"

I nodded. Metis knew all about the dagger and the fact that my mom had hidden it from the Reapers. She and my mom had been best friends years ago when they'd gone to Mythos Academy.

"Well, that would certainly explain the full-frontal assault," Nickamedes said in a dark tone. "The Reapers will do anything to get their hands on that dagger."

Nobody said anything. We all knew the dagger was the last remaining seal on Loki's mythological prison. If the Reapers ever found the dagger, they could use it to free the god and set him loose in the mortal realm once more. I was kind of fuzzy on exactly *how* they were supposed to use the dagger to do that, but I knew people would die if Loki ever got free—so many people.

So many people had died already today.

"I wonder why they thought the dagger was here?" Metis asked. "The Crius Coliseum isn't known for its artifacts collection. Its pottery and art, certainly, but not high-end, magically powerful artifacts and especially not weapons."

"Maybe this will help." I used the edge of my hoodie sleeve to pull the white square of paper out of my jeans pocket. "The Reaper girl dropped this while we were fighting. I haven't touched it yet so I don't know what kind of vibes might be attached to it. After—after what happened today, I don't know that I want to touch it."

Metis, Ajax, and Nickamedes looked at each other, then Metis stepped forward and took the paper from me. Carson got to his feet, and she spread it out on the desk where he'd been sitting. We all gathered around and stared at the paper.

It had been folded several times and almost covered the entire desk by the time Metis finished spreading it out and smoothing down the edges. The paper featured a detailed map of—of something. I couldn't tell what, exactly. Something with a dome, judging by the round shape in the top left corner of the map. Small Xs had been drawn all over the paper in what looked like random positions. There was no pattern to the marks that I could see. All put together, it looked like squiggly gibberish. What was so important about this that the Reaper girl had almost let me take her head off rather than leave it behind?

Ajax let out a curse and turned away from the paper. Metis sighed and rubbed her head, as though it was suddenly aching. Nickamedes stayed where he was, though, still staring down at the paper, a thoughtful look on his face.

"What is it?" I asked. "What's wrong?"

"It's a map," Nickamedes said.

I rolled my eyes. Well, yeah, I could *see* that. But a map of what? Where? And why was it so important?

As if hearing my snide thoughts, the librarian looked up at me. "It's a map of the Library of Antiquities."

I frowned. "The library? Why would the Reaper girl have a map of the library?"

Nickamedes kept staring at me, and the answer popped into my head.

"The library," I whispered. "The Reapers think the Helheim Dagger is hidden somewhere in the Library of Antiquities."

"Apparently so."

I looked at Nickamedes. "Well?"

"Well what?"

"Well, *is* it hidden somewhere in there?" I demanded. "Have you known where it was this whole time?"

My voice got louder and sharper with every word. Logan walked over and put his hand on my shoulder, telling me to take it easy, but too many awful things had happened today for me to do that.

Nickamedes stiffened, then straightened up to his full height and peered down his nose at me. "I assure you that the dagger is *not* in the library. I know every inch of the place, and I would have discovered it long ago."

"Really? Like you knew that Jasmine Ashton was hiding in a storage room on the fourth floor with the Bowl of Tears last semester?" I sniped. "If I remember right, you thought some anonymous Reaper bad guy had stolen the bowl and smuggled it out of the library. But things didn't turn out that way, did they?"

Nickamedes's cheeks flushed an angry red, and he opened his mouth, ready to argue with me some more. Metis stepped in front of him, putting her hand on his chest.

"Enough," she said. "That's enough, both of you. Bickering among ourselves isn't going to solve anything. I'm sure Nickamedes is right and that the dagger isn't hidden in the library. Otherwise, someone would have stumbled across it years ago."

"But that's why the Reapers were here today, isn't it?" Coach Ajax rumbled in his deep voice. "Because most of the weapons and artifacts on display were on loan from the library. For whatever reason, the Reapers think the dagger is hidden in the library. They must have thought that Nickamedes didn't recognize it, that maybe it was labeled as something else and he packed it up and brought it to the coliseum to be displayed. At the very least, the Reapers knew they'd have an easier time breaking in here than they would the library."

"Well, who knows what the great mind of Grace Frost came up with," Nickamedes muttered in a snide tone. "Or where she hid the dagger to start with. I never understood some of the choices she made. Grace was a fool, if you ask me, about a great many things."

Anger exploded like fireworks in my chest at his harsh words. "And what would you know about my mom?" I snapped, my hands curling into fists. "She's dead, remember? Murdered by the Reapers because she was trying to keep the dagger safe from them. So don't you dare say another word about her!"

Nickamedes eyed me, his blue gaze dark. Logan tightened his grip on my shoulder, his fingers pressing into my skin through the fabric of my clothes. The librarian looked at me another second before his gaze skipped over to his nephew. Nickamedes's lips pulled down into another frown.

"The dagger isn't in the library," he insisted once more. "I don't even know why we're bothering to discuss this. I'm going to see if the parents of the injured students have arrived yet."

The librarian grabbed the office door and slammed it behind him as he stalked out of the room and down the hallway.

"What is with him and his bad attitude?" I muttered.

Metis shook her head. "It's a long story."

The professor stared at the map again, looking at all the Xs marked on it. Now that I knew it was a map of the library, I recognized some of the spots covered by the Xs. The checkout counter where I worked, the spot where the Bowl of Tears had once stood, the coffee cart set up to provide snacks to the students. Strange. Hundreds of kids tromped by those places every single day. I would have thought the Reapers would have marked more out-of-the-way spots, places more likely for my mom to have hidden the dagger and for it to have stayed safe all these years.

We looked at the map for a few more minutes before Metis took it over to the copier in the corner and made several duplicates of it, probably to give to the Powers That Were at the academy. Once that was done, the professor held out the original piece of paper to me, a clear question in her eyes.

I sighed. I didn't feel like using my Gypsy gift. Not now, not after everything that had happened, but I didn't have a choice. I needed to find the dagger before the Reapers did, and my psychometry magic was the best chance I had of doing that.

So I sat down on a chair, closed my fingers around the paper, and waited for the memories and emotions associated with the map to fill my mind.

The first image that popped into my head was one of the Reaper girl. She wore the same black robe and rubber mask she'd had on today, and she stood in an opulent living room. Dark wooden furniture, heavy, antique sofas, large paintings on the walls, crystal vases full of red and black roses. I watched as the Reaper girl leaned over the map, which was spread out on a table in front of her.

"Are you sure the dagger's in the library?" she asked.

She turned her head, and I realized that she was talking to a man. He wasn't wearing a robe and mask like she was, so I could see his face, but he wasn't one of the academy professors or staff members, so I had no idea who he was.

"I'm sure," he said. "All the locating spells we've done confirm it. The Helheim Dagger is hidden somewhere in the Library of Antiquities."

The Reaper girl looked up at a painting on the wall, one that showed a Black roc. I'd seen pictures of the gigantic bird in my myth-history book before, but this painting showed exactly how large and fierce it was. The roc was big, just as big as other mythological creatures like Nemean prowlers and Fenrir wolves, with curved, black talons that were capable of plucking a man off the ground—or tearing him to pieces. Its entire body was a glossy black, although this painting emphasized the bloody red tinge to the creature's feathers and the red spark that burned in the depths of its liquid black eyes.

The Reaper girl stared out at the rest of the room, and I realized that practically every piece of furniture and knickknack had an image of the bird painted on or carved into it. The chairs, the tables, several vases, a pair of bookends, even a marble statue in the corner. Someone was a little obsessed.

"Well, then," the Reaper girl said in a smirking voice. "If the dagger's in the library, I guess we should go get it, shouldn't we?"

The two of them started discussing where the dagger might be hidden and how they could go about pinpointing its exact location. Apparently, whatever security spells Nickamedes had placed in and around the library were blocking the bad guy's magic, which was why he couldn't be more specific about the dagger's location.

I frowned. Maybe I wasn't concentrating hard enough, but it seemed like there was something slightly off about the memories attached to the map. Something obvious I was missing. Something that didn't seem quite . . . real, like it wasn't a genuine memory or feeling. But try as I might, I couldn't figure out what it was.

Slowly, the flickers and flashes of images and feelings faded away, telling me that I'd gotten all the memories I could from the map. I opened my eyes and looked at the others.

"The Reapers have used some kind of magic mumbo jumbo to track the dagger," I said. "They can't zoom in on its exact location, but they've narrowed it down to somewhere in the library."

"If they think it's hidden in the library, then they'll do whatever it takes to breach campus security so they can search for it themselves," Ajax said. "I need to tell Nickamedes about this. Raven, too."

Metis nodded, and Ajax left the office to go look for the others. Then, the professor let out a weary sigh, sounding just as tired as Ajax had a few minutes before.

"What's wrong?" Daphne asked. "This is good, right? That we know where the dagger is?"

A grim smile curved Metis's lips. "Yes and no. It's good that we have a place to start looking for the dagger, but the library is enormous, and it could be anywhere inside. Even if you had an army of people at your disposal, it would still take years to thoroughly, completely search all seven floors, not to mention the patios and balconies outside and the surrounding grounds."

"There's something else, isn't there? Something else bad?" Carson asked.

Metis looked at him and nodded. "The bad is that not only do we now know where the Helheim Dagger is, but the Reapers do, too—and they'll do whatever it takes to find it first."

I thought of all the awful things I'd seen today. The Reapers storming into the coliseum and killing everyone within arm's reach; Carson getting stabbed; Daphne screaming; Morgan crouching over Samson's dead body;

the blood that now seemed to coat everything inside the coliseum.

Metis was right. The Reapers wanted the Helheim Dagger, and they didn't care what they had to do or whom they had to kill to find it.

Which meant that everyone at Mythos Academy was in serious, serious danger.

Chapter 5

We left the office and went back out to the main floor. The bodies had been cleared away, but the Mythos students who'd survived the attack clustered together in small groups, watching the men and women in the black coveralls take photographs and do other forensic-type stuff. Raven stood next to one of the pillars, supervising the evidence collection and cleanup.

Some of the kids who lived in or near the city were waiting for their parents to come get them and take them home, while others were going straight to the academy. I'd called my Grandma Frost and told her what had happened, and she was on her way here. She'd dropped Daphne and I off at the coliseum earlier, where we'd met Carson, who had taken a cab from the academy.

Logan, Daphne, Carson, and I drifted over to one side of the coliseum, not standing with the other kids, but not too far away from them either. Some of the students were still crying or just sitting on the floor with dazed looks on their faces. A few, like Abigail Rose, a smart Valkyrie who was in my English lit class, were trying to help the others. Abigail moved through the crowd, passing out bottles of water and tissues and keeping everyone calm. She noticed me watching her and gave me a small smile, which I returned.

My eyes scanned over the other students. To my surprise, more than a few looked back at me, and I realized that people were staring at my friends and me.

By now, everyone knew we'd fought a group of Reapers and had killed several of them. To the others, I suppose that made us heroes, although all we'd been trying to do was just survive. The four of us had been lucky we'd been in the weapons room. If we'd been out here on the main floor, we would have been injured like the other kids were—or worse.

One girl in particular kept staring at me. She was about my size, with a body that was lean and strong. Her hair was a rich, auburn color and frizzed out like crazy, just like mine did, but she had the most amazing golden eyes, like two perfect topazes had been set into her face. Even with a red, runny nose, splotchy face, and tears sliding down her cheeks, she was still quite beautiful. She wore designer clothes like all the kids at Mythos, but she kept tugging at her sleeves, like her shirt was too tight, even though it hung loosely from her shoulders. The girl noticed me watching her. Her cheeks flushed, and she looked away.

"Who's that?" I asked, jerking my head in the girl's direction.

Daphne looked over my shoulder. "Oh, that's Vivian Holler. She's a second-year student, too. An Amazon, I think. She's friends with Savannah and Talia."

"I don't think I've seen her before."

Daphne shrugged. "Vivian's kind of quiet from what I know. Doesn't say much, reads a lot, gets good grades, but isn't so good with weapons. Kind of like you, Gwen."

"Gee. Thanks," I said in a dry tone.

Daphne rolled her eyes and laid her head on Carson's shoulder. She hadn't let the band geek get more than a few steps away from her since the attack. Carson hugged Daphne to his chest, and a few pink sparks of magic shot off her fingertips and flickered in the air between them. Whatever else had happened today, at least Carson was okay. I don't know what Daphne would have done if he'd died. I don't know what *I* would have done.

Logan grabbed my arm and pulled me away from the others.

"You know, this isn't how I wanted school to start," Logan said. "Or how I pictured seeing you again after the break, Gypsy girl."

He gave me a small, sad smile. No, nothing about today had gone the way I'd hoped it would.

"Me either." I bit my lip. "Do you—do you think this is my fault? The attack?"

Logan frowned. "Why would you say that?"

My stomach twisted, but I drew in a breath and forced myself to get the words out. "Because I haven't found the Helheim Dagger yet like Nike wants me to.

Maybe if I'd found it by now, none of this would have happened. Maybe no one would have gotten hurt today. Maybe Carson wouldn't have almost died. Maybe— maybe Samson and the other kids would still be alive."

The Spartan put his hands on my arms. The heat of his body chased away some of the chill that had sunk into my bones. "That's crazy and you know it, Gypsy girl. None of this is your fault. This is how it's been ever since the other gods trapped Loki in that prison realm. The Reapers have been trying to free him, and they've been killing warriors like us ever since. Even if they hadn't been looking for the dagger, they probably would have come here today anyway, just so they could attack the other students and steal the artifacts. So don't you ever think for one second that any of this is your fault."

I nodded, although I didn't really believe him. No matter what he said, I couldn't help thinking that if only I'd been smarter, I would have found the dagger by now. If only I'd been quicker, I could have kept Carson from being stabbed. If only I'd been stronger, I could have killed the Reaper girl and avenged my mom.

If only . . .

Sometimes I thought those were the two most horrible words in the world.

Logan drew me into the strong circle of his arms. I put my head on his shoulder, and he wrapped his arms around me, just holding me—

"Bitch," a voice behind me muttered.

Still in Logan's arms, I raised my head and turned around to see Savannah Warren glaring at me from a few feet away. Savannah was a lovely Amazon with gorgeous green eyes and red hair that tumbled down her back like a copper waterfall. She also happened to be Logan's ex-girlfriend, the one he'd broken up with before the holiday break.

Savannah clutched two bottles of water in her hands, and her fingers tightened around one of them, like she wanted to throw it at me. With her Amazon quickness, she could bean me in the head with the bottle before I'd even realized she'd thrown it—or could even think about ducking.

Thanks to the gossip that had gone around campus before the holidays, I knew Savannah blamed me for Logan's breaking up with her. I supposed she had a right to feel that way. After all, I'd demanded that the Spartan kiss me or let me go during the Winter Carnival trip the students had taken a few weeks before the break.

I'd thought nothing could make me feel any worse today than I already did, but then I saw the hurt that filled Savannah's face as she looked at Logan holding me. I knew that pain—it was the same sharp, longing ache I'd felt whenever I'd seen Logan kissing the other girl. I'd only wanted the Spartan to care about me like I did him. I'd never intended for Savannah to get hurt—but she had.

What a mess I'd made of everything. I stepped out of Logan's arms, even though it was already too late.

"Savannah?" Vivian asked in a soft voice from her spot on the floor several feet away.

The Amazon glared at me another second, then walked over to her friend. She handed Vivian a bottle of water, which the other girl opened with shaking hands and started gulping down. Some of the water spilled onto Vivian's shirt, and Savannah handed her friend a couple of tissues to mop it up. Every few seconds, though, Savannah's angry eyes would cut to me.

Logan sighed. "I'll go talk to her."

I shook my head. "No, she's got a right to be mad at me."

"Oh, yes, she does," another voice drifted over to me. "Because everyone knows how crazy Logan is about you, Gwen. Why, it's almost the stuff of legend at Mythos. How the Gypsy girl tamed the wild, bad-boy Spartan."

Footsteps sounded behind me, and Morgan moved to stand beside me. She looked at Savannah, who was still glaring at me while she talked to Vivian in a low voice.

"Careful, Gypsy," Morgan murmured. "Savannah might look sweet and innocent, but the Amazon has a temper. She's not someone you want to mess with. You know, if you keep this up, you'll turn into me pretty soon. The school slut who goes around stealing other girls' boyfriends."

The Valkyrie let out a harsh, ugly laugh, and a few green sparks hissed in the air around her. Morgan had a reputation for hooking up with any guy who caught her eye, one that had only gotten worse after everyone found out she'd been sneaking around with her best friend's boyfriend.

I'd never figured out how much Morgan remembered of the night Jasmine had tried to sacrifice her to Loki. Jasmine had used a powerful artifact called the Bowl of Tears to basically turn Morgan into a mindless puppet, and Morgan had claimed not to know what had happened. But I had a hunch that she remembered everything Jasmine had done to her, because Morgan had changed since then. She didn't seem as cold and cruel anymore, and she'd even helped me during the Winter Carnival when I'd decided to sneak into another kid's room. Now, the Valkyrie was almost someone I thought I could be friends with because she'd gone through some of the same terrible things that I had.

"I don't think you're the school slut, Morgan," I said in a quiet voice. "I think you kept it together today when the Reapers attacked. You knew you couldn't fight so many of them, so you hid instead. I think that makes you really brave and really smart."

The Valkyrie stared at me in surprise. After a second, her eyes narrowed, but there was a hint of a smile on her face. "You know what? You're actually okay, Gwen."

Morgan headed off to the other side of the coliseum. A soft snort caught my attention, and I realized that Savannah was still glaring at me. She must have heard Morgan's comment about Logan's being crazy about me, because anger once again twisted the Amazon's face.

But the weirdest thing was that Savannah's eyes were glowing red.

Okay, okay, so they weren't really *glowing,* but it seemed to me like a bit of fire flickered in her eyes for the briefest second, the kind of eerie crimson color I'd come to associate with Reapers.

I blinked. As suddenly as it had appeared, the red spark was gone, and Savannah's face was normal once more, making me wonder if I'd only imagined the whole thing. I rubbed my head, which was suddenly aching—

"Gwen!" a familiar voice called out. "Gwen!"

I stood on my tiptoes. An older woman threaded her way through the crowd of people in the coliseum. She looked out of place with her lavender silk shirt, black pants, and black shoes with toes that curled up, like a genie that had somehow escaped from her bottle. Silk scarves covered her body, flowing around her in waves of purple, gray, and green. Silver coins jingled together like musical fringe on the ends of the scarves, the noise echoing to the ceiling and back down again. A coat hung off her shoulders. It matched the iron-gray color of her thick hair, although her eyes were a bright violet in her wrinkled face—the same violet that mine were.

Yeah, my grandma, Geraldine Frost, might have looked out of place in the bloody chaos of the museum, but the sight of her couldn't have made me happier.

Grandma spotted me and hurried in my direction.

I broke away from Logan and threw myself into her open arms. "Grandma!"

She hugged me tight. "It's okay, pumpkin. I'm here now. Everything's going to be all right."

I didn't know if anything would ever be all right again, but I closed my eyes and hugged her even tighter, pretending it was just for this one moment.

Grandma hugged me for several minutes before finally letting me go. Then, she looked over at Logan, who was standing behind me.

"I take it this is the Spartan boy you've been telling

me so much about?" She smiled. "Why, he's even more handsome than you said. You've been holding out on me, pumpkin."

A fierce blush flooded my cheeks. "Grandma!"

She gave me an amused look. "He was going to meet me sooner or later, pumpkin. Trust me on that. I just didn't think it would be today—or in this awful way."

She was right, and there was nothing I could do now but make the introductions. "Logan Quinn this is my grandma, Geraldine Frost. Grandma, this is Logan. My, uh, friend."

I winced as I said the last word. I didn't know that we were just *friends,* but Logan hadn't exactly declared me to be his true love either. Or even just his girlfriend. We hadn't even been out on a date yet.

The two of them shook hands. Logan started to let go, but Grandma Frost clasped both of her hands around his. After a second, her violet eyes took on an empty, glassy look, like she was staring at something very far away, and I felt this presence stir in the air around her—something old, watchful, and knowing.

Grandma Frost was a Gypsy like me, which meant that she had a gift just like I did. In grandma's case, she was psychic and could see the future. Now, it looked like she was getting a glimpse of Logan's.

"It's not your fault, Logan," Grandma murmured to the Spartan. "It wasn't back then, and it won't be in the future."

Logan's face paled at her words, like he knew exactly what she was talking about. He opened his mouth like he wanted to ask my grandma a question but then clamped his lips shut.

After a moment, the invisible force swirling around Grandma faded and so did the vacant look in her eyes. She dropped Logan's hand and stepped back.

"What did you see?" I asked her.

For a moment, I didn't think she was going to answer me, but Grandma finally turned to me and smiled.

"Nothing to worry about, pumpkin," she said. "Besides, you know I don't share other people's fortunes. Client confidentiality and all that."

Client confidentiality? Grandma was a fortune-teller, not a lawyer. She almost always told me about her psychic visions—unless they had something to do with me. It was hard for Grandma to have visions about family members and friends, since the closer she was to a person, the more her feelings for them clouded and influenced what she saw. Even when she did see something about me, she didn't often share what it was. Grandma always said that she wanted me to make my own decisions and follow my own path, instead of relying on a future event that might or might not come to pass. Still, something about the tightness in Grandma's face made me wonder exactly what she'd seen—and how terrible it had been.

Logan stared at my grandma, a wary, almost hurt look in his eyes, like she'd just shared his deepest, darkest secret with the whole world. I wondered if Grandma had seen what I had when I'd touched Logan a few weeks ago—the Spartan standing over the bodies of a woman and a girl. I'd been concentrating on his fighting skills when we'd kissed, but I'd seen that image as well, even though I hadn't been actively searching for it. I wondered if what Grandma Frost had said to Logan had something to do with that memory, if maybe she'd figured out what secret he was keeping from me, the terrible thing he thought would change the way I felt about him. The secret I was bound to discover when my fingers, when my skin, touched his.

I didn't get the chance to figure out what they were keeping from me since we split up after that. Carson headed back to Mythos Academy with Logan and Nickamedes, while Grandma Frost drove Daphne and me to her house a few streets over from downtown Asheville. The separation wouldn't be for long, though, since classes started in the morning, despite the tragedy today. Apparently, the Powers That Were at the academy had decided that being on campus was the safest thing for students right now. After what had happened at the coliseum, I couldn't blame them. For once, I'd be happy to see the stone sphinxes that guarded the school gates.

Grandma parked her car on the street, and the three of us trooped up the gray, concrete steps to her lavender-painted house. A brass sign beside the front door read PSYCHIC READINGS HERE, which was how Grandma used her Gypsy gift to make extra money. Side jobs were sort of a habit in the Frost family, and I used my psychometry magic to find things the other kids at Mythos lost—laptops, cell phones, keys, purses, wallets, jewelry, bras, briefs and boxers.

With my Gypsy gift, it wasn't too hard for me to find

lost objects. Of course, once something was lost, I couldn't actually touch *it,* but people left psychic vibes everywhere they went on almost everything they touched. Usually, all I had to do to find a guy's missing cell phone was run my fingers over the furniture in his dorm room to get an idea of where he'd last put down the phone. And if I didn't immediately flash on the phone's location, then I just kept touching stuff in his room—or wherever the images led me—until I did.

While Daphne went into the living room to call her parents and tell them what had happened, Grandma Frost and I headed into the kitchen. With its sky blue walls and white tile, the kitchen was the brightest, cheeriest room in the house. But today, even it seemed cold, dark, and somber. I pulled out a chair and slumped over the table.

"I made an apple pie while you were at the coliseum," Grandma said. "Do you want some, pumpkin?"

She gestured to a tin she'd put on the counter to cool. The pie sat in between a couple of cookie jars—one shaped like a giant chocolate chip cookie and the other like a blue snowflake. The snowflake jar had been my Christmas present to Grandma, as per our holiday tradition of giving each other something with a snowflake on it. Sort of a natural thing to do when your last name was Frost. This year, Grandma had bought me a long, dark gray wool scarf, gloves, and a matching toboggan, all patterned with glittery silver snowflakes.

"Pumpkin? The pie?" Grandma asked again.

"No, thanks. I don't think I could eat anything right now."

Grandma Frost had some mad baking skills, and I had a serious sweet tooth, but even the warm, sugary pie couldn't tempt me today. It just seemed wrong. To do something as simple as eat dessert after what had happened.

"I know, pumpkin," she said. "I don't feel much like eating myself."

Grandma sat down at the kitchen table and clasped my hand in hers, just the way she'd done to Logan earlier. I closed my eyes and let the warmth of her love fill me up and wash away the awfulness of the day.

"Does it ever get any easier?" I asked in a soft voice, opening my eyes. "Knowing how the Reapers hurt other warriors? Seeing . . . what they do to people? After facing down Jasmine and Preston Ashton, I thought I knew what the Reapers were capable of. But today at the coliseum, it was just . . . horrible."

Grandma shook her head. "I'd like to tell you that it does get easier, that you get used to the blood and violence, but I'd be lying. All I can do is be here for you, Gwen. I'll always be here for you, no matter what—you can count on that."

I thought about my mom and how she'd told me the same thing. That she loved me no matter what and that she'd always be here for me, too. But my mom had been taken away from me, brutally murdered by the Reaper girl.

My mom's death wasn't going to go unpunished.

I didn't care what I had to do, but I was going to find out who the Reaper girl really was—and then I was going to kill her. Maybe that made me no better than the Reapers, but I didn't care. Not after what I'd seen today, not after the Reaper girl had laughed in my face about murdering my mom.

But I forced myself to push those dark thoughts away, at least for now. Today, I was in Grandma Frost's kitchen, and that was what I wanted to focus on. To-morrow, I'd go back to Mythos Academy and start my search for the Helheim Dagger, but for today, we were safe. I was going to enjoy the calm while it lasted.

Grandma and I sat there in the kitchen, just holding hands, for a long, long time.

Chapter 6

Daphne finished her call to her parents and came into the kitchen, but none of us felt like talking or eating. The Valkyrie was still tired from her magic's quickening and healing Carson, so she took a hot shower and went to bed even though it wasn't even eight o'clock yet. Grandma did the same, and so did I.

I wiped the steam off the bathroom mirror and stared at my reflection. Wet, wavy brown hair, a few freckles on my winter-white skin, and eyes that were a strange shade of violet. I'd washed off all the blood that had spattered on me during the attack and thrown my clothes in the trash, but the awful memories were still there, lurking just below the surface of my mind. I shivered and dropped my gaze from the mirror.

Since I couldn't sleep, I wrapped myself in my purple flannel robe and trudged up the stairs to the third floor. Really, it was an attic, although Grandma had put some furniture up here for me. After my mom had died, I'd spent hours up here, just staring out the window, crying, and wondering why my mom had been taken from me so suddenly, so cruelly. I must have asked myself *why* a thousand times, but there was never any answer.

It wasn't any easier now that I knew the real reason why.

I snapped on a lamp. Stacks and stacks of battered cardboard boxes formed a zigzag maze through the attic, stretching from one side of the house to the other. Most of the boxes held your usual clutter, old magazines Grandma had never gotten around to throwing out, worn-out clothes that didn't fit anymore, Christmas decorations we'd put away until next year.

But there were some newer boxes in the mix—boxes full of my mom's things. Her clothes, her books, her jewelry, even her makeup and a bottle of her favorite lilac perfume. Everything my mom had left behind in our old house when she'd been murdered last year. All the pieces of her daily life she'd never use again, thanks to the Reaper girl.

I hadn't looked at the boxes since her death, but now it was a necessity. Over the holiday break, I'd been going through the boxes and the items inside, one by one, trying to find something, anything that would tell me where my mom had hidden the Helheim Dagger. I'd used my psychometry and touched every single item in every single box, hoping my mom had left me a clue somewhere, that I'd pick up something, get a vibe off it, and see exactly where she'd hidden the dagger.

It had been one of the hardest things I'd ever done.

Everything I touched, every sweater I held or necklace I brushed my fingers across brought back a memory of my mom. In a way, it was like I was seeing a condensed version of her life and all the things she'd seen, done, and felt along the way. It was fun flashing on her favorite toys as a kid and seeing her playing with them, her brown hair in pigtails, and freckles dotting her face just like they did mine. But it also reminded me of how much I missed her—and how I'd never see her smile or laugh or talk to her again.

In a way, touching her things was like losing my mom all over again—a dozen little deaths packed into each and every box.

But I was determined to do it. My mom had hidden the dagger back when she'd been going to Mythos and had been the Champion of Nike, the Greek goddess of victory. Now, as the goddess's current Champion, it was my job to find the dagger—before the Reapers did.

My hope had slowly dwindled as I opened box after box and didn't find what I was searching for, until now there was only one box left I hadn't been through. I pulled it over to an old, gray velvet loveseat in the corner, opened the top, and started going through the items inside. Clothes, a worn-out slipper, some dried-up markers, a few books, a roll of quarters my mom had forgotten to take to the bank. It was an odd mix of items.

One by one, I touched everything in the box, wrapping my fingers around the items and reaching for my pyschometry magic, straining to see everything I possibly could with my Gypsy gift. All I got were a few weak flashes of my mom buying the clothes in the store or shaking the markers and grumbling because they were out of ink. Pretty standard stuff. Most of the time, I didn't get much of a vibe off common, everyday objects that had a specific purpose or function or ones that tons of people used every day like pens, computers, or paper clips. I only got the big, high-def flashes, the major whammies of memories and feelings, when I touched something a person had a deep, emotional connection to, something she'd imprinted a piece of herself on, like a treasured family heirloom ring or a favorite Christmas ornament someone had made when he was a kid.

Still, one by one, I went through the items in the box, looking into the pockets on the clothes and shaking the books in case something had been slipped between the pages. Nothing. I pulled out the final sweater in the box and set it aside, ready to give up, when I noticed there was something underneath it—an old shoebox. I grabbed it and popped off the top, expecting to find a pair of winter boots my mom hadn't worn in ten years.

Instead, a small, leather-bound diary nestled in tissue paper lay inside the box.

Curious, I reached down and pulled out the diary. From the tissue paper, I got a small flicker of my mom packing away the book, but that was all. The diary's gray leather cover was worn and faded, and the edges of the pages looked wavy and crinkled, as though someone had spilled water on them. Bits of silver glinted dully on the cover, swirled into the curlicue shapes of vines and leaves that ran onto the spine and then flowed over the back of the diary.

I'd never known my mom had kept a diary, but now that I'd found it, I couldn't wait to see what memories it held—and what secrets my mom might have left behind.

So I drew in a breath, pushed the tissue paper aside, stroked my fingers over the soft leather cover, and closed my eyes.

My psychometry magic immediately kicked in, and images of my mom flooded my mind. Mostly, the memories showed her sitting at a desk in a dorm room, doodling and scribbling in the diary. She was young then, about my age, seventeen or so, her brown hair pulled back into a loose ponytail, and I realized that she must have kept the diary when she was attending the academy. One by one, the images of my mom flashed before my eyes, showing her writing in the diary in various places on campus—on the grassy upper quad, in the upscale dining hall, even while she was sitting on the steps outside the Library of Antiquities.

I concentrated on that last image, grabbing hold of and really focusing on it, pulling everything into sharp detail, hoping to see something that would tell me where the Helheim Dagger was. But the memory just showed her sitting on the main library steps in between the two stone gryphons that guarded the entrance. My mom turned her head and stared at the gryphon on the right side of the steps, then abruptly looked away. Nothing weird there. The statues always creeped me out, too. Apparently, the image hadn't been as important as it had seemed.

I let go of that memory and surfed through the others attached to the diary, but there was nothing out of the ordinary. Just my mom writing and doodling.

After a few minutes, the images and feelings started to fade, telling me that I'd learned all I could from the diary—at least by using my Gypsy gift. I opened my eyes and flipped through the first couple of pages, my fingers skimming over my mom's beautiful, flowing handwriting. Even if there wasn't a clue in the diary about where my mom had hidden the dagger, it was still a piece of her, and I wanted to read it. I wanted to know what she'd done when she'd been at Mythos, how she had felt about the school, who her friends and enemies had been, the cute guys she'd crushed on, and mostly especially how she'd found the courage to be Nike's Champion and fight Reapers. I wanted to know, well, everything—all her secrets.

Since there was nothing else in the box, I packed all the clothes and other odd items back inside. Well, except for the quarters. I'd spend those.

Cradling the diary in the crook of my arm, I turned out the light and walked down the attic stairs to my room on the second floor. Daphne was already asleep, and I lifted the covers and crawled into bed next to her. The Valkyrie murmured something in her sleep, then rolled away from me. A few pink sparks crackled on her fingertips at the motion before winking out. I lay still, and Daphne let out a quiet sigh and sank deeper into sleep. I put my mom's diary on the nightstand within easy reach. Then I snuggled deeper under the covers, determined to go to sleep so I wouldn't be totally exhausted tomorrow.

Slowly, my body relaxed, my mind started to drift, and the comforting blackness began to rise, drowning out the horrors of the day. I was almost asleep . . . when a low, angry growl sounded outside my window.

My eyes snapped open.

I'd heard growls like that before, and they usually meant one thing—that something was about to try and eat me.

I lay there in bed, covers pulled up to my chin, straining my eyes and ears, scarcely daring to breathe, but all I heard was Daphne. The Valkyrie snored like she had a chainsaw stuck in her throat, which was super, super annoying. I was beginning to think I'd just dreamed the growl and was starting to sink back into sleep . . .

When I heard it again.

This time, I couldn't pretend I'd just imagined it. I slipped out of bed, reached down, and grabbed my scabbard. I slid Vic out of the leather with a whisper and crept over to the window.

"What's going on?" Vic mumbled, his half of a mouth stretching into a wide, jaw-cracking yawn.

"I think there's something outside," I muttered.

The sword blinked his one eye, which glowed like a purple moon in the darkness of my room. "You *think?* You don't know? Gypsy, how many times have I told you? Only wake me up when there's trouble—or Reapers lurking around that I can kill."

Vic snapped his eye shut and went back to sleep. I glared at the sword, tempted to shake him awake, but I'd learned there was nothing I could do to get Vic to behave. He might be a mostly inanimate object, but he definitely had a mind of his own.

I made sure I had a good grip on the sword, then pulled the curtain back and peered outside.

I didn't see anything—not a thing.

No, that wasn't quite true. I didn't see anything *suspicious*. The window looked out into the backyard, where a tall maple stood guard, the tree's branches reaching all the way over to tap against the glass. When I was a kid, I used to climb outside, sit in the tree, and read my comic books. It had scared my mom to death. Grandma, too. They'd both thought I'd slip, fall, and break my neck, but I never did. Climbing was actually something I was good at. Thanks to my Gypsy gift, I'd always been able to flash on the branches and tell which ones were the strongest and which ones would snap under my weight.

Right now, though, the branches bobbed back and forth like a tornado-force wind had just whipped through them. Weird. Nothing else was moving, and the wind wasn't rattling the bushes in the backyard, but the tree looked like a whole flock of birds had suddenly erupted out of the top of it.

Maybe it was the idea of birds, but I looked up just in time to see a shadow move across the sky in a lazy pattern—almost like it was circling the house.

My mind flashed back to all those carvings and figures of Black rocs I'd seen when I'd picked up the Reaper girl's map. Was it possible she'd sent a roc to spy on me? To peer in my window? Perhaps even to peck its way inside through the glass, grab the map she'd dropped, and kill me? I shivered and tightened my grip on Vic.

I peered into the night, my eyes gliding right, then left, up, then down, looking for a roc, a Nemean prowler, or any other mythological creature that might be lurking about in the clouds above or the shadows below. I didn't see anything. It wasn't that late, but a dark frost had already painted the landscape in cold, silvery shards. I would have thought the sight pretty, if I hadn't known just how much the shadows could hide—

The growl sounded again.

I froze, waiting for the sound to cut off like it had before. But this time, it just kept going and going, rumbling along like a car idling by the curb. So I focused, this time really listening to the growl instead of letting myself be frightened by it, and I realized it wasn't a Nemean prowler like I'd feared. Otherwise, the sound would have been more of a hissing yowl. No, this growl sounded more like . . . a dog. A very large, very angry dog.

A shadow detached itself from the garage behind the house, slinked into the bushes, and disappeared through a gap in the picket fence. Beyond that, the landscape gave way to a hill covered by a wild tangle of briars and brambles, but my eyes locked onto that one shadow, trying to figure out exactly what it was.

Something with four legs and a tail slipped into the thicket and vanished from sight. It could have been a stray dog—or a Fenrir wolf.

Not too long ago, I'd helped a Fenrir wolf when it had been injured; afterward, it seemed to regard me as almost a friend. But I hadn't seen the wolf since I'd left the Powder ski resort. Metis and the other professors had searched for it, but the wolf had escaped into the surrounding mountains. In a way, I was glad. Even though Preston had trained, beaten, and ordered it to kill me, the wolf wasn't all bad. I'd hoped it would find a pack of wild Fenrir wolves to run and play and live with deep in the mountains.

But why would the wolf be outside my window tonight? How would it have tracked me here all the way from the ski resort? And why now?

Then another, more chilling thought entered my mind. What if it wasn't *my* wolf, the one I'd helped, but instead another one sent by the Reapers to kill me? Daphne had told me that once you pissed off the Reapers, they didn't stop coming until you were dead. I'd done plenty to annoy them in the short time I'd been at Mythos Academy.

I crouched there by the window and watched, but nothing else moved in the tree, the sky, or the shadows below. I breathed a sigh of relief. Whatever had been out there, it looked like it had left, at least for this night.

Still, it was a long time before I went back to bed— and longer still until I finally fell asleep.

Chapter 7

Early the next morning, Grandma Frost drove Daphne and me to Mythos Academy. Normally, I would have just taken the bus that shuttled tourists from Asheville up to the posh suburb of Cypress Mountain, where the academy was located. But after the attack yesterday, Grandma insisted on driving us—and she made me promise her that I wouldn't sneak off campus to see her during the week like I usually did. Since I didn't want her to worry, I reluctantly agreed.

Grandma dropped us off in the parking lot behind the gym, joining a long line of limos and drivers who were doing the same. Kids got out of the cars and grabbed their designer luggage before hopping onto golf carts and zooming toward their dorm rooms across campus. By the time Daphne and I got our bags out of the trunk, all the carts were full, so we had to wait for someone to come back with an empty one.

"Everybody's so quiet," Daphne murmured, holding her three bulging suitcases in one hand like they didn't weigh any more than the pink purse hanging off her other arm. "It's strange."

She was right—everyone was being quiet. Eerily so. Normally, kids would have been laughing, texting, and gossiping about who'd hooked up and split up over winter break, but this morning, all the kids had their chins tucked down into the tops of their expensive jackets and their hands shoved deep in their pockets, instead of messing with their phones. Even the kids who hadn't been at the coliseum yesterday were feeling the fear and pain of the Reapers' attack. It had been a brutal reminder of why we were all here at Mythos to start with.

Finally, a couple of golf carts came back, and we were able to leave. Daphne and I put our stuff in our dorm rooms, and at seven thirty that morning, I once again found myself fighting for my life. But this time, it was only in the gym with Logan and his two Spartan friends, Oliver Hector and Kenzie Tanaka.

Slash-slash-slash.

I moved Vic through a series of quick maneuvers swinging my sword a little closer to Logan's head every single time.

"Ha!" I shouted as I flashed the blade at him. "Take that!"

Logan grinned, his blue eyes practically glowing in his face. Nothing made the Spartan happier than sparring—especially since he almost always won.

"Not bad, Gypsy girl," he said. "You're finally learning how to attack instead of just defend. But what are you going to do against something like this?"

Clang-clang-clang.

The Spartan launched into a series of even quicker, more complicated moves, and ten seconds later, his sword hovered against my throat.

"And things were going so well up until now," Vic grumbled.

"Shut up, Vic," I said with a smile on my face.

Yeah, Logan had just mock killed me again, but for the very first time since he'd begun training me, there was a bit of color in his cheeks. The Spartan wasn't breathing hard, but he'd actually had to put a little effort into beating me that time. I was starting to hold my own against him, and that was saying something, considering he was the best fighter at Mythos.

Of course, when I'd kissed Logan a few weeks ago, I'd flashed on him and basically absorbed all of his fighting skills. Using my psychometry magic to see and tap into Logan's memories and make them my own was how I'd kept Preston from killing us, but I never used my magic or Logan's prowess against him while we were sparring. I wanted to develop some fighting skills of my own, something it finally seemed like I was doing.

I glanced over at Kenzie and Oliver, who were sprawled across the gym bleachers.

"Time?" I asked.

Kenzie checked his phone. "Two minutes, one second. Up more than a minute from our last session before the break."

"Looking good, Gypsy," Oliver said, grinning and giving me a thumbs-up.

I grinned back. Logan and I headed over to the bleachers. We'd been fighting with swords for half an hour now, and it was time to move on to ranged weapons, like bows, something Kenzie and Oliver used more than Logan did. While Kenzie and Logan set up the archery target and decided what kind of bow we'd practice with today, I walked over to where Oliver sat texting on his phone.

"So," I asked the Spartan. "How was your holiday?"

"Good," he said. "Lots of food, lots of family stuff, you know, the usual."

"And did you meet anyone cute over break?"

Oliver looked down at his phone, and a blush started to stain his cheeks. "Maybe."

I smiled. "Really? That's great! You'll have to give me all the juicy details."

Oliver shook his head and ran his fingers through his sandy blond hair. "I think it's too soon for that. I mean, I'm not dating the guy yet or anything. Besides, I still have feelings for Kenzie."

Oliver glanced over at his best friend, who was debating the merits of different types of crossbows with Logan. Kenzie didn't make my heart pound like Logan did, but he was cute in his own right, with his glossy black hair and dark eyes. Before the holiday break, I'd learned that Oliver had a serious, serious crush on him, though Kenzie, who was not gay, had no idea.

"You want to talk about it?" I asked in a soft voice.

Oliver shook his head. "Nah. I'll get over Kenzie, really, I will. It will just take some time." Another grin creased his face. "Maybe *you'd* like to talk, say, about that pretty new necklace you're wearing? How are things with you and Logan?"

I ran my fingers over the silver strands wrapped around my throat. My gaze went to Logan, who was still talking to Kenzie. "It's complicated. I mean, we didn't exactly get a chance to talk yesterday, you know?"

Oliver's face darkened. "I know. Logan called Kenzie and me last night and told us what had happened. I can't believe the Reapers attacked the coliseum like that just because they thought the Helheim Dagger might be there. That was vicious, even for them."

I was about to answer him when one of the doors at the far end of the gym creaked open and three kids stepped inside—two girls and a guy.

They stood in the doorway, eyes wide, peering into the gym like they were expecting to see something really cool inside. I glanced around, wondering what they could be so interested in, but the gym looked the same as it always did. Championship banners in fencing, archery, and other sports dangling from the high ceiling, wooden bleachers jutting out from two of the walls, several racks of weapons stacked up against one another.

But the kids must have seen what they were looking for because the three of them walked forward, their shoes scuffing on the thick mats that covered most of the floor.

"Who are they?" I asked. "And what do you think they're doing here?"

Oliver glanced over at them. "Some first-year students. I'm not sure what their names are, but I've seen them around campus."

At Mythos, the students ranged from the first-years, who were sixteen, all the way up to the sixth-years, who were twenty-one. The upper-class students mixed and socialized, but nobody had much to do with the first-years, not even the kids in my class, who were only a year or so older.

The three kids tiptoed forward and took seats on the bleachers a few feet away from Oliver and me. Then, they just sat there, staring at us like they were waiting for something amazing to happen. I noticed the guy was carrying a staff in addition to his backpack, while the girls both had scabbards that held swords. Nothing unusual there. Practically all the kids took their weapon of choice to classes with them. At Mythos, your weapon told everyone what kind of warrior you were, what kind of magic you had, and what you could do with it, and the swords, staffs, and bows were status symbols just as much as having the latest phone or laptop.

Logan and Kenzie finished setting up the archery target and headed back to the bleachers. Logan looked at the kids, then at Oliver and me. We both shrugged. We didn't know who they were or what they wanted. Usually, it was just the four of us in the gym this early in the morning before classes started.

"Do you guys need something?" Logan asked.

"Oh, we thought we would, um, watch you," one of the girls said. "Someone told us that Logan Quinn trains every morning in the gym. That's you, right?"

Logan frowned. "Yeah, but why would you guys want to watch me? It's just weapons training. The same stuff we do in gym class every day."

"Because you killed Reapers at the coliseum yesterday," the guy explained, his eyes bright with excitement. "How awesome was it? I mean, actually getting to fight them? I bet it was supercool."

His words unleashed a flood of memories, and for a moment, I was back at the coliseum. The image of the Reaper stabbing Carson flashed through my mind, while Daphne's screams echoed in my head. And the blood—all the blood that had splashed everywhere. The coppery stench of it filled my nose. My stomach twisted, and my heart pounded as if it had all just happened a second ago.

"Awesome?" I snapped. "It wasn't *awesome* at all. It was hard and scary and dangerous, and I thought I was going to throw up the whole time. There was nothing *awesome* about it, and if you think there was, then you're an idiot."

The guy's mouth fell open, and he let out a huff. "Oh, please, you're just jealous you didn't kill as many Reapers as Logan did. I heard you just got one, while he killed, like, a dozen."

A dozen? Where was he getting that ridiculous number from? Logan had only killed two Reapers—not a dozen. Actually, Daphne had taken out the most Reapers, since the Valkyrie had killed three of them.

"Is that little punk impugning your fighting skills?" Vic muttered. "Why don't we go show him who's boss, eh, Gwen?"

I gripped Vic tighter, muffling the sound of his voice, but his words only made me that much angrier. So much so that I didn't realize I'd taken a menacing step forward until I felt Logan's hand on my arm.

"Gypsy girl," Logan said in a soft voice. "It's all right. Calm down. He doesn't mean anything by it."

I drew in a breath and let it out. "Well, he shouldn't talk about things he doesn't know anything about."

The guy gave me a haughty look that turned into an arrogant smirk when Logan told them they could stay and watch us train. I moved over to the archery target and started shooting arrows with a bow, while Kenzie and Oliver stood off to one side, calling out tips and suggestions.

Maybe it was the fact that we had an audience or maybe it was because the first-year guy had pissed me off, but all my good mojo from earlier vanished, and I missed the target as many times as I hit it. Every miss made me angrier and that much more frustrated.

"Geez," I heard the guy say after one of my arrows flew past the target and weakly *thumped* off the wall. "How did *she* ever manage to kill a Reaper? She totally sucks."

The two girls murmured their agreement.

"I don't know," one of the girls said. "There's got to be something special about her, right? Isn't she the one who survived the avalanche during the Winter Carnival? That weird Gypsy girl?"

"Well, maybe she does better with the weather than she does with weapons. She certainly couldn't do any worse." The guy snickered at his lame joke.

My hands curled around the bow, and I seriously considered stalking over to the bleachers and bashing him over the head with it.

"Don't let them get to you," Oliver said in a quiet voice, handing me another arrow. "They don't know what they're talking about. They don't know how great you're doing, especially considering the fact that you haven't been training your whole life like the rest of us."

I knew what Oliver said was true, but it didn't quiet the snickers that rang up from the bleachers behind me—or soothe my anger. Still, I gritted my teeth and raised the bow up to my shoulder, determined to get through the rest of training time as quickly as possible. I lined up my shot and let the bowstring go.

Another shot, another miss. Behind me, the snickers grew even louder, seeming to echo all the way up to the top of the rafters and back down again.

I sighed. I wasn't psychic, not like Grandma Frost, but I had a feeling it was going to be that kind of day.

After the humilation of weapons training was finally over, I left the gym and stepped outside. The main upper quad was the center of Mythos Academy and featured the five buildings where the students spent most of their time—English-history, math-science, the gym, the dining hall, and the Library of Antiquities. Each one of the buildings sat at a different edge of the quad, reminding me of the points of a star.

From a distance, the structures all looked old and pretentious with their dark gray stone and tall, slender windows. But if you took a closer look, you'd notice how the heavy vines of ivy clutched at the doors and windows like green, bony fingers, while balconies, towers, and parapets bristled out like sword points from the sides and tops of the structures. The sharp angles glittered in the winter sun, and it always seemed to me like the towers were stretching up to stab the sky.

And then there were the statues.

Gryphons, gargoyles, dragons, a Minotaur, chimeras, and dozens of other mythological creatures covered every single one of the buildings from top to bottom. A claw here, a pair of fangs there, teeth that were longer than my fingers. The sinister statues were lifelike replicas of the creatures they represented, right down to depicting all the ways the real things could tear you to pieces. But what made them especially creepy to me was the fact that the statues' open, lidless eyes always seemed to track my movements, like there was something lurking underneath the stone just waiting to break free and gobble me up. No matter where I went on the quad or how fast I walked, I could never get away from the creatures' cold, fixed gazes.

But today, the statues weren't the only ones watching me.

I'd thought my ordeal would be over after weapons training, but to my surprise, it continued all day long. Ever since I'd started going to Mythos, I'd been pretty much invisible to the other students, since I wasn't as rich, pretty, powerful, and popular as everyone else seemed to be. If the other kids even noticed me at all, it was only because they knew me as Gwen Frost, the Gypsy girl who touched stuff and saw things. Well, that, or they wanted me to find something that was missing, like their phone, laptop, or a six-pack of beer they'd smuggled into their dorm room.

But today, it was completely different.

In between every one of my classes, all the other kids on the quad turned their heads to stare at me, like I was some kind of circus freak they'd gathered to see. The bearded lady they couldn't quit staring at. I kept my head down and hurried on to my next class, as if that would somehow protect me from all the curious looks.

But things weren't any better inside than they were out. In every one of my classes, the other kids looked at me and whispered to each other behind their hands, or worse, they texted their thoughts across the room, until everyone's phone lit up with the news. Apparently, word had gotten around that I'd been at the Crius Coliseum yesterday and that I'd killed a Reaper. Some of the kids gave me small, encouraging smiles, but just as many snorted, shook their heads, and rolled their eyes in disbelief. Like I'd just been lucky I'd killed a Reaper. Maybe I had, but that didn't give them the right to judge or make fun of me.

The rumors going around campus were just absurd. Everything from the Reapers robbing the coliseum to hock the gold and jewels on the artifacts, to them murdering everyone inside the museum, to Logan's going into full-on battle mode, killing two dozen Reapers, and scaring the others so much that they'd all run away crying. Nobody seemed to care what had really happened. The more outrageous the story was, the faster it got sent from one phone to the next.

By the time lunch rolled around, I'd had enough of the furtive looks and snarky whispers. I hadn't realized just how much I'd enjoyed being invisible until today.

"I wish everyone would quit staring at us," I grumbled. "I don't see what the big deal is. Don't they know that we just got lucky?"

"I think most of them know we were lucky," Carson said. "But almost everyone at Mythos has lost someone to the Reapers. For you, Logan, and Daphne to actually kill some of them in battle, well, it makes the kids who've lost their parents and friends feel a little better, you know? Like we were actually able to get the upper hand on the Reapers for once. Like we were able to strike back a little for all of them."

"Even though Samson and the others kids still died yesterday?" I asked.

The band geek shrugged. He didn't have an answer for that anymore than I did.

I sighed and stabbed my fork into the delicate china bowl on the table in front of me. I wasn't sure exactly what was in the bowl. Oh, there was some elaborately shaped pasta floating around in there and what looked like seared steak mixed with a spicy marinara sauce, but you could never really tell at Mythos. Here, the mystery meat was just as likely to be escargot as anything else.

Yep, escargot. That's what the dining hall served for breakfast, lunch, and dinner, along with things like liver, veal, and lobster. Seriously, liver for breakfast. Yucko. But the academy chefs would be more than happy to whip up a liver-and-onions omelet flavored with goat cheese and some obscure, bizarre spices if that's how you wanted to start your day. I don't know why the Powers That Were didn't lighten up and serve some regular food—or have it catered in. Some days, I would have happily done extra homework just to have a triple chocolate milkshake from the Pork Pit restaurant.

Given the slim pickings and lack of normal food on the lunch line, I usually opted for some sort of grilled chicken salad. It was kind of hard to mess up raw vegetables, but the chefs at Mythos did their very best, cutting the carrots, lettuce, and tomatoes into froufrou shapes and marinating them in weird sauces. Today, I'd wanted something warm, given the January cold outside, so I'd opted for the pasta. Now, I was regretting my decision.

I pushed the bowl away and reached for the dessert I'd grabbed—chocolate mousse, one of my favorites. At least, I thought it was chocolate mousse. The parfait glass was so small there was only about a spoonful of dessert actually inside it. The Powers That Were totally skimped on portion size when it came to the sweet stuff.

I supposed I should be grateful that a chef hadn't come over and tried to flambé the mousse. For some reason, the chefs at Mythos liked to play with fire, and there was always at least one dessert on the menu that needed to be blowtorched before you were allowed to eat it. The chefs here *so* could have learned a thing or two from Grandma Frost when it came to baking.

A series of high-pitched giggles caught my ear, and I looked for the source of the sound. Like everything else at Mythos, the dining hall was totally pretentious, and there were more suits of armor in here than there had been in the entire Crius Coliseum. The metal knights clutched their gleaming swords and battle-axes, standing guard against the walls, right under the oil paintings that showed all sorts of mythological feasts.

Round tables covered with fine white linens, dainty dishes, platinum silverware, and crystal vases full of fresh narcissus flowers filled the dining hall, which looked more like a five-star restaurant than a school cafeteria. Adding to the atmosphere was the open-air indoor garden that took up the center of the room. Olive, almond, and orange trees towered up out of the black soil, while a series of grape vines twisted over and through them all. Here and there, statues of wine, food, and harvest gods like Dionysus and Demeter peeped out from behind the trees, their stone eyes fixed on the students scarfing down their expensive entrees.

The giggles sounded again, and this time, I was able to pinpoint the origin—the table where Logan was sitting. A girl, one of the first-year students who'd been in the gym this morning, hovered by the table the Spartan was sharing with Kenzie and Oliver. The girl said something to Logan, then handed him a pen and a piece of paper. The Spartan shifted in his chair, looking uncomfortable, but Kenzie and Oliver had their hands over their mouths, like they were about three seconds away from laughing.

"Did Logan just give that girl an autograph?" Daphne asked, drumming her fingers on top of the table and making pink sparks of magic shoot out everywhere.

Carson hesitated. "That's what it looks like."

The girl gave Logan another smile before giggling

again and rushing off. She hurried over to the table where her own friends were sitting and showed them the piece of paper. This time, they all erupted in a fit of giggles.

"Geez," I muttered. "It's a wonder they all don't just go over there, take off their shirts, and ask him to sign their bras."

Daphne raised an eyebrow. "Jealous, much?"

I sank a little lower in my chair. "Not jealous. Well, not exactly. It's not like I have any claim on Logan. We haven't talked, you know, about anything."

I'd wanted to talk to the Spartan this morning during weapons training, but Kenzie and Oliver had shown up before I'd had the chance. Afterward, Logan had rushed out of the gym, saying he needed to go back to his dorm room before classes started. I got the feeling Logan was trying to avoid me as much as possible. I wondered if it had anything to do with what Grandma Frost had said to him yesterday—about how something hadn't been his fault in the past and wasn't going to be his fault in the future, either.

The Valkyrie raised her eyebrow. "Oh, suck it up, Gwen. The Spartan gave you a diamond necklace for Christmas. I'd say that's a pretty good indication he likes you. And he did fight by your side in the coliseum."

I sighed. "I know, I know. I just wish—I just wish I knew where things stood between the two of us. Once and for all."

I watched as another girl from the table of first-year

students got up, walked over to Logan, and got him to give her an autograph as well. I rolled my eyes.

"You'd at least think they'd ask us all for autographs," I muttered. "We were there, too, and you saved Carson's life."

"Something I will be forever grateful for," Carson said, squeezing Daphne's hand.

Instead of being pleased by the band geek's soft, sweet words, something uncertain flashed in Daphne's eyes. After a moment, she slipped her hand out of his.

"I just remembered I need to run over to the library and get a reference book for my next class," Daphne said. "See you guys later."

The Valkyrie got to her feet, grabbed her Dooney & Bourke purse, and stalked out of the dining hall, leaving pink sparks of magic flashing in her wake.

"What's wrong with her?" I asked.

Carson shrugged his lean shoulders. He didn't know either. Daphne could be quick to anger, and she definitely had a temper, but she'd never just gotten up and walked away before—especially when she didn't seem to be mad about anything. Strange.

More giggles sounded, and my fingers tightened around my fork as yet a third girl approached Logan.

I wasn't the only one who noticed the Spartan's new fan club. A few tables over from where Carson and I sat, Savannah glared at Logan. Savannah was sitting with Talia Pizarro and Vivian Holler, and I remembered what Daphne had said about the three of them being friends.

I actually knew Talia since we had gym class together and often ended up as sparring partners. Sometimes she dropped by when I was doing my early morning weapons training with the Spartans since she was dating Kenzie. Talia was tall and lithe with ebony skin and black hair that was cropped into a cute pixie cut. She was talking and gesturing about something, but Savannah wasn't paying attention to her. Neither was Vivian, who had her head bent down over a thick book and was fiddling with a piece of her frizzy auburn hair. The first day back at school, and she was doing homework already? Even I wasn't that dedicated—or geeky.

Savannah must have felt me staring because the Amazon turned her head and looked in my direction. Our gazes locked across the dining hall.

Once again, I thought I saw a burning flash of red in her eyes—Reaper red, as I'd come to think of it.

An uneasy feeling slithered up my spine. I'd only seen that crimson spark a few times before and always in the eyes of Reapers or the creatures they trained. Could Savannah—was it possible—could Savannah be a Reaper?

Maybe even *the* Reaper girl? Loki's Champion?

I don't know where the strange thoughts came from, but they popped into my head, and I couldn't push them away. It was like someone was pounding the ideas into my skull with a hammer. My head started to ache, and my heart began to burn with anger at the thought of the Reaper girl and how she'd killed my mom. My hand tightened around my fork again, and I pictured myself shoving it into Savannah's chest. I didn't really consider myself to be a violent person, but that thought made me happy in a way that nothing else had in a long, long time—

"Gwen?" Carson asked. "Are you okay? You have this really angry look on your face right now. Did I do something to upset you?"

His soft, worried voice penetrated my anger. I dropped my eyes from Savannah and shook my head. Almost immediately, the rage I'd been feeling vanished, although my head kept aching, like I was getting a migraine. Great. Just what I needed.

I suppose it served me right for freaking out and being totally paranoid. Savannah wasn't a Reaper. No way. She'd been there at the coliseum with Vivian yesterday, and she'd been attacked just like all the other kids. Savannah was a victim, just like everyone else.

Savannah's mouth flattened out into a hard, thin line, and she said something to Talia. Soon, the other Amazon was glaring at me, too. Even Vivian shot me dark looks every time she flipped a page in her book, although her golden gaze was a little less hostile than the others' were.

I sighed and turned away from them. Yeah, I knew Savannah blamed me for Logan's breaking up with her, and I had plenty of guilt over that, but the other Amazon really needed to give it a rest with the dirty looks. It wasn't like I'd done it on purpose. Besides, I didn't even know what was going on with Logan and me, if we were a couple or just friends or something in between. The uncertainty was making me crazy—so crazy that I was imagining that Savannah was a Reaper. Geez. *Get a grip, Gwen.*

Suddenly tired of well, everything, especially the weird way I was feeling, I got to my feet and grabbed my gray messenger bag.

"Where are you going?" Carson asked.

Another giggle echoed through the dining hall as yet another girl fawned over Logan. The sound made my headache that much worse. "Someplace quiet where you can't get autographs."

Chapter 8

The rest of the day dragged by, but finally, it was time for my sixth period myth-history class. I slid into my seat behind Carson just as the bell rang.

A minute later, Professor Metis stepped into the classroom and closed the door behind her. Bronze skin, stocky body, silver glasses, black hair pulled back into a tight bun. Metis looked the same as she always did, although today, her eyes seemed dull and weary, and her shoulders drooped in exhaustion. Daphne might have healed Carson yesterday, but Metis had been responsible for patching up all the other students who'd been injured. It looked like the professor was still feeling the aftereffects of the attack, just like the rest of us were.

Metis shuffled over and arranged some papers on a podium that was almost as tall as she was. Then, she turned her attention to the students.

"I'm sure you've all heard by now about the Reaper attack," she said. "About the students who were killed, the ones who were injured, and the others who fought back against the Reapers."

Metis's eyes focused first on Carson, then me, and all the other students turned to look in our direction, too. Carson sighed, while I sank a little lower into my seat. I didn't know why Metis was making me out to be some kind of hero, when I knew that I wasn't—and would never be.

"The students at the coliseum were all very brave," Metis said. "And we can all learn something from what happened. As horrible as the attack was, it's reminded me and the other professors what we are here to do. To teach you—all of you—how to best use your magic and skills to protect yourselves and your loved ones, and to fight against the Reapers should you ever be unlucky enough to encounter them like your classmates did."

The professor looked from one kid to the next, until finally, her green eyes met mine. After a moment, I dropped my gaze. All I wanted to do was forget about what I'd seen yesterday, even though I knew I never would.

"I was going to quiz you today about the artifacts you were supposed to have gone to the coliseum to view over the winter break," Metis said. "But that doesn't seem fair, considering the circumstances."

Everyone breathed a sigh of relief. Metis's quizzes were always tricky, no matter how much you studied.

"Instead, I'd like you to turn your books to page 269," Metis said. "Today, we're going to discuss some of the unique architecture that can be found on the academy grounds."

Architecture? That sounded *totally* boring, but I flipped over to the appropriate page and found myself looking at the Library of Antiquities. The black-and-white photograph made the building look darker and even more ominous than it usually did.

"We'll start with the library, since it's the largest building on campus," Metis began. "As you can see, the library has a number of balconies, not to mention the towers on the roof. . . ."

For the next thirty minutes, Metis talked about everything from the library's many features to the architectural styles that had influenced them to the net worth of the gold and gems that made up the frescoes covering the building's interior dome. Answer: Close to five million big ones. Except for that fun, larcenous fact, the information was all seriously, seriously eye-glazing, and I had to pinch myself a few times just to stay awake. I was about to zone out again when Metis finally moved on to a slightly more interesting topic.

"Now, let's discuss the various statues that can be found at the library," she said. "Please turn over to page 273."

Pages rustled, and once again, I found myself staring at another black-and-white photo. Only this time, it was a close-up shot of the two gryphons that guarded the steps outside the Library of Antiquities.

They looked just as fierce in my myth-history book as they did in real life. The gryphons sat up straight, their eagle heads held high and their wings tucked in tight behind their enormous lion bodies, like they were getting ready to salute—or snap at you with their hooked beaks and sharp claws.

As I stared at the page, the photo began to blur and

melt, like the ink was still wet and about to smear everywhere. I sighed. Not again. The statues were creepy
enough by themselves—I didn't need my psychometry
to kick in and make them seem any more lifelike and
frightening than they already were, but that was exactly
what was happening. Sometimes my Gypsy gift went a
little haywire and made me see things that weren't really
there. I didn't know exactly why.

Even though I knew what was coming, I couldn't help
staring as the gryphons in the photo began to move,
arch, and stretch, like two cats waking up from a long
winter's nap. The gryphons curved their bodies this way
and that, their lion tails lashing back and forth, claws
sheathing and unsheathing, beaks screeching open and
snapping shut with loud *clicks*. Then, the creatures'
heads swiveled around to me, their narrowed, lidless
eyes staring out at me from the photo. The gryphons
started stalking toward me, like I was their intended
prey—

I shook my head. The gryphons snapped back into
their original positions, and the photograph returned to
normal. I carefully leaned back from my myth-history
book, keeping my gaze away from the gryphons. Creepy.

"Like all the statues on campus, the gryphons are
meant to be guardians," Metis continued her lecture.
"That's what they symbolize—protection, dedication,
devotion to a higher cause."

"You mean like the sphinxes perched on either side of
the main gate?" an Amazon asked from across the
room. "The ones that supposedly break out of their

stone shells and attack if a Reaper tries to sneak onto campus? That's what's meant to happen, right?"

Metis nodded her head. "Exactly like that. All of the statues, the gryphons and sphinxes included, are imbued with magic and wards to protect the campus and keep Reapers from entering. Even if the Reapers were to somehow get past the outer defenses and mount an attack, the statues would still trigger an alarm, a siren that would alert everyone on campus as to what was happening."

I noticed that the professor didn't exactly answer the girl's question about whether or not the sphinxes would really come to life and rip the Reapers to shreds. After what I'd seen the Reapers do at the coliseum, that's exactly what I hoped would happen. I'd been hanging around Vic too long—I was starting to get as bloodthirsty as the sword was.

"Now, nothing is foolproof, but I want you all to know that you are as safe at the academy as you can possibly be," Metis said. "That's why I wanted to talk about the statues today and to mention that all of the staff are dedicated to protecting you—even more so now, given the tragedy at the coliseum."

One by one, Metis looked at all the students again, before her gaze finally locked with mine. I wanted to believe the professor, really I did, but after what I'd seen the Reapers do yesterday, I knew that none of us were safe, not even behind the stout walls of Mythos Academy.

"And now, for your next essay assignment."

A chorus of groans sounded, but Metis ignored them.

"For your next essay, I want you to pick a statue, research it, and write a report on its history, architecture, and so on," she said. "I expect several sources and a full bibliography. From *real* books in the library, people, and not some pseudo mythological quotes you found on your friend's academy profile page."

More groans rippled through the room, but the bell rang, drowning them out. The other kids got to their feet and started packing up their things, but I stayed seated, my gaze once again going to my myth-history book and the photograph there.

The gryphons, I decided. I'd do my report on the gryphons. It was time I got over this weird, paranoid fear I had of them and all the other statues.

Besides, writing about something that creeped me out was probably the only way I'd stay awake long enough to finish this assignment.

I started to go up to Metis after class to ask if she, Nickamedes, or Coach Ajax had turned up anything on the Reapers that had attacked the coliseum. Who they really were, where they might be hiding, if the Reaper girl was with them. I also wanted to ask Metis what she and the others were going to do about the Helheim Dagger—if they were going to organize groups to start searching the library for it. The professor had let me keep the original map, just in case I could get any more vibes off it, but she'd taken the other copies so she, Nickamedes, Ajax, and supposedly Raven could study them.

To my surprise, the professor packed up her briefcase and left the classroom before half the students did. I wondered where Metis was off to in such a hurry, but I didn't want to be a total freak, shove through the crowd, chase after her, and ask.

So I eased into the flow of students streaming down the hall, pushed through the closest door, and walked down the steps of the English-history building. It was cold on Cypress Mountain, even for January, and the frosty air blasted through my heavy, purple plaid coat like a battering ram. There should have at least been snow on the ground if we had to endure some frigid Arctic blast, but of course, there wasn't. I don't know why that put me in such a grumpy mood, but it did.

I took my gloves out of my pockets and pulled them on, then wrapped my gray wool scarf with its glittering snowflakes around my neck. I also yanked the matching toboggan down over my flyaway hair, but the extra layers didn't help as much as they should have.

Still thinking about the cold, Metis, and the Reaper girl, I left the upper quad behind, stalked down the hill, and hurried across the lower quads. I tucked my chin down into my scarf and didn't stop walking until I reached the edge of campus and the twelve-foot-high wall that separated Mythos Academy from the outside world.

The iron bars on the gate loomed up in front of me, reminding me exactly where I was—and that I wasn't supposed to be here. Not today, anyway. Most afternoons, I slipped through the bars, walked over to the bus stop, and rode down into the city to see Grandma

Frost, but I'd forgotten that I wasn't going to leave campus today, that I'd promised Grandma I wouldn't because of the Reaper attack. Even though I really wanted to see her, I didn't want my grandma to worry about me any more than she already was.

Sighing, I glanced at my watch. I still had plenty of time to kill before I had to go to the Library of Antiquities to work my regular shift. Despite the cold, I didn't feel like going back to my dorm room and obsessing about Logan, the Reaper girl, where my mom had hidden the Helheim Dagger, and everything else that was on my mind right now.

I called Daphne, hoping I could hang out with the Valkyrie, but she didn't pick up. Weird. My best friend was one of those obsessive people who *always* picked up their phones. Even when someone texted her, Daphne would usually just go ahead and call them back. I wondered what was up with the Valkyrie. First, she'd bolted out of the dining hall during lunch, and now, she wasn't answering her cell. It wasn't too hard to figure out it had something to do with what had happened at the coliseum. I just couldn't imagine what it could be, though. Yeah, the attack had been scary and horrible, but we'd come through it okay. That was what I was focusing on, or at least trying to, even though Samson Sorensen's dead face and those of the other kids had flashed through my mind more than once today.

Since I didn't have anything to do or anywhere to be for a while, I decided to wander along one of the ash gray cobblestone paths that ran parallel to the wall and see where it took me. Usually, I just walked straight down to the gate and ran over to the bus stop. I'd never stopped to explore what was just inside the wall, so I set off on one of the paths, heading to the left.

Purple pansies and other small winter flowers struggled to keep their colorful petals spread wide, despite the chill in the air. Above them, the trees stretched their bare, skeletal branches out in all directions, creating a dark wooden canopy that screened out what little sun there was. A few iron benches were tucked away in the blackening shadows, while a small creek that snaked alongside them had completely iced over.

And of course, there were more statues.

The statues were made of the same dark gray stone as the ones on the main campus buildings, although these were much smaller, no more than two or three feet high. A small group of them was clustered around a stone footbridge that arched over the frozen creek. The largest figure had a man's torso, along with goat's hooves and a short tail. Two horns curled up out of his stone hair, and he held a flute to his lips, like he was getting ready to blast out a cheery tune. I recognized the statue as Pan, the Greek god of the shepherds and a whole bunch of other things, depending on which myth-history book you picked up in the library.

Several other stone statues of wood nymphs and dryads were arranged around him, their arms wide and feet high, flowers clutched in their fingertips, like they were dancing to Pan's phantom song. The more I stared at them, the more it seemed like the nymphs were looking back at me, their eyes narrowing to sly slits, their lips drawing back to show their teeth, their fingers strangling the delicate petals in their grasps.

I sighed and looked away. Sometimes I thought if I never saw another statue again, it would be too soon. And now I had to do a stupid report on them for Metis's class. Ugh.

I kept walking, passing more benches and more statues, but what surprised me was the fact that several more gates were set into the stone wall that circled the academy. So far, I'd only been through the main gate and the secondary one at the end of the parking lot behind the gym, but iron bars were spaced into the wall every few hundred feet. A pair of stone sphinxes perched above them all, looming over either side of the open spaces. I supposed there were so many gates in case the students ever needed to leave campus in a hurry—like if the Reapers ever attacked the academy in a group the way they had the coliseum. The thought made my stomach knot up.

Despite my brisk pace, the winter chill continued to creep through my clothes and seep into my bones. I'd just turned around to head back to my warm dorm room when a low growl sounded.

I froze, suddenly colder than ever before, wondering if I'd only imagined the sound—and really, really hoping I had. In my experience, growls were never, ever good. Growls usually meant that large, scary creatures like Nemean prowlers were lurking around and intent on tearing into me with their teeth and claws. I was *so* not fond of the oversize, black panther-like creatures—

especially since the Reapers trained them to be deadly, kitty-cat assassins.

The growl rippled through the air again, shattering any hope I'd had of it just being my imagination or my Gypsy gift gone wild. I slowly turned my head to the right—and saw the Fenrir wolf.

Chapter 9

The Fenrir wolf was hunkered down in a pile of leaves on the other side of the gate I was standing in front of. The creature was even longer than I was tall, with a thick, powerful body and razor-sharp teeth and claws to match. Its fur wasn't quite black, but more like the dark, deep, smoky color of ashes. The shaggy coat helped it blend in with the shadows cast by the towering trees. The last time I'd seen a Fenrir wolf, I'd noticed that its fur had crimson strands glistening in it, but I didn't see any in this creature's coat. Its eyes were a rusty red, although the color was far dimmer than I remembered it being and without the creepy burning glow that had told me just how much the wolf had wanted to gobble me up.

My gaze roamed over the creature, and my eyes caught on its ear. A small V was grooved into the wolf's right ear, and I knew it was my wolf after all. The one I'd met at the ski resort, the one that had kept me from freezing to death after we'd both been caught in the avalanche Preston had set off. The wolf had gotten the V-shaped scar that day.

"Um, puppy?" I asked in a tentative voice, since that was all I'd ever called the wolf. "Is that really you?"

At the sound of my voice, the Fenrir wolf sprang to its feet, and its muzzle creased back into what looked like a—a *smile*. Okay, that was a little creepy. Usually, mythological creatures weren't any happier to see me than I was to notice them stalking me and licking their chops at the thought of sinking their teeth into my body. But the wolf actually seemed glad I'd noticed it, like— like it had been waiting here for me to walk by.

The wolf let out a soft whine and crept closer to the gate, making the leaves crackle underneath its enormous body. I walked over to the iron bars. I hesitated, then stretched my hand out through one of the gaps. The wolf paced back and forth for a few seconds before heading toward me and shoving its head underneath my hand.

As soon as my fingers brushed its fur, images of the wolf began to fill my mind. Flashes of the crushing avalanche that had almost buried us both, then one of the branch that had pierced the creature's leg and of me shoving the sharp wood out so the wolf could walk again, even a memory of me facing down Preston and the wolf spoiling the Reaper's aim when Preston had tried to kill me with a crossbow.

More images zipped through my mind, of snow and trees and the wolf running through the forest, along with the creature's feelings. There was only one emotion, really—happiness. Pure, fierce, intense happiness that it was finally free of the Reapers who had caged it, hurt it, tortured it for so long. Tears burned my eyes at the intensity and depth of the wolf's elation.

Then, the image of another wolf popped into my head, a second Fenrir wolf, although this one didn't have the Reaper red tint to its gaze or fur. It must be one of the wild Fenrir wolves that Metis had told me about, the ones who lived deep in the mountains and were rarely seen by members of the Pantheon. At first, my wolf was cautious around this other creature, but soon, the two of them were hunting through the snow together. Playing, mock fighting, even snuggling together.

For the first time, I realized my wolf was actually a she, and I also got the sense that it—no, *she*—wanted me to help her.

"I don't understand," I murmured, opening my eyes and staring at the wolf. "Why are you here? Why did you leave your mate? You were so happy with him. What could you possibly want here with me?"

The wolf let out a little snort, like she couldn't believe I was so dense. Kind of sad when a mythological creature thought it was smarter than you. The wolf pulled away and walked back and forth in front of the gate, almost like she was parading around for me. I stared at the creature, wondering what she was doing, what she was trying to show me.

After a few seconds, I realized the wolf was much fatter than I remembered her being before—especially around the middle. I reached out and put my hand on the creature's stomach. It took a second, but another little flicker filled my mind, another little spark that told me the wolf wasn't exactly by herself anymore.

"Oh," I said. "*Oh*. You're going to have a baby puppy . . . or whatever."

I didn't know how much of my words the wolf understood, but she almost seemed to nod her head, like *finally, the silly mortal girl understands what I'm trying to tell her.*

I didn't know much about animals, but it seemed to me the wolf was much bigger than she should have been, given the fact that I'd only seen her a few weeks ago. Did mythological creatures have their babies faster than regular animals did? Was that why the wolf was so large already? How soon would she have her puppy? I didn't know the answers to any of the questions swirling in my mind.

"But I still don't understand. Why come here? How did you even find me in the first place?" I asked.

The wolf made a loud snuffling sound, and her black nose quivered.

"So . . . you smelled me out? You somehow . . . tracked me all the way back here from the ski resort?"

Again, the wolf nodded. Okay, so the Fenrir wolf had been following me. That was kind of freaky.

My eyes narrowed as another thought occurred to me. "Were you outside my Grandma Frost's house last night? The big purple house with the gray steps?"

Another nod.

"Why?"

Instead of nodding, this time the wolf made a growling sound in the back of her throat—the sort of low, harsh growl that told me that she'd like to sink her teeth into something and not let go until it was good and dead. I kept my hand on the creature's stomach, reaching out with my Gypsy gift, trying to figure out what had angered her enough to make that sound, but all I could see and feel was the puppy moving around inside her.

Frustrated, I dropped my hand and crouched down beside the gate. Thinking. Okay, so the Fenrir wolf that I'd helped weeks ago had somehow tracked me down, going over several mountains and a lot of miles to do it. Now, said wolf was here at Mythos Academy, pregnant, and apparently expecting me to take her in, like she was just a cute little corgi, instead of a mythological creature with more teeth than I had brain cells.

I'd seen and done a lot of freaky stuff since I'd come to Mythos, but this was rapidly moving to the top of the list of weird.

The wolf stared at me, almost like she could tell what I was thinking. Her ears drooped, and she let out a sad whine that pierced my heart like a Reaper's sword. I had to do *something* to help her. Yeah, maybe the creature had originally intended to kill me per Preston's orders, but the wolf had kept me warm after the avalanche, and she'd kept Preston from putting a crossbow bolt through my chest. I owed her for that.

As for why she'd come to the academy, well, I didn't know. Maybe she didn't want to have her puppy in the mountains. Maybe there were Reapers after her. Or maybe there was something else going on that I was completely missing. Either way, the wolf had helped me

as best she could. I figured I should return the favor. It
was the right thing to do.

First, though, I had to clear it with the Powers That
Were—namely, the two sphinxes perched on the stone
wall on either side of the iron gate. I'd been so focused
on the wolf I hadn't noticed that the sphinxes seemed to
have grown larger and more imposing in the last few
minutes, their features becoming sharper and more pro-
nounced, their claws glittering in the weak winter sun,
as if whatever was lurking beneath their stone facades
was a breath away from leaping down and tearing the
wolf to pieces.

Professor Metis had told me the sphinxes were designed to keep things out of the academy—Bad, Bad
Things like Reapers, Nemean prowlers, and, well, Fenrir wolves. I didn't know exactly how well they worked,
though, since Jasmine Ashton had said there were other
Reapers at Mythos besides her—kids and professors. I
suppose the Reapers had some way of hiding their true
nature from the sphinxes, some sort of loophole that let
them walk by the statues without getting attacked.
There were lots of loopholes like that at Mythos, especially when it came to all the magic mumbo jumbo stuff.

But Metis had also claimed the statues wouldn't hurt
me or anyone else who was supposed to be here. I just
hoped they'd give a pass to my new furry friend as well.

"The wolf's with me," I told the sphinxes. "She doesn't
belong to the Reapers. Not anymore."

The sphinxes glared down at me, their stone eyes
seeming to narrow at my words, as if they were judging
whether or not they were true. I waited a few seconds,

but nothing happened. The sphinxes didn't relax their rigid stance, but they didn't spring to life and attack the wolf either. Instead, they just kept staring at me. Okay, it looked like it was up to me to make the next move.

I stretched my hand out through the bars and gestured at the wolf. "Come on, girl. Come here."

The wolf paced back and forth a few seconds, eyeing the sphinxes in much the same way they were her. Finally, though, the wolf stepped forward. I dug my hand deep into her shaggy fur and gently tugged her toward the gate, keeping contact with her body the whole time. My theory was that if the sphinxes wouldn't attack me, then maybe they wouldn't harm whatever or whomever I was touching either.

The wolf crept forward and stuck her head through the gate. Maybe it was my imagination, but the sphinxes seemed to twitch, and a few chips of stone slid off the top of the wall and banged into the iron bars. The wolf flinched at the harsh, ringing sound, but I kept my hand on her back and looked up at the sphinxes.

"I told you that she's with me."

The sphinxes continued to glare at me, but no more stone chips tumbled off the wall.

A few seconds passed. When nothing else happened, I tugged on the wolf, urging her forward before the statues changed their minds. She tentatively slid one of her front paws inside the gate, then the other one.

"That's it," I whispered. "They won't hurt you as long as you're with me."

The wolf let out another huff, like she didn't really believe me, but she kept moving forward. It was a tight squeeze, especially around the middle, but the creature shimmied through the iron bars to the other side, knocking me over in the process.

Then, she plopped down on her butt, her long tail slapping from back and forth, like she'd just done the coolest trick ever. Maybe she had.

I looked up at the sphinxes, who were still glaring at me, their lidless eyes narrowed to slits. "Thanks," I said. "You know, for not ripping us both to pieces."

The sphinxes didn't do or say anything, but for a second, I felt that force stir around them—that ancient force that seemed to hover around all the statues on campus. Then, it faded away, and the sphinxes were just stone once more.

Beside me, the wolf let out another low, threatening growl, like she was showing the sphinxes that she wasn't *really* afraid of them.

"Come on," I said, rubbing her ears. "Let's get you settled in my dorm room before anyone sees you. Scary stone sphinxes are one thing, but professors are another."

I got to my feet and set off through the trees, with the wolf loping along behind me.

Chapter 10

It wasn't easy, sneaking the Fenrir wolf across campus to my dorm, but I managed it, mostly by skulking from tree to tree. Really, I was way easier to spot than the wolf. With her dark fur, the wolf was able to almost completely blend in with the shadowy landscape. Me in my purple coat, jeans, and sneakers? Not so much.

Once we got to my dorm, Styx Hall, things got much easier, since my room was the only one on the third floor, stuck in a separate turret that had been tacked onto the rest of the building. A bed, some bookcases, a desk, a small fridge. It looked like your typical dorm room, although I'd added my own personal touches, like the framed photos of my mom that stood on my desk, right next to a small replica statue of Nike.

Vic had said he wanted to take a nap, so I'd brought him back to my room before myth-history class. The sword hung in his black leather scabbard in his usual spot on the wall, right next to my posters of Wonder Woman, Karma Girl, and The Killers. His eye snapped open at the sound of me opening the door and stepping inside.

"Well, it's about time you got here—"

Vic's twilight-colored eye widened at the sight of the Fenrir wolf, and his mouth fell open. Actually, I imagined that it would have fallen off completely if, you know, it wasn't forged together with the rest of his face. I sighed. I knew what was coming now.

"Gwen Frost, have you lost your bloody mind?!" Vic roared.

"Sshh!" I put a finger up to my lips. "Do you want everyone in the whole dorm to hear you?"

"What is that—that *thing* doing here?" Vic snapped, glaring at the wolf.

The wolf's eyes narrowed, and she let out a low growl, her eyes fixed on the weapon like she wanted to leap up, snatch Vic off the wall, and give him a vicious shake.

"It is not a *thing,* it is a *wolf*. A female wolf, as a matter of fact. One who is going to have a, um, puppy very soon."

"Well, I can *see* that," Vic sniffed. "She's as big around as a bloody cow."

The wolf's growl got a little deeper and uglier. I put a hand on her back and started stroking her fur. That seemed to calm her down, although she kept growling at the sword.

"Well, apparently, she's decided that she wants to stay with me . . . or something," I said. "I found her down by one of the gates, like she was waiting for me to show up."

Vic's mouth dropped open again. "So you let her inside the academy grounds? Why would you do that?"

"I didn't let her inside," I said in a cross voice. "The sphinxes did . . . after I told them that she was with me."

The sword stared at me.

"If I had a hand, I would slap it to my forehead in disbelief," Vic grumbled. "No, actually, I'd use it to slap some sense into *you*, Gwen. That is a bloody *Fenrir wolf*, not a puppy with sad eyes that you spotted at the pound and just had to bring home. In case you've forgotten, that is the same wolf that would have been more than happy to make mincemeat out of you at the ski resort."

I sighed. "I know all that. I also know the wolf kept me from freezing to death during the avalanche, and she kept Preston from killing me with his crossbow. Surely you remember *that*, since you were there."

Vic sniffed again. "I recall no such thing. Except that I was brilliant in battle, as always."

"Anyway," I said through clenched teeth. "If the wolf wants to stay here with me for a while, then I'm going to let her. At least until I can figure out what she really wants. She's gone through a lot since she escaped from Preston, and I don't exactly speak wolf."

Vic huffed and snapped his eye shut. Discussion over. I sighed again. Now the sword was in one of his *moods*, and he probably wouldn't speak to me again until I coaxed him to—or bribed him by turning the television to some action-movie marathon. Maybe it was his bloodthirsty nature, but Vic absolutely loved watching bad guys getting beaten, bloodied, and blown up. The James Bond marathons were his favorites.

But the good thing about Vic's not speaking to me was he couldn't back talk me, or worse, tell me what a colossal mistake I was making, trusting a creature the Reapers had trained to kill warriors like me. But I knew the wolf wasn't like that anymore. My Gypsy gift had shown me what was in her heart—relief at finally being free of the Reapers. She wouldn't hurt me now.

I went into the bathroom, filled a bowl with water, and put it at the foot of my bed so the wolf could get a drink if she wanted to. Then, I hunkered down on the floor beside her.

"You stay here. I have to go out for a few hours, but I'll get you something to eat and bring it back, okay?"

The wolf let out a little grumble of pleasure as I rubbed her ears.

"You know, I really need to think of a name for you if you're going to be hanging around for a while," I said. "Would you like that? A name?"

Her ear, the one with the ragged V in it, twitched. I took that as a yes. I stared at the wolf, wondering exactly what kind of name you gave to a mythological creature. Somehow I didn't think Fido or Fluffy would cut it.

"How about Nott?" I finally said, remembering a name from one of my myth-history books. "She's the Norse goddess of the night, and your fur makes you look all dark, shadowy, and mysterious."

The wolf sat there a second, then her face split into a

happy grin, and her tongue lolled out of the side of her mouth. It was the same rusty red as her eyes were, instead of the bright crimson I remembered it being.

"Nott, it is," I said.

The wolf leaned forward and licked me on the cheek. I laughed and playfully pushed her head away, before getting to my feet and heading out.

The first thing I did was go over to the dining hall, grab a tray, and pile it high with every single meat dish on the dinner menu. Tonight's offerings included seared lamb chops, grilled filet mignon, and mounds of spaghetti topped with spicy veal meatballs. I know, I know, you aren't supposed to give animals people food. But Nott was a mythological creature, one that could actually eat *people*. So I figured the meat would be okay. Besides, it was the best I could do tonight.

The chef who packed my food into a brown paper bag looked at me a little strangely, apparently wondering how much I thought I could eat at one time, but I gave him a bland smile. I just hoped Nott liked veal better than I did. Yucko.

I'd been so busy with the wolf that I'd lost track of time, and I had to hustle to make it over to the Library of Antiquities for my shift. The library sat at the head of the upper quad, the top point in the star formation, and dwarfed all the other buildings. It just had the most of everything—the most windows, the most balconies, the most towers.

The most statues.

According to Metis's lecture, more statues could be found on the library than on any other building on campus. Mythological creatures covered the structure, from the bottom, open-air balcony that wrapped all the way around the building to the spear-like points on the towers on the seventh and topmost floor. My steps slowed, and I stopped at the bottom of the library stairs, staring at the two gryphons perched on either side.

The statues looked the same as they did in my myth-history book. Eagle heads, lion bodies, killer claws, curved beaks. They loomed over me, their outlines sharp and crisp against the gray, gloomy, winter sky, their lidless eyes locked onto me, tracking my steps.

I flashed back to the image of my mom that I'd seen when I'd picked up her diary, of how she'd been sitting on the library steps in between the two gryphons. I wondered what my mom had thought of the statues— and if she'd been as creeped out by them as I was. Even more than the sphinxes who guarded the gates, it always seemed to me that the gryphons were seconds away from coming to life, shaking off their stone shells, and ripping me into bloody pieces.

I pushed that disturbing thought away and headed up the stairs, through a door, and down a hallway before stepping inside a pair of open double doors. An aisle unrolled like a marble carpet down the center of the library, before spreading out into an open space that featured tables where students could sit and study, as well as the glassed-in offices of the librarians.

Instead of going down the aisle to my usual post behind the checkout counter, I turned and walked back into the stacks until I came to a certain spot. Once, a glass case had stood here, the one that I'd grabbed Vic out of during my desperate fight to the death with Jasmine. Of course, the case was long gone, since the evil Valkyrie had smashed it to pieces, but that wasn't what I was here to see anyway.

No, I was here to visit a goddess.

I tilted my head up and stared at a figure above me. A balcony wrapped all the way around the second floor of the library, and slender columns separated statues of all the gods and goddesses from all the cultures of the world. Greek gods like Psyche and Persephone. Native American deities like Coyote and Badger. Celtic gods like Balor and Branwen. All the members of the Pantheon could be seen, except for a single empty spot. That's where the statue of Loki would have stood, but there were no statues of the Norse god of chaos anywhere on the Mythos campus. Not hard to figure out why, since the evil god had tried to take over the world and his Reapers of Chaos enjoyed killing warriors more than anything else.

I pulled my eyes away from the empty spot and stared up at the figure directly above me—Nike, the Greek goddess of victory. The goddess's statue looked exactly like she did in real life. Hair falling past her shoulders, a toga-like gown flowing around her body, wings peeking up from behind her back. To me, the goddess was cold, beautiful, strong, and terrible all at the same time. That's what I felt whenever I was in her presence—the raw power that rolled off her in fierce, frosty waves.

I supposed she seemed that way to me because Nike was the embodiment of victory, something that could be a bitter, bitter thing in the end. That's how I felt about what had happened at the coliseum. Sure, my friends and I had survived—but other kids had died. I would never, ever forget that.

It had certainly been that way as well for the members of the Pantheon when they'd battled Loki. Sister had turned against sister, warrior against warrior, god against god, until the whole world had been on the brink of destruction. If Loki ever got free, that's what would take place again—another long, bloody Chaos War. But that wasn't going to happen, I vowed. Now that I knew where to look, now that I knew the Helheim Dagger was hidden in the library, I was determined to find it—no matter what.

"Well, in case you didn't notice, it looks like I have a new, um, pet, for lack of a better word," I said. "You want to give me a clue about why Nott decided to track me down?"

The statue didn't move, didn't blink, didn't twitch, didn't do anything to indicate that Nike was in there somewhere—or that the goddess was actually listening to me in the first place. Still, saying hello to Nike and talking to her, even if she didn't talk back, always made me feel a little better. Like maybe she really was up there on Mount Olympus or wherever the gods hung out these days, looking down and watching over me.

"I know, I know," I said. "You can't really tell me anything because of the pact the gods made not to interfere with mortal affairs. Still, if you ever wanted to slip me a clue on the sly, I'd be more than happy to listen."

The statue didn't move, but for a moment, it seemed like Nike's lips curved up into a smile. Well, I supposed there were worse things than amusing a goddess.

I left the statue behind, stepped out of the stacks, and headed for the checkout counter. The main space in the Library of Antiquities was a huge room with a dome-shaped ceiling that arched all the way up to the top of the seventh floor. It always seemed to me like the library was taller than that, though, like it just kept going up and up and up.

I craned my neck back, trying to get a glimpse of the frescoes painted on the curved ceiling, the ones adorned with the millions in gold, silver, and jewels that Metis had mentioned during her myth-history lecture, but all I could see were shadows. Maybe that was for the best. No doubt the frescoes were just as creepy and lifelike as the stone statues that decorated the rest of campus. There was only so much weird I could handle in one day.

The checkout counter stood in the middle of the library in front of the offices that split the domed room in two. Students huddled at the study tables near the counter. Despite the fact that this was only the first day back from the winter break, every single table was packed—and not because we all had so much home-work to do already.

The library was one of the main places to Hang Out and Be Seen at Mythos. Kids were here to study, sure, but they were also eyeing everyone who came and went, talking, texting, and gossiping as fast as their fingers and mouths would move. I supposed the library was so crowded tonight because everyone wanted to get caught up with his or her friends about everything that had happened over winter break. Not to mention all the rumors still flying around about the Reaper attack—and my part in it. Once again, more than one kid stared at me before he turned and whispered something to his friends. Great. Just great.

I stepped behind the checkout counter and put my messenger bag in a slot underneath the long counter. I'd barely had time to sit down on the stool next to one of the computers when a door in the office complex squeaked open.

"You're late, Gwendolyn," a low voice said. "Yet again."

I rolled my eyes and swiveled around on the stool. Sure enough, Nickamedes stood behind me. The librarian had his arms crossed over his chest, and he was tapping his right fingers against his left elbow, a clear sign he was upset with me—again. But really, when wasn't he upset with me? I couldn't do anything right as far as Nickamedes was concerned, and I had no idea why.

I looked at the sundial-shaped clock that hung on the outermost glass wall. "No, I'm not. I'm right on time."

Nickamedes pushed back the sleeve of his black sweater and looked at his own watch. "No, you're not. It's one minute past the top of the hour, which means that you are late."

I rolled my eyes again. "One minute? Seriously? You're going to yell at me for being one minute late?"

The librarian's blue eyes narrowed. "It doesn't matter if it's one minute or one hour. Late is late, Gwendolyn. I suppose you were busy sneaking off campus so you could go see your grandmother, even though you know students aren't supposed to leave the academy grounds during the week."

His snide tone grated on my nerves. Yeah, maybe that's what I usually did, but today I'd stayed at the academy, just like Grandma Frost had wanted me to. Even when I did what I was supposed to, I just couldn't catch a break where the librarian was concerned.

"Actually, I was walking around campus like a good little girl," I snapped at him. "I didn't set one foot outside the walls today."

A hand, yes. A foot, no. Although I wasn't about to mention that or Nott to the librarian.

Nickamedes arched his black eyebrows and gave me a sour look. He obviously didn't believe me.

I wanted to growl just like Nott. First, Daphne had gone off during lunch in her weird mood, then Professor Metis had bolted before I could talk to her, and now, Nickamedes was giving me grief over being one lousy minute late. I was so tired of people and their attitudes today, especially Nickamedes, who'd openly despised me from the first moment I'd stepped into the library.

All of my anger and frustration bubbled up, burning like acid in my chest, and I opened my mouth without really thinking about what I was doing.

"Why do you hate me so much?" I asked. "What did I ever do to you that was so terrible? I'd really like to know."

For a moment, Nickamedes seemed shocked, like I wasn't supposed to notice how much he disliked me or how he went out of his way to needle me about every little thing. Please. Even if I didn't have my Gypsy gift, I still would have felt the cold anger that blasted off him whenever he set eyes on me, and it seemed like the librarian's hatred of me had only gotten worse since he'd seen me with Logan at the coliseum. It was like Logan's and my being friends—or whatever we were—made Nickamedes even more upset with me, for whatever reason. Like I'd gone out of my way to personally offend him or something.

Nickamedes stood there, staring at me, his lips pressed into a tight, thin line.

"Well?" I snapped. "Are you going to answer me? Or are you going to yell at me some more? Because I've got work to do, and I really don't have time for your mind games today."

An angry flush blossomed in Nickamedes's pasty cheeks, but I saw something flicker in his cold eyes—something that looked a lot like sorrow. Like he'd lost something once upon a time and could never get it back, so he took his anger out on everyone else as a result. The librarian opened his mouth like he was going to say something, but at the last second, he clamped his lips shut. Nickamedes pivoted on his heel, stalked into the office complex, and slammed the door behind him so hard the glass rattled.

I sat there and watched him go into his office, sit down at his desk, and start shuffling papers around, pointedly ignoring me. It seemed like I'd actually gotten the best of the uptight librarian. For some reason, though, it didn't make me as happy as I'd thought it would.

Chapter 11

I put Nickamedes out of my mind and spent the next hour working. Checking out books, looking up info for other kids, helping them find the reference materials they needed to do their homework.

After about an hour, things slowed down enough for me to do what I really wanted to do tonight—start searching for the Helheim Dagger. I pulled the Reaper girl's map of the library out of my bag and spread it out on a shelf below the checkout counter, out of sight of any students walking by. I didn't want anyone to get too interested in what I was doing, especially since the other kids kept staring at me. That made me feel uncomfortable enough already. Besides, I was already something of a freak at Mythos. I didn't want to be known as Gwen Frost, that weird Gypsy girl who studied maps in her spare time.

I hadn't had much of a chance to look at the map since yesterday, so I spent about fifteen minutes just studying it, memorizing every single line, every little squiggle, every single smear of ink and odd, random crinkle. Thanks to my Gypsy gift, I never forgot anything I saw. Now, the map was in my head, and I'd be able to pull up the image of it whenever I wanted to, which would be way better than dragging the paper through the stacks as I searched for the dagger. Carrying a map around was a sure sign you were up to something, and I wanted to keep what I was doing under the radar.

Especially since I didn't know if there were any Reapers watching me tonight.

It wasn't out of the realm of possibility. In fact, I'd say the odds were pretty good that at least one Reaper was in the library, among all the Amazons, Romans, Vikings, and Valkyries. Given their failure to find the dagger at the coliseum, I was pretty sure the Reapers—whoever they really were—were out in full force this evening, especially since I'd seen way more students than usual slip into the stacks.

Of course, some of those kids were just going back there to find a quiet corner to do the nasty. At Mythos, doing the deed in the library was regarded as some kind of thrill. Whenever I dusted the books and artifact cases back in the stacks, I always found several used condoms. Yucko.

I pushed those thoughts out of my mind and concentrated on the map, especially the Xs that marked various spots in the library. Some of the places I recognized, like the cart that sold coffee, energy drinks, and sugary snacks to students so they didn't have to leave the library to get something to eat while they studied.

Raven, the old woman who'd overseen the collection

of the students' bodies at the coliseum yesterday, also manned the coffee cart. I'd never really paid much attention to Raven before, but it seemed like she was everywhere I turned these days. White hair, white dress, wrinkles. Raven perched on a tall stool behind the cart, reading a celebrity tabloid and seeming to be completely engrossed in the gossip-filled pages. She didn't notice me staring at her, my narrowed gaze going from the bottles of syrup to the cups to the silver espresso machine squatting next to her elbow.

Still, no matter how strange Raven was, I didn't think the dagger was hidden in her cart with the blueberry muffins and granola bars, so I turned my attention back to the map.

Another X marked a spot on the main floor where a glass case had once stood holding the Bowl of Tears. I'd managed to use Vic to destroy the artifact, and the case was long gone, smashed to pieces by Jasmine when she'd first stolen the bowl.

The dagger wasn't hidden there either, so I moved on to the next X. One by one, I examined all the marks on the map, getting a little more disappointed and disheartened with each location. Either the Reaper girl wasn't as clever as I thought she was or there was something wrong with the map, because every single X was in a place where the dagger just *couldn't be*. Like the coffee cart or part of the floor that I knew was completely empty. Weird. Very weird. Why mark up a map with hiding spots that weren't really hiding spots to begin with?

I was just about to put the map aside as a lost cause

when I realized there was a final X that I'd over-looked—one that marked a location on the second floor balcony. I looked up, trying to match the X on the map to the actual spot in the library. It took me several seconds to realize the X actually pointed to one of the statues, Sigyn, the Norse goddess of devotion—and Loki's wife.

Centuries ago, when Loki had first started making trouble and caused the death of Balder, the Norse god of light, the other gods had chained Loki up beneath a giant snake that continuously dripped venom onto his handsome face. The Bowl of Tears was what Sigyn had used to keep the venom off him as much as possible, even though it had spattered onto her too. But Sigyn had kept right on standing there, holding and emptying that bowl for years—until Loki had somehow tricked the goddess into helping him escape and then had left her behind.

At first, I'd thought Sigyn was kind of dumb for trying to help Loki for all those years, but now, I just felt sorry for her. All she'd done was love the guy. She wasn't responsible for his being such a monster. Still, Sigyn always seemed to get a bad rap in all the myth-history books. It was like people blamed her for Loki's getting loose and starting the Chaos War. I figured it wasn't her fault her husband turned out to be a psychotic criminal mastermind. Besides, Grandma Frost always told me that people made their own choices. I figured it was the same when it came to the gods.

I peered closer at the map. Sigyn's statue was in a part

of the library on the second floor that I didn't go to all that often. It was bad enough the gryphons and other outside statues always seemed to stare at me—I didn't want to think that the figures of the gods were watching me, too.

Still, as I looked at the X, my heart started to pick up speed. Sigyn's statue was in a remote spot in the circular Pantheon, away from the stairs that led up to the second floor. It would be the perfect place to hide something like the Helheim Dagger. I doubted even Nickamedes went to that part of the library more than once or twice a year. Maybe he'd been wrong. Maybe the dagger was in the library after all. I'd love nothing more than to go up there, find the dagger's hiding spot, and show the librarian just how wrong he'd been—

"Are you Gwen?" a soft voice asked.

I looked up to find Vivian Holler standing in front of the checkout counter. Frizzy, auburn hair, pretty face, golden eyes. Vivian stood on her tiptoes, trying to peer over the counter and see what I was doing.

"What are you looking at?" she asked.

I quickly folded half of the map on top of the other, hiding the squiggles from sight. "Nothing. Just some homework for myth-history. You know Professor Metis. She's always giving us something to do."

"But you're Gwen, right? Gwen Frost?" Vivian asked. "The Gypsy girl?"

"Yeah, that's me. Gypsy girl extraordinaire. Can I help you? Do you need help finding a book or something?"

She shook her head. "Not a book, but I heard that you can find other items. Stuff that's been lost . . . or maybe even stolen."

"Yeah, I do that from time to time."

Actually, more like twice a week, given the fact that the Mythos students went through cell phones like most people did tissues. Not to mention all the other things they lost, misplaced, or swiped from other students.

"What have you lost?"

"Or had stolen." Vivian winced, as if she didn't like saying the words out loud or as if she might somehow make them true just by speaking them. The ugly thought was definitely at odds with her soft, sweet, melodic voice.

I raised my eyebrows. "Okay, what have you had stolen?"

She bit her lip. "Well, I don't know that it was *stolen* exactly. It's just that I'm usually really careful with my stuff, you know? I like to know where everything's at all the time."

Okay, it sounded like Vivian had some neat-freak issues going on, but that was okay. So did I, from time to time.

"So what's gone missing?" I asked. "Cell phone, keys, your credit cards?"

She shook her head. "Nothing like that. You're going to think that it's silly, really, but I lost a ring. A very special ring."

"What does this ring look like?" I asked. "Do you have a photo of it? And what's so special about it?"

These were the standard questions I asked every time

someone wanted me to find a lost item. It helped if, you know, I actually knew exactly what I was looking for, instead of just some vague description like *a ring* or *my cell phone* or *my favorite black bra*. Most of the time, though, I ended up working blind, so to speak, since few people ever thought to take photos of the things they cherished, like jewelry. So I was pleasantly surprised when Vivian pulled her cell phone out of her purse and started scrolling through the pictures on it.

"Here," she said. "Here it is."

She turned the phone around so I could see the picture, and I leaned forward to get a better look. In the photo, Vivian had her arm around Savannah, and the two of them were smiling. Vivian was hugging the Amazon, and I could see a band on her right ring finger. It was a simple enough ring, made out of solid gold, although the band formed two small faces, one turned left and crying, the other turned right and laughing.

"The way you were talking about the ring, I figured it would have diamonds or something all over it, but that's a cool design. What is it?"

Centuries ago, the gods and goddesses on both sides of the Chaos War had rewarded their Champions and warriors with gold, silver, and jewels for their loyal service. Over the years, the warriors had kept the gravy train of wealthy going, investing and whatnot, which is why the Mythos students had parents who were so loaded and could afford to give their kids the very best of everything. Most of the kids at the academy, especially the girls, had more bling than Hollywood movie stars.

"Thanks," Vivian said. "The design is theater masks from ancient times. Sometimes they're called Janus masks, after the Roman god. I have the ring because I'm in the drama club, just like my mom was when she went to Mythos."

She blushed and dropped her head, almost like she thought I was going to make fun of her for telling me so much about herself. Daphne was right. Vivian was even more of a shy, insecure geek than I was. I wondered how someone so quiet could survive at a place like Mythos, where finding new ways to be mean and vicious was considered an art form.

"Well, I think it's cool you're in the drama club," I said. "I like comic books, myself. You know, super-heroes, villains, that sort of thing. I like how the good guys always win at the end of the story."

"Cool."

Vivian gave me a small smile, which I returned.

"So what happens now?" she asked. "Do I pay you before you find the ring? Or after?"

"I charge a retainer of a hundred bucks," I said. "You can give that to me tomorrow afternoon, when I come over to your dorm room and start looking for the ring. If I find it, you owe me another hundred bucks. But if I can't find it, I give you the hundred bucks back. Does that sound fair?"

She nodded, then frowned. "But I already looked in my dorm room. I looked everywhere for the ring. Trust me. I pretty much tore my room apart searching for it."

"I'm sure you did," I said. "But I have my own special way of tracking down stuff. So I need to look in your room first, okay?"

I didn't tell her about my psychometry or about how I planned to walk around her room tomorrow, touch stuff, and see what kind of vibes I got off her things. I'd learned it was better to keep information like that on a need-to-know basis, especially now that I was Nike's Champion. Grandma Frost had told me that being a Champion was like having a target painted on your back, and I was already feeling shaky enough, thanks to the Reaper attack.

Vivian frowned. "Well, okay, I guess it couldn't hurt to look in my room again."

"Great," I said. "When do you want me to come over?"

We made plans to meet in her dorm, Valhalla Hall, after sixth period tomorrow. Then, Vivian gave me another shy smile and headed back to the table she'd been sitting at with Savannah and Talia. The three friends packed up their books and left the library, although Savannah stopped long enough to give me a nasty look on her way out the door. I sighed. I wished the Amazon would just chill about the whole Logan situation already.

But there was nothing I could do that would get Savannah to give me a break, and I had more important matters to think about anyway—namely, where the Helheim Dagger might be hidden. So I unfolded the Reaper girl's map and started studying it again, wondering if I'd overlooked anything that might lead me to the dagger.

Chapter 12

Finally, at about eight thirty, students started filing out of the library for the night. The latest juicy gossip had been spread, the frantic texts had been sent, and it was time to get some rest before everyone did the same thing again tomorrow.

Nickamedes was still sulking in his office, which meant that I could finally leave the checkout counter and search for the dagger. And I knew just the place to start.

The library seemed to be deserted, and even Raven had closed down her coffee cart and left for the night, but I decided to be as incognito as possible. So I grabbed a metal cart full of books that needed to be shelved and pushed it back into the stacks. The wheels *squeak-squeak-squeaked* with every turn I made, but since all the wheels on all the stupid carts squeaked, I figured the sound would help me blend in. It would have been strange if the wheels *hadn't* screeched.

For the next ten minutes, I pushed the cart back and forth in the stacks, shelving all the books that needed to be put away, before steering the cart over to a set of stairs that led up to the second floor. I looked around again, but I didn't see or hear anything. Of course, that didn't mean much in the library, which in my experience was one of the most dangerous places on campus. I grabbed the last book off the cart and climbed the stairs, like the slender volume belonged in the stacks up there instead of downstairs in the main collection. Actually, it did go in the archives on the second floor.

If there was one word that described the statues ringing the second floor balcony, it was *impressive*. All of the gods and goddesses stood thirty feet tall and were carved out of marble so white and smooth that it just gleamed. I felt very small and very shabby in comparison to the elegant carvings. My sneakers slapped softly against the floor as I hurried along the balcony, and every few steps I paused and looked around, listening for any footsteps or rustles of clothing behind me.

Nothing. I heard and saw nothing.

Finally, I reached the statue of Sigyn. To my surprise, the Norse goddess stood in the spot right next to Nike's statue. How had I not noticed that before? Then again, on the rare occasions that I did venture up to the second floor, I always came to see Nike, not any other goddess.

The statue of Sigyn was just as tall and imposing as the others were. The Norse goddess of devotion wore a long gown, her bare feet just peeking out from underneath the draped folds. Strangely enough, the gown looked torn and tattered in places, as if her statue had been continuously chipped away over the years, although I don't see how that could have happened in the library. Her hands and arms looked especially pitted and pockmarked. A spiderweb swooped from one side of the statue to the other, looking like a glistening silver necklace that had been strung around the goddess's throat. Sigyn's features were pretty enough, but there was such sorrow in her face, as if she was somehow responsible for all the sadness in the world. It made me want to reach out and comfort her.

I stood there for several seconds, just staring into Sigyn's stone eyes, before shaking my head and coming back to myself.

"All right, Gwen," I muttered. "Focus."

I put the book I'd been carrying down on the floor. Then, I drew in a breath, leaned forward, and brushed my fingers against the cold stone, waiting for my psychometry to kick in, for the images and memories to fill my mind.

Instead of flashing on the statue and all the people who'd seen and walked by it over the years, I felt nothing—nothing at all. No flickers of feeling, no memories, nothing. It was like no one had ever touched the statue—not even the artist who'd carved it in the first place.

I frowned. My Gypsy gift always let me see *something,* always let me feel *something* whenever I touched an object, no matter how big or small it was. The only time I hadn't flashed or couldn't flash on an object was when it was an illusion, and there was nothing really there to start with. That's how Jasmine had tricked me into thinking she was dead—she'd created an illusion of her body lying on the library floor.

I rapped my fist on the stone, and the dull *thump-thump-thump* of my knuckles on the marble echoed around the balcony. Nope, the statue was as real as I was. Maybe nobody had touched it in so long that all the memories attached to the statue had faded away. That could happen sometimes with objects, like if they were put into storage and weren't used for long periods of time.

Since I hadn't gotten any vibes off the stone, I decided to keep searching the old-fashioned way—I ran my hands up and down the statue and tapped my knuckles on every spot I could reach, searching for a secret compartment. Okay, okay, so maybe I'd watched too many old *Scooby-Doo* cartoons over winter break, but I figured it was worth a shot.

Nothing—I found nothing. Sigyn's statue was solid marble. I even dragged a ladder over to the statue so I could reach even higher, but I still came up empty. I didn't know why the Reaper girl had marked Sigyn's statue on her map, but the dagger wasn't here. Maybe the dagger wasn't in the library after all.

Disappointed, I climbed off the ladder, dragged it over to the wall, and put it back in its spot next to a tall, skinny bookcase. Similar ladders could be found all over the library to help kids reach books on high shelves. I also retrieved the book I'd laid on the floor at Sigyn's feet, glanced at the call number on the spine, and headed toward the spot where it should be shelved.

I found the appropriate case and slid the book into its proper slot. I was just turning around to head down the stairs to the first floor when a silver plaque on the wall beside the case caught my eye. ARCHITECTURAL COLLEC-TION #1–13. The plaque made me think of the essay I had to write for myth-history. While I was up here, I might as well grab a couple of reference books, since Metis wanted *real* sources for the essay.

One by one, I tugged books off the shelves and opened them up, scanning the tables of contents. I didn't get any real vibes off the books, just faint, vague flashes of other students flipping through the faded pages. Most of the books hadn't been touched in years, and what-ever memories were associated with them had long since faded away.

What I did stir up was all the dust that had gathered on the volumes. Soon, clouds of dust motes swirled in the air around me, reminding me of the sparks of magic Daphne gave off. I'd texted the Valkyrie again while I'd been working, telling her that I'd found a possible loca-tion for the dagger and was going to check it out, but she hadn't responded, not even to text me back and say she was busy tonight. I didn't know what was going on with my best friend, which worried me.

Most of the books focused on the academy buildings, rather than the statues, but I finally found a few that seemed useful, including one that had a gryphon em-bossed on the front cover in silver foil. I looked at the title. *The Use of Gryphons, Gargoyles, and Other Mythological Creatures in Architecture.* Well, that cer-tainly sounded pretentious enough for Metis's class. I flipped through the pages and saw several photos of stone gryphons, including one that showed the two stat-ues outside the Library of Antiquities. Jackpot. I closed the book and tucked it under my arm. Who knew? Besides using it for a reference source, maybe something in the book would tell me why the statues seemed to be watching me all the time—

The *squeak* of a sneaker made me freeze.

It was a small, soft sound, one that I wouldn't have heard at all, if it hadn't been so absolutely quiet on the second floor. I looked down and noticed a shadow sliding up on the floor beside me, creeping closer and closer. I kept my head bent, like I was still scanning the shelf in front of me, and tightened my grip on the gryphon book. The shadow kept coming and coming, until it was right next to me. I whirled around and raised the book up high, ready to bring it down as hard as I could on whomever was sneaking up behind me.

But there was no one there—no one at all.

I snapped my head back and forth, looking around the balcony. Nobody appeared, and nothing moved, not even the statues. I really, really wanted to call out and ask if there was someone there, but since that was how everyone always died in horror movies, I decided to keep my mouth shut. Instead, gripping the gryphon book even tighter, I tiptoed over to the stairs, eased down them, and stepped back out onto the first floor.

I slid through the stacks, my eyes scanning left and right as I headed toward the checkout counter. Yeah, Nickamedes might be a pain, but listening to him yell at me was better than standing around waiting for a Reaper to sneak up and attack me. I was *so* getting tired of fighting for my life in the library.

I didn't see anything but books, books, and more

books, but for some reason, I felt like I wasn't alone, like there was another presence hidden among the tall stacks, creeping around in the shadows. Worse than that, my head started to pound, as if a set of invisible fingers were slowly stabbing their way deep into my brain.

Gypsy... A raspy voice echoed through the library. *Oh, Gypsy... I'm coming to kill you....*

I froze again, my heart leapfrogging up into my throat and choking me from the inside out. It wasn't the whispered words that creeped me out so much; it was the person who'd said them who really frightened me— Preston Ashton, when he'd been stalking me through the construction site at the Powder ski resort. Even worse, Preston had threatened to go after my grandma and kill her the same way he'd helped the Reaper girl murder my mom.

But Preston couldn't possibly be running around campus. He just couldn't. Preston was locked up in the academy prison in the bottom of the math-science building. I wasn't sure where the idea came from, but suddenly I was thinking of the prison and all the locks and magical wards you had to go through to even get to the door, calling up my memories of them and visualizing them in my mind. The pounding in my head intensified, and for a moment, I had trouble letting go of the images, but there was nothing to worry about. Preston was trapped so far underground he could never claw his way out.

Right?

Gypsy...

The voice kept echoing through the library, growing louder and louder with every cold, raspy whisper. Maybe the voice was supposed to scare me and make me start screaming. And yeah, part of me was shaking with fear. But then I thought about what I'd seen at the coliseum. Creepy voices were one thing—flesh-and-blood Reapers were another. After the attack yesterday, someone's trying to scare me with whispers seemed like child's play—*a bloody annoyance,* as Vic would say, more than a real threat.

"All right, creepy voice," I muttered. "Let's see how raspy you are when my hands are around your throat."

Still holding on to the gryphon book, I kept sneaking through the stacks, stopping to look and listen every few feet, and trying to pinpoint exactly where the voice was coming from. I didn't see anything, but the voice kept whispering over and over again, like a bell that was stuck inside my head, bringing a fresh wave of pain with it every single time it chimed. I gritted my teeth, trying to pretend I didn't hear the sound and ignore the growing ache in my skull.

For a second, I wondered if it was all in my head, but I pushed that thought away. I'd seen a lot of Bad, Bad Things over the years with my Gypsy gift, one of the worst being a girl who was being abused by her stepdad. If I had actually lost my mind and was just imagining all this, well, there were worse things I could be thinking about than a creepy voice saying it was going to kill me.

I kept roaming through the stacks, peering around the edges of the bookshelves, looking for the source of the voice. I was just about to give up and go back to the checkout counter, when something rustled a few shelves over.

Still gripping the gryphon book, I slithered in that direction. My sneakers barely made a scuffle on the marble floor, but I still paused every few seconds, looking and listening. Finally, I reached the section where I'd heard the rustle. I peeked through the books just in time to see a figure rounding the far corner, his back to me.

"Gotcha," I muttered.

I darted around the corner of the bookshelf, raced down the aisle, and headed out into the main library space. A figure was walking in the other direction toward the checkout counter. I raised the book high, ready to bring it down and bash him on the head from behind—

He must have heard the whisper of my sneakers, because at the very last second, he turned and grabbed my wrist. A moment later, I was flying through the air. The next thing I knew, I was lying on my back on the floor, aching all over and desperately trying to breathe and remember what I'd been doing in the first place.

Something scuffed, a shadow fell over me, blocking out the light, and a pair of boots planted themselves beside my head. Not good—so not good. I flailed around on the floor, my fingers searching for the gryphon book, which had fallen out of my hands, but I didn't feel it anywhere. Cold, sweaty panic filled me. I needed that book. I needed some sort of weapon to fight off a Reaper, to keep Preston from killing me like he'd promised—

"Gypsy girl? Are you okay?"

His words made me freeze for a third time. Even if I couldn't see his face, I still recognized the voice, enough to know it wasn't Preston standing over me.

Oh, no. Logan had just kicked my ass instead.

Chapter 13

It took me a couple of seconds to get my breath back enough to answer him.

"Sure," I wheezed, trying to keep the library from spinning around and around. "I'm fine for a girl who just got flipped over a Spartan's shoulder and slammed to the floor."

Logan winced, leaned down, and helped me sit up. "Sorry about that," he said, a sheepish look on his face. "I saw you out of the corner of my eye, and, well, instinct took over. Especially after what happened yesterday."

Yeah, that was the thing about Spartans—they all had that killer instinct. It was a wonder Logan hadn't taken the gryphon book I'd been holding and stabbed me with one of the pointed edges. The Spartan could totally do freaky stuff like that, thanks to his ability to pick up any object and immediately know how to kill someone with it. Seriously. Logan was the kind of guy who could skewer you with a paper clip. That's what made him such a great fighter.

When I felt steady enough, Logan grabbed my arm and helped me onto my feet. The Spartan put his hands on my waist, and I felt the scorching heat of his fingers all the way through my gray hoodie and T-shirt. Suddenly, I felt dizzy once more, but for another reason entirely than getting thrown onto the floor and the air knocked out of my lungs.

"Are you sure you're okay?" he asked, his eyes bright with concern.

I smiled. "I'm feeling better all the time, Spartan, especially since you've got your arms around me."

A grin crept across Logan's face, and he pulled me a little closer, staring down into my face. As much as I wanted to just forget the last few minutes, I couldn't help wondering what had happened to the creepy whispers. They'd disappeared the second I'd attacked Logan. My head still throbbed, but the invisible fingers that had seemed to be drilling into my skull had vanished.

"Logan?"

"Yeah?" he asked in a husky voice, staring at my lips.

"When you first came into the library, before you saw me, did you hear any . . . whispers or anything like that? A voice, maybe?"

The Spartan shook his head. "I didn't hear anything until you started sneaking up on me. You shouldn't wear sneakers, you know. They always seem to squeak no matter how quiet you're trying to be. But why are you asking about voices?"

I bit my lip. I didn't want to admit to the Spartan that I'd thought I'd heard voices or whatever those weird whispers had been. I didn't want him to think I was losing my mind, even if it seemed that way to me. Still, I couldn't help feeling that someone else had been in the library—someone who'd known exactly what Preston had said to me at the ski resort. But how was that even possible? Besides me, Logan had been the only other person there, and I knew the Spartan wouldn't try to scare me like that.

"Are you okay, Gypsy girl?" Logan asked. "You look sort of distracted."

I pushed all thoughts of the creepy whispers away and focused on Logan. "I'm fine. I just thought I heard someone moving around in the library. That's why I, uh, attacked you. Or tried to, anyway."

Logan grinned at me again. "Well, no harm done, right?"

"Right."

"So," he said. "Would this be a good time to talk about . . . us?"

I blinked at the abrupt change in subject. "What?"

For a second, he looked uncomfortable. "You know, *us*. As in you and me, and what's going on between us."

Confused, I just kept staring at him.

He sighed. "Girls always seem to want to talk about stuff like that. All the time. So I thought I'd bring it up first. For a change." He muttered the last few words under his breath.

Okay, so this wasn't exactly the starry, romantic talk I'd been hoping for, but Logan had said the word *us*. That would have given me a little bit of hope except for one thing—the fact that Logan had a secret he was keeping from me. One that he thought would make me stop caring about him. One that was going to come out sooner or later, once we started touching.

If we started touching.

I drew in a breath. "I'd love for there to be an *us*. I want that more than anything. I mean, it's kind of obvious how I feel about you. How I've felt about you for a while now. I'm crazy about you, Spartan. Even when you were with Savannah, I was still crazy about you, and my feelings haven't changed any over the holidays."

If anything, they'd only gotten stronger, but I didn't tell him that.

Logan frowned. "I'm sensing a *but* in there."

I drew in another breath. "*But* it's not that simple. You know how I feel about you, and I think I know how you feel about me. *But* we both know you're keeping something from me. Your big secret, remember?"

Logan's features tightened, and his face grew guarded. "What about it?"

"I'm going to find out your secret, Logan. Not because I want to," I added in a hasty voice, noticing the anger starting to cloud his face. "But because of my magic, because of my Gypsy gift. The second I touch you for any length of time, my psychometry's going to kick in, and I'll know everything there is to know about you—whether you want me to or not."

"But can't you just...turn it off or something?" Logan asked, the frustration making his voice harsh. "At least while we're together?"

I shook my head. "I can't, and believe me, I've tried dozens of times over the years. But my magic is a part of me. It's what makes me a Gypsy, just like your killer instinct makes you a Spartan. I wouldn't be *me* without my magic."

And now, it was time for the most difficult part, the thing I'd been dreading telling him for weeks now. "I've seen part of it already. Part of your secret."

Logan dropped his hands from around my waist and stepped back. A panicked light flared in his eyes. "What are you talking about?"

"When we kissed in the construction site at the ski resort, when I kissed you so I could tap into your fighting skills and defeat Preston, I saw more than just you battling other kids," I said in a low voice. "I saw you as a little boy—standing over two bodies. A woman and a girl. They looked like you, and there—there was blood all over them."

"You saw that?" he whispered.

I nodded. "Bits and pieces of it. First, I saw you in a closet, clutching a sword. You were so scared of what was going on outside the door, of all the shadows and screams you heard. Then, the memory shifted, and you were standing over the two bodies . . . crying. That was all I saw before the kiss ended."

Logan turned away from me. The Spartan ran his hands down over his face, like he could scrub the memory out of his own mind with the motion. After a second, he snapped back around and stabbed his finger at me.

"You had no right to do that. You had no right to go snooping through my head like that. No right at all, Gwen."

Uh-oh. The Spartan only called me *Gwen* when he

was serious about something—or seriously pissed off like he was now.

"I didn't do it on purpose. It just . . . happened."

The hard, angry look on Logan's face told me that he didn't believe me—that he didn't believe the memories had just come to me and that I hadn't gone looking for them on purpose. Yeah, sometimes I used my Gypsy gift to figure out what other people were hiding, what their secrets were, but I would never do that to Logan. *Never*.

"Will you at least tell me who they were?" I asked in a soft voice, trying to reach out to him. "The woman and the girl?"

Logan let out a bitter laugh. "I suppose I don't have a choice now, do I? Because I know you, Gypsy girl. Once you get your teeth into something, you never let go. Once you find out someone's keeping something from you, you're even more determined to figure out what it is, what their precious secret is."

I flinched at his words.

"You want to know what happened back then, Gypsy girl?" Logan snarled. "I'll tell you."

The Spartan's hands tightened into fists, and his whole body trembled with rage as he glared at me, his face as hard and fierce as I'd ever seen it.

"Reapers came to our house one afternoon, and they killed everyone they could get their hands on, just like they did at the coliseum. Except, in this case, that everyone was my mom, Larenta, and my older sister, Larissa. The Reapers came in, and they butchered them like cattle, even though neither one of them even had a weapon."

I'd thought it must have been something like that, but my heart still twisted at his pain, at the raw, naked grief shimmering in his eyes. "Oh, Logan. I'm so, so sorry. I know what it's like to lose your mom. To have her taken away from you. I'm sure that you did everything you could to help your mom and your sister. I'm sure you did everything you could to try and save them—"

He let out another harsh laugh, cutting off my words. "You don't know anything. Not a damn thing. Not about me, not about being a Spartan, nothing," he growled. "Your mom and grandma kept you out of all this, sheltered you from Loki and Reapers and everything else. You have no idea what it's like to grow up in our world, to deal with the threat of them *every single day*. To you, it's like it's all a big game or something. Even when Metis and Nickamedes tell you to be smart, to stay safe, you go right back to poking your nose into other people's business. When are you going to realize this obsession you have with finding out people's secrets is going to get you killed?"

I opened my mouth to say it wasn't true, that nothing he was saying was true, but the words just wouldn't come. Because really, deep down, I was *exactly* like that. I'd totally scoffed at the idea of Loki and Reapers of Chaos when I'd first come to Mythos, despite all the magic I'd seen around me. Even now, when I knew the Reaper girl was targeting me, I still wanted to beat her at her own game. I wanted to find the Helheim Dagger and keep it safe from her and all the other Reapers. I wanted to be worthy of the power and trust Nike had given to me. I wanted to be as smart, strong, and brave as all the other Frost women who had served the goddess of victory.

But most of all, I wanted to make the Reaper girl pay for murdering my mom.

"I don't know why I thought you would be different. I don't know why I thought you might understand. I don't know why I thought this would work," Logan said. "I'm sorry, Gwen. I just—I just can't do this. Not even for you. *Especially* not for you."

The Spartan turned around and stalked toward the double doors that led out of the library.

"Logan? Logan!"

But the Spartan didn't stop. If anything, he quickened his pace—and he didn't look back. Not even once.

I stood there in the middle of the library stunned—simply stunned. By the awful thing that had happened to Logan's family and by the awful things he'd said to me. Things that were a little closer to the truth than I would have liked them to be. Tears burned my eyes, and a sob rose in my throat, but I swallowed it down. How had Logan and I gone from talking about us and what we could be to breaking up before we even got together?

"Ahem." Someone cleared his throat.

I swiped the tears from my eyes and turned to find Nickamedes standing behind me, holding my messenger bag in front of him like a shield. From the look on his face, it was obvious the librarian had heard everything Logan had said to me.

"I bet you just loved that, didn't you?" I snapped, trying to keep the tears from running down my cheeks. "Your nephew telling me exactly what a horrible person I am. Did you give him pointers on that little speech? Or does being mean just run in the family?"

Nickamedes stared at me, his face blank and neutral. "I'm ready to close the library for the night, Gwendolyn. I thought you might want your things before you left."

He held out my bag, and I stalked forward and grabbed it from him, fully intending to run out of the library before he saw me cry. Except I didn't get a great grip on the strap, and the bag fell to the floor, spilling my stuff everywhere. The perfect ending to a perfectly miserable night.

I got down on my hands and knees and started scooping everything back into the bag. Pens, notebooks, the latest comic books I was reading, the bag of food for Nott. I'd just crawled over to the gryphon book I'd dropped earlier, when I heard Nickamedes shuffle on his feet behind me.

"Where did you get this?" he asked in a low voice.

I looked up to find the librarian clutching my mom's diary in his hands, a strange, twisted look on his face, like the leather cover burned his skin and it hurt him just to look at the journal. I got to my feet, stalked over, and yanked it out of his fingers, wondering if the damage had already been done, if he'd already imprinted his hatred for me on the diary.

"Give me that," I hissed. "That was my mom's, and I don't want you touching it. Not for one *second*."

The librarian frowned, but he didn't say anything.

Maybe for once he realized exactly how angry and hurt I was—if he even cared about such things. Instead, Nickamedes's gaze fell to something else on the floor, something that had slid under one of the tables, and he walked over to it and bent down.

I stood there a second, clutching the diary and reaching out with my psychometry. Once again, all I felt was my mom's presence, and the only images filling my mind were of her writing in the diary. Nickamedes hadn't touched it long enough to leave any piece of himself behind. Good. I didn't want him to ruin this for me, too.

"Gwendolyn, wait," Nickamedes said, still crouched down.

But I was in no mood to be lectured or whatever else the librarian had in mind, so I slung the strap of my bag across my chest and hurried out of the library as fast as I could.

I stalked across campus back to my dorm, trying not to cry about what had just happened between Logan and me—and failing miserably. For once, I was glad shadows covered the upper quad and the cobblestone walkways that led to the dorms. I didn't want anyone to see me like this, or worse, take a stupid picture with his or her cell phone and text it to everyone at the academy.

I passed a few kids heading to their own dorms for the ten o'clock curfew, but I was able to make it back to Styx Hall without anyone's getting a good look at my red, splotchy face. I used my student ID card to open the front door of the dorm and thumped up the stairs to my room on the third floor. I unlocked that door, too, and stepped inside. I threw my bag down on my desk, then went over and flopped onto my bed.

On the floor, Nott let out a little whine and lashed her tail from side to side. Vic's eye snapped open at the sound of me coming into the room. The sword stared at me for a second, his purplish gaze dark and suspicious.

"What's wrong?" Vic asked. "Why have you been crying?"

"It's nothing, Vic," I said and let out a hiccup.

For some stupid reason, I always started hiccupping after I cried. Another thing that made me a freak, right along with my psychometry. For once, I wondered why I couldn't have been blessed with a different kind of magic. Why couldn't Nike have made me superstrong like a Valkyrie? Or superquick like an Amazon? My psychometry was what was keeping Logan and me apart. No, correction, it was what had *driven* Logan and me apart. After the way the Spartan had lashed out at me tonight, I doubted anything I said or did would make him give me another chance—would make him give *us* another chance.

I didn't understand why. I'd told Logan that I'd seen his secret, that I knew what he was hiding, what made him so achingly sad, despite the fact that he tried to hide his pain with sly teasing and devilish grins. Instead of being relieved, Logan had only become angrier when he heard my confession. I didn't understand what was wrong with the Spartan—or me.

Logan and I were over before we'd even gotten started. Sometimes I thought that was the story of my life. My dad, Tyr, had died when I was two, before I'd even had a chance to know him. My mom had been murdered and had never told me about Loki, Reapers, or being Nike's Champion. And now, I couldn't find the Helheim Dagger so I could protect it from the Reaper girl. Yep, tragic loss and epic failure definitely seemed to be the stories of my life.

I rolled over onto my back, and Nott got up from her spot on the floor. The Fenrir wolf was so tall that she easily managed to put her head on the bed. She looked at me with her dull rusty eyes—eyes that weren't Reaper red anymore but weren't quite brown either—and let out another whine. Trying to comfort me, I supposed.

I sighed, reached out, and stroked her silky ears. Nott let out a grumble of pleasure and shoved her head farther underneath my fingers. For some reason, petting her made me feel a little better—even if she was big enough to eat me. Sighing, I got to my feet. Just because I was suffering didn't mean the wolf should, too.

While Nott ate the meat I'd brought her from the dining hall, I took a shower, then went downstairs and grabbed some blankets and pillows from one of the closets where the extra bedding was kept. I carried the blankets up to my room and made a nest for Nott in between my bed and my desk.

"You never made me a cozy bed like that," Vic said from his spot on the wall. "And I'm far more useful than a bloody wolf."

Nott stopped eating long enough to growl at him.

"That's because you have a cool leather scabbard," I told the grumpy sword. "It's your own little nest."

"Hmph!" Vic snapped his eye shut once more.

I sighed and went back downstairs, this time grabbing a bucket from underneath the sink in the common kitchen that all the girls in the dorm shared. I carried the bucket back up to my room, filled it with water, and let Nott drink as much as she wanted. Then, when most of the lights in the dorm had gone dark and everything was quiet, I snuck the wolf down the stairs and let her do her business outside the dorm before the doors automatically locked down for the night.

Finally, we were safe in my room. I thought about cracking open the gryphon book and getting started on the essay for Metis's myth-history class, but instead, I found myself digging my mom's diary out of my bag and curling up with it in bed.

Nott and Vic were both asleep, but I was too wound up to settle down, so I snapped on a light over my bed and started reading.

Today, I started my second year at Mythos Academy.... Those were the words on the diary's first page. I snuggled down below my comforter a little more, ready for a long night of reading and hopefully forgetting about my own problems.

The diary went on from there, detailing the things my mom had done when she was seventeen and a second-year student at the academy like me. She wrote of her teachers and classes and how much she disliked Mrs. Banba, the moody economics professor.

I smiled, hearing my mom's voice in her words, almost like she was here reading the diary to me like a bedtime story. It comforted me. I especially liked the pages that talked about her friendship with Metis. Apparently, the two of them had been quite the trouble-makers during their days at Mythos. Mom even complained about getting a talking to by the Powers That Were at the academy after one of their stunts. A few photos had been stuck in the diary, too, mostly of my mom grinning at the camera or her and Metis with their arms around each other. I set those aside. I'd frame them later and put them with the other photos on my desk.

Still, as much as I enjoyed reading the diary, it didn't give me any clues as to where my mom had hidden the Helheim Dagger. She never wrote anything about the artifact at all. The closest she came was when she mentioned *an important mission* she'd received from Nike. I thought she might have meant the dagger, and I scanned the surrounding pages, but she didn't write anything else about the mission—not even if it had been a success or not.

But the diary did tell me one thing about my mom: She liked to doodle. Sketches and drawings could be found on almost every page, but they weren't the usual hearts and flowers you'd expect to find.

Instead, my mom had drawn statues—all the statues that covered the buildings at Mythos Academy.

Gargoyles, Minotaurs, basilisks, dragons, chimeras, Gorgons. All those and more littered the diary, peeking out at me from the tops and bottoms of the pages or stretching down the spine. For whatever reason, my mom had especially seemed to like the gryphons that guarded the library steps. There were more drawings of the two of them than there were of all the other statues combined. Maybe my mom had been given an assignment like I had to research and write about the statues. That was the only reason I could think of for why she'd drawn them over and over again.

Despite the weird doodles and my frustration at not being able to find the dagger, just reading through my mom's diary, just listening to her voice in my head and staring at her beautiful handwriting, made me feel a little better about, well, everything. Or maybe that was because I was holding the diary and soaking up all the images and feelings associated with it—everything my mom had felt and done. All the good times she'd had at the academy, and the bad ones, too. It was all a part of her and let me see my mom in a way I never had before, like watching old home movies of her as a teenager.

I didn't want the feeling to end, so when I finally quit reading and turned out the light, I slid the diary under my pillow, curling my fingers around it. And I stayed like that until I drifted off to sleep.

Chapter 14

The next day was exceptionally average. Except, of course, for my aching heart. I made sure I was at the gym for weapons training ten minutes early, hoping to talk to Logan before the others arrived, hoping to tell him . . . something, anything that would fix this problem between us.

For once, the Spartan didn't show up.

"Sorry, Gwen," Oliver said, slinging his bag onto the bleachers. "Logan texted me and said that he felt a little under the weather this morning."

"He's not the only one," I muttered.

I knew the Spartan was avoiding me, and it looked like Oliver and Kenzie knew it, too, from the sympathetic looks they gave me. As if that wasn't bad enough, we once again had an audience of first-year students, with even more kids than had been here yesterday. At least until they found out Logan wasn't going to be training. After that, all the girls left.

I gritted my teeth and clutched Vic so hard my fingers

went numb, just trying to get through the hour of torture.

The rest of the morning passed by in a boring blur of classes, lectures, and homework assignments until it was finally time for lunch. Carson had a special practice session to attend for the upcoming winter concert. The band geek was a Celt and had a magical talent for music, like a warrior bard. He automatically knew how to play every instrument he picked up.

So it was only Daphne and me at our usual table in the dining hall, although the Valkyrie just picked at her curried chicken salad croissant and ambrosia fruit salad.

"... and then he told me that I didn't understand, that I would never understand, and basically broke up with me before we even got together. Can you believe it?" I muttered, griping about Logan.

I waited a second, but Daphne didn't say anything. Instead, the Valkyrie stabbed another heart-shaped strawberry on her plate, although she didn't actually eat it.

"And then Logan and I totally made out right there on top of one of the tables in the middle of the library," I finished. "In front of Nickamedes. What do you think of that?"

"Awesome," Daphne muttered. "Just awesome."

I waved my hand in front of the Valkyrie's face, finally getting her to look at me. "What is wrong with you? You've barely said a word during lunch, and you're not listening to me at all."

"Sure, I am," Daphne said. "It's the same stuff you always talk about. You and Logan and your star-crossed relationship, and this big, important thing you have to do for Nike, because you're her freaking Champion. Give it a rest, Gwen. You are not the absolute center of the universe. The rest of us have problems, too, you know."

I stared at the Valkyrie, shocked and a little hurt by her snarky words. "What's wrong with you? Why would you say something like that to me? You're supposed to be my friend—my best friend."

Daphne glared at me, causing sparks to shoot out of her fingertips. For a moment, she stared at the pink sparks of magic flickering all around her, and her black gaze hardened.

"Forget it," she muttered. "You wouldn't understand anyway."

Then, the Valkyrie got to her feet, grabbed her tray, and stalked out of the dining hall without another word.

I sat there and watched her go, wondering what that had been about. Daphne had been quiet and distracted ever since we'd sat down, but I thought her mood just had to do with the attack at the coliseum and almost losing Carson. Almost watching your boyfriend die, then healing him with magic you suddenly developed was enough to shake up anybody, even the tough, sassy Valkyrie. But it seemed like there was something else going on with my friend, and I had no idea what it was. For the second time in two days, someone had told me that I just wouldn't understand. Well, I wasn't a mind reader. I *couldn't* understand if they wouldn't tell me what was going on in the first place.

Things didn't get any better the rest of the day, especially since I was paired with Talia in gym class. We sparred with staffs, and the tall Amazon went out of her way to kick my ass, sweeping my feet out from under me and busting my knuckles as many times as she could. I knew it was because Talia was friends with Savannah.

I wondered if it would make Savannah feel better to know that I'd taken Logan away from myself, too, just by being me.

Even Professor Metis was in a weird mood in myth-history class, and she rushed out the door the second the last bell of the day rang.

I walked over to my dorm room to check on Nott and gave the Fenir wolf some meat from the dining hall, along with some fresh water. Then it was time for me to meet up with Vivian Holler at Valhalla Hall.

Valhalla Hall was the plushest dorm at Mythos and home to most of the Valkyrie mean-girl princesses, although a few Amazons like Savannah lived there, too. I headed up to the second floor, where Vivian's room was, and knocked on the door.

A second later, Vivian opened it and gave me a shy smile. "Come on in."

I stepped inside the room, and Vivian shut the door behind me. For a second, I just stood there, staring at everything. A bed, a desk, a dresser, some bookshelves, a nice vanity table. Vivian had the same dorm room furniture that most of the girls did.

Vivian had said she was in the drama club, but she hadn't told me just how into it she was. Posters from popular musicals like *Beauty and the Beast* and *The Scarlet Pimpernel* covered the walls, along with smaller, framed playbills from a couple of plays the Mythos students had staged, including *The Odyssey* and *The Iliad.* There were more Janus masks in here, too, from the bronze bookends that propped up a stack of textbooks to the glittery gold stickers that decorated the mirror over the vanity table to a notepad on the desk. I thought I was a little obsessive about comic books, but I had nothing on Vivian.

I eyed the bookends. It was cool that Vivian was so into theater stuff, but all those crying and laughing faces kind of creeped me out a little—

"So are you ready to get started?" Vivian asked, cutting into my thoughts. "Because I've got to meet up with Savannah and Talia in a few minutes."

"Sure," I said, pulling my eyes away from the masks. "Where do you last remember seeing the ring? Do you remember having it in your room? Or do you think you lost it somewhere on campus?"

I really, really hoped it was just here in the room. If Vivian had dropped it on her way to one of her classes, it could take me days to find the ring—if I ever did.

Vivian hesitated. "The last time I remember seeing the ring was in here. Savannah and I were watching TV and hanging out Sunday night, and I remember taking it off and putting it down on my vanity table, right next to my jewelry box. But it's not in there now, and I can't find it anywhere."

She gestured at the jewelry box, which was also shaped like a pair of faces. It was carved out of onyx and had a slick, glossy surface that reminded me of a piano. Maybe it was a trick of the sunlight sliding in through the window, but for a moment, it seemed like the onyx faces melted into a puddle of black blood that oozed all over the glass-topped table—

I blinked, and the image vanished. The box was just a box once more.

"Gwen?" Vivian asked. "Are you okay? You have this strange look on your face."

"I'm fine," I said. "Can you show me exactly where on the vanity table you put the ring?"

She gestured to a spot right next to the jewelry box. I drew in a breath, leaned over, touched the surface of the vanity table, and waited for the images to fill my mind.

Nothing happened.

I didn't see anything. No memories, no flashes of feeling, no flickers of emotion, nothing. I moved my fingers all around the table, until I'd touched the entire surface, along with the jewelry box, but I still didn't get any vibes off it. I stared at the table and realized just how brand-new it looked—and not at all beat up like dorm room furniture usually was.

"Is this a new table?" I asked.

"Yeah," Vivian said. "My dad had it delivered this morning. New furniture was part of my Christmas present this year. Everything in here is new, including the jewelry box."

That seemed like kind of an odd Christmas present to me. Given how lavishly most of the warrior parents spoiled their kids, I would have expected Vivian to get something like a diamond tennis bracelet, an Aston Martin, or a custom-made sword for Christmas. Then again, I'd bought my grandma a cookie jar for the holiday, so I couldn't judge too harshly.

Still, the fact that Vivian's furniture was all new was a problem, since she hadn't used it enough yet to leave any imprints of herself behind. That meant I couldn't get any vibes off her furniture and that I wouldn't be able to use my Gypsy gift to follow the trail of psychic flashes to her ring, wherever it was.

It was rare, but every once in a while, I just couldn't find a missing item. Sometimes there wasn't much of a trail to follow. Keys slid out of pockets, phones fell out of purses, and watches slipped off wrists every day in every place you could think of. Sometimes the items were just lost for good and no amount of magic or snooping on my part would make them reappear.

"Is something wrong?" Vivian asked.

I shook my head. "Nah. I just realized this isn't going to be as easy as I thought."

Vivian gave me a strange look, but she didn't say anything else. Instead, she sat on the bed and watched while I crawled around the room, running my hands over all her books, makeup, and furniture, searching high and low for her ring.

I didn't find the ring, and I didn't get a single usable vibe off Vivian's things—not one. Oh, I got a few faint flashes of her reading through her favorite books or putting on her makeup when I touched those items, but those were just the same ordinary vibes I always saw when I touched stuff like that. Almost everything else in her room was new, shiny, and pristine. Good for her, but bad for me since I was trying to use my Gypsy gift.

Finally, I admitted defeat and climbed to my feet, dusting my hands off on my jeans. "Well, you're right. I looked under and behind every piece of furniture, and your ring isn't in here anywhere. Do you think you might have lost it somewhere else on campus? Maybe you took it off before weapons training and left it in one of the gym lockers?"

She hesitated, a troubled light filling her topaz eyes. "That's the thing. I'm not so sure that I lost it. I think— I think someone might have taken my ring."

I arched an eyebrow. "Really? Who? I find stuff for kids all the time, and in my experience, if you think someone stole your ring, then you're probably right. It happens more than you would think."

It always surprised me how totally klepto some of the warrior whiz kids were. Most of them had all the money in the world, but they still stole things from other students and even their friends out of hate, jealousy, or spite. I supposed that actually, you know, paying for something you wanted was *so* last year.

Vivian picked at a loose thread on her comforter. "It's so silly, though. She's my friend. She would never do anything like that. She would never steal from me, especially not that ring. She knows how much it means to me."

"What's so special about the ring?"

Vivian bit her lip and dropped her head. "It belonged to my mom. She gave it to me right before she died."

"Oh. I'm so sorry."

I couldn't think of anything else to say, and I knew that whatever I said wouldn't really make a difference anyway. My words wouldn't bring Vivian any kind of real comfort. Nothing anyone had said to me after my mom was murdered had helped.

She shrugged. "It happened when I was thirteen. Reapers, you know."

My thoughts drifted to Logan, and how his mom and older sister had been murdered by Reapers, too, probably the same way Vivian's mom had been. Thinking about the Spartan made my heart ache, but I forced myself to focus on the girl in front of me.

"Come on, Vivian. You might as well tell me who you think stole your ring. It'll make it that much easier for me to find it if I have a place to start looking."

She sighed. "Savannah. I think it was Savannah. Like I said before, the last time I remember having the ring was in my room when we were hanging out two nights ago. She left right before the ten o'clock curfew, and yesterday morning I couldn't find my ring. It was just . . . gone."

Vivian's voice trembled, and she put her hand up over her eyes. Like just the thought that Savannah might have taken the ring was enough to make her cry.

I frowned, thinking about her soft words. Why would Savannah steal from her friend? Yeah, kids stole from other kids at Mythos all the time, but usually only the superexpensive, high-end items—TVs, platinum watches, emerald earrings the size of quarters. Taking such a simple gold ring, especially when Savannah knew how much it meant to her friend, well, that sounded like something a Reaper would do just for meanness.

I thought of that flash of red I'd seen in Savannah's eyes, first at the coliseum and then again yesterday in the dining hall. Could—could Savannah be a Reaper? Could she even be *the* Reaper—the Reaper girl who'd murdered my mom? Loki's Champion?

I didn't know where the thoughts came from, but once they popped into my head, I couldn't seem to stop thinking about them. For some reason, the ideas just wormed deeper and deeper into my mind, burrowing into my brain like cold, grasping fingers—

"So what's next?" Vivian asked.

Once again, a dull ache started in the back of my skull, but I finally shook off my suspicions about Savannah. "You give me the hundred-dollar retainer, like we agreed on. I track down some leads and report back to you in a few days. If I find your ring, you pay me the rest of the money, but if I can't find it, I give you back your hundred bucks. Okay?"

Vivian nodded, got her wallet out of her designer purse, and passed me a crisp hundred-dollar bill. I held on to the money for a moment, but I didn't get much of a vibe off it. Just the feeling of it being handed from one person to another until it had wound up with Vivian.

"Thanks," I said, stuffing the money into my jeans pocket. "I'll try to have some news for you in a day or two."

I'd done all I could for Vivian, so I headed toward the door. I started to reach for the knob, but Vivian beat me to it and opened the door instead. Well, that was polite of her.

"Thanks," I said.

She nodded. "You're welcome. And thanks for looking for my ring, Gwen. You have no idea how much it means to me."

I smiled at her. "Hey, that's why I'm the Gypsy girl."

I left Vivian's room, and she shut the door behind me. On my way toward the stairs, I passed Daphne's room. Like the other Valkyrie wannabe princesses, Daphne also lived at Valhalla Hall. I hadn't talked to the Valkyrie since our fight at lunch, and she hadn't called or texted me. I didn't know what was going on with her, what had upset her so much, but I already missed her. I hadn't even thought to tell her about Nott showing up yet, and I needed someone to talk to about the wolf, Logan, and most especially about whether or not Savannah could really be a Reaper.

I hesitated, then knocked on Daphne's door. No answer. I didn't hear any music playing inside. No sounds of typing, either. The Valkyrie wasn't in there working on one of her many computers. Disappointed, I plodded down the stairs, left the dorm, and headed across campus to the English-history building, where Metis had her office.

Today was Tuesday, which meant it was time for me to pay a visit to Preston Ashton. Ever since the Reaper had been imprisoned at the academy, I'd been using my Gypsy gift to peer into his mind, to try to find out what the other Reapers were up to. Now, of course, I wanted to know what he knew about the Helheim Dagger and if he had a clue as to where it might be hidden. Maybe it was irrational, but I also wanted to see for myself that Preston was still in the academy prison. After hearing that creepy voice whispering to me in the library last night, I wanted to make sure Preston was locked away where he couldn't hurt anyone—especially not my Grandma Frost.

I entered the building and walked down the hallway to Metis's office. To my surprise, the door was cracked open, and I could see two figures inside through the frosted glass. I'd just raised my hand to knock when a voice drifted out to me.

"But I don't want to be a healer," someone muttered. "I *never* wanted to be a healer."

I frowned. That sounded like Daphne. I eased to one side so I could look in through the crack and realized that it *was* Daphne. The Valkyrie stood in front of Metis's desk, her hands on her hips, princess pink sparks of magic snapping in the air around her.

"I'm afraid you don't have a choice, Daphne," Metis said in a gentle voice. "Your magic has quickened. There's no reversing it. We've met after classes two days in a row now, and nothing's changed."

Well, that explained where Metis had rushed off to after myth-history.

Daphne threw her hands up, causing the sparks to cascade over her like raindrops falling from the sky. "But it only quickened because I was so upset about Carson. Because the Reaper stabbed him, and he was going to die."

"And your magic's quickening then, emerging then, was what let you save him," Metis said.

Daphne didn't say anything, but she slumped down in the chair in front of the professor's desk. "You don't understand. None of the other Valkyries in my family are healers. My mom has fire magic, and so did my grandma before she died. I thought that's what kind of power I would have, too. Something strong, something powerful. Not this—this *useless* thing."

Daphne held up her fingers and concentrated. After a moment, the pink sparks bled together, forming a rosy, healing glow that coated her entire hand. Once again, I had the strangest sensation that I could reach out and grab hold of her magic, that I would be able to feel it pouring into me, if only I were to touch the Valkyrie. It was the same feeling I'd had at the coliseum, when I'd grabbed Daphne's hand and had seen that brilliant pink light burning in her heart—that beautiful, beautiful spark.

"And then, there's this," Daphne muttered.

The Valkyrie leaned down. When she straightened back up, I realized she was clutching two things in her hands—the onyx bow and the quiver with its single golden arrow. The weapons she'd used to fight the Reapers. I blinked. I'd thought Daphne had left those behind at the Crius Coliseum after the attack.

"What am I supposed to do with these?" Daphne snapped. "I've given them back to you twice now, but every time I go to my room, there they are, lying on my bed. And the same thing's happened with Carson and that stupid horn he picked up at the coliseum."

She laid the weapons on the desk and shoved them at Metis. After a moment, the professor reached over and picked up first the bow, then the quiver. She examined them both for several seconds before putting them down.

"Daphne, do you . . . see anything on the bow or quiver? Any words or symbols?" Metis asked in a soft voice.

My breath caught in my throat. I knew what Metis was really asking my friend—if Daphne could read some sort of saying on the weapons. Every Champion was given a weapon by the god or goddess she served, and only a Champion could read the words on her specific weapon. Back in the coliseum, I remembered Daphne's saying the bow and quiver had once belonged to Sigyn, the Norse goddess of devotion. Could—could the goddess have picked Daphne to be her Champion? Was that why the weapons kept showing up in the Valkyrie's room? Was that why Carson still had that strange horn, too?

Daphne sighed and picked up the bow and quiver, looking them over. "I don't see anything."

"Well, maybe you will someday soon," Metis said. "Until then, it appears there is some magic binding the weapons to you, so you might as well keep them—and use them, should the need arise."

"Whatever," Daphne muttered. "Are we done? Because I've got an essay to write for English lit."

Metis nodded, and Daphne got to her feet and grabbed her things, including the onyx bow and quiver. I barely had time to back up before the Valkyrie yanked open the door and saw me standing in the hallway. Surprise filled her face, but it was quickly replaced by anger.

Daphne glared at me. "Geez, Gwen. Can't you keep your nose out of anyone's business for five minutes?"

I stiffened at her harsh tone. "I wasn't here because of you. I'm supposed to go see Preston today. To find out if he knew anything about the Reaper attack or knows where the dagger is hidden."

The Valkyrie snorted. "Great. So you're going to dig through a Reaper's head instead of spying on the rest of us. Well, that's a change, I suppose, from eavesdropping on your friends. Have fun with that, Gypsy."

Daphne shoved past me and stormed off down the hall without another word.

Chapter 15

I stood there, mouth open, and watched her go. Yeah, the Valkyrie could be volatile sometimes, but that was the second time today she'd been nasty to me. Okay, okay, so maybe I *had* been eavesdropping on Daphne and Metis, but that was just because I was concerned about Daphne. Sue me for caring about my best friend.

Metis stepped out of her office, her green eyes soft and kind.

I sighed. "I take it you heard that?"

The professor nodded. "Daphne's just upset. She thought her magic would be one thing, and it's turned out to be another instead."

"Yeah, but why is she taking it out on me?"

Metis tilted her head to one side. "Because your magic is exactly what it's supposed to be. You fully embrace your power, Gwen, and you try to do good with it. That's one of the things that makes you so strong. Don't worry about Daphne. She'll be all right. It'll take her a little time to adjust, but she'll come to understand that everything happens for a reason. That the gods give us the gifts we need when we need them the most."

The professor stared off into the distance. "I was the same way when I was her age. I hoped that my magic would be physical instead of mental."

"What do you mean?"

Metis sighed. "Magic is basically divided into two categories—physical and mental. Physical magic involves things like the fire magic Daphne said her mother has. Usually, physical magic can be used to hurt someone else, while mental magic is often more of a protective magic, like my healing power."

"So what you're saying is that physical magic has some kind of actual form or shape, right? Like rain from a storm?"

Metis nodded back. "Right. Rain from a storm would be a physical form of magic, something you can actually see and feel and touch, whereas telekinesis or telepathy would be a mental form, something you can't necessarily see or touch."

For some reason, the word *telepathy* seemed to resonate in my head, like a bell softly chiming, although I had no idea why. As far as I knew, I'd never met anyone with telepathic magic. Lots of kids at Mythos had the physical magic Metis had described, like the ability to shoot lightning out of their fingertips or summon up gusts of wind with just a wave of their hands. I supposed the enhanced senses so many of the students had would be considered a form of mental magic.

"But what about my magic?" I asked. "What about my touch magic?"

That's what some people called my psychometry— touch magic.

"Your touch magic is different," Metis said. "It's one of the rare abilities that can be both physical and mental at the same time."

"What do you mean?"

Metis tapped her fingers against her lips, like she was struggling over how to explain it to me. "Well, obviously, you know about the mental part. That's when you touch objects and see things, as you put it. When you get flashes of other people's memories and emotions in your own mind."

I nodded.

"But there's a physical aspect to touch magic as well," Metis said. "You can get vibes off objects easily enough, but those with touch magic like yours can also influence people. I imagine if you tried hard enough, Gwen, you could push your thoughts and feelings into someone and make her see and feel exactly what you wanted her to. In theory, you could do even more than that. Your psychometry lets you see people's memories, lets you feel what they feel. Who's to say that you couldn't reach even deeper inside them? Perhaps even tap into someone's magic while you were fighting him and turn it against him? There are some very interesting theories about touch magic out there, although few of them have ever been proven, since it's such a rare gift."

Metis's words made me flash back to the Reaper attack. I remembered seeing that spark inside Daphne and trying to reach out and grab it with my own magic. For a few seconds, it had almost felt like that was what I was doing, like I was channeling her healing energy, before the Valkyrie had toppled over from exhaustion. Maybe that was *exactly* what I'd done, since all the cuts and bruises I'd gotten during my fight with the Reaper girl had vanished then. I wondered if that was what Metis was talking about, if tapping into Daphne's or even someone else's power was one of those mysterious *other things* I might be able to do with my Gypsy gift.

Basically, though, the professor had told me the same thing my Grandma Frost had a while back—that my magic would keep getting stronger and keep growing and that I'd be able to do more and more things with it. I wondered how it all worked, though. I'd never tried to take more than memories and feelings from an object, and I'd certainly never tried to exert my will over anyone else.

I opened my mouth to ask her another question, but Metis cut me off.

"Let me get my jacket, and I'll take you down to the prison," she said. "I'm interested to hear what Preston has to say for himself today. And don't worry about Daphne. She'll be okay."

The professor stepped back inside her office. Once again, I thought about Daphne's harsh words and the anger simmering in her eyes. Somehow I doubted the Valkyrie would come around as quickly as Metis thought she would.

* * *

Metis and I left the English-history building and walked across the upper quad to the math-science one. I tucked my chin down into my gray scarf to try and keep warm, but the air seemed to grow colder and colder with every step I took, like there was a storm blowing in.

I followed Metis into the math-science building, and then down, down, down we went, going through a series of doors coded with keypads and magical locks, until it seemed like we were so far underground, we would never see the sun again.

Finally, we came to an enormous door that was made out of the same dark gray stone as the rest of the building. Thick iron bars crisscrossed over the door, and two sphinxes had been carved into the stone facing each other. The creatures looked even fiercer than the ones on the gates outside did, like their sole reason for being was to keep whatever was behind the door from getting out. No matter how many times I came down here, the sight of the glaring sphinxes always made me uneasy. I shivered and looked away.

Metis fished a large skeleton key from her jacket pocket and slid it into the lock. The door opened with a loud *screech,* and we stepped through to the other side.

The prison had a dome-shaped ceiling, just like the Library of Antiquities, and seemed much larger than it should have been, considering how far underground we were. Glass cells made up the circular prison walls, stacking up to form three floors. It always struck me as kind of funny that this was one place at the academy that didn't have any statues of gods, goddesses, or mythological creatures. Instead, a hand holding an enormous set of balanced scales had been carved into the stone ceiling. That didn't make it any less creepy, though.

A desk squatted right inside the door. Usually, Raven sat there, reading one of her celebrity gossip magazines, but today, her chair was empty. Metis saw my questioning look.

"Raven had to go over to the dining hall to get some supplies for her coffee cart," she said. "Besides, it's not like Preston's going anywhere. If the other Reapers had wanted him free, they would have come for him by now."

Her explanation made sense, but it didn't make me feel any better about being here. Nothing ever did. I put my bag down on Raven's desk and turned toward the center of the prison.

Preston Ashton slumped over a stone table in the middle of the domed room, right underneath the hand-and-scales carving. Despite the fact that he was wearing an orange jumpsuit and paper shoes, Preston was a handsome guy with white-blond hair, pale blue eyes, and chiseled features. At least, I'd thought he was gorgeous until, you know, he'd tried to kill me a couple of times. Now, when I looked at Preston, all I saw was the Reaper red spark that burned in the bottom of his eyes.

Preston sat up at the soft whisper of our footsteps on the floor, and his lips curled back into a sneer.

"Why, Gypsy," he said. "You haven't been down here in weeks. I was beginning to think you'd forgotten about me over the holidays."

As if I could ever forget about Preston and the awful thing he'd promised to do to my Grandma Frost if he ever got free. But there was no point in letting the Reaper know just how much he scared me—that would only make him happy.

"Actually, I put you completely out of my mind during the holidays," I said in a cool voice, dropping into the stone chair across from him. "It was rather refreshing not to go digging through your depraved memories for a few weeks."

Preston jerked toward me, but the chains that shackled his arms to the table and his legs to the floor kept him from moving more than an inch.

"Temper, temper," I mocked him.

Preston sat back in his chair and gave me a cold smile, although his cheeks still burned with anger. "We'll see who's laughing soon, Gypsy. We'll see."

I ignored the chill his smirking tone always made me feel, grabbed his hands, and reached for my magic. I spent the next fifteen minutes digging into Preston's mind, sorting through his memories, the things he'd seen and the horrible, terrible, sickening things he'd done as a Reaper. The people he'd killed, everyone he had tortured, everyone he'd ever hurt, I saw it all—and it was all very, very bad.

"Are you getting anything?" Metis asked.

I shook my head. "Nothing. Just the same memories I've seen before. I don't think he knows anything about the attack at the coliseum or where the Helheim Dagger might be hidden."

Preston raised an eyebrow. "Still searching for the

dagger, Gypsy? I would have thought a clever girl like you would have found it by now."

"Shut up, Reaper," I said and reached for his hands again.

Once again, I got nothing. No hint that Preston had known about the attack and no clue that he had any idea where the dagger was. I'd just let go of his hands when Metis's cell phone rang. The professor pulled the phone out of her pocket.

"Hello? Hello?" Metis pulled the phone away from her ear and shook her head. "It cut off. I can never get good reception down here. I'll have to go upstairs to call back."

Metis told me to take a break, since she also needed to update Nickamedes and Coach Ajax about the big, fat lot of nothing I'd found out. The professor excused herself, saying she would be back in a few minutes. She left the prison, leaving me alone with Preston.

Since I didn't want to touch the Reaper without Metis here, I got up and roamed around the prison, looking into all the cells. There wasn't much to see. Some of the cells featured cots, sinks, and metal toilets, while some were just empty rooms. That's where they would keep the creatures, I thought. The Nemean prowlers, the Fenrir wolves, and the Black rocs the Reapers used to do their dirty work for them.

Preston didn't say anything while I walked around, but he kept his hate-filled eyes on me, just watching—which creeped me out more than if he'd been screaming curses at me the whole time.

Finally, I couldn't stand the silence anymore, and I

headed for the door. I'd wait outside until Metis came back and then I'd try looking into Preston's mind again. I opened the door to step out into the hallway—and found the Reaper girl there waiting for me.

"Hello, Gypsy," she said in a nasty tone. "Miss me?"

Before I could move, before I could react, before I could even scream, the Reaper girl stepped forward and punched me in the face. I staggered back and fell to the stone floor, but the Reaper girl didn't stop there. She kicked me in the ribs, and I let out a moan and rolled away from her. Still, despite the pain, I couldn't help wondering how she had gotten down here in the first place past all the doors and locks.

"Forget about her!" Preston screamed from across the room. "Get me out of these chains! Quick! Before Metis comes back!"

The Reaper girl vaulted over me and darted over to the table where Preston was chained. She wore the same black robe and rubber Loki mask that she'd had on during the coliseum attack. I didn't know where she'd gotten it from, but the Reaper girl pulled out a key from the folds of her robe and started fiddling with the lock on Preston's chains. A second later, the lock snapped open— and I knew that I was in big, big trouble.

I scrambled to my feet and lurched over to Raven's desk. The Reaper girl saw what I was doing and raced back over to me just as I drew Vic out of my bag and yanked the sword from his leather scabbard. I always brought Vic with me whenever I came to the prison, since he made me feel a smidge safer. The Reaper girl responded by drawing her own sword from underneath the billowing folds of her black robe.

"Lucretia!" Vic hissed at the sight of the other sword.

Lucretia's burning red eye narrowed with hate. "Vic!" she snarled right back.

That was all they had time to say before the fight started.

Slash-slash-clang!

My sword locked with the Reaper girl's, the blades throwing red and purple sparks everywhere as the two weapons shouted taunts and insults at each other.

"Butter knife!" Lucretia crowed.

"Rusty spoon!" Vic snapped.

I tuned out the swords' chatter and focused on the Reaper girl, trying to anticipate what she would do next, how she would attack me. Behind me, metal clanked and rattled as one by one, Preston opened the locks on his chains—and then he was free.

Out of the corner of my eye, I saw Preston head toward me, his hands curled into fists and a murderous look on his handsome face. His eyes were glowing even brighter now—that bloody, eerie Reaper red.

I lashed out with my sword, making the Reaper girl momentarily retreat, and then turned, so that my back was to one of the glass cells. I wouldn't last a minute if I let the Reaper girl and Preston attack me from two sides at once. Logan had taught me that. My heart squeezed in on itself. *Logan.* I wished he was here right now. The Spartan would know what to do—he'd know exactly how to defeat the Reapers. I'd be lucky if I survived another minute.

Instead of launching himself at me like I expected him to, Preston stopped short and glared at me.

"Go!" the Reaper girl shouted at Preston. "Go! Go! Go!"

Preston gave me a cruel smile, then raced out of the prison. I started after him, but the Reaper girl blocked my path and raised her sword again.

Slash-slash-clang!

Back and forth we dueled for the better part of two minutes before my sneakers skidded on the smooth stone floor. The Reaper girl took advantage of my slip to punch me in the face again. The force of her blow sent me flying back into one of the cells. My head snapped against the glass, and pain exploded in my skull. Dazed, I slumped to the ground, barely managing to hold on to Vic.

"Gwen!" Vic shouted. "Get up, Gwen! Get up before she kills you!"

But I was too dazed to do that—I was too dazed to do anything. The Reaper girl stood there, her sword in her hand. All she had to do was raise it up, bring it down, and I'd be dead.

Simple as that.

She stood there, hesitating, like that's exactly what she wanted to do. But instead of finishing me off, the Reaper girl turned and ran out the open prison door.

Chapter 16

I scrambled to my feet and tightened my grip on Vic. Ignoring the pulsing pain in my head, face, and ribs, I darted out the prison door after the Reapers—but they'd already disappeared.

I hurried to the end of the hall and starting racing up the stairs and through all the open doors. Up, up, up, I went, climbing as fast as I could, but I was already too far behind. I didn't even hear the hollow echo of Preston's and the Reaper girl's footsteps ringing on the stairs above my head.

"Come on, Gwen!" Vic shouted in an encouraging voice. "You can catch them!"

Finally, I climbed the last of the stairs, raced out of the math-science building, and skidded to a stop on the upper quad. My head snapped left, then right, as I stood there panting, but Preston and the Reaper girl were nowhere to be seen. Neither was Metis. Kids milled around on the quad like usual, laughing, talking, and texting as they headed for their after-school activities.

A few kids gave me strange looks, eyeing my flushed

face and the giant gulps of air I was sucking down, but I ignored them. What would Preston and the Reaper girl do now? Where would they go? *Think, Gwen, think!*

Then, the answer came to me.

You'd better finish me now, Gypsy. Or I'll get free one day, and I'll go kill that doddering old grandmother you love so much.

Grandma Frost, I thought, remembering Preston's awful, awful promise to me.

Somehow I knew that's where they were headed. Preston wouldn't miss a chance to hurt me by killing my grandma—he just wouldn't. And Grandma had no idea he was coming or the horrible danger she was in.

Terror twisted my heart at the thought, but I forced myself to push past the fear and think. I didn't know how the Reaper girl had gotten past all the security measures to get down to the prison in the first place, but if she'd been smart enough to do that, then she had to have thought out Preston's escape as well. She'd get him off campus as quickly as she could, and since the Reapers were leaving the academy grounds, I doubted the sphinxes would try to stop them. And then—and then what?

A car, I thought. She'd have a car waiting outside the academy walls to whisk Preston away, but the Reaper wouldn't immediately go into hiding. No, he'd stop by Grandma Frost's house first. I knew he would, which meant that I needed a car, too, if I had any chance of saving her.

I sucked in another cold breath and started to run.

* * *

I pulled my cell phone out of my jeans pocket as I ran. Since I couldn't text, run, and hold on to Vic all at the same time, I settled for hitting the numbers in my speed dial. First, I called my Grandma Frost.

"Pick up," I panted as I ran. "Please, *please* pick up."

But she didn't.

The terror rose up in my throat, choking me, but I forced it down. The Reapers couldn't have gotten to her house yet, so Grandma must be doing a psychic reading for one of her clients. She never answered the phone then. The answering machine clicked on, and I left her a garbled, frantic message telling her about the Reaper girl's freeing Preston and asking her to call me the second she got this message. I would have kept talking, but the machine clicked, cutting me off.

Cursing, I went to the next number on my list, which was Daphne. But apparently, the Valkyrie was still mad at me and screening her calls because she didn't answer. I tried Logan next, but the Spartan didn't answer, either.

Why did everyone have to pick today to be pissed at me?

So I went to the fourth person on my list. For once, *for once,* someone decided to answer his freaking phone.

"Hey, Gypsy," Oliver's smooth voice filled my ear. "What's going on?"

"I need you to get your car and meet me down by the main academy gate. Right now!"

"Gwen?" Oliver's voice sharpened as he heard the panic in my tone. "What's going on?"

"Preston just busted out of the academy prison," I

said in between panting breaths. "I think he's headed to my Grandma Frost's house to kill her. I need you to drive me down there, so meet me at the front gate as soon as you can. And bring some weapons. We'll need them."

"Gwen—"

I hung up before Oliver could say anything else. I knew the Spartan would help me. That's what friends did for each other.

I kept running, trying Grandma Frost, Daphne, and Logan again and again—but nobody answered me. I cursed some more. What good were cell phones if nobody picked them up? Finally, just as I was running on fumes, I reached Styx Hall. It took me far longer than I would have liked to yank my student ID card out of my jeans pocket, scan it through the machine, open the door, and sprint up the three flights of stairs to my room, but there was something else I had to do before I met Oliver, another way I could maybe save my grandma.

"Nott!" I said, barging into my dorm room. "Nott, I need you!"

The Fenrir wolf had been napping in her nest of blankets, but she sprang to her feet at the sound of my frantic voice.

"What are you doing, Gwen?" Vic said. "You're wasting time."

"Shut up, Vic," I said, laying the sword down on the bed and shoving my cell phone into my jeans pocket. "I need to concentrate."

While I'd been sprinting across campus, it had occurred to me that the wolf could run much faster than I could—much, much faster. I was sure that Oliver was racing toward his car right now, but it would still take him time to get it and more time still for us to drive down the mountain.

It was time Grandma Frost just didn't have.

I dropped down beside the wolf, wondering if my crazy plan was going to work. Maybe Vic was right and I was just wasting time. But I had to try—I *had* to.

Metis had told me that I could do more with my Gypsy gift than just touch stuff and see things—that I could make other people see and feel things, too. I just hoped she was right.

Still sucking down big gulps of air, I carefully put my hands on either side of Nott's massive head and looked into her dull eyes—and then I reached for all the memories I had of my Grandma Frost. All the kindness and caring she'd shown me over the years, all the big and small ways she'd cared for me, especially after my mom had been killed, all the love I felt whenever I held her hand.

I concentrated on those memories, pulling them up in my mind, and then I sort of . . . shoved them at Nott. Instead of touching something and letting the images fill my mind, I did the opposite—I took the memories I already had and consciously pushed them out in another direction, into another mind.

Somehow it worked.

The wolf flinched, and I could feel her confusion at the jumble of memories and thoughts that weren't her own crowding into her brain. After a few seconds, she relaxed when she realized I wasn't going to hurt her, that the thoughts weren't going to hurt her. Then, I focused on my grandma's house and pushed that image into the wolf's mind as well.

"I need you to go to my grandma's house and protect her until I get there," I said. "Please. Can you do that? Do you even understand me?"

Nott stared at me a second longer. Then, she leaned forward, licked my cheek with her tongue, and headed for the door.

"I'll take that as a yes," I said, grabbing Vic off the bed and scrambling after her.

I led Nott down the stairs and through the dorm, not caring who saw me or what they thought about it. For once, I got lucky, and we didn't run into any other students. I opened the back door of the dorm, and the wolf raced outside. In a moment, she'd disappeared from view.

I sucked in another breath and started my own sprint, racing down to the main gate. I didn't even spare the sphinxes a glance as I slipped through the iron bars to the other side. Oliver had been quicker than me, because the Spartan was already parked across the street in his black Cadillac Escalade.

I ran over to the SUV, yanked open the door, and threw myself into the passenger's seat.

"Gwen?" Oliver said, putting the car into gear. "Are you sure about this?"

"No," I said. "But I can't take a chance with my grandma's life. Now, drive."

Oliver peeled away from the curb without another word. I laid Vic across my lap, then pulled my phone out of my jeans pocket. Once again, I tried Grandma Frost's number. Once again, she didn't answer. My red-hot panic slowly melted into cold, sinking fear. I had to get to her before Preston and the Reaper girl did. I couldn't lose my grandma like I had my mom. I just *couldn't.*

"I called Logan and Kenzie to come and help," Oliver said, zipping down the mountain as fast as he could. "But they didn't answer me."

My heart sank a little lower in my chest. I bit my lip and nodded, resisting the urge to scream at Oliver to drive faster. Logan and Kenzie didn't matter right now. If we didn't get to the house before Preston and the Reaper girl did, my grandma was as good as dead.

It seemed to take *forever* for Oliver to zoom down the mountain, although he made better time than the bus ever did. He turned onto the street that fronted my grandma's house and parked outside. I was out of the SUV before the wheels stopped rolling. Oliver cut off the engine, opened his own door, and raced after me.

What I saw on the porch made my blood run cold. The PSYCHIC READINGS HERE sign beside the front door barely clung to the side of the house, like someone had taken a crowbar and tried to pry it off. Even worse was the fact that the door had been kicked in, the frame splintered in at least three places.

"Gwen! Stop!" Oliver hissed, grabbing the back of my hoodie before I could sprint into the house. "You don't know who or what is in there."

Even though I wanted nothing more than to race inside, I made myself stop. The Spartan was right. My rushing into the house blind could make a bad situation worse.

So I tightened my grip on Vic and brought the sword up into an attack position. Beside me, Oliver slapped a bolt into the crossbow he'd brought along. The Spartan nodded at me, telling me to take the lead and that he had my back. Together, we stepped into the shadows.

The inside of the house was a disaster. Everything that could be overturned was, from the curio cabinet that displayed Grandma's good china to the blue sofa to the entertainment center that held the TV. Everything was smashed, stomped, and broken, like someone had taken great glee in destroying every single thing he could.

Preston, I thought darkly, and moved on.

Oliver pointed to another splintered door, and I tiptoed over to it and peered inside the room where my grandma gave her psychic readings. The beaded curtains that hung on the windows had been torn down, and the gray silk-covered table had been split into two pieces. My grandma's crystal ball had also been shattered, the splintered shards glistening like teardrops on top of the gauzy cloth.

A cold fist of fear wrapped around my heart and squeezed tight. I turned around and shook my head at Oliver, telling him the room was clear. We tiptoed through the rest of the downstairs, stepping over more smashed furniture, before we finally headed toward the kitchen. My heart pounded at the thought of what we might find in there, and I had such a death grip on Vic that my hands ached.

Something crunched in the kitchen. Oliver and I stopped where we were in the hallway—listening. A series of rustles and scuffles sounded, telling us that someone was moving around in the kitchen. Oliver put a hand on my shoulder, silently asking me if I was okay. I nodded, drew in a breath, and eased forward, peering into the room.

The sight there stunned me.

Grandma Frost stood in the middle of the kitchen, a bloody sword in her hand, Nott sitting off to her right, and a dead Reaper at her feet.

Chapter 17

"Grandma?" I whispered, hurrying forward. "Are you okay?"

Grandma Frost gave me a grim smile. "Well, as much as I can be with a dead Reaper bloodying up my kitchen and an overgrown wolf wanting a treat."

Nott let out a soft whine, apparently agreeing with my grandma. I laid Vic on the kitchen table, then hugged my grandma as hard as I could. Her wrinkled hand smoothed down my hair and brushed across my cheek, and the warmth of her love filled me, driving away the cold, cold fear.

"I'm all right, pumpkin," she whispered. "I'm all right."

Tears of relief slid out of the corners of my eyes. I pulled back and brushed them away.

"What happened?" I asked. "How many Reapers were there? How did you fight them off by yourself?"

"Sit down, and I'll tell you all about it. As for how I fought them off..." Grandma swung her bloody sword in a vicious arc that even Coach Ajax would have been proud of. "You forgot one thing, pumpkin—I used to be Nike's Champion, too."

Then, she grabbed a dishtowel and started wiping the Reaper's blood off the sword as if it was just another stain to be cleaned up.

Fifteen minutes later, Grandma Frost slid a pan of homemade apple cinnamon rolls out of the oven. The warm smells of melted butter, brown sugar, and sweet cinnamon blasted into the kitchen, making it feel as inviting and cozy as ever—except for the dead body on the floor. Oliver had dragged the Reaper's body over to the far corner, and Grandma had put a gray sheet over it, but we all knew it was there.

Apparently, the body didn't bother Oliver, though.

"These are great," he said, taking a big bite of one of the hot, sticky rolls. "You've been holding out on me, Gwen. If I'd known your grandma made desserts like this, I would have come here ages ago."

Grandma Frost leaned over and patted the Spartan's hand. "You are welcome here anytime, Oliver. Just let me know when you're coming, and I'll make something special for you."

She winked at him. The Spartan grinned and took another bite of his roll.

I picked up my own roll but put it back down on my plate. I didn't have the appetite for it right now. "So what happened with the Reaper?"

Grandma stared at me, her violet eyes dark in her face. "I'd had a bad feeling all day that something was wrong, but I couldn't pinpoint exactly what it was. I'd just given my last reading of the afternoon and had walked my client to the front door when I saw a black SUV parked across the street. I looked at it, and I knew there was trouble inside—trouble that was headed my way."

"Then what happened?" Oliver asked, reaching for another cinnamon roll.

"I went to the closet and grabbed my trusty old sword," Grandma said, giving the weapon a fond pat. She'd cleaned the sword and had propped it up in a chair along with Vic, although it was just a regular sword and didn't have a face or talk like he did. "Then I came back here in the kitchen to wait for them. They came in through the front door, tearing up everything they could. I don't think they expected me to fight back, though. The first one there on the floor came in here like it was his kitchen instead of mine. I cut him down pretty quick, but that wasn't the end of them."

"How many more were there?" I asked.

"Two more," she said. "A boy wearing an orange jumpsuit and a girl wearing a black robe and a Reaper mask."

Preston and the Reaper girl. They'd come here just like I'd thought they would.

"I'll admit I'm not as young as I used to be, but I was holding my own," Grandma said. "But then, the Reaper girl tried to use her mind tricks on me."

I frowned. "What mind tricks?"

"She tried to confuse me, make me see things that weren't really there," Grandma Frost said. "She even tried to force her way into my mind and make me freeze up so that I'd stop fighting back. She had a lot of tricks, and she was strong in her magic. As strong as anyone I've ever seen with that kind of mental power."

I frowned. Mental power? The Reaper girl had some kind of mental magic?

"I was weakening, but then your friend there"— Grandma gestured at Nott—"came running into the kitchen. Well, the boy in the orange jumpsuit and the Reaper girl left lickety-split after that. Not even Reapers want to take on a Fenrir wolf."

"Good girl," I murmured, rubbing Nott's ears.

The wolf sighed with pleasure. Sometimes I thought she would have let me pet her forever. No wonder. Preston had never done anything but beat and whip Nott while she'd been in his control. I knew. I'd seen his memories of the wolf and all the horrible things he'd done to her.

"So now what?" Oliver asked. "Because I assume you don't want a dead body sitting in your kitchen for the rest of the day."

Grandma looked over at the Reaper's body. The man's boots just peeked out from under the edge of the white sheet. "Now, we call Aurora," she said. "And tell her what happened."

Grandma called the academy, and Metis, Nickamedes, and Coach Ajax arrived about thirty minutes later, along with several men and woman wearing black coveralls. I half expected Raven to show up as well, but she didn't appear. Maybe if she'd been in the prison like usual, then Preston wouldn't have escaped and come after my grandma. Maybe if Metis had stayed there with me, we would have been able to capture the Reaper girl, too. I didn't know who I was angrier at right now—Preston and the Reaper girl for escaping, or Raven and Metis for not being around when I needed them.

Right before they arrived, I took Nott outside and put her in the garage behind the house. I didn't know how Metis and the others would react to seeing the Fenrir wolf, and I didn't want them to hurt her or try to take her away. Grandma agreed with me since Nott had helped save her life, too. She gave me some blankets and a bucket of water, all of which Oliver carried to the garage for me. The Spartan went back inside the house while I put the soft fleece down on the concrete floor, trying to make Nott as comfortable as possible.

When I finished, the wolf plopped down on the blankets and let out a long sigh. Her ears drooped, and her rust-colored eyes were dimmer than usual. She seemed tired. I ran my fingers over her body and reached out with my psychometry, wondering if she had an injury we'd overlooked, but the wolf was fine. I could feel that running down the mountain had worn her out, but for the first time, I got the sense that something else was wrong with her—something more than just being exhausted. It almost seemed like something was eating away at the wolf from the inside, sapping all her strength. I reached out with my Gypsy gift again, but I just couldn't figure out what it was.

So I spent a few minutes petting Nott, then slipped back inside.

While the people in the coveralls cleaned up the mess in the front of the house, the rest of us gathered in the kitchen. Metis used her magic to heal the injuries Grandma Frost and I had gotten fighting the Reapers. When the professor finished with us, Ajax drew back the sheet, revealing the dead guy's face. I didn't recognize him, and to my surprise, he hadn't been wearing a Reaper mask. Probably because Preston and the Reaper girl had thought my grandma wouldn't be around to tell anyone what the guy looked like. The thought made my heart clench with fear.

I stared down at the dead guy. After a moment, I frowned. Something was nagging at me. Something about the Reaper girl and her mask, something she'd said or done in the memory I'd seen of her looking at the map of the Library of Antiquities. I used my psychometry to reach for the memory. The Reaper girl staring at the map, talking to the man beside her about the Helheim Dagger, all the creepy paintings and carvings of Black rocs in the room with them. I played the images over and over again in my head, but I couldn't quite figure out what was wrong with them.

"Gwen?" Metis asked. "Do you think you could see what you can get from the dead man? It might be useful. He might know where Preston was heading or who the Reaper girl really is."

Surprised, I looked at her. "You want me to touch the dead guy? Why? You didn't ask me to touch any of the dead Reapers at the coliseum."

Metis glanced at Ajax and Nickamedes. "We thought about asking you to do it then too, but we didn't want to put you through that when you'd just seen your class-mates die. But now . . ."

"Now we don't have a choice. Not if we want to find Preston and the Reaper girl before they hurt anyone else," I said in a bitter tone.

Metis nodded. "When I left the prison to return the call I got, nobody picked up. I think the Reaper girl was the one who phoned to lure me away from the prison so she could free Preston. We need to know what they're planning and where they may be going next, and you're our best hope of getting that information at this moment."

I knew her request was perfectly reasonable, but that still didn't make it any easier. If there was even the smallest chance of catching Preston and the Reaper girl, then I had to use my magic to try and find out what I could, even if it meant touching a dead man. I wanted the two of them captured and locked away—for good this time. So I drew in a breath, leaned down, and took the dead man's hand in mine.

The images and feelings flooded my mind, the way they always did.

I'd never touched a dead person before, but I got the sense that all the memories and feelings associated with this man were quickly fading away, right along with the warmth of his body. Try as I might, I could only see and feel what the Reaper had experienced during his last few minutes. The rest of him was already gone. So I focused on the last memory I could see—the three Reapers sitting in a car.

"Are you sure about this?" the dead man asked, staring across the street at my grandma's house. "I mean, this broad might be old, but she used to be a Champion. *Nike's* Champion. You know how much trouble they've given us over the years."

"Relax, Stuart," Preston sneered in a confident voice. "There's no way one old lady will be able to take out three Reapers, especially since we've got the element of surprise on our side."

Preston turned around to look at the Reaper girl sitting in the backseat. I couldn't see her face because of the mask she wore, but a spark of red flashed in her eyes through the slits in the rubber.

"You've been awfully quiet back there," Preston said. "What are you? Scared?"

The Reaper girl tapped her finger on her lips. Well, okay, they weren't really *her* lips, but Loki's melted ones. The motion caused something gold to glint around her finger, something that had a familiar shape—

"No, I'm not scared," she said in a low, throaty voice. "But perhaps it would do you good to be a little more careful, Preston. After all, you're the one who's spent the last few weeks locked up because of Nike's Champion."

"That Gypsy bitch," Preston snarled. "You should have let me kill her in the prison."

The Reaper girl shook her head. "We stick to the plan, remember? We're only here because you're so determined to kill the grandmother, and it doesn't interfere with anything else. If you knew what was smart, you'd go straight to the safe house like I told you to."

The girl's tone was casual, but there was no mistaking

the authority and power in her voice or the fact that she was the one in charge. Preston shrank back a little in his seat.

"No," he said. "Not until I keep my promise to Gwen. That Gypsy has spent the last few weeks digging through my brain. I'm going to hurt her where she'll feel it the most. So let's go."

Preston opened the car door and headed toward the house. The others followed him. After that, the dead man's memories grew more and more disjointed. There was a blur of movement, the shatter of breaking glass, and then finally, a bright, agonizing flash of pain as Grandma Frost stabbed the Reaper with her sword. After that, the world slowly faded to black until there was nothing else to see or feel—and no more secrets left to discover.

I let out a breath and opened my eyes. The others stared at me, their faces tight with concern and questions. I let Grandma Frost help me up and then I fell into a chair and slumped over the kitchen table.

"Did you get anything?" Ajax asked in his deep, rumbly voice.

I shook my head. "Not much. I only got a few snatches of conversation, mostly Preston and the Reaper girl sniping at each other, although she did mention something about a safe house. Do you think they're still in the area?"

Nickamedes nodded his head. "It's likely. It's only been a few hours, so the Reapers probably haven't had a chance to smuggle Preston out of the country yet so he can be reunited with his parents, wherever they're hiding."

Metis, Nickamedes, and Ajax started talking, with Oliver and Grandma Frost chiming in, about where the Reapers might be hiding Preston and what their next move would be to get him to safety.

Maybe it was wrong, but I felt like everything that had happened so far had gone exactly the way the Reapers had wanted it to. Sure, the Reaper girl had dropped the map at the museum, so we knew the Helheim Dagger was hidden in the library, but other than that, we had nothing. Several kids had been killed at the coliseum, I hadn't found the dagger, and now Preston had escaped and was free to terrorize people once more. I'd say it was Reapers 100, Gwen 0.

And it didn't look like the score was going to change anytime soon.

Chapter 18

By the time we straightened up Grandma Frost's house and put everything back in some semblance of order, it was after dark. Metis tried to get me to go back to the academy, but I refused, wanting to stay with my grandma for the night. Grandma said that she didn't see Preston and the Reaper girl coming back, according to her psychic visions, but I couldn't shake the feeling they might try to hurt her again, so I stayed, along with Nott, who was still hidden in the garage. Metis also said that she'd post a few guards—the men and women in the coveralls—outside on the street to keep an eye on things.

Several hours later, Grandma came up to my room to tuck me in for the night. I lay on the bed, staring at the ceiling and brooding.

"Uh-oh," Grandma said, sitting on the edge of the bed. "I know that look. What's wrong, pumpkin?"

I sighed. "There was something else, something else I saw when I touched the dead man earlier today, something I didn't tell the others."

Grandma nodded. "I thought as much, given how

quiet you were after that. What did you see, Gwen? You can tell me. You can tell me anything."

I rolled over onto my side to look at her. "When I was fighting the Reaper girl in the academy prison, she had a chance to kill me—but she didn't. In the memory I saw of her, she told Preston that she didn't kill me because the Reapers have some sort of plan. What do you think it could be? Do you—do you think it involves me somehow? Because I would never help them. *Never.* But what she said scares me just the same."

Grandma Frost reached down and threaded her fingers through mine, but for once, the warmth of her touch didn't soothe me. "I know you would never willingly help the Reapers, pumpkin," she said. "There's no telling what that girl meant. She could have just been showing off for Preston."

"But I feel like it's important," I insisted. "Like I'm missing something obvious about everything that's going on. It's like I have all the pieces of the puzzle, but they just won't fit together, no matter how hard I try to make them."

"I know, pumpkin. Sometimes I feel that way about my visions, especially when I only see a part of someone's future. You'll figure it out," Grandma said. "The answer will come to you in time. I have faith in you, and your mom and Nike do, too. Never forget that."

She kissed my cheek, and the familiar softness of her love washed over me again. "Now, try to get some sleep," Grandma said and left the room.

Even though I didn't really think I could sleep, I did as she asked and snuggled deeper under the covers. I supposed I was just as exhausted as Nott because I was asleep in minutes.

A jumble of images filled my mind, everything and everyone I'd seen over the last few days. Sometimes my mind went all wonky like that, as my brain struggled to process all the information my Gypsy gift downloaded on a daily basis.

The attack at the coliseum. The Reaper girl and the flash of red in her eyes. The feel of Vic in my hands and the sound of the sword snarling as I used him to battle the Reapers. The cruel whispers in the library and the horrible, aching sensation of fingers digging into my mind. All the images of Black rocs I'd seen in the Reaper girl's living room suddenly transforming into the real creatures, taking flight, and throwing themselves at me, pecking at me with their sharp beaks, suffocating me with their thick, black wings.

Then, finally, I saw the gryphons, the ones guarding the entrance to the library. They stared straight at me like usual, but instead of being stone, their eyes were red—Reaper red. I watched, horrified, as the statues began to move. One of them, the right one, hopped down from its perch and began to slowly stalk toward me—

I woke up in a cold sweat, thrashing at the covers that had twisted around my body like a snake curling around its victim. After a few seconds, I realized I was awake and that the gryphons, the rocs, and all the rest of it had just been a dream. *Just a bloody dream*, as Vic would say. I looked over at the nightstand where I'd propped up the sword. Vic's eye was closed, and his mouth was loose and slack. A series of soft mumbles sounded, telling me he was asleep.

"Bloody Reapers," the sword muttered. "Kill them all. . . ."

Every once in a while, Vic's eye would twitch, like he was chasing after the Reapers that haunted his dreams. For once, the sword's bloodthirsty attitude made me smile. It was nice to know I could always count on Vic's being, well, Vic. Even when he was asleep.

Since I couldn't go back to sleep, I got up and dug my mom's diary out of my messenger bag. I'd left the bag in the academy prison when I'd chased after Preston and the Reaper girl, but Metis had brought it to me. I snapped on a light and flipped through the crinkled pages, but even my mom's words couldn't bring me any comfort tonight.

I put the diary aside, but there was another book in my bag—the gryphon book I'd picked up last night in the library. *The Use of Gryphons, Gargoyles, and Other Mythological Creatures in Architecture*. Still remembering my strange dream of the statues stalking me, I opened the book, settled down under my comforter, and started reading.

For the most part, the book was super, super *boring*. If you were into architecture or old buildings, yeah, it might be cool, but to me, it was a total snooze. After a few eye-glazing pages, I gave up reading and just flipped through and looked at the photos, which were way more interesting. Basically, the book featured pictures of the creature-feature statues on famous buildings in the mythological world. I didn't recognize most of the structures, but the Crius Coliseum was included—and so was the Library of Antiquities. Lots of photos of the library's statues were shown. Of those, the two gryphons by the front steps got the most space, having their own two-page spread in the book.

Height, weight, type of stone used. All that and more about the gryphons was chronicled in dull little info boxes. The statues were estimated to be seven feet tall and weigh in at a whopping three tons each. Only seven feet tall? Really? The statues always seemed so much bigger to me. Even in the photos, they looked larger than that, but I couldn't decide if it was just a trick of the light playing across the pages.

I sighed. I didn't know why I was wasting my time looking at the gryphons. They were just statues after all. The Helheim Dagger was what I was really after, even though I was no closer to finding it than when I'd first started. Not to mention the fact that the Reaper girl had beaten me twice this week, Preston was free, and Logan and Daphne weren't speaking to me.

Right now, I didn't feel like Nike's Champion. I didn't feel brave or strong or smart. I didn't feel like I'd done a single thing that had been worthwhile. I was just Gwen Frost, that Gypsy girl who always messed up.

Disgusted with myself, I put the book aside, snapped out the light, and brooded in the darkness.

Grandma Frost drove me back to the academy the next morning. Nott took up most of the backseat, her enormous gray head stuck out the window like she was just a regular dog out for a ride in the car. The wolf made me smile when absolutely nothing else had these past few days.

Before we'd left the house, I'd asked Grandma if she wanted me to leave Nott with her, to help protect her in case the Reaper girl or Preston came back to the house. Grandma Frost had stared at the Fenrir wolf, and she'd gotten that empty, glassy look in her violet eyes again.

"No," she'd murmured. "I think the wolf should go back to the academy with you, pumpkin. Nott came to you, not me. She belongs with you."

I said good-bye to Grandma Frost and snuck Nott back to my dorm room. Then, it was time for me to head to the gym for weapons training. Kenzie and Oliver were already there waiting for me—and so was Daphne.

The Valkyrie was sitting on the bleachers talking to the two Spartans, but she got to her feet as soon as she saw me. She was wearing one of her favorite pink argyle sweaters over a black skirt and black tights. She stalked over and stared at me a second, before lurching forward and giving me a bone-crushing hug.

"Daphne...," I wheezed, my back cracking. "I... can't...breathe...."

"Oops. Sorry about that. How are you?" she asked, pulling back and giving me a critical once-over. "Oliver called me last night and told me what happened. I was going to call you, but I didn't know if you'd pick up or not because of what happened outside Metis's office yesterday."

I shrugged. "I'm okay, I guess. Metis healed the bumps and bruises I got fighting. My grandma's fine too—that's the most important thing. I still can't believe the Reaper girl managed to free Preston from the academy prison."

Daphne's eyes narrowed. "Do you have any idea how she did it?"

I shook my head. "Not a clue. But I opened the door, and there she was, larger than life, like she'd had every single one of the door codes and magic mumbo-jumbo passwords she needed to get past the locks. Even Metis isn't really sure how she managed it. And of course I was stupid enough to open the door to the prison for her. Apparently, that's why the sphinxes carved into the door didn't attack or do whatever they were supposed to do. That's what Metis said, anyway."

At my grandma's house, Metis had taken me aside and said that Preston's getting free wasn't my fault, that she should have stayed in the prison with me, especially since Raven hadn't been there. I'd realized that I wasn't really angry at the professor for leaving me alone. No, I was mostly upset at myself for not being strong and smart enough to stop Preston and the Reaper girl. Some Champion I was turning out to be.

"Tell me everything," the Valkyrie said, walking me over to one of the bleachers.

We sat there, and I told my best friend about Preston's getting free, his attacking my grandma, and how I'd raced to save her. I also told her all about Nott, since I hadn't mentioned the wolf and her reappearance to the Valkyrie yet.

"I, uh, got your calls," Daphne said, cringing a little.

"I thought you were just calling to talk. Or maybe to yell at me for all the things I accused you of. If I'd known your grandma was in trouble, I would have picked up."

"I know," I said. "How are you? How do you feel about your magic? You could have told me, you know, that you were freaking out about being a healer. I would have listened."

"I know you would have listened," Daphne said in a low voice. "I just—I wanted someone to blame, you know? I wanted it to be someone's fault that my magic didn't turn out like I thought it would. That it's this instead."

The Valkyrie held up her hand and that rosy glow coated her palm again. I leaned over and touched my fingers to hers. Once again, I felt the healing power emanating from her.

I thought about what Metis had said about my own magic, about how I could maybe use my psychometry to tap into other people's powers. I don't know exactly how, but I reached out and gave a little yank with my mind, and I felt the tiniest bit of Daphne's magic pour into me.

It wasn't just that the Valkyrie's magic healed a person's body. There was also a soothing quality to it, which reminded me of the feeling I got whenever I was around Metis. Vic always claimed the professor's lectures put him to sleep, but to me, they were just calming. Even when Metis was talking about Reapers, Loki, and other horrible things, they seemed distant and far away. I got the same sort of soothing feeling from Daphne's magic. It was kind of funny, since the Valkyrie could be so quick to anger—

"Gwen?" Daphne asked, the glow on her palm dimming. "What are you doing?"

I dropped my fingers from hers, and the feel of her magic vanished. "Nothing. Just—nothing."

I didn't feel like explaining things to her, not when I was still trying to figure them out for myself. The Valkyrie closed her hand into a tight fist, and the rosy glow disappeared in a shower of pink sparks. The tiny flickers of magic cracked and hissed before slowly winking out one by one.

"I don't like it, but I guess I'm stuck with it," Daphne said, shaking her head. "Me, a healer? Can you imagine it?"

I could, maybe more than my friend realized. There was so much strength in her, so much goodness. Now, she had a way to share her power with others. "I think your magic is amazing, and I'm sure you're going to do amazing things with it."

Daphne stared at me, her lips splitting into a wide grin. We didn't say anything for a few moments. Finally, the Valkyrie cleared her throat.

"Anyway, I'm sorry that I've been such a total bitch this week," she said. "It was just Carson's getting stabbed and my magic's quickening and everything. It made me a little cranky."

I'd say *cranky* was an understatement, but I let it slide. I'd been so wrapped up in my own problems that I hadn't exactly been the greatest friend, either. "That's okay. That's what best friends are for, right? So we can be cranky together."

Daphne gave me another grin, then playfully punched me in the shoulder, her Valkyrie strength almost making me fall off the bleacher. We both started laughing, and just like that, everything was right between us again.

We were still talking and joking around when the door to the gym opened—and Logan stepped inside.

Chapter 19

Logan strode toward me, and my heart rose up in my chest. By now, the Spartan was sure to have heard what had happened with my grandma, Preston, and the Reaper girl. I hoped he, well, I didn't know exactly what I hoped. I was just glad he was here.

I got to my feet and started to smile at the Spartan—until I realized that he was trailed once more by his first-year student entourage. The kids, including several more girls than before, hurried after the Spartan, like groupie fans trailing after a rock star. I rolled my eyes.

Logan said something to one of the first-year guys, who herded everyone else over to the bleachers so they could watch us practice. Only I didn't know if we were even training today. I hung back, holding Vic, and waited for Logan to make the first move.

"Hey," the Spartan called out, going over and grabbing a sword from one of the racks of weapons.

"Hey," I said, playing it cool.

On the bleachers behind me, Daphne let out a loud

snort. "Oh, just go ahead and kiss and make up already," the Valkyrie said. "You know you both want to."

I would have liked nothing better. But we couldn't kiss—not without my flashing on Logan and learning the rest of his secret. Finding out what he was so afraid to tell me, the deep, dark thing he thought would change my feelings for him. I could see the same thought filling the Spartan's eyes. That, yeah, maybe he would have liked to kiss me, but he didn't want to give up his secret just to touch me. It hurt, knowing his secret was more important to him than I was. It hurt more than I ever could have imagined it would.

Tears pricked my eyes, but I blinked them back. Once again, my Gypsy gift was what was keeping us apart. I'd always loved my magic and the secrets it revealed to me, but for the first time, I wondered what it would be like not to have it. To be able to just let go and not worry about whom I was touching and what I might see. To just step into Logan's arms without any kind of fear of learning that he didn't care about me as much as I did him or the secrets he just didn't want to share.

The Spartan swung his sword from side to side, getting a feel for the weapon as he walked over to my position in the center of one of the mats. Logan stopped in front of me. Even now, when I knew how angry he was at me, my heart thudded at the sight of him. Black hair, blue eyes, strong body. All that was missing was his usual teasing grin.

I smiled at him, hoping he'd smile back and I'd know that everything was going to be all right between us. Instead, Logan's eyes were ice-cold as he raised his sword and lightly kissed the blade against my weapon.

"Ready, Gypsy girl?" he asked in a neutral voice.

My heart quivered with pain, but I nodded and tightened my grip on Vic.

For the next hour, we sparred, with Logan mock killing me again and again. Too bad the deadly Spartan couldn't put a dagger in my feelings for him as well.

Logan left the gym as soon as we finished training, followed by his entourage. I stood in front of the bleachers and watched him push through one of the doors. The Spartan didn't look back at me—not even once.

"Don't worry, Gwen," Oliver said as he packed up his things. "He'll come around. You'll see."

I thought of the coldness in Logan's eyes this morning and the things he'd said to me the other night. I didn't think there was anything I could do or say to Logan to make him forgive me. Not this time.

"Gwen?" Oliver said.

"Yeah, I'm sure you're right. Logan will come around sooner or later." I forced myself to smile at my friend, even though the lie burned my tongue like acid.

The rest of the day passed by like it always did. Classes, lectures, homework assignments, the usual froufrou food in the dining hall. Finally, the last bell rang after myth-history class. Metis glanced in my direction like she wanted to come over and make sure I was doing okay, but I didn't have time for the professor today. I

had a hunch that I wanted to check out—and unfortu-
nately, Daphne insisted on going with me.

I brushed my brown hair back off my face and jiggled
my hand, shaking off a stray spark of her magic that
had decided to cling to my skin instead of winking out.
A second later, that princess pink spark was replaced by
a dozen more. Daphne always gave off more magic
when she was nervous, worried, or upset.

You'd think she'd never broken into someone's room
before.

And she thought I was a freak. Please. I could totally
keep my cool when the occasion called for a little breaking and entering. And blackmail. And, well, several
things that weren't exactly on the up and up. My Gypsy
gift and all the Bad, Bad Things I'd seen with it had
made me a little jaded that way. Okay, okay, *totally*
jaded that way.

"Will you hurry up with that already?" Daphne
hissed. "She could come back any second. I don't see
why we're even doing this in the first place."

I slid my driver's license in between the doorframe
and the lock that was keeping me out of Savannah Warren's room. "Well, it would go a lot faster if you'd keep
quiet and quit asking me to hurry up. I can only concentrate on one thing at a time."

"And here I thought you were such a brilliant multi-
tasker," Daphne muttered, glancing down the empty
hall toward the stairs like she had ten times in the last
minute.

I rolled my eyes and started to snap back at her, when

my license slid exactly where I wanted it to go, and the door clicked open.

"Bingo," I whispered, turned the knob, and stepped inside.

Daphne hovered in the doorway, an uncertain look on her face. I rolled my eyes again.

"Well, don't just stand there," I said, grabbing her arm and dragging her inside. "The key to breaking and entering is to actually *enter* after you break. Not stand around in the hall where everyone can see exactly what you're doing."

"Sorry," Daphne muttered. "I haven't had quite the experience at this as you have, Gwen."

Yeah, we were totally sniping at each other, but I didn't mind because this was as close to normal as we'd been since the Reaper attack.

"Tell me again why we're in here?" Daphne asked, tiptoeing forward to stand beside the bookcase that hugged the wall inside the door.

"Because Vivian hired me to find her ring, and the last time she remembers seeing it is when she was with Savannah."

Yeah, yeah, I knew there were more important things I could be doing, like seeing if Metis and the others had figured out where Preston and the Reaper girl were hiding. But I'd taken Vivian's money to find her ring, and I owed it to her to try to do that, especially since it meant so much to her, since it had been her mom's ring, too. I knew what it was like to lose your mom, how you wanted to hold on to every piece of her you had left.

Besides, I wanted to do *something* right this week.

Maybe finding Vivian's ring would be it. At the very least, maybe it would take my mind off all my other problems—for a little while anyway.

"So what?" Daphne said. "Savannah probably just borrowed it without telling her. Friends do that all the time."

I raised an eyebrow. "Really? So if I was to borrow, oh, I don't know, your favorite purse without telling you, then you'd be perfectly okay with that?"

Her eyes narrowed. "I'd be okay with it, but you might not be if you wanted to live long enough to finish the semester."

"That's what I thought," I said, going over to the vanity table. "Now help me look for Vivian's ring."

"Fine," Daphne huffed, stepping forward. "But I'm doing this under protest."

"So noted. Now shut up and start looking."

We spent the next ten minutes tossing Savannah's room. Okay, okay, so maybe *tossing* wasn't the right word, but we did look in every cubbyhole, crack, and crevice that we could find, along with all the usual hiding spots kids thought were so clever, the places where no one would *ever* think to look for their supersecret stash of candy bars, beer, cigarettes, or whatever their vice of choice was. Under the mattress. Taped to the bottom of a drawer. Tucked in a plastic bag and stuffed into the back of the toilet. I knew all the good hiding places, and my mom had told me about even more she'd discovered as a police detective.

"Nothing," Daphne said when we finished. "See? I told you Savannah didn't have the ring. Now, can we please get out of here before she comes back? Savannah's supposed to meet Talia and Vivian in her room this afternoon. That's what I heard her say when I was standing in line behind her in the dining hall."

Daphne's telling me what she'd overheard at lunch was the reason I'd decided to break in here, since it was kind of hard to look for lost or stolen property when the thief was still in her room.

Frustrated, I put my hands on my hips and looked at the room again. For some reason, I felt like Vivian's ring was in here somewhere, like I could almost feel it calling out to me. I wasn't ready to give up, so I went through the room again, more slowly and methodically this time, despite the fact that Daphne threw off more and more sparks of magic the longer we stayed.

The Valkyrie was just about to forcibly drag me out into the hallway when I grabbed a book and accidently banged it into the side of the bookcase—and the ring slipped out from the case and fell to the floor.

I leaned forward, staring at the inside of the book-case. I'd pulled out all the books and had looked through and behind them, but the ring had been wedged into a hollow space where one of the wooden shelves didn't quite meet the side of the case. Not too shabby, as far as hiding places went. Definitely a little more creative than the back of the toilet.

Daphne bent over, picked up the ring, and turned it around and around in the palm of her hand.

"This? You really think Savannah stole *this*? It's just gold. There aren't even any diamonds on it. No rubies, no sapphires, nothing. It doesn't even look like it's worth more than a couple hundred bucks. And those two faces are really ugly." Her critique finished, the Valkyrie sniffed and handed it over to me.

Images filled my mind as soon as I touched the ring.

I'd expected to get a few vibes off the ring, especially since Vivian had told me how special it was to her and how it had been her mom's ring. And I did see those memories. A younger Vivian standing by a bed. An older woman reaching up, her bloody hand shaking as she handed over the ring. Vivian crying and slipping the gold band onto her finger. I could feel Vivian's emotions, too. Her sadness that her mom was dying, her anger at the people who'd killed her. They made my own heart ache for the other girl. I knew how hard it was to lose your mom—especially to the Reapers.

I also saw other flashes, images of Vivian wearing the ring and growing up over the years. But then, the images changed and shifted. For a second, I felt like something was wrong. Like there was some feeling, some emotion attached to the ring I couldn't quite grasp, that my Gypsy gift couldn't quite show me, for whatever reason. It was the same vague, uneasy feeling I'd had when I'd touched the map the Reaper girl had dropped in the coliseum.

Then, a new image filled my mind—one of Savannah putting on the ring.

The pretty Amazon sat at the vanity table in her room, staring down at her hand and admiring the Janus ring and the way the gold glinted. I felt Savannah's smug satisfaction that the ring was hers now, that she'd taken what she wanted and that no one was the wiser.

Greed. The feeling made me sick to my stomach. So Vivian was right, and Savannah had stolen her ring after all. Some best friend she was.

I'd thought that would be the end of the memories, but the image didn't fade away. Instead, it sharpened, hammering into my head, and Savannah reached over and picked up something on top of the vanity table—a Reaper mask.

Horrified, I watched as Savannah put on the mask, then grabbed a black robe from the floor and draped it over her shoulders. She looked at her reflection in the mirror and smiled, a bit of Reaper red fire flashing in her eyes.

I recognized her then. How could I not?

I was so shocked that the rest of the vision slipped away, splintering into shards that felt like they were stabbing deeper and deeper into my brain. I gasped in pain and opened my eyes. The ring slipped from my trembling fingers and hit the floor again.

"What? What is it?" Daphne said. "Why do you have that weird, sick look on your face?"

"Because Savannah didn't just steal Vivian's ring," I said in a whisper, staring at my best friend. "She's a Reaper, too. And not just any Reaper. She's the Reaper girl, Daphne. Loki's Champion. The one who murdered my mom."

Chapter 20

"Savannah Warren? A Reaper?" Daphne shook her head, making her blond ponytail swish from side to side. "No, I don't believe it. No way."

"But she has the ring," I said.

I looked down at the ring lying on the floor. The sunlight streaming in through the window made the gold gleam, causing another thought to pop into my head. I remembered somewhere else I'd seen a flash of gold recently. I reached for the memory of the Reaper girl sitting in the car outside my Grandma Frost's house and focused in on it, playing the images again in my head. I hadn't paid much attention to it before, but there it was on her right hand, winking at me like an evil eye when she tapped her fingers against her lips.

I stabbed my finger at the ring. "I saw the Reaper girl wearing that in my vision of her attacking my Grandma Frost's house. It's the same ring Vivian says she thinks Savannah stole from her room."

Daphne shook her head again, pink sparks flying off

her fingertips. "No, Gwen. You don't understand. There's no way Savannah could be a Reaper."

"Why not?"

Daphne stared at me. "Because Reapers killed her entire family."

"What?"

The Valkyrie sighed. "You know that practically everyone at Mythos has lost somebody to the Reapers, right? Their parents, an aunt, an uncle, a friend, somebody."

I nodded.

"Well, a little over a year ago, just after we started as first-year students, Savannah's family was murdered by Reapers. Her parents, her kid sister, even some cousins. The Reapers broke into her parents' summer house in London and slaughtered them all. Even for the Reapers, it was *vicious*. The only reason Savannah wasn't killed too because she was here. She pulled out of school after that and went to stay with her aunt. She didn't come back until after the holidays last year. So I'm telling you there is *no way* Savannah is a Reaper. It's just not possible."

Daphne looked at the ring on the floor. The Valkyrie might not have my psychometry magic, but she didn't want to pick it up any more than I did. Not if it belonged to a Reaper. "What about Vivian?"

"What about Vivian?"

Daphne gestured at the ring. "It's her ring, right? So maybe the images you saw were her. Maybe your magic got mixed up or something, and she's really the Reaper."

I eyed her. "You really think someone like Vivian Holler could be a Reaper? You saw how scared she was at the coliseum after the attack, and you told me yourself that she sucks with weapons. The Reaper girl, whoever she really is, definitely does not suck with weapons. I had the cuts and bruises to prove it. She's beaten me twice now. Do you think Vivian could do something like that?"

Daphne shrugged. "But it's her ring, so the memories attached to it should all be hers, right?"

"I don't know," I said. "I saw some images of Vivian's mom giving her the ring and Vivian wearing it. But then, the images changed, and it was Savannah wearing the ring, and Savannah putting on a Reaper mask. Not Vivian."

"You didn't see anyone else wearing it?"

I shook my head.

"So it's got to be one of them, right? Maybe the memories are messed up because they've both worn the ring."

I stared down at the gold band. "I don't know. I just don't know. If Vivian's the Reaper, then why would she hire me to find her missing ring? Supposedly, the Reapers know all about my psychometry magic. She'd have to realize that I'd flash on her being a Reaper as soon as I touched it."

"Who knows why Reapers do what they do?" Daphne said, finally bending down and picking up the ring. "They're all about head games. Anyway, we're not going to figure it out standing around here. Let's go before Savannah comes back. I don't think she's a Reaper, but I don't want to take a chance I'm wrong about it, either."

We left Savannah's room, walked down the hall, and went into Daphne's room. I grabbed my messenger bag and pulled out a plastic bag. Using the edge of my hoodie sleeve, I took the ring from Daphne, careful not to touch it with my bare fingers, and slid it inside the plastic. The gold masks gleamed at me, looking bright and sinister at the same time.

"So what are you going to do with it?" Daphne asked.

I shrugged. "I guess I'll give it back to Vivian. What else can I do? It's her ring. Besides, I don't want to tell Metis that I think either Savannah or Vivian is really the Reaper girl and Loki's Champion in disguise. At least, not without proof."

"Well, how do you think we could get some proof?" Daphne asked.

I thought about it. "I'd have to touch them. Savannah and Vivian. Objects can get so many images and feelings attached to them that it can sometimes fuzz up everything else, just like you said. But I don't think there's any way a Reaper could hide what she really was if I touched her. At least, not that I know of. I think it's worth a shot, anyway. Then, I can tell Metis which one of them it is."

"All right, so who do you want to start with?" Daphne asked.

"Vivian," I said. "That'll be easier. I have a reason to

see her now that I found her ring. Getting close enough to touch Savannah will be trickier, seeing as how she hates me so much."

Daphne and I made plans to meet up later at the library, and she promised to bring Carson along for backup. I also texted Vivian to meet me at the library so I could give her the ring. Then, I went to my dorm room, grabbed Vic from his spot on the wall, and told him what was going on.

"Well, it's about bloody time you discovered the Reaper girl's real identity," the sword said. "I'm looking forward to sinking my teeth into Lucretia again."

Vic made a chomping sound with his mouth. I frowned and held him out at arm's length. Did the sword even have teeth? I'd never thought to look, and I wasn't so sure I wanted to now.

While Vic crowed on and on and *on* about how he was going to cut Lucretia to ribbons, I sank down onto the floor and started petting Nott. Maybe it was just my Gypsy gift, but the wolf looked like she'd doubled in size since I'd seen her this morning. Her eyes were duller, too, as though she was still tired, even though she'd been in my room all day resting. What was wrong with her? Why was she always so exhausted?

"How are you feeling, girl?" I murmured.

Nott thumped her tail and leaned into my touch. I closed my eyes and concentrated. Once again, I could feel that spark of life in her stomach, the pup waiting to be born, although I had no idea when that might happen or what to do to help her. With everything that had been going on, I'd kind of forgotten Nott was a mom-to-be. I'd have to call Grandma later and get some advice on how to make the wolf more comfortable. Grandma had been raised on a farm. She'd know what to do. She always did.

I made sure Nott had enough water and gave her all the meat I'd been able to get from the dining hall at lunch today. After she ate, the wolf curled up in her nest of blankets and went to sleep. I petted her a final time before grabbing Vic. I left the door open a crack so Nott could get out and have more room to roam around if she wanted to, then walked across campus to the library.

Once more, I stopped outside the building, staring at the gryphons that crouched on either side of the entrance. It seemed like I was seeing the gryphons everywhere I went these days. First, in my mom's diary, then in the architecture book I'd found, and now here again in real life. If only the Helheim Dagger was as easy to find.

As I stared at the gryphons, I wondered what I always did—what would happen if I actually touched one of the statues, if my psychometry would somehow make it actually spring to life and attack me the way I'd seen it do in my dream last night.

I looked around at the other kids moving in and out of the library, laughing, talking, and leaning against the other statues like it was no big deal. The other students sat next to and even on the gryphons and other stone creatures on campus all the time. Surely, they wouldn't bite me . . . or whatever.

Suck it up, Gwen. That's what Daphne would tell me

if she was here, and my friend was right. I'd been creeped out by the gryphons and other statues ever since I'd first started going to Mythos. Enough was enough. It was time for me to realize the statues were just made of stone—nothing else. Determined to put my weird phobia to rest once and for all, I reached out with my fingers to touch one of the gryphons—

"Late again, I see," a snide voice murmured behind me. "Usually, you actually make it *inside* the library before you start wasting time."

I sighed and dropped my hand. "Yes, Nickamedes?"

The librarian strode up beside me, carrying several books. "Here," he said, dumping the books into my arms. "Make yourself useful and go shelve those. I've got another load to bring over from the English-history building."

"Yes, master," I muttered, but the librarian had already turned and walked away, so he didn't hear me.

I thought about putting the books down on the stairs and going through with my plan to touch the gryphon before I went into the library to work my shift—

"Now, Gwendolyn!" Nickamedes called out from across the quad.

I sighed, juggled the books so they'd fit better in my arms, and headed inside before he could yell at me again.

The evening passed the way it always did. I checked out books, helped students look up others, and even got some of my own homework done on the side. I finally decided to start writing the architecture essay for Metis's class, and I scanned through the gryphon book, looking for information I could use.

But I couldn't concentrate. Over and over again, my eyes kept going back to the other book in my bag—my mom's diary. Something about the diary was slowly working its way up from the bottom of my brain. I knew better than to rush it, though. That would only give me a headache, and I'd already had plenty of those this week.

Daphne stepped into the library at about six, along with Carson. The Valkyrie came over to the checkout desk, like she was just hanging out a second. I quickly finished eating the cherry granola bar I'd bought from Raven's cart earlier and polished off the rest of my bottled water.

"You ready?" she said in a low voice.

I nodded. "Yep, I've got the ring right here, and Vivian just texted me to say she's on her way. So hang back, and we'll see what happens."

Daphne nodded and moved over to a study table where Carson was waiting. I'd just gone back to my architecture book when Logan walked into the library.

The sight of him took my breath away, despite how cold and distant he'd been this morning during weapons training. I expected him to go sit at one of the study tables or maybe get a snack from the coffee cart, but to my surprise, Logan headed over to me, as if I was the person he'd come here to see all along. The thought made my heart start hammering in my chest, but I told myself not to get my hopes up.

"Gypsy girl."

"Spartan."

We stared at each other for several seconds before Logan sighed.

"Look, I've been thinking about the other day, and I just wanted to say I'm sorry. I know that your having the kind of magic you do isn't your fault. It's just . . . frustrating. That you can know all these things about me with just a brush of your fingers. It scares me."

"I'm sorry," I said. "I wish I could turn it off—for you."

His lips twitched up into the barest hint of a smile. "I know, but I didn't have to be such a dick about it either. Or act the way I did this morning in the gym. I was wondering if we could just start over and rewind to how things were at the coliseum before the Reapers attacked. Do you think we could do that?"

I looked into his blue, blue eyes, and I knew I would do anything for him—even forgive him. "I'd love that, Spartan. I really would."

He grinned, and suddenly, everything was right in my world again. I wanted nothing more than to lean across the checkout counter and hug him tight, but I forced myself to be cool and make things work this time. As long as Logan was hiding something, we were still on shaky ground. I wanted the Spartan to tell me his secret in his own way, in his own time, and I didn't want to do anything to mess up what we had between us until then.

"Maybe we should take things slow," I said. "You know, sit down and actually talk instead of fighting

Reapers and going from one crisis to the next. Maybe we can finally get that coffee we've been talking about for a while now."

Logan's grin widened. "I'd like that. As for taking it slow, that's fine, too—as long as you can control yourself around me, Gypsy girl. I have a reputation for being irresistible, you know."

I rolled my eyes, and he laughed, a low, warm, deep chuckle that made my toes tingle.

My good mood didn't last long, because Vivian entered the library, along with Savannah and Talia. The three Amazons put their stuff down on one of the study tables, then Vivian walked over and stepped up behind Logan, apparently thinking the Spartan was in line to check out a book.

"We'll talk later," I said. "There's something I need to take care of right now, okay? Call me later."

He gave me a crooked smile. "You got it, Gypsy girl."

Logan winked at me and walked away, but instead of leaving the library, he stopped at Daphne and Carson's table and started talking to them. The Valkyrie spoke to Logan, but she kept staring at me, waiting to see if I'd touch Vivian and freak out when I realized that she was really the Reaper girl. Only one way to find out.

"I got your message," Vivian said, stepping up to take Logan's place. "You said you found my ring?"

I pulled the plastic bag with the ring in it out of my bag and showed it to her.

Vivian's whole face lit up at the sight of the ring, like it was the most important thing in the world to her. Maybe it was, given the attachment she had to it. I didn't believe she could be the Reaper girl, no matter what Daphne thought. I just didn't see how Vivian could fake that level of shy niceness. Plus, her voice was so soft and sweet. It didn't sound anything like the Reaper girl's low, harsh tone. Then again, neither did Savannah's voice.

Vivian put the other hundred bucks she owed me on the counter. I touched the money and concentrated, but I only got the familiar, faint vibe off it, the feeling of the bill going from one hand to another until it had wound up in mine. No clue there, so I tucked the money into my jeans pocket.

"So where was it?" Vivian asked. "Where did you find the ring?"

"I found it in Savannah's room," I said in a neutral tone.

This was always the hardest part, telling someone her friend had taken what rightfully belonged to her—and not by accident.

I watched her closely, but all the usual emotions flickered across Vivian's face. Surprise. Confusion. And finally, cold knowledge as she realized what my finding the ring in Savannah's room really meant.

"Oh," she said, her face paling. "Oh."

That was all a lot of people could say when they found out something like that about their supposed best friends. I waited for Vivian to do or say something else, but she just stood there, a miserable expression on her face and tears shining in her eyes. After a second, she snapped out of her daze and held out her hand to me.

I handed over the bag with the ring in it, accidentally-on-purpose letting my fingers touch her hand so I could flash on Vivian and see if she was really the Reaper girl.

Various images of Vivian filled my mind. Her sitting in class this morning, eating lunch in the dining hall, walking over to the library. But mainly what I felt was a sense of hurt and confusion over Savannah's betrayal. Apparently, it had affected Vivian more than she was letting on because the emotion blocked out everything else.

There was no hint she was a Reaper, and I didn't sense any sort of hate or malice in her at all. That was a little strange. Even the nicest girl could be a total bitch sometimes. If I'd just found out that my best friend had stolen something from me, well, I'd be royally upset about it. But all Vivian felt was sad, disappointed confusion. She was a far better person than I was. By this point, I would have dug my fingers into Savannah's red hair and started pulling out clumps of it until she confessed to stealing the ring.

Before I could get any more vibes off her, Vivian pulled back, breaking the connection between our fingers.

"Well, thanks for finding it," she said in a tight voice.

"Sure. Anytime."

Vivian turned and walked back to the table where she was sitting with Savannah and Talia. Savannah asked Vivian something, but Vivian gave her a strange look and turned away from the other girl.

Across the library, Daphne looked at me, her eyebrows raised in a silent question. I shook my head, telling her I hadn't gotten any flashes off Vivian that told me she was the Reaper girl. The Valkyrie shrugged back at me.

But I wasn't done yet. I grabbed some books to shelve and wandered over to the table where Vivian, Talia, and Savannah were still sitting. Talia and Savannah were talking about something, but Vivian just sat there, keeping quiet and staring at the ring she'd slipped onto her finger.

I did my accidentally-on-purpose thing again, only this time, I dropped a book onto the table, right into the middle of the three Amazons.

"Whoops! So sorry about that. Let me get that out of the way."

I reached down and grabbed the book, touching Savannah's hand along the way. Memories and emotions rushed into my mind, everything from Savannah's sitting in class to eating lunch in the dining hall to the Amazon's smiling up at Logan as the Spartan walked her across campus when they'd been going out. A soft, warm, fizzy feeling swept over me then, telling me just how much Savannah had liked Logan—and just how hurt she'd been when he'd broken up with her.

That last feeling made my own stomach tighten with guilt, but I forced myself to keep touching her, to keep concentrating and keep looking for any hint that Savannah was the Reaper girl.

I didn't find anything.

Oh, Savannah was plenty pissed at me for a lot of things—for taking Logan from her, for the way the Spartan looked at me, even for dropping the book practically in her lap a few seconds ago. The Amazon wouldn't have minded working out her anger and frustration by sparring with and beating me a few times in the gym, but she didn't have any cold, dark, murderous rage toward me, and I didn't sense any of that feeling in the echoes of her heart.

Mystified, I drew back, clutching the book. By this point, all three girls were looking at me like I was a complete freak. Right now, I supposed I was.

"Sorry," I mumbled again and hurried off to shelve the books like I was supposed to.

The three Amazons watched me the whole time, putting their heads close together and whispering. I gritted my teeth and ignored them, pretending I didn't see them talking about me. On the way back to the checkout counter, I stopped by the table where Daphne was sitting with Carson and Logan.

"Anything?" the Valkyrie whispered.

I shook my head. "I didn't get any big vibes off either one of them. Vivian was upset Savannah took her ring, and Savannah was mad at me as usual. If one of them is the Reaper girl, she's found some way to hide it."

She tried to confuse me, make me see things that weren't really there, Grandma Frost's voice whispered in my mind. *She had a lot of tricks, and she was strong in her magic. As strong as anyone I've ever seen with that kind of mental power—*

"Savannah's not a Reaper," Logan said, interrupting my thoughts. His face tightened. "Trust me on that."

I opened my mouth to ask how he could be so sure, but I realized what his answer would be—because Savannah's family had been brutally murdered just like his mom and older sister. I bit my lip and kept my mouth shut. Logan and I had just established this new beginning between us. I didn't want to wreck it with my suspicions. Still, the Spartan gave me a sharp look, like he knew exactly what I was thinking.

"Anyway, I think I've done enough snooping for one night," I said. "You guys can leave if you want to. I've still got a few more hours left to work."

"Are you sure you'll be all right?" Carson asked, his eyes dark and worried. "What if the Reaper girl is lurking around in here somewhere?"

I started to answer him when I noticed Nickamedes glaring at me from the doorway to the library offices. He stabbed his finger at the kids milling around the checkout counter.

"Gwendolyn!" Nickamedes called out in a sharp voice. "Why are these students still standing in line?"

I grimaced and looked at Carson. "Don't worry. I think Nickamedes is grouchy enough to keep even the Reaper girl away."

I scurried back to the counter. Under Nickamedes's watchful eyes, I spent the next hour checking out books, shelving, and helping the other students with whatever they needed. Daphne and Carson hung around for a few more minutes before grabbing their stuff and leaving.

Logan sat at their table a little while longer, his face troubled as he looked back and forth between Savannah and me. Finally, the Spartan got to his feet. He stared at me, his expression blank, before turning and walking out of the library. I sighed, wishing things could be different between us, wishing things could just be *easy*. Just for once. I cared about Logan, and he cared about me, too. So why was it so difficult for us to be together?

One by one, the rest of the students packed up and headed out. Everyone must have decided to call it an early night because I was the only one left in the library by eight o'clock, except for Nickamedes, who'd gone back into his office to do whatever he did when he wasn't busy yelling at me.

With the library empty, I thought about once again using the Reaper girl's map to try to find the Helheim Dagger, but what was the point? I could spend years searching the library and never figure out exactly where the dagger was. Although, I supposed if I couldn't find the dagger, then neither could the Reaper girl. That thought didn't cheer me up, though.

After I finished shelving the books, there was nothing left to do but sit behind the counter and wait until my shift was over. Since I was totally bored, I opened the architecture book again so I could work on my essay. Once more, I turned to the pages that featured the gryphon statues. Height, weight, type of stone used. The information was the same as before, but I couldn't quit staring at the photographs of the statues. I couldn't get rid of this nagging feeling that something was wrong with the photos or maybe even the statistics on the page.

I glanced down and noticed my mom's diary peeking out of the top of my bag. She'd drawn the statues when she'd been a student. Maybe her diary could help me figure out why I was so obsessed with them now. I grabbed the diary, flipped over to the right pages, and compared my mom's drawings of the gryphons to the photos in the architecture book.

For the first time, I noticed an arrow pointing to the base of one of the statues.

The arrow was on my mom's drawing. It was so tiny that I hadn't noticed it before but just thought it was part of the rest of the random doodles and squiggles on the page. But the more I looked at the arrow, the faster and harder my heart started to pound. Why would my mom draw an arrow there? Why in that particular spot? What was so special that she'd felt the need to mark it that way? My eyes flicked back and forth between her drawing and the photographs in the architecture book.

It took me a few seconds to realize that only one of the statues had a base.

The right statue, the one I'd seen my mom stare at when I'd first touched the diary and flashed on the image of her sitting on the library steps. That gryphon sat on a square slab of stone that was maybe three inches high, while the other statue looked like it had just been plopped down beside the steps with no slab to support its heavy weight.

My heart picked up speed, racing as fast as my thoughts. What if—maybe—just maybe—my mom hadn't hidden the dagger inside the Library of Antiquities after all? What if she'd hidden it *outside* instead? What if she'd tucked it away in the base of the gryphon statue so it would be safe?

No, I thought. That was stupid. The answer couldn't be that simple. Hundreds of kids walked by that statue every single day. Surely, someone would have found the dagger by now if it had really been hidden there. My imagination was working overtime, and it was another false lead, just like all the Xs on the Reaper girl's map of the library.

I closed the diary and the architecture book and stuffed them back in my bag, but I couldn't stop fidgeting and thinking about that arrow—that one tiny arrow pointing at the gryphon. The more I tried to fight the urge to go outside and look at the statue, the more the feeling welled up inside me that I absolutely had to—that I *needed* to right this very second.

I bolted off the stool.

I ran around the library counter, down the long, main aisle, through the double doors, out into the hallway, and then finally outside. The night was cold, so cold that the air burned my lungs, and a dark frost had already coated the entire quad, painting everything a sinister, shadowy silver. The area was deserted, and I was all alone except for the frost, the darkness, and the statues. Even now, I felt like they were watching me from the shadows, tracking my movements.

But I only had eyes for the gryphon statue, the one sitting on the right side of the steps. I bent closer to peer at the statue, comparing it to the left one. Just like in the photographs and my mom's diary, the right statue stood on a base while the left statue didn't.

I stood there a second, staring at the statue, wondering if I was right and if I should really do this. I'd always felt there was a force lurking beneath the stone of the statues, especially the gryphons outside the library.

What if I touched it and the statue sprang to life? No one was on the quad, so no one would hear me scream. Even if by some miracle Nickamedes did hear the sound from inside the library and came to investigate, well, there wouldn't be much left of me by the time he arrived.

But I had to do this. According to Nike, finding the dagger and moving it to another, safer location was the key to keeping Loki locked away in his prison. Protecting the dagger was what would prevent the evil god from gathering his army of Reapers together and trying to take over the world again.

I'd already seen people die this week, students I went to school with, kids my own age who hadn't deserved to have their lives cut short. I'd seen the tears and fear of the other students and everyone else on campus, and I could only imagine what the families of the murdered kids were going through, the grief eating away at their hearts. I didn't want anyone else to get hurt; I didn't want anyone else to go through that kind of pain ever again.

I thought of my mom and how clever and brave she'd been hiding the dagger to start with. Even though she was gone, I still wanted to make her proud of me. Her and Grandma Frost and all my other ancestors who'd served Nike over the centuries. I wanted to be worthy of the magic the goddess had gifted me with, and protecting the dagger from the Reapers was one way I could do that.

But first, I had to find the dagger, and this was my best lead so far—and maybe my last chance. All I had to do was lean forward and touch the stone, and I'd get the answers to my questions—one way or another.

Heart hammering, I drew in a shaky breath, brushed my fingers against the cold stone, and waited for my magic to come to life—and maybe the gryphon along with it.

Chapter 21

The images and memories immediately slammed into my mind, like a tidal wave washing away everything else.

I got the sense that the gryphon was old, ancient even, in the same way that Vic was. And like Vic, there was a—a *spark* in the statue, some sort of force or spirit that I could feel staring at me from deep, deep inside the stone. The force reminded me of the burning red eyes—Loki's eyes—that were always watching me whenever I used my psychometry to slip into Preston's mind. But the statue didn't radiate the same malevolence the Reaper and the crimson eyes did. Instead, what I felt was more of a . . . watchful presence. Like the gryphon was guarding not only the library but all the kids who passed by it on a daily basis and even the academy at large, just like Metis had said. It filled me with a sense of peace, safety, and comfort.

I stood there, eyes closed, my hand pressed against the cold stone, trying to make sense of all the images flashing through my mind. There were thousands of them, stretching back and back and back in time. Seasons came and went in the blink of an eye. Snow melted into spring, the summer sun beat down, fall leaves swirled by, and then the snow came again. All through the seasons, all through the long years, kids leaned on the statue and walked past it and a few even stuck used pieces of gum on it. Yucko.

After a few seconds, the first, overwhelming rush of memories and feelings faded away, slowing to a steady stream, and I was able to start sorting through the images, looking for a specific one attached to a very specific person. I ignored the flashes of guys touching, leaning against, or sitting on the statue, instead focusing on the ones of all the girls who'd been close to the gryphon over the years. Not her or her or even her . . . but her!

The memory almost slid by before I could grab hold of it, but I managed to catch it before it disappeared into the dark of my mind. I ignored the other images still slipping by and brought the one I wanted into focus.

The memory took place on a cold night much like this one. A girl my own age stood in front of the gryphon statue. Brown hair, violet eyes, pale skin dotted with freckles. Her face was as familiar to me as my own was, although I would never be as beautiful as she'd been.

"Mom," I whispered, even though she couldn't hear me, even though it was just a memory.

My mom looked out across the empty quad, scanning

the shadows. *Violet eyes are smiling eyes.* That's what my mom had always jokingly said, but she wasn't smiling tonight. Instead, her lips were clamped down into a tight, thin line, and her whole body was rigid with tension and fear—fear that the Reapers searching for her would find her before she could complete her mission for Nike. My mom felt she was running out of time, but she was still going to stop a moment and look around. She was still going to be as careful as she could.

When she was sure she was alone and that no one was watching her, my mom pulled a piece of black cloth out of her backpack. She set the cloth down on the library steps, and something sticking out of the edge of it scraped against the stone. My mom froze, her eyes darting around, as if that one small noise would somehow draw the Reapers immediately to her.

But no one erupted out of the shadows, and after a minute, my mom relaxed and turned back to the statue. She ran her hands over the gryphon this way and that, like she was looking for something. Finally, she found what she was searching for. My mom reached forward and twisted the very end of the gryphon's tail. A second later, the base of the statue slid forward like a door hinging open, revealing a secret, hollow space inside.

My mom paused and glanced around, once again making sure no one was watching her. Then, she picked up the black cloth, pulled the edges together, slid it inside the hidden compartment, and twisted the gryphon's tail back the other way. The base of the statue closed, hiding the cloth from sight.

My mom sighed, and her body relaxed. It was done—her mission was complete. She took one more look around before she drew up the hood of her jacket, tucked her hands into her pockets, and hurried away from the library, melting into the shadows. . . .

I dropped my hand from the gryphon and opened my eyes. I let out a breath and was surprised to feel how weak my knees were. I had to sit down on the steps until the shaky feeling faded away. Then, I got back on my feet and approached the gryphon statue once more.

My eyes flicked to the creature's lion tail, and I bent down to study it. It looked like just another part of the statue, just another piece carved out of a single hunk of dark gray stone. If I hadn't seen my mom twist the end of the tail, I never would have thought to do such a thing—or that there was a hidden compartment underneath it.

I wondered how my mom had found it in the first place. If she'd listened to the same sort of myth-history lecture I had, if maybe that was how she'd discovered the statue's secret. It didn't really matter in the end, though. All that was important was finding the dagger and taking it somewhere safe—somewhere the Reapers could never get to it.

"You protected it well all these years," I murmured, talking to that spark of awareness I'd sensed deep inside the stone. "But the Reapers are closing in on the dagger's location, and now, I have to move it somewhere else. I hope you understand. I'll do my very best to protect it—I promise you that."

The gryphon didn't say anything, but its lidless eyes seemed to narrow in the faint golden glow cast by the lights that lined the library balcony. For the first time, the faint motion didn't unnerve me. Instead, it comforted me, like the gryphon knew it was time for the dagger to be moved, like it somehow recognized me as being connected to the girl who had hidden it here in the first place. After a moment, the gryphon dropped its eyes, and its head seemed to dip ever so slightly, almost like it was giving me permission.

Fingers trembling, I stretched my hand forward and twisted the end of the gryphon's tail.

It moved just as smoothly as it had for my mom, and the secret compartment slid open with the barest whisper. My hand shook so badly that I had to stop and curl it into a fist for a moment before I felt steady enough to open it back up and reach inside the hollow chamber. My fingers touched something soft and silky in the darkness, and another image filled my mind—my mom slipping the cloth into the same spot I was now pulling it out of.

I drew out the black cloth, then twisted the gryphon's tail again, hiding the secret compartment from sight. Fingers still trembling, I unwrapped one corner of the cloth, then the other—slowly revealing the Helheim Dagger.

The dagger was lighter than I'd thought it would be— much, much lighter. It barely weighed more than the silk it had been wrapped in. Instead of metal, the dagger was made out of black marble that glimmered with tiny bronze flecks. A single ruby was set into the hilt, but the gem was dark, like the light that had once been inside it had been extinguished. It took me a moment to realize that the gem was shaped like a single, narrowed eye. I wondered if the gem was Loki's portal to this realm, a window from his mythological prison. I wondered if the evil god could somehow look through the ruby and see me holding the dagger right now. I shivered at the thought and quickly covered the weapon back up with the black cloth.

For a moment, I just stood there, not quite believing I'd done it, that I'd actually found the dagger. A grin spread across my face, and I wanted to let out a wild whoop of triumph, but I clamped my lips together and pushed those thoughts away. I had other things to focus on, like what to do with the dagger now that I actually had it.

Nickamedes, I thought. I'd go back into the library and show the weapon to Nickamedes. He'd call Metis and Ajax, and then, we could figure out how to hide it again—

"Well, Gypsy," a low voice said behind me. "Thank you so much for finding the dagger for me. I was starting to wonder if you were up to the task."

Something rustled behind me, and I spotted a shadow sliding over the frost, rushing toward me. I whirled around, but it was already too late. The Reaper girl's fist connected with my face, and the world went black.

The first thing I was aware of was the throbbing ache in my cheek.

Pulse, pulse, pulse. It was a slow, steady pain, keeping perfect time to the beat of my heart. It hurt so much, but I focused on the pain, moving past it, shoving it into the back of my mind. Even though things were still fuzzy in my brain, I knew that I was in Big, Big Trouble. I could feel the hate emanating from the other people around me. The ugly emotion pressed down on my chest like a lead weight, suffocating me. I couldn't tell how many of them there were, but they all despised me. My stomach twisted at the rage that just kept flowing off them like waves slamming into the shore.

"Well," a familiar voice said. "I think the Gypsy is finally waking up."

I knew that voice, I thought, still feeling a little dazed, but I couldn't quite believe it was *her*. She'd seemed so nice, so much like *me*, but she was a Reaper, and she'd used me to help her find the Helheim Dagger. That much I knew, even if I didn't know exactly how she'd tricked me into doing her bidding.

I opened my eyes to find Vivian Holler perched on the desk in front of me.

"Hello, Gypsy," Vivian said. "Surprised to see me?"

I shook my head, but that just made my face ache even more. I wiggled my jaw, trying to get the worst of the pain over with. Slowly, the sharp, pulsing throbs faded into softer, more manageable twinges, and I was able to look around without a haze of white stars blurring my vision.

I was tied to a chair in an opulent living room filled with dark wooden furniture, antique sofas, and crystal vases full of roses. The overpowering scent of the black and blood-red petals permeated the air, making me gag, but I kept scanning the area. I turned my head and found myself staring at a gold statue shaped like a bird, its wings spread wide. An enormous painting featuring the same sort of bird with the same wings hung on the wall behind it. I realized where I was—in the living room I'd seen when I'd first touched the Reaper girl's—Vivian's—map of the Library of Antiquities.

"Wings," I mumbled, eyeing the statue next to me. "What's with all the wings?"

Vivian arched an eyebrow. "That's what you want to know? Not how I tricked you into finding the dagger for me? Really, Gypsy, I thought you'd say something more interesting than that. But if you absolutely must know, I'll be happy to show you."

Vivian let out a low, sharp whistle and turned toward a set of doors that led out onto a balcony. Even though it was dark outside, I could still see the black shape of something drop from the sky and land on the balcony. Vivian walked over, opened the doors, and stepped back.

A second later, a Black roc hopped inside the room.

The roc was enormous, easily as big as Nott—if not bigger. Its wings were a slick, shiny black, shot through with glossy streaks of red that gleamed like rivers of blood, and the roc's black, curved talons looked like they were almost as long as my arm. In myth-history class, Metis had once said that rocs were Arabian creatures that were strong enough to grab people and fly away with them. I'd thought the idea was ridiculous then, but now, I totally believed it. The roc definitely looked like it could eat me with two snaps of its sharp, pointed beak.

The roc's eyes were a bright, shiny black as well, but that ominous, Reaper red spark burned in the inky orbs. I shivered and looked away from the creature.

"You don't like my pet?" Vivian asked. "What a shame. My family has been raising them for generations, you know. Practically all the Reapers get their rocs from us. We're quite famous for breeding them to be especially vicious."

She let out another whistle and pointed at the balcony. The Black roc hopped outside, its talons scraping against the floor. Vivian shut the door behind it, although I could still see the roc lurking outside, peering in through the doors like it wanted to peck its way through the glass to get to me.

Footsteps whispered behind me, and a few seconds later, Preston stepped into view. Vivian resumed her perch on the desk, and Preston went over to stand beside her. Preston's orange jumpsuit was gone, and he was dressed in expensive clothes once more. Boots, designer jeans, a luxurious cashmere sweater, a leather jacket. All black, of course. Just like his rotting soul.

Preston smirked at me. "I told you I'd get the best of you one day, Gypsy. How stupid of you not to believe me."

I glared at him. "Oh, please. You wouldn't be standing here right now if it wasn't for Vivian, and we all know it. She's the one who's done all the work. She's the one who got you out of the academy prison."

I looked at the other girl. "Bravo on that, by the way. And the rest of this elaborate scheme. You've managed to pull it off quite nicely."

She brightened at my snarky tone. "I have, haven't I? Not that I'm one to gloat, but I really have outdone myself this time."

"Oh, just go ahead and tell me all about your evil master plan," I muttered. "You know you want to. That's why you haven't killed me already. The villains in movies and comic books always want to gloat, too."

I didn't add that that gloating was also always the villains' downfall—that cliché was the only bit of hope I had right now.

Vivian laughed. The sound grated on my ears just like the roc's talons had raked across the floor. "Well, that's one of the reasons, anyway. I'm not quite through with you yet, Gypsy, but we'll get to that in a few minutes. As for how I tricked you, you're supposed to be a clever girl. You were smart enough to defeat Preston, although that wouldn't take much doing. So why don't *you* tell me how I tricked you?"

I looked at her for a few seconds, then around at the room again. Thinking. The longer I kept Vivian talking, the longer someone might have to find and rescue me. Of course, I didn't know exactly *who* that someone would be. Nickamedes would probably think I'd just slipped out of the library early, instead of realizing that something had happened to me—if he even bothered to look for me. Given my history with the librarian, he'd probably be glad to come out of his office and find me gone.

"Gypsy?" Vivian asked, snapping her fingers in front of my face. "Are you still with us?"

Red sparks streamed out of her fingertips like raindrops. It was something I'd forgotten about these past few days, but during the fight at the coliseum, I'd thought the Reaper girl had to be a Valkyrie, given how strong she was and how much it had hurt when she'd punched me. But I'd never seen Vivian throw off sparks of magic like Daphne or the other Valkyries did.

I nodded at her fingers. "How did you hide that? The sparks and the fact that you're really a Valkyrie? Everybody at Mythos thinks you're an Amazon."

She shrugged. "The same way I hide everything. You want to know a secret?"

I always wanted to know secrets, and most especially hers, but I didn't say anything. Vivian leaned forward anyway.

She stared at me, and a flicker of red flashed to life in the depths of her golden gaze. "You're not the only Gypsy at Mythos, Gwen."

My mouth dropped open, and all the air left my lungs. I was just that shocked. Grandma Frost had told me there were other Gypsies out there, other families gifted with magic by the gods just like ours had been. She'd also told me that not all of the Gypsies were good like us, that some were lazy or indifferent or were even Reapers.

So far, I hadn't met any other Gypsies, but here I was, face to face with the most evil Gypsy of all—Loki's Champion. For as good as the goddess Nike was, Loki was equally bad, which meant that his Champion would be just as vicious and ruthless as the evil god was.

"What—what kind of magic did Loki give your family?"

I forced myself to ask the question. If I knew what kind of magic Vivian had, then maybe I could find some way to turn it against her and escape.

Vivian smiled. "Why, the most wonderful magic of all—chaos magic."

"What's that?" I'd never heard of that kind of magic before, and I hadn't seen any references to it in the myth-history books I'd been using to research my own touch magic.

Beside Vivian, Preston snorted. "It's not chaos magic. For the most part, it's just regular old telepathy."

"Telepathy?" I asked. "You mean like reading minds and planting thoughts in people's brains?"

"Exactly," Preston said. "Vivian can make people see and hear things that aren't there. Big whoop, if you ask me."

A dangerous light flared in Vivian's eyes, and that spark of Reaper red I'd seen before burned a little brighter at Preston's mocking words.

I thought of the Reaper red flashes that I'd noticed in Savannah's eyes and the hate that had filled her face whenever she looked at me. Vivian had done that, I realized, had made me suspect the other girl was a Reaper so I wouldn't focus on Vivian. That was probably how she'd changed her voice, too, so I wouldn't hear her talking and realize who she really was. I wondered what else she'd done to me this week. I had a bad, bad feeling that I was about to find out—and that it was going to get a whole lot worse.

"Actually, Preston's right," Vivian said. "I can make people see things that aren't really there, plant thoughts in their heads, even get them to follow my commands. Illusions, confusion, chaos. It's all the same really, but Loki made my family's telepathy magic particularly vicious. If I want to, I can look into a person's brain and make it seem like her worst nightmare has come to life. Would you like to see that, Gwen?"

My heart dropped into my stomach at her cold, cold words. My Gypsy gift had shown me so many awful things over the years. If Vivian looked into my head with her magic, she'd have plenty of nightmares to choose from.

"Of course you would," Vivian said.

She pushed off the desk and headed toward me. Vivian stopped in front of me and smiled—and then she turned around to stare at Preston.

He frowned. "What are you doing—"

That's all he got out before his face turned white, and he started screaming.

Preston screamed and screamed and screamed like he would never stop. Desperate, he lurched forward, like he could get away from Vivian's magic if only he could move. Preston's knees hit a table. He staggered back, then tripped on a rug and fell to the floor. He curled into a ball, covering his eyes with his hands like he could block out whatever it was he was seeing. But the defensive posture didn't help him, and Vivian smiled as his shrieks of terror filled the room.

"Preston's worst nightmare is quite interesting," she murmured, staring down at him. "It's you, actually. Apparently, he was never so scared in his life as he was when you told him there was nothing he could do to stop you from touching his hands and riffling through his memories with your psychometry magic. Preston's something of a control freak, you see."

Vivian kept staring at the other Reaper, and I felt this force rolling off her—an ugly, angry, malevolent force that got stronger and stronger with every one of Preston's screams, almost like his fear was giving her even more power, like his terror was making her *happy*. I could almost see the evil force in the air, slithering over and coiling around and around him like a snake with venom dripping off its fangs—venom that was penetrating Preston's brain and poisoning his mind with vision after horrific vision.

Finally, Vivian shook her head and turned away from him. The ugly, invisible force vanished, and after a moment, Preston quit screaming, although his whole body shook with violent sobs.

"Too easy," she said. "His mind is so simple. That was hardly a challenge. But you, Gypsy, you've been much more interesting to play with."

While Preston wept on the floor, I thought about everything that had happened the past few days.

"You planned this whole thing, didn't you?" I asked. "The attack at the Crius Coliseum, letting me see you there after the fact so I'd notice how shaken up you were, the creepy voice in the Library of Antiquities, even hiring me to find your lost ring. You did it all just so you could keep track of me while I was searching for the Helheim Dagger."

Vivian reached down and plucked the dagger off the desk. I blinked. How had I not noticed it lying there? She turned the dagger this way and that, making the bronze flecks in the marble shimmer. For the first time, I realized what had bothered me so much about the memories I'd gotten off the map that Vivian had dropped— the fact that she'd been wearing her Reaper mask in them to protect her real identity. Something she wouldn't have done if she hadn't been planning to leave the map behind the whole time.

"You dropped that map on purpose," I said. "You wanted me to have it. You wanted me to flash on it. Why?"

Vivian shrugged. "Some of the other Reapers had determined that the dagger's location was somewhere in or around the Library of Antiquities, but it would have taken years to search the building and find it, especially given my obvious limitations as a student. So I decided to let you find it for me. But since you didn't seem to know the dagger was in the library, I decided to give you a little push. Everyone always waits until the last second to do his or her homework. I figured you'd probably be at the exhibit the day before school started, so I convinced Savannah to go with me to finish my myth-history assignment."

"If you were just trying to get at me the whole time, then why kill those other kids?" I whispered. "Why did they have to die?"

Vivian shrugged. "I had to make it look like a real attack or you never would have bought the idea that I'd accidentally dropped the map. Besides, I never liked Samson Sorensen. He always thought he was so much cooler than the other guys at school—much too cool to date someone like me. I asked him out once, back before Jasmine got her hooks into him, but he just laughed and asked why I ever thought he'd want to go out with a mousy little girl like me. Well, he didn't laugh so much when I ran my sword through his chest, did he?"

Rage twisted her face, and her fingers tightened around the dagger, like she wanted to kill Samson all over again.

"And then in the library?" I asked, trying to keep her talking. "What was with the whole creepy voice thing?"

Vivian's face smoothed out a bit, and she shrugged again. "I needed Metis's door codes and magic passwords to get down to the prison to free Preston. I knew she'd been taking you to the prison to pry into his mind, and given your psychometry and the fact that you never forget anything you see or hear, I knew you had the passwords locked away in your brain. All I had to do was slip into your mind and make you think about Preston so I could find the information I needed. We know all about you and your touch magic. I must say it's come in quite handy so far. Helping me free Preston, then finding the dagger. Good job, Gwen. Good job."

I thought about all the headaches I'd had these past
few days and all the times it had seemed there were a
pair of fingers digging into my skull. That had been Vivian, using her telepathy on me. On some level, I'd
sensed what she was doing and had even tried to fight
back, although it hadn't worked. Then, another thought
popped into my head.

"You know about my touch magic—and what I'm
supposed to do with it," I said, echoing something Preston had once said to me.

Vivian snorted. "Please. As if you could ever kill Loki
with your pitiful psychometry."

Once again, all the air left my lungs, and white stars
exploded before my eyes. I thought I'd been stunned before, but that was nothing compared to the utter shock
I was feeling right now. "You think—the Reapers actually think—that I'm going to kill Loki with my magic?"

My voice was barely a whisper. I could hardly even
find the breath to ask the question. Kill a god? Me?
How could I do that with my touch magic? How could
anyone do that?

Vivian noticed the shocked look on my face and burst
out laughing. "You mean you didn't know? The great
goddess Nike didn't tell you? Oh, how wonderful."

Vivian kept right on laughing. Meanwhile, Preston
had finally quit shaking and crying and pushed himself
up to a sitting position. He gave Vivian a hate-filled
glare and wiped away the tears on his flushed cheeks.

"But what about the ring?" I asked, my mind spinning in a thousand different directions. "Why even bother to hire me to find it?"

Vivian held out her hand, admiring the ring glinting on her finger. I stared at the two faces in the gold band. Now, instead of one laughing and one crying, both faces seemed to be twisted and grinning at me with evil, malevolent glee.

"I should have known," I muttered. "The ring has two faces just like you do. It doesn't just represent theater masks, does it? Although you should buy something nice for Mr. Ovid, the drama teacher. He's made you into quite the little actress."

"True," Vivian agreed. "I'm much more talented than that stupid Amazon, Helena Paxton, will ever be, but Mr. Ovid always gives her the lead roles in our plays. You really need to brush up on your myth-history, Gwen. I told you before it was a Janus ring, as in the Roman god of beginnings and endings. He has two faces, one looking into the future and one looking into the past. The ring's been in my family for years as a symbol of our hidden loyalty to Loki. It was my mom's—until some members of the Pantheon killed her."

Her face scrunched up, and I remembered the image I'd seen of Vivian's mom handing her the ring and all the pain the girl had felt at her mom dying. I would have felt sorry for her—if she hadn't caused me the same pain by murdering my mom.

Then, another thought popped into my head. "That's why you had brand-new furniture in your dorm room, wasn't it? And why you rushed to open the door for me when I left the day I came over to look for your ring.

You couldn't take a chance that I'd flash on something in your room, like your vanity table, and realize who you really were. But why hire me to find the ring when it was never lost?"

"You're right about the furniture. As for the ring, I needed to hang around and see what you were doing, and I didn't want you to get suspicious of me before you found the dagger. So I made up the story about Savannah's stealing my ring and hid it in her room for you to find. Besides, I knew it would be easy to make you think that she was a Reaper. It's no secret the two of you are still fighting over Logan."

"So it was just a distraction. But you had to know I would touch the ring and flash on it, if only to make sure that Savannah had really stolen it," I said. "How did you twist the memories around to make it look like she was the Reaper instead of you?"

Vivian shrugged. "Chaos magic, remember? Confusion and illusions. In some ways, my magic is the exact opposite of yours, Gwen. You touch objects and see things. If I focus hard and long enough, I can actually imprint emotions and memories on certain objects. So it was easy for me to take an image of myself wearing the ring and make it look like Savannah."

"But—"

A series of low chimes sounded, cutting me off. My eyes flicked to the source of the sound—an ebony grandfather clock shaped like a roc that stood against one wall.

"At last, midnight," Vivian murmured. "Do you know what that means, Gwen?"

"What?"

Vivian smiled. "It means it's finally time for you to do what I brought you here for."

I had to force myself to ask the question. "And what would that be?"

Her smile widened. "Die."

Chapter 22

Another Reaper came into the living room—the man I'd seen when I'd first touched the fake map. He cut through the ropes that tied me to the chair, then he and Preston hauled me through the balcony doors and outside.

I started to fight back, but Preston held a sword against my ribs and told me that he would shove it through my heart if I so much as breathed wrong. So I decided not to breathe wrong.

Vivian led the way, while Preston and the man forced me down a set of stone steps and then out into the forest that lay beyond the mansion. I couldn't see much of the landscape in the darkness, but I got the sense that we were still in the mountains, still in North Carolina, still close to the academy. I don't know why that comforted me, but it did. If I was going to die, well, at least it would be close to home. Maybe the members of the Pantheon would at least find my body and bury it.

We trudged deeper and deeper into the woods, the frosted leaves crunching like brittle bones under our feet. The lights from the mansion behind us slowly disappeared, but they were replaced with new ones up ahead. The lights flickered and danced in the darkness, and I realized they were torches burning in the night.

We stepped through the trees and into a large clearing. An enormous circle made out of black marble had been set into the middle of the forest, with the trees rising up on all sides like the pillars of a great coliseum. Tall, skinny torches had been placed into small holes cut into the stone, and their crackling red flames leaped up into the air, like they were straining to set fire to the trees around them.

We hadn't passed anyone in the forest, but thirteen people had already gathered inside the stone circle, one standing by each torch—and every single one of them wore a Reaper mask and a black robe.

I stared out into the circle of people, my eyes going from one twisted Loki face to the next. I couldn't see who was behind the masks, but I thought I probably knew some of them, that they were kids or professors at Mythos. A sense of familiarity radiated off them, along with hate—so much hate. Every single Reaper in the circle would have been more than happy to step forward and kill me. I bit my lip and tried not to show just how terrified I was of them and what they were about to do to me.

"What is this place?" I asked.

"This," Vivian said in a satisfied voice, "is a Garm gate, one of hundreds located all over the world. It serves as a portal to other gates and even other realms—including Helheim."

"Helheim?" I whispered.

From researching the dagger, I knew that the weapon was named for Helheim, which was the Norse world of the dead—and the prison realm where Loki was trapped. Supposedly, it was a place that no one—god or mortal alike—could ever escape, but I had a sick, sick feeling that wasn't going to be true tonight.

Vivian looked at me, a mocking expression on her face. "Just putting it together now, are you, Gwen? Although I have to say I love that dawning look of horror on your face."

I wanted to ask her more questions, but I didn't get the chance as Preston and the man dragged me to the center of the stone circle. Something had been carved into the marble under my feet, and it took me a few seconds to realize what it was—a hand holding a set of balanced scales. The exact same hand and the exact same scales that adorned the roof of the academy prison.

Vivian strode into the middle of the circle as well. She stopped and looked out at the other Reapers who had gathered around.

"We've all waited a very, very long time for this moment," she said. "For centuries, our ancestors have served Loki faithfully, preparing for the day when we could finally free our god from the prison he's been trapped in for so long. Well, that time has finally come."

Yeah, I knew I was about to die, but I still couldn't help rolling my eyes at her formal, grandiose words. Practice in front of the mirror much, Viv?

"You all know what to do," Vivian said. "So let's get started."

Softly at first, very, very softly, the Reapers began to chant. I didn't know what magic mumbo jumbo they were spouting, but the sound of their low, guttural words sent chills up my spine. Slowly, their words grew sharper and sharper, until the air felt like it was full of cold knives that were pressing against my skin, ready to cut me open if I dared do more than breathe.

Vivian turned her attention back to me, twirling the Helheim Dagger in her hand like it was a cheerleader's baton instead of the powerful, dangerous artifact it was.

"I know you're wondering why I didn't just kill you in the academy prison when I had the chance or even when you first came to Mythos back in the fall," Vivian said. "The answer is simple—we needed you to find the dagger for us, and we needed your blood. Fresh blood and not what had already been spilt. Of course, Jasmine almost ruined that and so did her big brother Preston."

Beside me, Preston stiffened at her words, but he didn't say anything. I'd thought he couldn't despise anyone more than he did me, but even standing here among all the other Reapers, I could feel the special, jealous hate Preston had for Vivian.

Preston and the man held me still while Vivian approached me, the dagger glinting in her hand. My stomach twisted, and suddenly, I realized what she was going to do—Vivian was going to sacrifice me to free Loki from his prison.

Grandma Frost had said being a Champion made you a target for the Reapers. Nike had said the same thing, except she'd added that a Champion's blood had power—enormous power—since that person had been chosen by a god. It made sense, I supposed. Nike had helped imprison Loki in the first place, and now, Vivian was going to use my bloody death to free the evil god.

And there was absolutely nothing I could do to stop it.

If I tried to get away, Preston would stab me with his sword. If I held still, Vivian would gut me with the dagger. Either way, I was dead, dead, dead.

Vivian stopped in front of me, a cold, satisfied look on her face. How had I ever thought her sweet and shy? As I watched her, that red spark already flickering in the depths of her gaze began to burn brighter and brighter until her eyes gleamed with the same crimson fire as the torches.

"Hold out her hand," Vivian said.

My hand? What did she want with my hand? Why wasn't she going for my heart?

Preston forced my hand open and shoved it in front of me. Vivian slashed down with the dagger, opening up a deep cut on my right palm. I hissed with pain, but Vivian sawed the dagger deeper and deeper into my skin, until I thought she was going to cut my hand in half. I bit back a scream and tried not to vomit.

Blood poured out of my palm, coating the dagger in a sticky glaze. For a few seconds, nothing happened, but then, a red spark flared to life in the eye-shaped ruby set into the dagger's hilt—a hot, eerie, crimson light that I knew all too well.

"No," I whispered. "No, no, no."

Vivian shoved the dagger back into the cut, turning it over and over until it was completely covered in my blood. She pulled back, and I realized that instead of blood dripping off the end, the dagger was actually *ab-sorbing* my blood, sucking it up like a vacuum cleaner. The last drop of blood vanished into the stone, and the eerie crimson light spread out from the ruby. In seconds, the whole weapon was burning the same blistering red as Vivian's eyes.

Vivian carefully placed the dagger in a slot in the middle of the stone circle, right in the center of the hand holding the balanced scales, piercing it in the same place where she'd cut my palm. She stepped back to the edge of the circle, and Preston and the other man hauled me over there as well, Preston's sword still pressing into my side.

As I watched, the Helheim Dagger started to burn even brighter, giving off wisps of acrid black smoke, before it just...*melted* into the stone. One second the dagger was whole and solid; the next it was gone. The instant the hilt of the dagger disappeared, the ground started trembling, as if we were standing at the epicenter of the most violent earthquake ever. One by one, the torches went out before abruptly flaming to life again. The black stone under our feet began to buck and heave, like someone was pounding at it from below with a giant fist.

BOOM-BOOM-BOOM!

A few seconds later, the stone Garm gate gave way to whatever was hammering at it, and the circle splintered down the middle. The stone heaved again and split the other way, forming a giant X. A crimson cloud of smoke erupted from the giant fissure and spewed up like lava, burning even brighter and hotter than the torches, until it scalded my face with its intense heat. An acrid stench filled the air, like sulfur mixed with some sort of flowery perfume.

Then, as suddenly as it had all started, the trembling and the shaking stopped, and the smoke vanished. I blinked, trying to get my bearings, and that's when I realized that a figure had appeared in the middle of the stone circle right beside the center of the X.

He wore a long black robe, and he huddled on his knees. His body was cramped and twisted, his chest almost touching the ground, his neck cocked to the point of breaking, his right arm flung up at an awkward angle behind the rest of him. He clutched the Helheim Dagger in his right hand, the point turned up, like he'd used the weapon to stab through the stone above him.

I could just see the edge of his face, but it seemed sleek and shiny, like it was made of wax. Even more than that, I could feel the anger rolling off him in waves—anger, rage, and the absolute blackest sort of hate.

"Loki," I whispered in fear.

Chapter 23

The Norse god of chaos stayed still and frozen in the middle of the stone circle. Slowly, his fingers twitched, and his muscles spasmed, as though he'd been trapped in that one, agonizing position for a long, long time and was having trouble getting to his feet. His arm came down, his neck twisted back into the appropriate place, and his chest lifted as he got to his feet. His bones cracked and popped with every movement, matching the crackle of the torches. Each and every sound made me grind my teeth together and cower a little more in fear. I'd been face-to-face with a god before. Nike had come to me twice now, but this—this was different.

Because this was Loki, and he radiated pure evil.

Finally, the god straightened up to his full height—almost seven feet tall. He had his back to me, but his head pivoted left, then right, his bones snapping into place as he stared at the circle of Reapers in front of him. Then, the god lifted his hands into the air and let out a scream—a wild, wild scream full of all the hate and rage that had sustained him over the centuries he'd been trapped. A scream full of all the bloody chaos and harsh promises of death his Reapers had whispered about over the years.

It was the most awful sound I'd ever heard.

Just the faintest whisper of it would have been enough to make my head pound. Hearing the full force of it caused hot tears to slide down my cheeks and my whole body to ache, as though the god's scream was enough to peel my flesh from my bones. Maybe it was. Either way, I didn't think things could get any worse—until the god turned around and I got my first good look at him.

It was—he was—*horrible*.

Loki was the most horrible thing I'd ever seen and worse than anything I could have ever imagined. I'd seen drawings of him in my myth-history books, but they'd failed to show the god's true self. A piercing blue eye, a strong chin, a great cheekbone, an aquiline nose, alabaster skin. Half of his face was perfect, beautiful, gorgeous even, like he was one of the marble statues in the Library of Antiquities come to life. His hair flowed down like a river of gold, just brushing the top of his right shoulder.

But the left side of the god's face was just—melted. Like hot candle wax that had run together and mushed all the original, clean, straight lines of his features into something dark, ugly, and utterly twisted. Instead of being blue, the god's eye on that side of his face was red—Reaper red. His cheekbone was nothing more than a smushed piece of putty, and his nose looked like a hooked beak that was trying to dig its way into his chin.

The part of his skin that wasn't smooth and shiny was pitted with pockmarks, and the hair on that side of his head was black, with crimson strands glinting among the thin, matted, singed locks.

Loki was the most horrific thing I'd ever seen, and now, the god was finally free of his prison. And it was my fault—all my fault. People were going to die, and it was all my fault for being stupid enough to let the Reaper girl use me to find the Helheim Dagger. Somehow I swallowed down the hot, sour, bitter bile that rose up in my throat.

Vivian stepped forward and dropped to one knee before him. "My lord," she said in an awe-filled tone. "We have finally succeeded in freeing you, and now, after so many years, we await your instructions."

Loki looked at the Reaper girl on the ground before him. "Rise, my Champion, for you have served me well. And together, we will make sure that Chaos reigns once more here in the mortal realm."

Despite the god's twisted features, his voice was rich and smooth, with a low, throaty timbre. A soft, seductive voice, the kind of voice that could convince a person to do almost anything. Even though I knew how evil he was, even though I knew all the horrible things he'd instructed his Reapers to do, his voice was still beautiful, sweet, and pure, and I could feel the hypnotic pull of his words wrapping around me and trying to dig into my brain just like Vivian had done with her telepathy magic. I ground my teeth together and shoved the feeling away as hard as I could.

Vivian got to her feet, her eyes glowing an even

brighter red. The god handed her the Helheim Dagger, presenting it like it was a gift. Vivian bowed her head again to Loki, then lifted the weapon high.

"To Chaos!" she screamed.

"To Chaos!" the other Reapers shouted over and over again, their screams sealing not only my fate, but that of the world as well.

Finally, the wild echoes of the Reapers' screams faded away, and Loki looked at Vivian once more.

"Now," the god said. "I want to see the sacrifice you've brought me."

Vivian jerked her head in my direction. The god looked over his shoulder, staring at me with the beautiful half of his face. Loki's blue eye focused on me and narrowed, and the god turned and began striding in my direction. His bones snapped and popped with every step he took, and I realized he wasn't wearing any shoes underneath his long robe. The splintered marble didn't seem to bother him, although I knew the sharp shards had to be digging into his feet with every step he took.

Still, I got the feeling the god was not entirely well. There was a rigid stiffness in the way he moved, and he kept wincing, as if it pained him to be here in the mortal realm. Or perhaps he'd spent all these centuries being tortured, like he had been the first time the other gods had imprisoned him.

Loki stopped a few feet away. Preston and the other man dragged me forward into the flickering torchlight, and the god examined me.

"Another Frost girl," he said, his smooth voice dripping with hate. "I see Nike hasn't changed her tactics, despite all the centuries that have passed."

I had no idea what the god was talking about, and I didn't really care right now. I wanted nothing more than to curl into a ball and whimper at his feet, but I wasn't going to be cowed or frightened, not even by the evil god. I would meet my death bravely, if nothing else—just like my mom had.

It took me a moment to summon up my courage, but I finally looked up and raised my eyes to his. It was bizarre staring into his face, with one side so perfect and the other side so completely ruined. I decided to focus on the ruined side. After all, that's what Loki really was—ruined in every way possible.

"You may have gotten free," I said in the bravest, boldest voice I could muster. "But you haven't won yet. Nike and the other members of the Pantheon will rise up and defeat you just like they did before. They'll put you back down there where you belong—for good this time."

Loki stared at me, and I felt the seconds of my life slowly tick away as the god thought about what to do to me, how to make me suffer just like he had.

Tick-tick-tock.

Instead of smiting me with his burning red eye or whatever kind of evil magic mumbo jumbo he could do, the god threw back his head and laughed. I sucked in a breath and tried to keep from doubling over in pain. The mocking sound had the same effect as a vicious punch to the stomach. I'd felt Nike's cold, raw power before when the goddess had appeared to me, but it was nothing like Loki's evil. The god practically oozed malevolence, hate, and rage. I'd thought Nike was the strongest being I'd ever encountered, but now, I was wondering if I was wrong.

"Oh, Gypsy, poor, pitiful Gypsy," Loki murmured. "Having such misguided faith in your goddess, just like all your other ancestors have over the years."

The god leaned forward and stared at me, his face inches away from mine, his one red eye burning into both of my violet ones. "Don't you realize that I've already won? I'm free, and I've got you here. That's all I need to achieve my ultimate victory."

Before I could think about the god's words, Loki looked over at Vivian.

"Kill her," the god said.

A smile spread across Vivian's face. "With pleasure."

The Reaper girl walked toward me, slashing at the air with the Helheim Dagger, which she still had clutched in her fingers. As much as I wanted to, I didn't close my eyes as she approached. I would look her in the face while she killed me, just like my mom had done. Gwen Frost, Gypsy girl and brave to the bitter, bitter end.

Vivian came closer and closer, the crimson fire in her eyes burning a little brighter and a little hotter with every step she took. Finally, she stopped in front of me.

"Too bad it's over already, Gwen," she said. "I had such fun playing with you these past few days."

"Go to hell, bitch," I said through clenched teeth.

Vivian let out a merry laugh. "I think I'll send you there first."

She raised the dagger high overhead. The black blade

flashed for a second in the torchlight before it started its downward arc toward my heart—

A fierce growl sounded, and a large shadow leaped out of the trees and plowed into the Reaper girl, knocking her to the ground. The dagger skittered across the stone, and Vivian scrambled after it. But the creature wasn't done. It barreled into the ring of Reapers, snapping its jaws and swiping its claws at everyone within reach. In five seconds, two Reapers were dead. In another five, two more had joined them.

The creature turned to face an attack by one of the Reapers, and I finally recognized it for who and what it was.

"Nott," I whispered.

I didn't know how the Fenrir wolf had found me out here in the middle of nowhere, but I was glad she had— so, so glad. For the first time, a bit of hope rose up in me.

"Nott!" I said in a stronger voice.

The wolf paused her latest attack for a moment to stop and give me a goofy grin. Then, she was sinking her teeth and claws into another Reaper. Preston was so surprised to see the wolf that he lowered his sword from my side. I started struggling against Preston and the other man who was holding me. If I could just get free of them, I could run off into the woods and escape. Nott was here, and she was ripping through the Reapers like they were paper dolls. In another minute, there wouldn't be enough of them left to stop us from escaping—

A harsh *caw-caw-caw* rang through the treetops, sounding more like a scream than a bird's cry. I barely had time to look up before the Black roc attacked. I hadn't noticed the giant bird, but it must have been sitting in one of the trees during the whole creepy ritual, because it launched itself off a branch and down toward Nott's back, its talons outstretched and ready to tear into her.

The wolf sensed the other creature's attack and snapped her head around, taking a mouthful of feathers out of the roc, which let out another horrible *caw-caw-caw* before flapping up into the sky. Nott eyed the creature as it circled around for another attack. The wolf didn't notice that Vivian had picked up the Helheim Dagger and was creeping around to her blind side.

"Nott!" I screamed, still fighting to break free. "Look out!"

But it was too late. Vivian stabbed the Fenrir wolf in the side with the dagger, then pulled it out and stabbed Nott again. The wolf staggered back, then fell to the stone. Blood was just—*everywhere*. Nott looked at me and let out a low, pain-filled whimper. Tears streamed down my face, and I struggled as hard as I could, but Preston and the other man held me tight.

"Nott!" I screamed. "No! Nott! No!"

The wolf's eyes fluttered once then slowly closed. Blood continued to pour out of the ugly wounds in her side, matting in her dark fur. I kept crying and screaming and fighting, but it was no use. No matter what I did, no matter how I bucked and heaved and kicked and flailed, I couldn't get free of Preston and the other man.

Loki's lips twisted into a disgusted sneer at the sound of my screams. He turned to Vivian. "Shut her up—"

In the distance, a high, piercing note sounded. The bright, sharp sound echoed through the trees, like a clap of thunder rumbling over the land. It was just as loud as Loki's laugh had been earlier, but for some reason, this sound didn't scare me. It gave me—*hope.*

For a moment, all the Reapers froze, even the ones who were writhing and moaning in pain from the damage Nott had done to them.

"The members of the Pantheon!" one of the Reapers hissed. "They've found the safe house already!"

"Let them come," Vivian said, sweeping the dagger back and forth in a vicious arc so that Nott's blood slid off the end of it. "We'll end this war—once and for all."

The note sounded again, even louder and sharper this time. To my surprise, Loki staggered back at the sound, and the god clapped his hands over his ears.

Vivian stared at him, suddenly uncertain. "My lord?"

"It's the Horn of Roland," Loki rasped in a low voice. "After being trapped so long underground, the sound is like . . . daggers in my head."

The horn blasted a third time, and the god let out a shriek of utter agony, his body spasming with pain. One of the Reapers stepped up beside Vivian.

"Quickly," the Reaper said. "Get him on the roc before they blow the horn again. He's still weak, and we can't let them capture him. Not now. Not before he's ready for the transformation."

Transformation? What transformation? What was he talking about?

Vivian let out a sharp whistle, and the Black roc fluttered down to the ground once more. She passed the

Helheim Dagger to Preston and hurried over to the bird. Working quickly, she and the other Reapers put some kind of leather harness on the roc, loaded a still-writhing Loki onto the bird's enormous back, and strapped him down. Were they actually going to—to *ride* the creature? Vivian climbed up in front of the god and took the reins, answering my silent question. She held up the reins and started to slap them down against the bird's wings.

"Wait," Loki rasped. "One . . . more thing . . ."

The god looked down at me, and once more, I felt the full force of his hate, burning into me like I was standing on the surface of the sun.

"Kill the Frost girl," Loki said. "With the dagger. Now, before it's too late."

"Happily," Preston said.

Before I could blink, before I could even scream, Preston raised the Helheim Dagger high and stabbed me in the chest with it.

Chapter 24

For a second, I didn't feel anything.

Then, my brain caught up with the rest of my body. I screamed as Preston plunged the dagger into my chest, and I screamed again as he wrenched it free. The pain was—was—*unbearable*. Unending waves of agony roared through my body, each one a little larger and more awful than the last. I don't remember putting my hands over the wound, but I must have, because suddenly, I could feel the blood spurting out from between my fingers—warm, wet, sticky, and stinking of copper.

White stars exploded in front of my eyes, and the next thing I knew I was on the ground, staring up at Loki, Vivian, and the Black roc they were sitting on.

The evil god stared down at me, and a smile split his grotesque features. On the smooth side of his face, his lips curved up, but on the melted side, they turned down. The sight reminded me of the two faces on Vivian's ring—only much, much uglier.

"Well," Loki said, a harsh note of triumph ringing in

his voice. "That's one problem finally solved. Give my regards to Nike when you see her, little Gypsy. And tell her that it's only a matter of time now before the Pantheon falls and Chaos reigns once more."

Vivian tightened her grip on the Black roc's reins and looked down at Preston.

"Make sure the Gypsy dies, Preston," she ordered. "The rest of you, disappear into the woods. We'll regroup at the second safe house. And see if you can take some members of the Pantheon out along the way."

The other Reapers nodded and slipped into the forest. Vivian slapped the leather reins against the roc's back, and the enormous bird flapped its glossy black wings. The roc swooped up into the air just as easily as it had darted down from the trees. Despite the pain of my wound, I couldn't stop staring at the creature and the people riding it.

Vivian, the girl who'd murdered my mom, and Loki, the evil god I'd just freed against my will.

I don't know if Loki heard my agonized thoughts, but the god leaned over the side of the roc, his Reaper red eye burning into mine. Once again, I felt an emotion radiating off him—one of pure, swelling triumph. As if by ordering my murder, he'd achieved some long-secret dream, some great, final victory.

The evil god's half-melted face was the last thing I saw before the roc disappeared into the night sky.

Preston watched Vivian and Loki vanish into the darkness, a sour expression on his handsome face.

"It should have been me," he muttered. "I should have been chosen to be Loki's Champion. Not *her*."

Preston lashed out with his foot and kicked me in the side. The force of the blow rocked me over onto my stomach, and I moaned as a fresh wave of pain pulsed through my body.

"Well," he said. "At least I had the pleasure of killing you tonight. That's something, I suppose."

Preston crouched down on his knees, a mocking smile on his face. "You're not so tough now, are you, Gypsy? Not so brave and strong when you're not digging through people's memories while they're all chained up. But your pitiful psychometry magic can't help you now, can it?"

But your pitiful psychometry magic can't help you now, can it?

Maybe it was the haze of pain that wrapped around me, but Preston's words echoed through my mind again and again. Something about his words seemed... wrong.

I struggled to try and focus, to figure out what bothered me so much about the Reaper's words now, while I was dying and should be thinking about things like my immortal soul.

It took me a few seconds, but then, I remembered what Grandma Frost and Professor Metis had told me. About how there was more to my psychometry than just touching objects and getting vibes off them.

Your psychometry lets you see people's memories, lets you feel what they feel. Metis's voice rang in my head.

Who's to say that you couldn't reach even deeper inside them? Perhaps even tap into someone's magic while you were fighting him and turn it against him?

I thought about Daphne then, about how I'd been able to feel her healing power in the coliseum and then again in the gym, about how I'd been able to touch her power and feel it flow into my own body if only for a few seconds. Too bad the Valkyrie wasn't here now. I could have reached for her healing magic—

Then, the strangest idea occurred to me. Daphne wasn't here, but Preston *was*.

I thought about it, wondering if I could do the same thing to the Reaper that I'd done to Daphne...if I could touch him and somehow use his magic, his energy, to heal myself. It sounded crazy, but I'd do anything to stop the terrible, unending pain I was feeling—even touch the Reaper one last time.

Preston was right. I was dying. I could feel the life leaking out of me with every drop of blood that oozed over the broken black marble. Crazy or not, I had to try. It was all I could do.

So I drew in a shallow breath, put one trembling hand out on the jagged stone, and pulled myself forward a few inches. Then, I did the same thing with my other hand. It was hard—so freaking *hard*—but I did it anyway. After a few seconds, Preston noticed what I was doing. He let out a dark, ugly laugh.

"Still fighting, Gypsy? Still coming for me? It won't do you any good. That wound I gave you is a mortal one. You'll be dead in a few minutes. The only reason I don't use my sword to take off your head is that I want you to suffer, just like my sister Jasmine suffered when you killed her. Of course, I can't make your pain last nearly as long as it should, but this will do quite nicely."

I didn't bother responding. I didn't have the breath or the energy for it. All I was focused on was Preston. He was crouched down about two feet away from me. The bottoms of his pants had risen when he'd bent down, and I could just see the sliver of his pale ankle showing through the gap between his pant leg and his sock. Closer and closer I crept to the Reaper's foot, leaving smears of blood on the broken stone underneath my body, my eyes fixed on that tiny batch of bare skin.

Preston smiled at my pitiful struggles. Watching me worm my way toward him amused the Reaper. I seized onto that emotion and used it to fuel my own anger at everything that had happened tonight. Vivian's tricking me, freeing Loki, killing Nott.

I almost came undone at that last thought, at the idea that Nott was dead, but then I remembered the wolf's whimper and the way she'd looked at me, like she'd let me down when I was the one who'd failed her instead. Nott had thrown herself into a ring of Reapers to try and save me. The least I could do to repay her sacrifice was try my crazy plan, even if it didn't work. Besides, I had nothing left to lose.

So I gave myself a final push forward, reached out, and wrapped my hand around Preston's ankle—but all I felt was his sock.

The fabric was soft, smooth, and slippery underneath my bloody, grasping fingers, but it wasn't what I needed. I needed to touch his bare skin. I *had* to. That was the way my magic worked—and that was the only way my plan was going to work.

If it worked.

"Gypsy," Preston muttered. "What are you doing? Don't you know these are cashmere socks? And you've just ruined them. I should stab you again just for that."

Openly weeping now, I flailed at his ankle, my nails scratching, trying to pull down his sock so I could wrap my hand around his bare skin.

Preston frowned, as if he realized for the first time that I wasn't just berserk with pain and grief, that I was actually touching him for a reason. "What do you think you're doing—"

With the last spurt of energy I had, I surged forward another inch and shoved his sock down. My fingers closed around the Reaper's ankle, and then I *yanked*.

That was the only word I could think of to describe what I did. Preston's memories and feelings immediately flooded my mind, the way they always did whenever I touched another person. But this time, I pushed those thoughts and feelings aside and went deeper, looking for his magic, looking for the spark that made Preston, well, Preston.

And I found it.

It was harder than it had been with Daphne, so much harder, probably because Preston didn't have the Valkyrie's healing magic. I didn't know exactly what kind of magic the Reaper had, but I could feel it pulsing inside him, an ugly red spark that beat along with every steady pump of his heart. I imagined sticking my hand around his heart and closing my fingers around that energy, that feeling, that spark at the very center of his being. And then I yanked it toward me.

I mentally tugged on his magic, on that strong, pulsing feeling, with everything I had, taking it away from Preston and pulling it into my own body.

For a few seconds, Preston didn't realize what was happening or maybe that's how long it took for it to start working. But suddenly, he let out a ragged breath.

"What are you—what are you doing?"

I ignored the Reaper's questions. Really, I didn't know what I was doing either. All I was aware of was that the pain in my chest had started to ease, and I felt like I could breathe again.

After a few more seconds, the Reaper finally realized that something was seriously wrong. He tried to get to his feet and move away from me, but by that time, I felt strong enough to reach out with my free hand, pull his sock out of the way, and wrap my fingers around his other ankle. Preston jerked up, but his arms windmilled, and he fell back down on his ass on the stone.

The Reaper tried to kick me away, but I dug my nails into his ankles, drawing blood, and held on. I knew that if I let go, if he managed to wrestle away from me, my connection to him would be cut off. I wouldn't be able to touch him—or his magic—anymore, and then I'd die. All the while, I kept tugging and yanking and pulling on his energy, pouring it into my own body, imagining that it was flooding into the stab wound in my heart and pulling all the skin there back together the way it should be, just like I'd seen Daphne heal Carson in the coliseum.

Preston started to scream, but I blocked out the sound. My entire world had shrunk to holding on to the Reaper and using his magic to heal myself.

I don't know how many minutes passed before I noticed that Preston wasn't moving, that the Reaper wasn't fighting me, that he wasn't screaming anymore.

And that the wound in my chest wasn't hurting anymore.

I frowned, wondering what was wrong, wondering why I didn't feel Preston struggling, wondering why I didn't feel the Reaper's energy pouring into me. It was difficult, but I peeled my bloody fingernails from around Preston's ankles. Then, I turned over onto my back, unzipped my hoodie, and pulled up the T-shirt I had on underneath it. Blood coated my chest like I'd painted it for a football game, but the stab wound had healed. All that remained of it was a faint line slashed over my heart.

Somehow I'd done it—I'd used my touch magic to heal myself.

I shoved my shirt down, turned back over onto my stomach, and started crawling toward Preston. I might have healed the dagger wound, but I was still weak, and I had to stop and rest every other breath. But finally, I was able to see the Reaper's face.

Preston's sightless blue eyes stared up at the sky, his mouth twisted in a silent scream.

He was dead, and I finally realized exactly what had

happened. I'd killed the Reaper. I'd killed Preston with my Gypsy gift, used my psychometry magic to suck all the life right out of him.

I slumped to the stone and tried not to cry at the evil thing I'd done—I'd just committed murder.

Chapter 25

I don't know how long I would have lain there if a low whimper hadn't sounded, penetrating my hate, fear, and self-loathing. I looked up to find Nott staring at me, her eyes barely open.

"Nott!"

I crawled over to the Fenrir wolf as fast as I could. Somehow I forced myself to sit up and cradle her enormous head in my lap. The wolf weakly licked my fingers, and I felt her pain pulse through my body. It was even greater than my own had been, so great that I didn't know how she found the strength to keep breathing, to keep fighting. Her rusty eyes were completely dark now and covered by a thin, gray film.

"Don't you worry," I whispered. "I'm going to fix you."

I reached for my magic, but this time, I pushed it outward, trying to heal Nott the way I'd used Preston's energy to heal myself.

It didn't work.

She was too far gone, and I didn't have enough magic. Every bit that I fed her got soaked up immediately, and I could tell it wasn't making a difference. I was exhausted now. I'd barely had enough power to save myself, and Preston was already dead. In that moment, I wished the Reaper had still been alive. I would have dragged him over here and happily murdered him again with my magic if it meant saving Nott.

The wolf licked my fingers again, as if trying to tell me that it was okay, that she knew I'd done my best to save her.

"Nott?" I whispered. "Nott!"

The wolf laid her head down, closed her eyes, and let out what sounded like a happy sigh. Then, she was still—forever.

I put my head down on the wolf's neck and wept.

They found me at dawn, just as the last of the lavender twilight was fading away, and the world was preparing itself for a new day—the first day without Nott. I huddled there on the cold stone, stroking Nott's silky ears with my frostbitten fingers.

Clash-clash-clang!

Screams and shouts echoed through the forest, followed by the ring of blade on blade. Branches snapped and leaves crackled as several Reapers raced into the clearing. They stopped short at the sight of me huddled in the middle of the broken circle, my head still pressed against Nott's cold neck.

"Is that the Gypsy?" one of them said. "The one that Ashton stabbed to death? How is she still alive?"

"I don't know," another one muttered. "But she won't be for much longer."

The Reaper walked over to me and raised his sword high, ready to bring it down on my head—

He jerked, screamed, and arched his back a moment before falling to the ground beside me. A golden arrow quivered in his back. *Daphne,* I thought, and went back to petting Nott.

The other Reapers whirled around, and a moment later, my friends charged into the clearing. Logan carrying a sword, a shield strapped to his arm. Daphne with her onyx bow and quiver. Oliver, Kenzie, Metis, Nickamedes, and Ajax, all carrying weapons. Even Carson was here, clutching a staff and an ivory horn that reminded me of a miniature tuba, the same horn he'd picked up at the coliseum, the one that Daphne had said kept appearing in his room no matter how many times he gave it back to Metis. *The Horn of Roland,* I thought. That's what Loki had called it.

"Gwen?" Logan shouted, swinging his sword at the Reaper closest to him. "Gwen!"

I didn't raise my head, and I didn't respond to him. I just kept stroking Nott's ears. Nothing else mattered but that.

Clash-clash-clang!

The battle raged in the circle all around me, but it seemed distant and far away. The curses, the shouts, the smash of steel against steel. It was like a dim dream. Eventually, though, as my friends fought their way closer to the center of the circle, I began to make out their voices through the noise and chaos.

"Get out of the way, Spartan!" I heard Daphne snap. "Unless you want me to put an arrow in your back!"

"No!" Logan shouted back at her. "I have to get to Gwen before it's too late! I won't let her die like I did my mom and sister!"

I frowned. That wasn't right, I thought. Logan hadn't let his family die. He'd been a kid when the Reapers had murdered them. There was nothing he could have done to save them. If he'd tried, he would have been killed, too.

The sound of Logan's voice made me blink and raise my head. The Spartan froze when he realized that I was staring at him.

"Gwen?" he said in a shocked voice. "Gwen!"

Logan was so surprised that he did something I'd never thought he'd do—he stopped fighting. The Reaper he'd been battling raised his sword, ready to press this unexpected advantage. Panic rose up in my chest, breaking through the cold fog that clouded my mind. Logan was going to die because of me—just like Nott had.

I started to scream out a warning, but Nickamedes stepped forward, putting himself between Logan and the Reaper. The librarian parried the blow meant for his nephew, then drove his sword into the Reaper's chest. Logan pulled his eyes away from me and started fighting again.

A minute later, the battle was over, and all the Reapers were dead. My friends hurried over to me, stepping over the bodies that littered the cracked black stone.

"Gwen?" Logan said. "Are you all right?"

The Spartan stared at me, an anguished look on his face, but all I could see was the blood on him. It covered his sword, his shield, and his hands like a coat of fresh, glossy paint. Blood had even spattered onto his face, looking like crimson tears dripping from the corners of his blue, blue eyes.

My gaze moved past him. Daphne, Carson, Oliver, Kenzie, Metis, Nickamedes, Ajax. All of them were covered with blood—so much blood. They'd fought their way through the Reapers to get to me, someone who didn't deserve their friendship.

Someone who didn't deserve anything at all.

"Gwen?" Logan asked again, his voice dropping to a whisper. "What happened? Are you okay?"

"It was Vivian," I said in a dull tone. "It was Vivian the whole time. She has telepathy magic, illusion, confusion, and chaos powers. She tricked me into finding the Helheim Dagger for her, then used it and my blood to open a portal to Loki's prison. He's free. Loki's free, and Nott's dead."

I kept stroking the wolf's cold ears. "Poor Nott. She barely got a chance to live, you know? To be free. And now she's gone, all because of me. It's all my fault. My mom's murder, Vivian's freeing Loki, everything. You shouldn't have come for me. You should have just let the Reapers kill me. *I* should have let Preston kill me."

Logan stared at the others, then put down his sword and took off his shield. The Spartan dropped down on his knees beside me. He hesitated, then stretched out his arms, like he was going to hug me.

"Don't touch me!" I screamed, lurching away from him. "Don't you dare touch me!"

Confusion and hurt filled Logan's face, but he reached for me again. Somehow I was able to get to my feet and stumble away from the Spartan.

"Keep your distance!" I screamed, whirling around. "All of you! Don't come near me!"

This time, Daphne stepped forward, her eyes full of worry. "Gwen? Just calm down, okay? Nobody's going to hurt you now. We're your friends. We're here to help you."

I let out a bitter laugh. "It's not you that I'm worried about. It's *me*."

"Did the Reapers—did the Reapers hurt you?" Oliver asked in a low voice.

I laughed again, a little louder and harsher this time. "Yes, yes, they did. Vivian cut my palm open to the bone, and Preston stabbed me in the chest with the Helheim Dagger."

"But you look . . . okay," Oliver said in a hesitant tone, as if he wasn't sure it was really true. He glanced at the others for some kind of help, but they all looked just as shocked and uncertain as he did.

"Oh, sure," I said. "I'm fine now. Because I did that to Preston."

The others looked at the dead Reaper lying on the cold marble.

"What happened to him?" Carson asked. "I don't see any wounds on his body."

"What happened to him? I *killed* him, Carson. With my touch magic. My power that's so very rare and so very special. I just grabbed hold of Preston, and I pulled all his energy, all his magic, all his freaking *life,* into my own body. To heal myself, to save myself. Some kind of Champion, I am, huh?"

The band geek stared at me, his mouth open in a silent O.

I turned to Metis, my gaze harsh and accusatory. "You told me that I could influence other people and objects with my psychometry. You never said anything about killing them. You never said anything about *that.*"

"It'll be okay, Gwen," Metis said, slowly walking toward me. "It'll be okay. You'll see. We'll figure everything out. All that matters now is that you're safe."

I looked up at the sky, as if I could somehow see Vivian, Loki, and the Black roc they'd flown away on.

"None of us is safe," I muttered. "Not anymore."

As suddenly as it had come, all the fight and energy left my body. My knees buckled, and Logan's face was the last thing I saw before I passed out.

Chapter 26

Metis used her magic to heal me, and I woke up a few minutes later, still lying close to Nott. The next few hours passed in a haze of tears. Despite my demands to stay away from me, my friends put me on a stretcher and carried me out of the woods. They did the same for Nott, too, without my even asking.

They took me to Grandma Frost's house. I told my grandma the same thing I had the others—not to touch me. But of course, she didn't listen.

"You're my granddaughter," she said in a sharp voice. "You would never hurt me."

Then, Grandma cradled my bloody face in her hands, and I felt the warmth of her love wash over me, stronger than ever before. And I wept again.

Finally, I went upstairs to the bathroom, but instead of getting in the shower, I stared at myself in the bathroom mirror. My brown hair was matted and snarled, my clothes were ripped, and black smudges of exhaustion ringed my haunted violet eyes. Even my snowflake necklace seemed dull and tarnished around my throat. There was blood all over the silver strands—my blood, Nott's blood. I took it off and left it on the bathroom counter. I'd been so happy when Logan had given me the necklace, but right now, I couldn't stand to look at it. I couldn't stand to look at myself.

I took a hot shower and cleaned up, but really, I was just going through the motions. I sat at the table in Grandma Frost's kitchen, listening to the story of how the others had found me. Apparently, I had Morgan McDougall to thank for my rescue. She'd been skirting around the edge of the quad, going back to her dorm room for the night, and had seen the Reaper girl carrying my body away. Morgan had followed the Reaper girl all the way to one of the academy gates, where she had removed her mask, showing Morgan who she really was. When Morgan realized that Vivian was taking me off campus, she'd called Professor Metis and raised the alarm. Metis and the others had eventually realized that Vivian had taken me to her family's nearby estate and had fought their way through dozens of Reapers who had gathered in the mansion and on the grounds.

After Metis finished the story about Morgan, the professor and I went into the bathroom, and Metis once again examined my hand and chest where I'd been stabbed. But both wounds were completely healed, except for the thin white lines that marred my skin. Metis tried to get rid of those as well, but no matter how much of her healing energy she poured into me, the marks didn't fade away. She thought it was because they'd been made with the Helheim Dagger. Metis said that powerful artifacts like that could sometimes leave behind scars that would never heal.

Just like my heart would never, ever heal. I didn't need the scars to remind me of what had happened. I'd never forget it, and I'd never stop blaming myself for everything, for all my many miserable failures.

Late that morning, we buried Nott in my grandma's backyard, right next to a lilac bush that was bare and brown for the winter. Logan and Oliver volunteered to dig the grave, and I insisted on helping, even though I wanted nothing more than to curl up in bed and never come out again. Metis, Ajax, Nickamedes, and Grandma Frost came outside to pay their respects to Nott, along with Daphne, Carson, and Kenzie.

"Should we say something?" Oliver asked me in a quiet voice when we were through.

I stared down at the mound of loose, turned earth and shook my head. I would have liked to have said something, to talk about how gentle Nott was deep down inside, but my throat closed up, and I just couldn't get the words out. Grandma Frost squeezed my hand, and everyone else gave me sympathetic looks and said how sorry they were. Then, one by one, the adults and my friends went back inside, until only Logan, Grandma Frost, and I were left outside.

"I'll give you two a few minutes," Grandma finally said, squeezing my hand again before she headed into the house.

Logan and I stood there next to Nott's grave. The Spartan raised his arm like he wanted to put it around me but dropped it to his side instead. Besides Metis and Grandma Frost, no one else had touched me, and I didn't want them to.

I never wanted anyone to touch me again. Not after what I'd done to Preston. Not when I finally knew exactly what I was capable of.

I don't know how long we stood there, but the air turned colder, and fat flakes of snow started drifting down from the winter-white sky. The flakes gathered in my hair and mixed with the tears trickling down my cheeks. They still weren't as cold as my heart was, though.

"I'm a coward, Gwen," Logan said, breaking the silence.

That was the last thing I'd expected him to say, and I turned to stare at him.

"You're not a coward," I said. "I saw how you fought the Reapers in the clearing, and Ajax told me how you led everyone into battle against the ones at the mansion. He's so proud of you for that. So is Nickamedes."

Logan sighed. "I didn't mean today. I meant when I was a kid—the day my mom and older sister were murdered. That's my big secret, Gwen. That's what I never wanted you to find out. How much of a coward I was that day."

He hesitated, then stepped forward. I tried to jerk away, but Logan gently captured my face in his hands. He stared into my eyes, and the memory washed over me.

Logan as a young boy, hiding in a closet, clutching a

sword, terrified by the screams and curses he heard out-side the door. Then, the Spartan standing over the dead, bloody bodies of his mother and older sister. Logan lying in between them as the tears and grief over-whelmed him.

I'd seen these same images once before when I'd kissed Logan, but he kept his hands on my face, letting me go deeper into the memory, letting me feel his emo-tions, finally showing me his secret.

I saw it all through his eyes. Him playing outside with his toy sword, pretending that he was battling Reapers. Then, Logan actually seeing a group of black-robed Reapers climb over the stone wall at the edge of the woods. Logan running inside and yelling out a warning to his mom and older sister. His mom screaming back at Logan and his sister to hide. Then, the Reapers storm-ing into the house, his mom and sister stepping up to fight them, even though they knew they couldn't win. Logan wanting to help his family but instead turning and running deeper into the house . . .

Logan hated himself because he'd been scared that day. Spartans were the best fighters, the toughest war-riors. They weren't supposed to be scared or run away from a battle—ever.

Logan's self-loathing poured into me, making me feel sick to my stomach. Guilt, shame, disgust, fear. The Spartan felt all of those things because he'd run away and hidden in a closet instead of fighting the Reapers like his mom and sister had, like he was training to, like he wanted to. Part of him felt things would have been better if he'd at least tried to protect his family, even if he would have died along with them.

"Do you see?" Logan whispered. "Do you finally see what a coward I was? How I let my family die just to save myself?"

I shook my head and stepped back. His hands fell away from my face, breaking our connection. "You're not a coward. You were five years old when it happened. If you'd tried to fight them, they would have killed you, too, Logan. You have to know that. Your mom knew it. That's why she yelled at you and your sister to hide. She wanted you to be safe, even if it meant your leaving her behind. No doubt your sister felt the same way, that she had to help your mom protect you."

The Spartan gave me a sad smile. "Maybe that's true, but that's not how it feels to me. I feel like I let them down, like I let myself down. On that day, I vowed that I'd become the very best fighter I could be so I could protect other people. So I could stop the Reapers from killing someone else's family and the people I care about. The people I love."

The words hung in the air between us, seeming to drift up and down on the wind, along with the crystalline snowflakes. My heart soared at the Spartan's words, breaking free of my chest and swirling up into the sky. Logan cared about me just as much as I did him. He loved me just as much as I did him. For a moment, everything was bright and beautiful and perfect.

Then I realized that I didn't deserve Logan's love—not anymore.

Logan looked at me with such hope in his eyes, such intense longing. It took all the strength I had to turn away from him and shut out the happiness I felt at his confession.

The Spartan sighed. "I thought that's what you had realized when you told me you'd seen me standing over my mom and sister. That you'd seen just what a coward I really was. What you think about me matters—it matters a lot. That's why I was so upset that night in the library. That's why I said all those horrible things to you. Do you think you can forgive me, Gypsy girl?"

"There's nothing to forgive," I said. "I don't think you're a coward, Logan. I think you're one of the strongest, bravest people I know."

The Spartan put his arms around me, and I felt his breath kiss my cheek. But even that wasn't enough to drive away the cold that had seized my body, especially when I realized that his hands were perilously close to touching mine again. The image of Preston's dead face filled my mind, and my chest tightened with panic.

"Let go of me," I said. "Let go!"

Logan immediately dropped his arms and stepped back. "What's wrong? What did I do?"

I shook my head, trying to slow the rapid, painful beat of my heart. "Nothing. You didn't do anything wrong. It's me. It's always been me and my stupid psychometry magic."

The Spartan frowned, confusion filling his eyes. He didn't understand, and I didn't know how to explain that I was scared of hurting him just like I had Preston. Logan would insist that it wasn't possible, but the Spartan hadn't seen what I'd done to Preston; he hadn't felt Preston's panic and fear like I had. He didn't know that I'd ignored Preston's fear, and worse, that part of me had actually *liked* the way it had felt, that part of me had actually *enjoyed* the power I had over the other boy in that moment. Logan just didn't realize what I was capable of, and I never wanted him to find out.

Maybe that made me the real coward with my own secret to hide now.

"I'm sorry, Logan," I finally said. "Just—leave me alone. Please?"

I turned and ran back into the house before he could reach for me again.

Soon after that, everyone left to go back to the academy. I wanted to stay with Grandma Frost, but Metis insisted that I return to the academy, too, until she and the other members of the Pantheon could figure out how Loki's escape was going to affect us all.

"It's the safest place right now for you, Gwen," Metis said in a gentle voice. "Don't worry. I've arranged for some members of the Pantheon to come here and guard Geraldine."

So I went, even though I didn't really want to. I was back on campus by three o'clock. I stood outside the door that led to my dorm room, thinking how normal it looked, how normal everything looked. I wondered if I would ever feel normal again, if I would ever feel safe or happy again. The door was open, probably from where Nott had left my room to come find me. My heart ached at the thought of the wolf. I wondered if it would ever quit hurting, if I would ever quit hurting over everything that had happened.

"Gwen?" Daphne asked. "Do you want me to stay with you?"

The Valkyrie's words penetrated my daze. Daphne had walked up to my room with me, even though I'd insisted that I could make it by myself.

I shook my head. "I just need to be alone right now. Okay?"

Daphne didn't like it, but she nodded and bit her lip. My friend carefully put her arms around me and gave me a hug, just like the others had done. They'd all hugged or touched me before we'd left Grandma Frost's house, as if that would convince me I wasn't a threat to them. But nothing would do that—not now.

Daphne tried to be gentle with her hug, but her great Valkyrie strength still cracked my back. I stood absolutely still, careful not to let any part of my bare skin touch hers. Finally, she dropped her arms and stepped back.

"Call me later, okay?" Daphne asked in a worried voice.

I nodded, although I had no intention of doing that. I had no intention of doing anything. What was the point? I'd made such a mess of everything. Loki was free, and soon, he and his Reapers of Chaos would take over the world and kill and enslave the rest of us. What was the point in trying anymore?

I'd never felt so miserable in my entire life, and I knew I deserved to. This was my fault—all my fault. If only I'd realized what Vivian was up to, if I'd just left the dagger hidden where it was, it would have been safe, and Loki would still be trapped in his prison. Instead, I'd unleashed the evil god on the entire world. I wasn't Gwen Frost, that Gypsy girl who saw things. Not anymore. Now, I was just Gwen Frost, epic, epic failure.

Daphne left, and I stepped into my room and slung my messenger bag down on the floor. For the second time this week, Metis had brought the bag to Grandma Frost's house. I reached into the bag and drew out Vic, who was still sheathed in his black leather scabbard. I'd never even had a chance to use him against Vivian and the other Reapers. Some warrior whiz kid I was.

Vic's eye snapped open, and he regarded me for several long seconds. "It's not your fault, Gwen. None of this is your fault. Even Champions are not infallible."

Even Vic was being nice to me, which let me know just how royally I'd screwed up.

"Thanks, Vic," I mumbled and hung the sword on his spot on the wall.

The sword kept looking at me, and I flopped down onto the bed to avoid his steady stare. Loki, Vivian, Preston, Nott, Logan. All the images from the last day swirled through my mind, adding to my guilt. I don't know how long I would have lain there staring up at the pointed ceiling if a soft, familiar whimper hadn't caught my attention.

"Nott?" I whispered, sitting up.

The room was empty.

Then, I remembered. Nott was gone, and I'd seen the wolf die, held her in my arms while it happened. It was just my imagination, just my Gypsy gift playing a cruel,

cruel trick on me. I started to lie back down on the bed when the whimper sounded again.

I looked around the room again and noticed something moving in the pile of blankets that Nott had been sleeping on. It looked small, but I still grabbed Vic. Then, I tiptoed over to the blankets, leaned down, and carefully pulled one of them back.

A newborn wolf pup whimpered up at me.

My mouth dropped open, and all I could do was just stand there and stare at it. How—why—when—My jumbled thoughts didn't make any sense, but the answer finally came to me.

"Nott," I whispered.

The wolf must have had her pup while I'd been kidnapped. Then, somehow, someway, she'd sensed that something was wrong and had come after me. Grandma Frost had said the wolf and I had some kind of connection, but I'd never expected this.

In my hand, Vic's eye narrowed as he peered down at the wolf.

"Great," the sword muttered. "Just bloody great. Now, there's another one of them."

"Shut up, Vic," I said, putting the sword down and going back over to the pup.

The wolf pup had fuzzy, ash-gray fur and looked like it weighed maybe two pounds. Since I didn't know what else to do, I tentatively stretched my hand out toward it. I didn't know if it could smell me or not, if it had any idea who I was or what had happened to its mom, but the pup nestled its head under my hand and licked my fingers. All sorts of feelings flashed through my mind. The pup was confused and scared and hungry.

They were some of the most beautiful emotions I'd ever felt.

The feelings smashed at the cold, hard shell that had coated my heart ever since Nott had died, cracking it wide open. A smile spread across my face, and tears streamed down my cheeks. I wrapped the pup back up in the blanket, then fumbled for my phone. I was too excited to text, so I hit the number on my speed dial. She picked up on the second ring.

"Hello?"

"Grandma!" I shrieked. "You'll never guess what's happened!"

"Pumpkin?" Grandma Frost asked. "Are you okay? What's going on?"

I started to answer her, but that's when the wolf pup opened its eyes for the briefest second, for the barest moment of time. What I saw took my breath away and made me wonder if I was dreaming. The phone slipped from my fingers and thumped to the floor.

"Gwen? Gwen!" Grandma's voice rang out through the phone, but I wasn't paying attention to her anymore.

Instead, I was looking at the wolf. Once again, the pup opened its eyes for just a split second. I hadn't been wrong before, and I wasn't just imagining things.

The pup's eyes were the same color as Vic's—the soft color of twilight.

*   *   *

"A Fenrir wolf pup," Professor Metis said in wonder an hour later. "I've never seen one of them before."

Metis was in my room, along with Coach Ajax, and the three of us were staring at the wolf. Metis had brought over a cardboard box, which I'd lined with blankets. The professor had let me feed the pup using a bottle full of milk, and now, the pup—a girl—was sleeping. I reached down and stroked the wolf's tiny ears, and the pup's contentment filled my mind.

"Do you suppose that's why Nott came here?" I asked. "So I could take care of it? Do you think she knew she was going to die?"

Ajax shrugged his massive shoulders. "The world and the gods work in mysterious ways, Gwen. But Nott left something of herself behind, and we'll take good care of it. You can count on that."

"Hmph," Vic harrumphed from his spot up on the wall. "It's going to be a lot of trouble if you ask me, and it will shed *everywhere*."

I glared at Vic and started to tell him to be quiet again, when I realized that the sword's face had softened and that there was a gleam of a tear in his eye.

"I suppose the little bugger is kind of cute, though. At least for something covered in fur," Vic mumbled.

He sniffed a few times, and I got the impression that he would have reached up and wiped the tear out of his eye if he, you know, actually had had a hand to do that with. So I grabbed a tissue out of the box on my desk and dabbed at the sword's eye with it.

Vic smiled at me, and then the two of us turned our attention to the wolf pup once more.

"What are you going to name her?" Metis said.

I thought about it for a second. "Nyx."

"The Greek goddess of the night?" Ajax asked.

I nodded. "Yes, because she came out of the darkness just like Nott did."

In the box, the pup stirred a little, almost as if she could hear the sound of her mom's name, even though Metis had said that the wolf would be blind and deaf for at least a few days.

I kept right on stroking her tiny, silky ears, though, just like Nott would have wanted me to.

Chapter 27

I stayed with Nyx for the rest of the day, marveling at how small and perfect she was. Daphne and Carson came over, too, and the three of us just sat there looking at the pup. I thought about calling Logan, but every time I picked up the phone, Preston's face filled my mind instead. I just couldn't get over my fear I'd do the same thing to Logan that I had to the Reaper.

But there was something else I had to do, so I asked my friends to feed Nyx again while I went out for a while.

I walked across campus to the Library of Antiquities. Everything was normal inside. Students laughed, talked, and gossiped on the first floor, while Raven sold snacks and drinks at her coffee cart. Nickamedes stood behind the checkout counter, helping Mrs. Banba find some reference material. He, Metis, and Ajax had decided to go about their daily routines and pretend everything was normal until they heard from the Powers That Were on how they wanted to handle the news of Loki's escape.

I noticed the librarian staring at me, but I ignored him and climbed the stairs to the second floor. I stopped and looked down at all the kids studying below. They had no idea how much their world had changed overnight. I thought of the attack a few days ago at the Crius Coliseum. There'd been so much death, destruction, and deception already. And now, it would only get worse since Loki was free. There was a war coming—a war I had no idea how we were going to win.

I walked around the circular balcony until I came to a particular statue in the Pantheon—Nike, the Greek goddess of victory. She looked the same as always, although her face seemed to be a little sad today, with the corners of her mouth turned down instead of up. I wondered if it was because I'd failed her so miserably.

"I'm sorry," I said, tears filling my eyes once again. "So sorry. For everything."

I stood there, hoping the goddess would respond to me, but of course, she didn't. The gods only appeared to mortals on their terms. Still, I knew that Nike would come to me again, so I sat down beside the statue to wait.

I don't know how long I sat there, waiting for Nike to move, to blink, to speak, to just do something, anything to let me know that all hope wasn't lost.

But nothing happened.

Down below, Nickamedes announced that the library was closing for the night, and the few students remaining inside packed up their things and left. Not wanting to spend the night trapped in the library, I got to my feet, trooped down the steps, and headed toward the double doors on the first floor. I was just about to step through them when a voice called out behind me.

"Gwendolyn? A moment, please."

I sighed and turned around. Nickamedes stood behind me, holding something in his hand. He gestured at me, and I walked over toward him.

"What?" I mumbled. "Going to lecture me about what a mess I've made of everything? You don't have to. Trust me, I know how bad things are right now."

Nickamedes shook his head. "No, Gwendolyn, I'm not going to lecture you. I think you held up remarkably well, all things considered. I don't know that I would have been as brave as you were."

I blinked. The librarian never complimented me— *never*. I'd thought he'd rant and rave about how I'd pretty much doomed the entire world, since that was exactly what I'd done. Instead, the librarian gestured for me to take a seat at one of the study tables. Bewildered, I did as he asked, and Nickamedes pulled out a chair and sat across from me. It occurred to me that this was the first time the librarian hadn't stared down his nose at me. But instead of looking at me, he kept his eyes on the thin piece of paper in his hand, like it was the most important thing he'd ever seen.

Finally, Nickamedes cleared his throat. "A few days ago, you asked me why I hated you so much."

"And now you're going to tell me? Terrific," I muttered.

The librarian shook his head. "No, I'm not going to tell you because I don't hate you, Gwendolyn. I never have."

"Then what's with all the attitude every time I come in here? Because you sure act like you hate me."

Nickamedes sighed. "It's . . . complicated."

"Most things are at Mythos," I said in a snide tone.

I would have said something else snarky if I hadn't noticed the pained look on the librarian's face. "What's the matter? What have I done wrong this time?"

Nickamedes finally looked up at me. "Nothing. You haven't done anything wrong, but I admit that it's been . . . difficult for me to work with you, Gwendolyn. And your perpetual tardiness isn't the only reason."

He drew in another breath. "I knew your mother, you see. Back when we both went to Mythos. We were actually quite good friends, Grace, Aurora, and I."

Nickamedes flipped over the piece of paper he'd been clutching, and I realized that it was actually a photo— one of my mom, Metis, and Nickamedes sitting on the library steps, laughing about something.

My breath caught in my throat. "Where—where did you get that?"

"It slipped out of your mother's diary when you dropped your bag in the library a few nights ago," he said. "The photo slid underneath one of the tables. I tried to give it back to you then, but you'd already left."

So that's what he'd been calling out to me about that night. I'd thought he'd just wanted to gloat about Logan's dumping me.

"You were friends with my mom?" I asked. "Really?"

He nodded, and a smile curved his lips. "Really. Grace, Aurora, and I were as thick as thieves. We had big dreams back then, you see, of how we were going to take on the Reapers and change the world, how we were going to make it safe for all the other warriors out there, so that maybe we wouldn't have to be warriors anymore."

"What happened?" I asked, sensing the story didn't have a happy ending.

Nickamedes shrugged. "We did fight Reapers, the whole time we were at Mythos, and Grace and Aurora were chosen as Champions. But then, things started to change. We all started to change. By the time graduation rolled around, we weren't the same people that we were in this photo. Your mother was . . . tired. Tired of fighting Reapers, tired of being a Champion, tired of all the blood and death and responsibility."

I knew exactly how she had felt. I'd only been Nike's Champion for a few months, but it seemed that no matter what I did, no matter how hard I fought, the Reapers just kept coming and coming and coming. And now, with Loki free, it would only get worse—so much worse.

"Anyway, right before graduation, your mother and I . . . argued," Nickamedes continued. "I wanted to join up with other members of the Pantheon. The Pantheon has its own police force, you see, with members stationed all over the world, dedicated to finding Reapers and putting them in prison where they belong. Joining their ranks had been my dream as long as I'd been at Mythos. It had been Grace's dream, too."

"But she changed," I said, picking up on his feelings. "And she didn't want to fight anymore, did she? After graduation."

Nickamedes shook his head. "No, and I couldn't understand why, since she was a Champion, since she had so much power, so much magic. I said some things to her. . . . Well, let's just say they weren't very nice. Basically, I called her a quitter and told her that she didn't deserve to be Nike's Champion."

I winced. "Sounds kind of harsh to me."

Nickamedes gave me a sad smile. "It was, and I regret it more than you'll ever know. We went our separate ways after graduation. Eventually, I decided to come back here and look after the artifacts in the library."

"And my mom became a cop in the mortal world."

"I guess she fulfilled our dream in a way after all," Nickamedes said. "I thought about her quite often, wondering where she was and what had become of her, if she was living the Reaper-free life she'd wanted. Then one day last spring, Aurora came to me and told me that Grace had been murdered. That she had a daughter and that you were going to start attending Mythos in the fall. I immediately told Aurora that I wanted you to work here in the library with me."

I frowned. "But why? Why would you do that?"

Especially given how you've treated me. I didn't say the words, but they hung in the air between us, angry and unspoken.

"Because you're Grace's daughter," Nickamedes said in a quiet voice. "And I loved your mother very much."

The revelation stunned me. Uptight, prissy Nickamedes and my—my—*mom*. Together? As a couple? In love? It didn't make any sense. Then again, I supposed Logan and I didn't make much sense either. The fierce Spartan warrior and the Gypsy girl who was just learning how to fight.

"I'm sorry I've acted the way I have toward you," Nickamedes said. "Our breakup was rather . . . messy, as you can imagine. I'd thought I'd gotten over your mother, or at least gotten over my anger at her for leaving, but then you came to Mythos. And you look so much like her, especially when you smile. More than that, you're smart and strong, just like she was too."

The librarian's face softened, and for a moment, I got a glimpse of what he had been like when he was younger—of the guy my mom had fallen for all those years ago. Then, Nickamedes cleared his throat again, and the image vanished.

"I suppose I've been taking my anger at your mother out on you, Gwendolyn, and that's not fair. I wanted to apologize for that. It won't happen again."

I didn't say anything. I didn't know what *to* say. Nickamedes loving my mom; my mom wanting a normal life; my mom quitting as Nike's Champion. It was a lot to take in, and a thousand different questions filled my mind.

"Anyway," Nickamedes said. "I thought you should know why I've treated you the way I have, and I wanted you to have this."

He held out the picture, and my fingers trembled as I took it. My psychometry kicked in immediately, and I felt all the things my mom and Nickamedes had, since they'd both handled the photo. Mainly, I got flashes of my mom's fond memories and her aching regret over the way things had ended between the two of them. They were the same feelings Nickamedes had, although his were now mixed with the determination to do right by me—to protect me the same way Metis had sworn she would.

"Thank you for this, but I think you need it more than I do." I held the photo out to him. "Keep it as a re-minder of my mom. I think she'd want that."

Nickamedes nodded and took back the picture. His fingers lingered on my mom's face, and I could tell he was thinking about her again and wishing things had been different between them. Finally, the librarian raised his gaze to mine once more, his blue eyes that were so much like Logan's.

"And now, for the last thing I wanted to say to you tonight. You can't give up, Gwendolyn," Nickamedes said. "You have to keep on fighting just like the rest of us do."

I sighed. "What's the point? Loki's free because of me. Because I failed to protect the Helheim Dagger, he and the other Reapers are going to kill people. You know, start another Chaos War, plunge the world into eternal darkness, that sort of thing."

I'd been kind of out of it back in the forest, but I knew that Oliver had found the dagger beside Preston's body. I had no idea what would happen to the artifact now. Maybe the Powers That Were would put it on display here in the Library of Antiquities as a reminder of my epic failure.

"You listen to me, Gwendolyn Cassandra Frost," Nickamedes said in a sharp tone.

I blinked, wondering how the librarian knew my middle name, but I decided not to ask him since he was glaring at me—*again*.

"You're Nike's Champion just like your mother was before you," the librarian snapped. "And I will not have Grace Frost's good name dragged through the mud because you're too busy moping and brooding to do what needs to be done. There's a war coming, and we're going to do our best to win it, which means you need to start polishing up that talking sword of yours. Do you understand me?"

Maybe it was Nickamedes's prissy tone or the fierce look on his face. Or maybe it was because I'd felt all the same things he did for my mom—all the love and all the aching regret. But for this moment, this one instant, he gave me a flicker of hope that maybe it wasn't too late. That maybe we could figure out a way to defeat Loki after all.

That maybe I could actually kill the god, like I was supposed to.

"I understand," I said.

"Good," Nickamedes said.

Our talk was over. I got to my feet, and Nickamedes did the same. I told him good night, then turned and headed out of the library.

"And don't be late for your shift tomorrow!" the librarian called out just as I stepped through the double doors.

Instead of annoying me, his words actually made me smile. It was comforting to know that no matter how bad things got, some things would never, ever change.

Chapter 28

I left the library and walked down the steps. I stopped a moment to stare at the gryphon statue, the one that had protected the Helheim Dagger for so long.

"I'm sorry," I whispered. "I failed you."

Maybe it was just a trick of the moonlight, but it seemed that the gryphon dipped its head in disappointment. I sighed once more. Despite Nickamedes's pep talk, there was no getting over the fact that things had not gone well the past twenty-four hours. Not well at all.

I turned to look back at the library a final time—and that's when I saw her.

She stood at the top of the library stairs, perfectly framed by a slice of moonlight. Bronze hair flowed down past her shoulders, the thick waves matching the folds of the white, toga-like gown that covered her lean, strong body. Her face was as beautiful as ever, although her features looked as cold as marble in the darkness. I focused on her eyes—eyes that weren't quite purple but not really gray either. Even now, here, they reminded me of the color of twilight.

"Nike," I whispered.

"Hello, Gwendolyn," the goddess said.

The Greek goddess of victory glided down the steps to me, her feet barely seeming to touch the stone. Her wings arced up over her back like the two halves of a heart, the feathers ruffling with her elegant, graceful movements. As the goddess neared me, I once again felt her power—the cold, beautiful, terrible power that rolled off her body in unending, unstoppable waves.

"Hello, Gwendolyn," Nike said again, giving me a soft smile.

The goddess's serene expression didn't comfort me. Not at all. Not after I'd failed her so miserably.

I swallowed. "I suppose you're here to take back Vic and that you'll take my magic away, too, while you're at it and give it to someone else. Someone who deserves it."

She frowned. "Why ever would I do that?"

I swallowed again, but I just couldn't seem to get rid of the tight knot that clogged my throat. "Because I failed you," I whispered. "Because I wasn't able to hide the dagger again. Because Vivian used it and my blood to free Loki. Because now, he's going to plunge the world into a second Chaos War. Because people are going to die, and it's all my fault."

I couldn't stop the tears from sliding down my cheeks again. "All my fault."

"Oh, Gwendolyn," Nike said, moving forward. "It's

not your fault. This was what was always going to happen."

I frowned. "I don't understand. How is Loki's getting free what was always going to happen? Did you—did you know about all this? That the Reapers would find the dagger and free him in the end?"

The goddess slowly nodded her head, her eyes steady on mine.

Confusion filled me. "But—but *why?* Why would you let that happen? If you knew that I was going to fail, then why would you tell me to look for the dagger? Why not let it stay hidden? If you knew I wouldn't succeed, why didn't you pick someone else to be your Champion?"

Instead of answering my questions, Nike settled herself on the stone steps, right in between the two gryphon statues. She arranged her gown over her knees, then patted the step beside her, her fingers leaving faint marks in the dark frost that had already gathered there. Bewildered, I sank down next to the goddess, careful not to touch her. Nike might claim that she wasn't going to strip me of my magic or incinerate me on the spot, but she could always change her mind.

"What your myth-history books don't tell you is that Loki's prison was always meant to be a temporary solution," Nike said. "But time has a different meaning to mortals than it does to gods, and as the centuries passed, and Loki remained imprisoned, most members of the Pantheon thought that meant he was gone for good—that he would stay imprisoned until the end of time itself."

"Okay," I said, trying to understand. "So the other gods' trapping Loki wasn't meant to last forever but was more like putting duct tape on something until you can get it fixed for good. But why tell me to find the dagger? What good did that do?"

"It was a necessary part of the chain of events," Nike said.

I stared at the goddess. "Necessary? What was *necessary* about all this? I almost died, and I killed someone in the process, using the magic *you* gave me. And Samson and the other kids at the coliseum and Nott *did* die. What was the point of all that? Of all that pain?"

Nike gave me a sad look. "Pain is a part of life, Gwendolyn, for mortals and gods alike."

"We're all just game pieces to you, aren't we?" I muttered in a bitter voice. "Little dolls you can move around and play with however you like."

Suddenly, I knew why my mom had quit being Nike's Champion. I could imagine exactly how she felt, day after day, year after year, fighting against the Reapers, trying to do the right thing but having no clue as to what the gods where really up to behind her back or how it would impact her. No wonder my mom had left Mythos Academy and the mythological world it represented far behind. No freaking wonder.

"Your mother felt that way, too," Nike said, almost like she could hear my thoughts. "She felt as though I was using her to reach certain ends."

"Were you?"

The goddess gave me a wry smile. "It is a difficult

business, trying to save the world. Some people must make sacrifices so that others can live and prosper."

"But why me? Why do *I* have to be the one to make sacrifices?"

"Because you're strong enough to make them, Gwendolyn," Nike said. "You're strong enough to keep going no matter how dark and hopeless things get, even if you don't think you are. You could have given up when the Reaper stabbed you. Most people would have. But instead, you figured out a way to save yourself. That makes you very smart and very, very strong. That's why the Reapers fear you—that's why Loki himself fears you."

I seriously doubted that Loki feared anything, especially me, but I didn't argue with the goddess. We sat there in silence for several moments, watching the moon and clouds wisp across the night sky. Finally, Nike spoke again.

"Now, you have a decision to make, Gwendolyn—whether or not you wish to continue on as my Champion."

I eyed the goddess. "You'd actually let me quit? Just like that? Why? You're a goddess. I can feel the power you have. I imagine you could make me do anything you wanted me to."

"I could make you carry on as my Champion, but your heart wouldn't be in it, and you would soon come to hate me for it. You have free will, Gwendolyn, just like every creature, mortal, and god does. Remember that, because it's the most important thing I'll ever tell you. Never forget that, because it's the very thing Loki

and his Reapers are trying to take away from you—
your right to choose your own fate."

Nike hesitated. "I know you've lost much already,
that you've suffered much already, and if you wish to be
released as my Champion, then I will do that for you."

I wanted to say *yes* so badly. To pretend I'd never
heard of Nike, Loki, or any of the rest of it, just like my
mom had. To go back to just being Gwen Frost, that
weird Gypsy girl who touched stuff and saw things. But
I couldn't stop myself from asking the inevitable question.

"And what would happen if I quit?" I asked. "To the
academy? To my friends?"

Nike shrugged. "The academy will be overrun by the
Reapers and eventually destroyed—and so will your
friends."

She said it calmly, coldly, as if it were a foregone con-
clusion, as if there was a giant hourglass somewhere
and the sand had already started to trickle out of it to
seal the fate of my friends and everyone else at Mythos.

"And if I continue on as your Champion? What do
you want me to do now that Loki is free? How can I
stop him and the Reapers?"

"There is only one way to finally end the conflict between Loki, the Reapers, and the members of the Pantheon," Nike said in an ominous voice. "Someone must
kill Loki, and that someone is you, Gwendolyn."

Vivian had said the same thing to me back in the
mansion, but hearing it from Nike made it sound even
more impossible than before.

"But—but *how* am I supposed to do that?" I sputtered. "I couldn't keep the Reapers from freeing Loki in the first place. How am I supposed to kill him? He's a *god,* in case you haven't noticed."

Nike arched a delicate eyebrow at my harsh tone, but I didn't back down and I didn't look away from her. Kill a god. She actually expected me to kill a freaking *god.* I'd seen Loki, and I'd felt exactly how powerful he was, even though he'd been trapped in his mythological prison for centuries. I didn't think I could just walk up to him and stab him in the heart with Vic.

"Why can't *you* do it?" I asked, a pleading note creeping into my voice. "You defeated him once. Surely you can do it again."

Nike shook her head. "After Loki's actions led to the death of Balder, the other gods all banded together and made a pact that no god would be able to kill another. That's why I didn't kill Loki at the end of the Chaos War. That's why he was imprisoned instead."

The goddess looked at me. "But we never said anything about mortals, you see. If a mortal Champion is strong enough, if a mortal Champion is clever enough, then she can kill a god—even one as powerful as Loki. But you must act quickly, Gwendolyn. Right now, he is still weak from his imprisonment, but it won't be long before he starts gaining power—and still more followers."

"But I don't even know where he is, and neither does Metis or the other members of the Pantheon," I said. "How am I even supposed to find him?"

"You won't have to," Nike said. "His spies are everywhere, and he'll come to the academy sooner or later.

There are many artifacts here that he wants, many powerful things and people here that he needs in order to finally defeat us."

I wrapped my arms around myself, trying to ward off the chill I felt at her words, but it didn't work. My eyes swept over the quad, with its cluster of old buildings, iron benches, and towering trees. When I'd first come to Mythos, I'd hated the academy, but now, I couldn't imagine myself going to school anywhere else. Somehow, over the past few months, it had become like a second home to me, a place where I was slowly learning to fit in, a place where I was slowly learning to be strong.

And it would all be destroyed if Loki wasn't stopped—if I didn't figure out some way to kill the evil god.

"Now, Gwendolyn, I must have your answer. Will you continue to help me fight against Loki? Will you do what you can, what you must, to save us all?"

I thought of Logan, Daphne, and all my other friends. I thought of the academy grounds being overrun by Reapers, of Reapers killing everyone they could get their hands on. I thought of all the academy's statues and buildings crumbling to dust. I thought of darkness falling over the world the way it had in the clearing in the forest last night. And I knew what my answer would be—what it would always be, as long as I had breath left to fight.

"I'll do it. I'll continue on as your Champion." I looked at the goddess. "Just don't blame me if you end up being disappointed. You know, having the fate of the entire world on my shoulders is a lot of freaking pressure."

"I could never be disappointed in you, Gwendolyn," Nike said in a soft voice. "You're everything that is good about mortals. Your heart is pure, and you do the best you can, no matter how difficult a situation is. You always try, and that's all anyone can ask of a Champion."

I didn't know about the good and pure parts, but I wasn't going to argue with her. Not now.

Nike rose to her feet. "And now, I have a gift for you, Gwendolyn. A visit from an old friend."

Toenails clicked on the balcony above our heads, and I turned around, wondering at the sound. A moment later, Nott stepped into view.

"Nott," I whispered.

I raced up the steps and threw my arms around the wolf's neck. "Oh, Nott!"

Tears ran down my cheeks, and I started rubbing the wolf's ears. They felt real enough under my fingers. Nott let out a little grumble of happiness.

"I'm so, so sorry, Nott," I said through my tears. "I tried my best to save you."

The wolf licked my face, and I felt her gentle understanding and forgiveness fill my mind, along with another thought. With my arms still around the wolf, I turned to look at Nike. The goddess walked up the steps to where we were standing.

"You sent her to me, didn't you? But why? And how? I didn't think you could help me like that." Another thought popped into my head. "Is that why Nott had her pup so soon? Did you help her with that too?"

Nike nodded. "Yes, on both counts. I knew you would need aid in the forest when Loki was freed, and you had saved Nott before when you freed her from the Reaper boy. So I went to her and asked for her help. She agreed to trade her life for yours. And you're right. The gods can't interfere with mortals, but Nott isn't quite a mortal, now is she?"

A small, satisfied smile curved her lips, and I knew what she was really talking about—another loophole. Just like picking a Champion was a god's way of seeing that his or her instructions were carried out here in the mortal realm. Sometimes I wondered why the gods had bothered with rules in the first place since they were always looking for ways around them.

"But she died," I whispered. "Why would she want to die?"

"Nott was sick, Gwendolyn," Nike said. "Very few members of the Pantheon know this, but the Reapers use a potent drug, a poison really, to train the Fenrir wolves and other creatures. It's what turns their fur and eyes that eerie red color. The Reapers start feeding it to them the day they're born so they can control them. That's why so many of the wolves and other creatures obey the Reapers and don't try to fight against them—because the creatures need that daily dose of the drug to keep on living. Without it, the creatures slowly, painfully die."

I'd thought there was something wrong with Nott, given how tired she had seemed. I'd thought maybe it was because she was about to have a pup, but really, it had been the poisonous drug working on her the whole time, slowly eating away at her body.

"But surely there's an antidote," I said. "Some way to reverse the poison."

Nike shook her head. "Not in Nott's case. She'd been fed the poison for too long."

Another horrible thought filled my mind. "But what about Nyx? Will she be all right?"

"The wolf pup will be just fine," Nike said.

Relief filled me, and I stroked Nott's ears some more.

"But now, I'm afraid it's time for us to go," Nike said in a gentle voice. "Even now, Loki is starting to move against the other members of the Pantheon. I have preparations to make, old friends and allies to call upon."

I nodded and swiped the tears from my cheeks. "I'm going to miss you so much," I whispered to the wolf. "So much. But I'm going to take good care of Nyx for you. I promise."

Nott licked my hand, then moved away.

I got to my feet, and Nike approached me once more. The goddess leaned down and kissed me on the cheek. As soon as she touched me, I felt her power wash over me like waves of ice rippling against my skin. But it wasn't a bad feeling. If anything, I almost felt like I was sharing in her strength, if only for a moment. That sensation, the immense feel of her power, gave me the courage I needed to carry on, knowing what she expected of me, knowing what I had to do to save us all—find a way to kill Loki.

"Take care, Gwendolyn Frost," Nike said. "Be well and stay strong until we meet again, for you will be tested—sooner than you think."

Then, the two of them stepped back, melting into the moonlight, until there were only shadows and frost gathered around me once more.

Chapter 29

I didn't think that they would, I didn't think that they *could,* but slowly, things went back to normal. I went to class, took care of Nyx, and snuck off campus to go see my Grandma Frost. I even kept working my regular shifts at the Library of Antiquities. I wouldn't say that Nickamedes and I were besties now, but we didn't snap at each other every chance we got, either. That was an improvement, I supposed.

But the mood at Mythos Academy was tense. The Powers That Were had called a school-wide assembly and held a memorial service for the kids and other folks who'd died at the Crius Coliseum. After the service was over, the Powers That Were had told everyone that the Reapers had finally succeeded in freeing Loki, although they didn't mention exactly how it had happened or the part I'd played in things. The kids' reactions ranged from shell-shocked to scared to immediately wanting to go to war with the Reapers. I knew the feelings—each and every one of them—because they were the same ones I struggled with every day.

Only I was actually supposed to *kill* Loki, and I had no idea how to go about doing that—if it was even possible in the first place. I told Metis and Grandma Frost what Nike had said to me, what she'd told me I had to do, but I didn't share my mission with my friends. There wasn't any point in worrying them.

I was worried enough for us all.

A few days later, Daphne, Carson, and I sat in the dining hall. Daphne and Carson were kissing, and I was picking at the froufrou mystery meat the chefs had decided to whip up for lunch. Just another day at Mythos Academy, despite the fact that an evil god was on the loose.

Daphne let out another giggle, and a shower of pink sparks filled the air. I rolled my eyes and put down my fork.

"Okay, seriously? You guys are going to make out during lunch, too? Do you know how disgusting that is? Some of us are trying to eat," I muttered.

"Not anymore," Daphne said. "You put down your fork."

"Whatever," I said. "And Carson? You should know that you're wearing Daphne's lip gloss again."

Carson blushed, picked up a napkin, and started scrubbing his face with it. Daphne just giggled, leaned forward, and planted another kiss on the band geek's face. I rolled my eyes again, but I wasn't the only one eyeing the happy couple—so was Savannah.

The pretty Amazon sat at a table a few feet away from us, along with Talia and Morgan, who seemed to have become friends with them. I hadn't spoken to Savannah, but everyone at Mythos knew that Vivian was really a Reaper and Loki's Champion. The Powers That Were had told everyone about Vivian during the assembly. Savannah and Talia were both picking at their food, and Savannah had a particularly miserable expression on her face.

"I'll see you guys later, okay? There's something I have to do."

Daphne and Carson waved good-bye to me, then started kissing again. I grabbed my bag and walked over to Savannah's table. I stood there almost a minute before the Amazon decided to stop pretending that she couldn't see me.

"What do you want?" she finally muttered.

I drew in a breath. "I just wanted to say that I'm sorry about Logan's breaking up with you. I know how much you cared about him, and I know how much we both hurt you. I'm sorry for it, all of it."

Savannah blinked like she couldn't believe I'd just apologized to her. Talia looked just as shocked, although Morgan smiled at me. I wondered if the Valkyrie had ever wanted to tell Jasmine that she was sorry for messing around with Samson, but of course, it was too late now.

Apologizing to Savannah was something I'd been thinking about for a while. I didn't know if it would make a difference to the other girl, and I certainly didn't expect her to like or even forgive me, but it was something I needed to do for myself. Even though I hadn't meant to, I'd hurt Savannah, and I wanted to try to make it right.

Savannah stared up at me, her eyes narrowed, like she wasn't sure I was serious. Then, her gaze drifted over to the table where Logan sat with Oliver and Kenzie. Sadness filled her pretty face.

"I knew," she said. "I knew Logan liked you the first time I saw you together at the homecoming dance. I just wanted it to be me instead. You know?"

"Yeah," I said in a quiet voice. "I know."

"He's staring at you right now."

I didn't turn and look at the Spartan. I wasn't quite ready to face him. Not yet. Nobody spoke for a moment. All around us, the clink and clatter of dishes sounded, mixing with the talk of the other students.

"So are you guys together now or what?" Morgan asked.

I looked at the Valkyrie, and Talia jabbed her in the side with her elbow.

"What?" Morgan asked, wincing. "You guys know I can't resist a good piece of gossip."

"I don't know what we are," I said, answering Morgan. "But I care about him. I never thought I'd be the kind of girl to steal someone else's boyfriend, but I guess I turned out to be that person, after all. Just like you said I was at the coliseum."

Morgan looked at me, then smiled again, green sparks of magic flickering around her. "Nah, Gypsy. You've got a long way to go to catch up to me."

I smiled back at her.

"Besides," Morgan said. "I told Savannah and Talia about how you saved me from Jasmine that night in the Library of Antiquities. So they know you're not all bad, even if Talia won't admit it."

Talia glared at the other girl, and Morgan quickly scooted her chair back so she was out of range of the Amazon's quick, sharp elbow.

"You remember?" I asked. "What happened that night?"

A haunted look filled Morgan's hazel eyes. "I could see and hear and feel everything that was going on as it happened. I just couldn't do anything about it."

The other girls looked at her with sympathy, but Morgan pretended that she didn't notice their stares. We were all getting good at ignoring things we didn't want to see.

"Anyway," I said. "I just wanted you to know I'm sorry. I'll see you around."

"Gwen?" Savannah called out as I started to walk away.

I turned to look at her.

"Be good to Logan, okay?" she said. "He deserves it."

I thought about telling her that I didn't know if Logan and I would ever be together, that I didn't know if the Spartan even wanted to be with me anymore. Instead, I just nodded.

"Don't think this means I won't still be kicking your butt in gym class every chance I get," Talia growled.

I grinned at her. "I'd expect nothing less."

*   *   *

The next morning, I went to the gym for the first time since Vivian had forced me to free Loki. Oh, I'd come to the gym for my usual class, but I hadn't shown up for early morning weapons training with Logan, Kenzie, and Oliver—until now.

I also had on the snowflake necklace for the first time since Loki had escaped. Grandma Frost had gotten it cleaned for me, and not a speck of blood remained on the silver strands. Still, whenever I touched the necklace, all the horrors of that night came rushing back to me, since all my feelings and emotions had soaked into the smooth metal. But the delicate necklace had made it through that long night when it shouldn't have, just like I had. It was a sign of my survival—and the hope I had that Logan and I could overcome our troubles as well.

I was the first one in the gym, and I pulled my hair back into a ponytail. I paced back and forth in front of the bleachers where Vic was propped up and rehearsed what I was going to say to the Spartan.

"Oh, just tell the boy you bloody love him and be done with it," Vic growled. "This lovey-dovey stuff gives me heartburn. Don't you agree, fuzzball?"

Nyx barked, but I didn't know whether she was agreeing with Vic or angry at the nickname the sword had given her. The pup's twilight eyes were finally open, so I'd put her in my messenger bag this morning and had given her a tour of campus. I'd hoped that Nyx would stay in my bag during weapons training, but the pup had already climbed out. Now, she was trying to jump up onto one of the bleachers. Smiling, I bent

down, picked her up, and put her where she wanted to
go. Nyx licked my hand and started running up and
down, like a pirate sprinting along a wooden plank.

"She's cute," a low voice called out behind me. "Just
like Oliver said she was."

I whirled around. Logan stood behind me, wearing
jeans and a long-sleeved blue T-shirt that brought out
his icy eyes.

"Hi," I said in a soft voice.

"Hi," Logan said in a guarded tone.

We stood there. Logan didn't approach me; he didn't
tease me; he didn't do anything that would tell me what
he was thinking. Finally, I cleared my throat.

"So where's your entourage?" I asked.

Logan shrugged. "They quit coming a few days ago.
Everyone has more important things to think about
now that Loki's free."

I nodded.

"What are you doing here, Gypsy girl?" Logan asked,
his gaze on my face. "I've called and texted you a dozen
times, and you never once responded."

"I know," I said. "And I'm sorry about that. I came
over here this morning to apologize for, well, everything. But especially for how I acted outside my
Grandma Frost's house. You came to rescue me, you
risked your life to save me, and I didn't want to have
anything to do with you. I'm sorry for that. Sorrier than
you'll ever know."

I didn't make excuses, and I didn't bring up what I'd
gone through in the stone circle, everything I'd lost and
how much it had hurt me. Carson had told me more

than once that all the kids had lost someone to the Reapers. Now, I had, too. First, my mom and now Nott. Not to mention the bits and pieces of myself I'd sacrificed along the way just to stay alive. And there was more loss, suffering, and pain on the way—for all of us. I could feel it deep down in my bones.

Logan sighed. "I'm sorry, too, Gypsy girl. For that night in the library when I accused you of digging through my brain. I know you can't help it, that your magic makes you see things whether you want to or not. The truth was that I was afraid—afraid you'd see me for the coward I really was. But then when I found out you'd been taken by the Reapers, all that mattered was getting you back—and not being that coward again."

"You're not a coward," I said. "I never for one minute thought you were a coward. I'm the coward."

"Why would you say that?"

"Because I want you, but I'm afraid to be with you."

Logan started toward me, but I held up my hand, stopping him.

"I don't want to hurt you," I whispered. "With my—with my magic. You don't know what it felt like, to pull Preston's life out of him. What if I slip up and do it again? What if I touch you and do that to you? I'd *never* forgive myself. I don't know that I can forgive myself for doing it to Preston, even if it was the only way to save myself. The thought of ever hurting you, it just—it just makes me *sick*."

I wrapped my arms around myself and looked away. Logan reached out and cupped my hand with his cheek, raising my face to his. My eyes widened at his soft touch and all the emotions I felt pouring into me. His care, his concern, his understanding. The hot, pulsing warmth of his feelings took my breath away because it was exactly the same way I felt about him. The same way I'd always felt about him.

Logan gave me a crooked grin. "You won't hurt me. I know you won't."

"How can you be so sure?" I whispered.

His grin widened. "Because you're that Gypsy girl, and I'm the bad-boy Spartan. And I think it's time we were finally together, don't you?"

I stared at him, all of these emotions pouring through me, burning and burning, brighter and brighter, hotter and hotter, until they couldn't be contained and there was only one thing I could do. I stood on my tiptoes, wrapped my arms around his neck, and pressed my lips to his.

For a moment, the world just—stopped—and all I knew was the feel of Logan's lips on mine, the firm grip of his arms around me, the hard strength of his body pressing into mine. It was the most wonderful feeling in the world, and the kiss was everything I'd known it would be, everything I'd ever dreamed it would be— hot, sweet, sexy, intense.

But it was more than just a kiss. For the first time, Logan completely opened himself up to me. I saw and felt so many things, so many memories, so many emotions. All of Logan's doubts and fears, all of his insecurities, all of the worries that he worked so hard to hide from everyone else. I felt his strength, too—his determination to fight against the Reapers no matter what.

And most important of all, I realized just how much he cared about *me*.

I just felt—*everything*. The warm, fizzy, dizzying rush Logan got in his chest every time I smiled at him. The sly satisfaction whenever I laughed at one of his jokes. The lightness whenever we were teasing each other. Even the pride he had at how far I'd come as a warrior.

It all made me happier than I'd ever thought I could be.

When the kiss finally ended, the Spartan opened his eyes.

"Wow," he breathed out. "I know that I'm a great kisser, but you gave me a run for my money there, Gypsy girl."

I rolled my eyes, stepped back, and punched him in the shoulder. The Spartan just laughed. I started to hit him again, but Logan grabbed my hands, pulled me close, and kissed me again. The rest of the world just fell away—

"Woo!" someone whooped, interrupting us.

Surprised, we both drew back, breathless, and turned to see Oliver and Kenzie standing in the door to the gym, along with Daphne and Carson. Our friends all had smiles on their faces, and Daphne let out another loud whoop and started clapping, pink sparks dancing in the air around her.

"I guess the secret's out," Logan said.

"I guess so," I replied.

"Well, it's about bloody time," Vic muttered from his spot on the bleachers. "I was wondering if you two were ever going to wise up about each other."

Nyx barked, agreeing with the sword.

"Shut up, Vic," I said with a smile.

Logan put his hands on my waist and leaned down so that his forehead was touching mine. I marveled at the feel of his skin, at the strong circle of his arms, and especially at the fact that there were no more secrets between us.

Yeah, things were all kinds of messed up right now. Loki was out there somewhere, plotting against the Pantheon, along with Vivian, and the Reapers of Chaos were getting ready to rise once more. But right now, I was at the academy, safe, with Logan and my friends.

There would be time enough to worry tomorrow. About the Reapers, about Loki, and most especially about how I was supposed to kill the evil god. But today—today was about me and Logan and our feelings for each other.

"C'mon, Logan!" Carson called out from across the gym. "You can do better than that! Or do I need to come over there and show you how it's done?"

Logan turned around and glared at Carson, who just laughed. Then, the Spartan faced me again.

"What do you say we give them something to really cheer about, Gypsy girl?" Logan whispered.

I arched my eyebrow. "Bring it on, Spartan."

"Kids," Vic muttered in a fond voice.

And that was the last thing I heard before Logan lowered his lips to mine once more.

BEYOND
THE
STORY

Gwen's Report on the Artifacts Exhibit
at the Crius Coliseum
for Professor Metis's Myth-History Class

Given the Reaper attack at the coliseum, Metis didn't quiz us on the exhibit, but she did mention that we could write a paper on some of the artifacts we saw for extra credit. So here goes:

An Andvari coin: This gold coin is rumored to be from the stash of treasure collected by Andvari, a dwarf. Supposedly, Loki trapped the dwarf and took all of his gold. Seems like Loki was always doing sneaky things like that, even back before he was the ultimate evil.

Ariadne's ball of thread: It's a ball of silver thread. Sure, I imagine that Theseus found it useful when he was trying to find his way in and out of the labyrinth where the Minotaur was. But still, it's a ball of thread. I am not overly impressed.

Bastet's gloves: These gloves were supposedly worn by Bastet, the Egyptian cat goddess. They look like regular gloves, although they're made of a delicate gold mesh and the fingertips are tipped with curved onyx talons, like a cat's claws—except much, much sharper.

Coyote images: There were lots of drawings, carvings, and figurines of Coyote, the Native American god. All of the images were different, though, showing Coyote's trickster nature and supposed ability to change his shape.

Sigyn's onyx bow: It looks cool, and it's certainly shiny since it's made out of onyx. But I have to say that I'd prefer to fight with Vic, even if he is a little mouthy from time to time. Okay, okay, a whole lot mouthy pretty much all the time.

The Horn of Roland: I can't really play any musical instruments, so Carson was way more interested in this than I was. To me, it just looks like a miniature tuba. Supposedly, Roland was some great warrior who died in battle blowing this horn. Not sure what makes it so special if Roland didn't actually live through the fight though. . . .

Weapons, weapons, weapons: If I tried to list every single sword, bow, dagger, and staff that I saw at the museum, this report would go on . . . and on . . . and on. So I'll just say that there were lots of weapons on display and leave it at that. Sometimes, I wonder if all the professors and warrior whiz kids at Mythos care about anything else besides weapons.

Final thoughts: Many of the artifacts were destroyed during the battle with the Reapers, including much of the pottery, jewelry, and clothing that was in the main part of the coliseum. And, of course, my friends and I used some of the weapons and other artifacts to defend ourselves.

That's when Daphne picked up Sigyn's onyx bow and Carson got the Horn of Roland—things that it seems like my friends are stuck with, since the artifacts keep returning to them, no matter how many times they give them back to Professor Metis.

Kind of freaky, if you ask me, having something that you just can't get rid of. I suppose the bow and the horn have some sort of magic mumbo jumbo attached to them. I have a feeling that I'll find out before it's all said and done—and that maybe Daphne and Carson have their own roles to play in the war against the Reapers. . . .

Mythos Academy Warriors and Their Magic

The students at Mythos Academy are the descendants of ancient warriors, and they are at the academy to learn how to fight and use weapons, along with whatever magic or other skills that they might have. Here's a little more about the warrior whiz kids, as Gwen calls them:

Amazons and Valkyries: Most of the girls at Mythos are either Amazons or Valkyries. Amazons are gifted with supernatural quickness. In gym class during mock fights, they look like blurs more than anything else. Valkyries are incredibly strong. Also, bright, colorful sparks of magic can often be seen shooting out of Valkyries' fingertips.

Romans and Vikings: Most of the guys at Mythos Academy are either Romans or Vikings. Romans are superquick, just like Amazons, while Vikings are superstrong, just like Valkyries.

Siblings: Brothers and sisters born to the same parents will have similar abilities and magic, but they're sometimes classified as different types of warriors. For example, if the girls in a family are Amazons, then the boys will be Romans. If the girls in a family are Valkyries, then the boys will be Vikings.

However, in other families, brothers and sisters are considered to be the same kind of warriors, like those born to Spartan, Samurai, or Ninja parents. The boys and girls are both called Spartans, Samurais, or Ninjas.

More Magic: As if being superstrong or superquick wasn't good enough, the students at Mythos Academy also have other types of magic. They can do everything from heal injuries to control the weather to form fireballs with their bare hands. Many of the students have enhanced senses as well. The powers vary from student to student, but as a general rule, everyone is dangerous and deadly in their own special way.

Spartans: Spartans are among the rarest of the warrior whiz kids, and there are only a few at Mythos Academy. But Spartans are the most dangerous and deadliest of all the warriors because they have the ability to pick up any weapon—or any *thing*—and automatically know how to use and even kill someone with it. Even Reapers of Chaos are afraid to battle Spartans in a fair fight. But then again, Reapers rarely fight fair. . . .

Gypsies: Gypsies are just as rare as Spartans. Gypsies are those who have been gifted with magic by the gods. But not all Gypsies are good. Some are just as evil as the gods they serve. Gwen is a Gypsy who is gifted with psychometry magic, or the ability to know, see, and feel an object's history just by touching it. Gwen's magic comes from Nike, the Greek goddess of victory.

**Want to know more about Mythos Academy?
Read on and take a tour of the campus.**

The heart of Mythos Academy is made up of five buildings that are clustered together like the loose points of a star on the upper quad. They are the Library of Antiquities, the gym, the dining hall, the English-history building, and the math-science building.

The Library of Antiquities: The library is the largest building on campus. In addition to books, the library also houses artifacts—weapons, jewelry, clothes, armor, and more—that were once used by ancient warriors, gods, goddesses, and mythological creatures. Some of the artifacts have a lot of power, and the Reapers of Chaos would love to get their hands on this stuff to use it for Bad, Bad Things.

The Gym: The gym is the second largest building at Mythos. In addition to a pool, basketball court, and training areas, the gym also features racks of weapons, including swords, staffs, and more, that the students use during mock fights. At Mythos, gym class is really weapons training, and students are graded on how well they can fight—something that Gwen thinks she's not very good at.

The Dining Hall: The dining hall is the third largest building at Mythos. With its white linens, fancy china, and open-air indoor garden, the dining hall looks more like a five-star restaurant than a student cafeteria. The dining hall is famous for all the fancy, froufrou foods that it serves on a daily basis, like liver, veal, and escargot. Yucko, as Gwen would say.

The English-History Building: Students attend English, myth-history, geography, art, and other classes in this building. Professor Metis's office is also in this building.

The Math-Science Building: Students attend math, science, and other classes in this building. But there are more than just classrooms here. This building also features a morgue and a prison deep underground. Creepy, huh?

The Student Dorms: The student dorms are located down the hill from the upper quad, along with several other smaller outbuildings. Guys and girls live in separate dorms, although that doesn't keep them from hooking up on a regular basis.

The Statues: Statues of mythological creatures—like gryphons and gargoyles—can be found on all the academy buildings, although the library has the most statues. Gwen thinks that the statues are all super creepy, especially since they always seem to be watching her. . . .

Who's Who at Mythos Academy—
The Students

Gwen (Gwendolyn) Frost: Gwen is a Gypsy girl with the gift of psychometry magic, or the ability to know an object's history just by touching it. Gwen's a little dark and twisted in that she likes her magic and the fact that it lets her know other people's secrets—no matter how hard they try to hide them. She also has a major sweet tooth, loves to read comic books, and wears jeans, T-shirts, hoodies, and sneakers almost everywhere she goes.

Daphne Cruz: Daphne is a Valkyrie and a renowned archer. She also has some wicked computer skills and loves designer clothes and expensive purses. Daphne is rather obsessed with the color pink. She wears it more often than not, and her entire dorm room is done in various shades of pink.

Logan Quinn: This seriously cute and seriously deadly Spartan is the best fighter at Mythos Academy—and someone who Gwen just can't stop thinking about. But Logan has a secret that he doesn't want anyone to know—especially not Gwen.

Carson Callahan: Carson is the head of the Mythos Academy Marching Band. He's a Celt and rumored to have come from a long line of warrior bards. He's quiet, shy, and one of the nicest guys you'll ever meet, but Carson can be as tough as nails when he needs to be.

Oliver Hector: Oliver is a Spartan who is friends with Logan and Kenzie and helps with Gwen's weapons training. He's also one of Gwen's friends now too, because of what happened during the Winter Carnival.

Kenzie Tanaka: Kenzie is a Spartan who is friends with Logan and Oliver. He also helps with Gwen's weapons training and is currently dating Talia.

Savannah Warren: Savannah is an Amazon who was dating Logan—at least before the Winter Carnival. Now, the two of them have broken up, something Savannah isn't very happy about—and something that she blames Gwen for.

Talia Pizarro: Talia is an Amazon and one of Savannah's best friends. Talia has gym class with Gwen, and the two of them often spar during the mock fights. She is currently dating Kenzie.

Helena Paxton: Helena is an Amazon who seems to be positioning herself as the new mean girl queen of the academy, or at least of Gwen's second-year class.

Morgan McDougall: Morgan is a Valkyrie. She used to be one of the most popular girls at the academy—before her best friend, Jasmine Ashton, tried to sacrifice her to Loki one night in the Library of Antiquities. These days, though, Morgan tends to keep to herself, although it seems she's becoming friends with Savannah and Talia.

Jasmine Ashton: Jasmine was a Valkyrie and the most popular girl in the second-year class at Mythos Academy—until she tried to sacrifice Morgan to Loki. Gwen battled Jasmine in the Library of Antiquities and managed to keep her from sacrificing Morgan, although Logan was the one who actually killed Jasmine. But before she died, Jasmine told Gwen that her whole family are Reapers—and that there are many Reapers at Mythos Academy. . . .

Preston Ashton: Preston is Jasmine's older brother, who blamed Gwen for his sister's death. Preston tried to kill Gwen during the Winter Carnival weekend at the Powder ski resort, although Gwen, Logan, and Vic eventually got the best of the Reaper. After that, Preston was locked up in the academy's prison.

Who's Who at Mythos Academy and Beyond— The Adults

Coach Ajax: Ajax is the head of the athletic department at the academy and is responsible for training all the kids at Mythos and turning them into fighters. Logan Quinn and his Spartan friends are among Ajax's prize students.

Geraldine (Grandma) Frost: Geraldine is Gwen's grandma and a Gypsy with the power to see the future. Grandma Frost makes her living as a fortuneteller in a town not too far away from Cypress Mountain. A couple of times a week, Gwen sneaks off the Mythos Academy campus to see her grandma and enjoy the sweet treats that Grandma Frost is always baking.

Grace Frost: Grace was Gwen's mom and a Gypsy who had the power to know if people were telling the truth or not just by listening to their words. At first, Gwen thought her mom had been killed in a car accident by a drunk driver. But thanks to Preston Ashton, Gwen knows that Grace was actually murdered by the Reaper girl who is Loki's Champion. Gwen's determined to find the Reaper girl and get her revenge—no matter what.

Nickamedes: Nickamedes is the head librarian at the Library of Antiquities. Nickamedes loves the books and the artifacts in the library more than anything else, and he doesn't seem to like Gwen at all. In fact, he often goes out of his way to make more work for her whenever Gwen is working after school in the library. Nickamedes is also Logan's uncle, although the uptight librarian is nothing like his easygoing nephew. At least, Gwen doesn't think so.

Professor Aurora Metis: Metis is a myth-history professor who teaches students all about the Reapers of Chaos, Loki, and the ancient Chaos War. She was also best friends with Gwen's mom, Grace, back when the two of them went to Mythos. Metis is the Champion of Athena, the Greek goddess of wisdom, and she's become Gwen's mentor at the academy.

Raven: Raven is the old woman who mans the coffee cart in the Library of Antiquities. Gwen's also seen her in the academy prison, which seems to be another one of Raven's odd jobs around campus. There's definitely more to Raven than meets the eye....

The Powers That Were: A board made up of various members of the Pantheon who oversee all aspects of Mythos Academy, from approving the dining hall menus to disciplining students. Gwen's never met any of the board members that she's aware of, and she doesn't know exactly who they are, but that could change—sooner than she thinks.

Vic: Vic is the talking sword that Nike gave to Gwen to use as her personal weapon. Instead of a regular hilt, a man's face is inlaid into Vic's hilt. Gwen doesn't know too much about Vic, except that he's really, really bloodthirsty and wants to kill Reapers more than anything else.

Who's Who at Mythos Academy— The Gods, Monsters, and More

Artifacts: Artifacts are weapons, jewelry, clothing, and armor that were worn or used by various warriors, gods, goddesses, and mythological creatures over the years. There are Thirteen Artifacts that are rumored to be the most powerful, although people disagree about which artifacts they are and how they were used during the Chaos War. The members of the Pantheon protect the various artifacts from the Reapers, who want to use the artifacts and their power to free Loki from his prison. Many of the artifacts are housed in the Library of Antiquities.

Black rocs: These creatures look like ravens—only much, much bigger. They have shiny black feathers shot through with glossy streaks of red, long, sharp, curved talons, and black eyes with a red spark burning deep down inside them. Rocs are capable of picking up people and carrying them off—before they rip them to shreds.

Champions: Every god and goddess has a Champion, someone that they choose to work on their behalf in the mortal realm. Champions have various powers and weapons and can be good or bad, depending on the god they serve. Gwen is Nike's Champion, just like her mom and grandma were before her.

The Chaos War: Long ago, Loki and his followers tried to enslave everyone and everything, and the whole world was plunged into the Chaos War. It was a dark, bloody time that almost resulted in the end of the world. The Reapers want to free Loki, so the god can lead them in another Chaos War. You can see why that would be a Bad, Bad Thing.

Fenrir wolves: These creatures look like wolves—only much, much bigger. They have ash gray fur, razor-sharp talons, and burning red eyes. Reapers use them to watch, hunt, and kill members of the Pantheon. Think of Fenrir wolves as puppy-dog assassins.

Loki: Loki is the Norse god of chaos. Once upon a time, Loki caused the death of another god and was imprisoned for it. But Loki eventually escaped from his prison and started recruiting other gods, goddesses, humans, and creatures to join forces with him. He called his followers the Reapers of Chaos, and they tried to take over the world. However, Loki and his followers were eventually defeated, and Loki was imprisoned for a second time. To this day, Loki seeks to escape from his prison and plunge the world into a second Chaos War. He's the ultimate bad guy.

Mythos Academy: The academy is located in Cypress Mountain, North Carolina, which is a ritzy suburb high in the mountains above the city of Asheville. The academy is a boarding school/college for warrior whiz kids—the descendants of ancient warriors, like Spartans,

Valkyries, Amazons, and more. The kids at Mythos range in age from first-year students (age sixteen) to sixth-year students (age twenty-one). The kids go to Mythos to learn how to use whatever magic and skills they possess to fight against Loki and his Reapers. There are other branches of the academy located throughout the world.

Nemean prowlers: These creatures look like panthers—only much, much bigger. They have black fur tinged with red, razor-sharp claws, and burning red eyes. Reapers use them to watch, hunt, and kill members of the Pantheon. Think of Nemean prowlers as kitty-cat assassins.

Nike: Nike is the Greek goddess of victory. The goddess was the one who defeated Loki in one-on-one combat during the final battle of the Chaos War. Ever since then, Nike and her Champions have fought the Reapers of Chaos, trying to keep them from freeing Loki from his prison. She's the ultimate good guy.

The Pantheon: The Pantheon is made up of gods, goddesses, humans, and creatures who have banded together to fight Loki and his Reapers of Chaos. The members of the Pantheon are the good guys.

Reapers of Chaos: A Reaper is any god, goddess, human, or creature who serves Loki and wants to free the evil god from his prison. Reapers are known to sacrifice people to Loki in hopes of weakening his prison, so he can one day break free and return to the mortal realm. The scary thing is that Reapers can be anyone at Mythos Academy and beyond—parents, teachers, even fellow students. Reapers are the bad guys.

Sigyn: Sigyn is the Norse goddess of devotion. She is also Loki's wife. The first time Loki was imprisoned, he was chained up underneath a giant snake that dripped venom onto his once-handsome face. Sigyn spent many years holding an artifact called the Bowl of Tears up over Loki's head to catch as much of the venom as possible. But when the bowl was full, Sigyn would have to empty it, which let venom drop freely onto Loki's face, causing him great pain. Eventually, Loki tricked Sigyn into releasing him, and before long, the evil god plunged the world into the long, bloody Chaos War. No one knows what happened to Sigyn after that. . . .

Turn the page for a hint of
the adventures ahead
at Mythos Academy in

CRIMSON FROST,

on sale in January 2013.

Chapter 1

"I have a confession to make."

Logan Quinn looked over at me. "Really, Gypsy girl? What's that?"

I shifted on my feet. "I don't actually like coffee."

The Spartan stared at me a moment before his lips curved up into a teasing grin. "You probably should have mentioned that before now."

Yeah, I probably should have, since we were in a coffee shop. A large counter, lots of comfy leather chairs, wrought-iron tables, paintings of gods and goddesses on the walls, a display case full of blueberry scones, lemon-raspberry tarts, and decadent chocolate cheesecakes. Kaldi's Coffee Emporium looked like your typical java joint, except that everything was first-class and super-pricey all the way, from the fancy espresso machines that hissed and burped to the rich, dark aroma of the ridiculously expensive coffee that flavored the air.

Then again, such luxury was the norm in the upscale stores in Cypress Mountain, North Carolina. The Mythos Academy kids accepted nothing less than the best, and

Kaldi's was one of the most popular places to Hang Out and Be Seen when the students had free time, like we did today. Afternoon classes and activities had been canceled so all the kids could attend some big assembly at the academy's amphitheater. I wasn't sure what the assembly was going to be about. Probably some more hearty reassurances from the professors and the staff that all us warrior whiz kids were as safe as we could be at the academy, even though the evil god Loki was free.

For a moment, a face flashed before my eyes—the most hideous face I'd ever seen. One side so perfect, with its golden hair, piercing blue eye, and smooth features. The other side so completely ruined, with its limp strings of black hair, burning red eye, and melted skin.

Loki—the evil god that I'd helped set free against my will.

A shudder rippled through my body. Thanks to my psychometry magic, I never forgot anything I saw, but the image of Loki's double-face was burned into my memory. No matter what I was doing or whom I was with, no matter how hard I tried to forget what had happened, I saw the Norse trickster god's image everywhere I went. Gleaming in the windows of my classrooms, shining in the glossy surface of my dorm room desk, shimmering in the mirror, like a devil perched on my shoulder.

I shuddered again. It had taken all the strength I had not to scream when I'd brushed my hair this morning and had suddenly seen Loki grinning at me in my bathroom mirror, the perfect side of his face lifted up into a smile, and the ruined side turned down into a horrible, twisted grin—

"Gypsy girl?" Logan asked in a soft voice. "Are you still here with me?"

I pushed away all thoughts of Loki and made myself smile at the Spartan even though I wanted nothing more than to wrap my arms around myself and huddle into a ball in the corner.

"I know, I know," I grumbled. "I should have told you that I don't actually drink coffee. I just didn't want anything to ruin our first date, and when you suggested coffee . . ."

"You went along with it," Logan finished.

I shrugged.

Maybe it was thinking of Loki and his split face, but as I looked at Logan, I was once again reminded of how different we were. Simply put, Logan Quinn was gorgeous, with his thick, ink black hair and intense, ice blue eyes. His designer jeans, blue sweater, and leather jacket only highlighted how strong and muscled his body was.

Next to him, I pretty much faded into the background. The most interesting thing about my wavy brown hair was how frizzy it was today. You might look twice at my eyes, which were an unusual shade of violet, but the only thing special about me was the necklace I wore. Six silver strands wrapped around my throat before their diamond-tipped points formed a snowflake in the middle of the design. A Christmas gift from Logan, one that I almost always wore, even though it didn't exactly go with my plain gray sweater, purple plaid jacket, and not-so-designer jeans and sneakers.

And it wasn't just our looks and clothes that were different. Logan was a fierce Spartan warrior who was the best fighter at the academy. I was still trying to figure out how to wield a sword, even though I was Nike's Champion, the girl picked by the Greek goddess of victory to help her fight Loki and his Reapers of Chaos here in the mortal realm. Something I had failed at pretty miserably so far, since Loki was free and bent on plunging the world into a second Chaos War.

"You know what, Gypsy girl?" Logan said, once again interrupting my troubled thoughts. "Nothing could ruin this date. Ask me why."

"Why?"

He slung his arm around my shoulder and grinned. "Because I'm on it with you."

And suddenly, everything was okay, and I could breathe again.

That's why I was head over heels for the Spartan. Logan could be everything from fun and flirty to stubborn and infuriating, but then he went and said things like *that*. Was it any wonder I had such a massive crush on him?

Okay, okay, so maybe it had started out as a crush a few months ago, but given everything we'd been through, my feelings for the cute Spartan warrior had quickly deepened into something more: love. At least, that's what I thought it was; that's what it felt like to me—this warm, soft, fizzy feeling that filled my heart whenever the Spartan grinned at me, whenever he teased me or tried to make me forget about my worries, at least for a little while.

Like now.

I sighed and put my head down on his shoulder. Logan hugged me to his chest. He didn't say anything, but he didn't need to. Just being close to him was enough for me, after all these months we'd spent dancing around each other.

"You guys ready to order?" the barista asked.

We stepped up to the counter. The Spartan ordered a triple espresso since he loved the caffeine rush, while I got a hot, honey-pomegranate tea. Logan started to pull his wallet out of his jeans, but I beat him to it and handed the barista a twenty-dollar bill.

"My treat," I said. "After all, I'm the one who suggested coffee in the first place way back in the fall."

Logan nodded. "That you did. All right, Gypsy girl. Your treat—this time. The next round's on me."

We got our drinks and went over to a table in the corner of the shop next to a stone fireplace. Since the students had been given the afternoon off, we weren't the only Mythos kids who'd decided to come to Kaldi's and get something to eat and drink before the assembly started in another hour or so. I spotted several students I knew, including Kenzie Tanaka, Logan's Spartan friend, who was here on his own date with Talia Pizarro, a pretty Amazon in my gym class. I waved at them, and Kenzie winked at me before turning his attention back to Talia.

"What is *he* doing here with *her*?" A sneering voice drifted over to me.

I looked to my right to see Helena Paxton staring at me. Helena was a stunning Amazon with caramel-colored hair and eyes. Since Jasmine Ashton's death in the fall, Helena had established herself as the new mean-girl queen of the second-year, seventeen-year-old students at Mythos. She sat at a nearby table with two of her Amazon friends, all of them dressed in pricey jeans, stiletto boots, and tight, fitted sweaters; they had perfect hair, jewelry, purses, and makeup to match.

"I thought Logan's standards were a little higher than that. Guess I was wrong. Then again, guys will do any-thing—and anyone—to get some."

Helena's voice was low, but the cruel smile on her face told me that she meant for me to hear every word. I'd never done anything to Helena, except stand up for another girl she had been teasing, but that had been enough to put me on the Amazon's hit list. Now, every time she saw me, Helena went out of her way to be snotty to me. Try as I might, I could never seem to get the best of the Amazon, not even dream up a quick comeback to get her to just shut up.

Helena murmured something else to her friends, and they all started snickering. My hand tightened around my mug of tea. Not for the first time, I wished that I had an Amazon's quickness so I could bean Helena in the head with my mug. But she would only catch it and throw the mug back at me before I could blink.

"Ignore them," Logan said in a low voice. "They're just jealous that you're here with me."

I rolled my eyes. "Yeah. You and your ego."

Logan's grin widened, and I couldn't help laughing.

No matter how bad things got, the Spartan could always make me laugh. Something else that added to that warm, fizzy feeling in my chest.

We sat there in silence, listening to the murmurs from the other kids and the gurgles of the espresso machines. After all the battles we'd survived recently, it was nice to just sit with Logan without worrying about what was going to happen next, what new crises would pop up, or what Reapers might be lurking around, masquerading as students, professors, or even the coffee shop staff.

But after a few minutes, the reality of the situation hit me. I was on a date with Logan freaking Quinn, one of the cutest guys at Mythos Academy—and I had no idea what to say to him.

"So . . . what do people talk about on dates?"

Logan looked up from his espresso. "What do you mean?"

I shifted in my seat. "I mean you have a lot more experience at this than I do."

In fact, Logan had a reputation for being a total manwhore who went from one girl at the academy to the next. Me? I'd had exactly one boyfriend for a grand total of three weeks before I'd met Logan. So going on a date was still sort of a new experience for me. Besides, the Spartan had this natural, easy charm that made everyone like him—girls and guys alike. Me? I was about as charming as a wet sock.

"I mean, I know what we talk about at the academy all the time. You know, weapons training, where Loki might be hiding at, when he's going to come and kill us all, how we're supposed to stop him."

Actually, that last one was more like how *I* was supposed to kill the evil god. Yeah, me, kill an actual, living, breathing, walking, talking *god*. And not just any god, but Loki, who was pretty much evil incarnate.

But that was the seemingly impossible mission Nike had given me the last time I'd seen her a couple of weeks ago—something I hadn't shared with Logan or any of my friends. Kill a god. I had no idea how Nike expected me to do that. I had no idea how *anyone* could do that, especially me, Gwen Frost, that weird Gypsy girl who touched stuff and saw things.

Logan kept staring at me, and I found myself opening my mouth once more.

"I mean, I guess we could talk about how I'm actually getting a little better at using weapons, although I doubt that I'll ever be in your league. Or we could talk about Nyx, and how totally cute she is. Or Daphne and her healing magic. Or Carson and how obsessed he is with the winter concert the band is putting together . . ."

Babbling. I was finally out on a real date with Logan, and I was babbling like a windup doll someone had cranked into high gear.

Logan reached over and put his hand on top of mine, which was still wrapped around my mug. "Relax, Gypsy girl. Relax. You're doing just fine. We don't have to talk about anything if you don't want to. I'm just happy to be here with you and relax, especially with everything that's been going on these past few weeks. You know?"

His fingers felt warm and firm against my own, but more than that, I felt the warmth in Logan's heart—and all his feelings. His strength, his bravery, his determination to fight Reapers and to protect me no matter what. All those images, all those feelings flashed through my mind, driving away the doubts I felt about me, Logan, and everything else that was going on right now.

My psychometry magic let me know, see, and feel the history of any object I touched, and the same was true when it came to other people. More than once, my hand had brushed against someone else's, and I'd realized that what they said didn't match what they felt. That's what had happened with my first boyfriend. He'd kissed me, and I'd realized that he was really thinking about another girl instead.

But I didn't have to worry about any of that with Logan. I knew all the Spartan's secrets, and he knew mine. Well, except for the whole *Gwen's-supposed-to-kill-Loki* thing. I still wasn't sure exactly how to bring that up, and I wasn't going to. Not today. There would be time enough to obsess and worry about that later. Right now, I just wanted to enjoy my date with Logan.

"How is it that you always know just what to do and say to make me feel better?" I said.

Logan grinned. "Just another part of that Spartan killer instinct. I can slay the ladies just as well as I can Reapers."

I rolled my eyes and leaned over to punch him in the shoulder—and managed to knock over his espresso and my tea. Liquid cascaded all over the table, most of it spilling off the far side and into Logan's lap. The Spartan jumped up, but he didn't have an Amazon's quickness, so he couldn't avoid getting soaked.

"Sorry!" I said, getting to my own feet. "I'm so sorry!"

I reached for the silver holder on the table, intending to rip some napkins out of it, but instead, I ended up knocking it to the floor as well. The napkin holder *clang-cla-cla-clanged* across the floor.

By the time it skidded to a stop and the noise had faded away, all the people in the shop had stopped their conversations and work and turned to stare at us. Embarrassment made my cheeks burn, while Logan looked like he'd had water dumped all over him.

"Sorry," I mumbled again.

"It's okay," he said, holding his hands out to his sides to keep from touching his now-sticky clothes. "I'll just go get cleaned up."

He headed off toward the bathroom. I sighed, grabbed some napkins out of the holder, and started mopping up the mess I'd made. After a few seconds, most people went back to their conversations—except for Helena and her friends. They were too busy laughing at me to talk.

I put my head down, ignored them, and cleaned up the liquid as fast as I could before wiping off my hands. I threw all the used napkins into a nearby trash can, then sat down at my table and slumped as low as I could in my chair. So far, this date hadn't exactly been a big success—or even just the fun time I'd wanted it to be. Once again, I'd messed up everything without even trying. Sometimes I thought that was my specialty in life.

I was so busy brooding that I didn't pay any attention when the door to the coffee shop opened and three men trooped inside. Once again, all conversation stopped, and I felt a collective emotion ripple off everyone in the shop: fear.

"The Protectorate," I heard Helena whisper.

The Protectorate? What was that? Who were these people? I'd never heard of them before, but apparently they knew me because the men walked in my direction, their eyes fixed on my face.

I tensed, then sat up in my seat, wondering who the men were and what they wanted. Could they be Reapers come to attack the students in the shop? I'd wanted to be alone with Logan, so I'd left Vic, my talking sword, in my dorm room. Stupid of me not to bring the weapon with me, even though we'd only been getting coffee. I should have known by now that nothing was simple at Mythos—not even my first date with Logan.

My eyes scanned the nearby tables, looking for something I could use as a weapon, but the only things within arm's reach were the two empty mugs and the napkin holder. I wrapped my hand around the napkin holder and put it in my lap under the table and out of sight of the men.

This wouldn't be the first time Reapers had attacked me. If these men decided to do the same, well, I'd fight back as hard and fiercely as I could. Besides, one good scream, and Logan would come running out of the bathroom. I had no doubt the Spartan could hold his own against the men—and then some.

One of the men stepped up and stared down at me.

He was handsome enough, with blond hair and pale blue eyes, but his mouth was fixed in a firm frown, as if he constantly found fault with everything and everyone around him. He looked at me, and I stared at him a moment before my gaze moved to the two men flanking him. One of them was tall and slender, while the other was short, with a body that looked fat but was really all hard muscle.

The strangest thing was that the men all had on dark gray robes over their winter clothes. The robes reminded me of the black ones the Reapers always wore, although the men weren't sporting the hideous, rubber Loki masks the Reapers did. Instead, a symbol was stitched into their robes in white thread on their left collars close to their throats—a hand holding a set of balanced scales.

I'd seen that symbol before. It was carved into the ceiling of the prison in the bottom of the math-science building on campus, and it had also been in the middle of the Garm gate that Vivian Holler had used to free Loki. My unease kicked up another notch. Nothing good was ever associated with that image, as far as I was concerned.

"So you're her," the first man said. "Nike's newest Champion. Not quite what I expected."

His voice was soft, smooth, and cultured, but there was obvious power in his words, as if he was used to being obeyed no matter what.

"Who are you?" I snapped, my fingers tightening around the flimsy napkin holder. "What do you want?"

"And you don't even have the good sense to know when you're in trouble," the man murmured, as though I hadn't said a word.

I snorted. Oh, I knew I was in trouble. I was almost *always* in trouble these days. The only question was how bad it would be this time—and if I could somehow manage to get out of it alive once again.

The man kept staring at me with his cold, judgmental eyes, and I lifted my chin in defiance. Whatever happened, whatever these men wanted with me, whatever they tried to do to me, I wasn't going to show him how confused and scared I was. Reapers thrived on that sort of thing. I didn't think these men were Reapers, since no one in the shop was screaming or trying to get away from them, but they weren't here for anything good. I could feel the hostility emanating from them in waves, especially from the leader.

The man tilted his head to the side. "I wonder what he sees in you." After a moment, he shrugged. "No matter. It won't change anything."

"Change what?" I asked. "Who are you? What are you doing here? What do you want with me? And why are you wearing those ridiculous robes?"

Anger made the leader's cheeks take on a faint, reddish tinge. The short, muscular man choked back a laugh. The leader turned to glare at him, and the other man pressed his lips together, although I could see his chest shaking, as though he was trying to swallow the rest of his amusement. The third man seemed bored, like this was an errand he was eager to get over with.

Okay, this was getting weirder by the second. I was looking past the men, wondering what was taking Logan so long, when the leader stepped even closer to me, his eyes glittering with anger.

"Gwendolyn Cassandra Frost," he said in a loud, booming voice. "You are under arrest."